# AN UNEXPECTED PROPOSAL

The windowpane rattled again. This time Andrew did not glance away. Instead, he kept his eyes fixed on the young widow. He continued walking until he was only inches from her. Though the wariness in her eyes deepened, she did not move. She did, however, put her hand on Dora's shoulder, whether to comfort or protect her, Andrew did not know.

"There may be a way," he said slowly, hating himself when he saw hope leap into her eyes. She would never agree to his proposal. Never. "You need my services," he said, nodding toward the girl, "and I find that I need yours."

As Andrew forced his gaze to move slowly from the top of her head to the serviceable boots that peeked from beneath the shabby gown, he watched her flush, then turn pale.

"What do you mean?" she asked.

"I would expect you to live here for a year," he said smoothly.

Though her green eyes deepened with a fear so intense that it was almost palpable, she said nothing.

"A year," Andrew repeated. He paused for a long moment, then said, "As my housekeeper."

# North Star

# Amanda Harte

LEISURE BOOKS  NEW YORK CITY

A LEISURE BOOK®

September 2000

Published by

Dorchester Publishing Co., Inc.
276 Fifth Avenue
New York, NY 10001

ISBN 0-8439-4764-0

*For Catherine Lynn Bailey,*
*who shared my childhood and my dreams.*
*Happy Birthday, Cathie.*
*I'm so glad you're my sister.*

# Chapter One

*March 1853*

She couldn't run. Not now.

Beth Simmons crouched next to the little girl, putting her arms around the child and forcing herself to smile. How could she have forgotten even for an instant the reason they had come? Whatever else she was, Beth was not a coward. She would not run away, not when they were so close.

She rose and shook her long skirts, trying to brush off the worst of the dried mud. Though walking twenty miles and sleeping in barns had taken its toll on the black serge, she could not enter a mansion looking like an impoverished fugitive. She straightened her shoulders, trying not to wince at the pain that raced up her back. *I am not a fugitive,* she reminded herself. *I am a widow with a young child. I have every right to be here.*

Dora tugged on her hand again. Beth managed another smile for the little girl, who was so sensitive to her moods. "Upsie daisy," she said, gathering the child into her arms once more.

The weather was changing. The sky, which had been clear that morning, had turned hazy, dimming the afternoon sun. A bitterly cold wind, so laden with moisture from the nearby lake that it penetrated even the heavy woolen cloak Beth wore over three layers of clothing, mocked the calendar's claim that this was the first day of spring. Snow or sleet seemed imminent. Beth shuddered as she hugged the child, hoping her own body heat would warm Dora. Soon they would reach their destination, and there they would find something even more important than warmth. They would find the man who could work miracles, the only one who could help them.

There it was. Though the house at the southern side of Niagara Square seemed a mile from the street, light spilled onto the front porch, a welcoming beacon that told the world the doctor was home. "We're here," Beth said softly, more to herself than to the child, as she opened the front door. The foyer was magnificent, its walls and floor expanses of polished oak that directed the viewer's eyes up a curving staircase to a stained-glass window of incomparable beauty.

Beth took a deep breath, willing her hands to stop trembling. It would be all right. The house was not meant to intimidate. It was a positive sign, proof of the doctor's success. Everything would be fine. This man was not like the others. He would help them. But, try though she might, Beth was unable to convince herself. Dora, overly sensitive Dora, looked up, her brown eyes mirroring the fear Beth was battling.

"It's all right, honey," she said, and ushered the child into the surprisingly austere waiting room. Though the maroon carpet was thick and the furniture of good quality, no paintings or plants softened the angles. Beth led Dora to one of the four chairs along one wall. Made of unadorned wood, they were clearly designed for overflow seating, while the two stuffed chairs on the opposite side appeared more comfortable. A slender, dark-haired woman with one of the most beautiful faces Beth had ever seen sat in one of them, her fur-trimmed cloak draped over the other.

Though the young woman's expression was as chilling as the March air, Beth nodded a greeting to her before she settled Dora into one of the empty chairs.

The woman raised one eyebrow. "Are you lost?" Were it not for her petulant expression, Beth would have said that the doctor's other patient was perfection personified. She wore an emerald-green gown of a fabric so lustrous that Beth thought it might be silk. The perfect fit announced that it had been made for her, unlike Beth's own black serge, which had had two previous owners. The other woman's hair was perfectly coifed, and her hands were smooth and white, the hands of a woman who had never washed clothes, chopped wood, or carried a child for twenty miles.

Beth raised her chin ever so slightly. She would not let this woman cow her. "No, ma'am, we're not lost." She and Dora were exactly where they needed to be. As Dora started to whimper, Beth pulled her onto her lap, stroked her dark curls, and murmured reassuring words.

When she looked up, Beth saw the woman frowning as she stared at Beth's left hand. The wedding ring. For some reason, that simple gold band appeared to disturb the woman, for she flushed as she looked down at her own bare finger. A faint smile touched Beth's lips. How ironic that this beautiful, obviously wealthy woman was impressed with a piece of jewelry that Beth would have given almost anything not to be wearing.

"Look, Mrs. . . . ." The woman paused.

"Simmons."

"Mrs. Simmons." She repeated the name, her voice haughty with disdain. "The clinic is on Swan Street."

Beth shook her head, dismissing the idea of a clinic. "I am here to see Dr. Muller."

The brunette's smile was little more than a sneer. "The doctor doesn't see the likes of you."

As Dora squirmed, Beth shook her head again. He had to. A child's welfare depended on him.

The inner door opened.

"Doctor." For the first time the other woman's smile was genuine.

Beth looked at the man she had traveled so far and taken such risks to consult. Unbidden, disappointment rose in her throat. He was too young to have done all the things with which he was credited. The doctor should have been as old as her father, yet he appeared less than thirty, with blond hair unstreaked by gray and a face devoid of lines. It was a strong face, its wide forehead and square chin evidence of his Germanic heritage. It was a handsome face, its classic features enlivened by a cleft in his chin. And yet the face seemed at odds with the doctor's reputation. He should have looked experienced and compassionate, not callow and cold. Though his was a handsome face, when he smiled at the dark-haired woman, no joy touched his eyes. Indeed, as he turned his gaze toward Beth, she felt more chilled than she had battling Lake Erie's brutal wind.

The doctor took a step toward her, and Beth had the feeling that he was comparing her undeniably disheveled appearance with the other woman's perfection. "Are you lost, madam?"

"No, Dr. Muller, I'm not lost. I'm Elizabeth Anne Simmons and . . ."

Before Beth could complete her sentence, the brunette rose gracefully. "I told her to go to the clinic," she announced with another warm smile for the doctor.

Nodding, he gestured toward the inner room. "I'll be with you in a moment, Miss Fields." When the door had closed, he turned to Beth again. "Now, madam, what can I do for you?"

Beth stood and placed her hand on Dora's shoulder as the girl looked up, her wary expression telling Beth she sensed her tension. "I haven't come for myself," she said. "It's my child." Somehow she managed to speak calmly, as though those were words she said every day. "Dora cannot hear." She stroked the girl's head, smoothing the unruly brown curls that were so different from Beth's own straight reddish gold hair.

For the briefest of moments, the man's face softened, and he smiled at Dora as though to reassure her. Then he turned back to Beth, his blue eyes once again cold and assessing. "You expect me to cure her deafness." It was a statement, tinged with more than a little irony.

The room was so quiet Beth could hear the fire crackle in the stove and the windowpanes rattle behind the heavy velvet draperies. Ordinary sounds, sounds she and the doctor would barely notice, but ones Dora might never again hear.

"I heard," Beth said, emphasizing the verb, "that you were the best physician in Buffalo and that you had more success treating hearing problems than anyone in New York State."

There was another moment of silence, and though it was one of the most difficult things she had done, Beth refused to drop her gaze. If he was a bully, he would take advantage of any hint of weakness. She could not afford that.

"What you have heard is true." The man nodded, accepting the accolades as his due. "I must tell you, though, that my fees are commensurate with my skills." When Beth did not reply, he continued. "Let me be blunt, madam. How do you propose to pay for my treatments?"

It was a question that had plagued her, part of the endless nightmare of the past three weeks. "I have some money," she replied, "and I'm willing to work. I assure you that I will pay you eventually."

"I see." As he frowned, the cleft in his chin deepened. "You expect me to spend my time—my very valuable time— on the chance that one day you might repay me." He looked at Dora again, and Beth saw the firm line of his lips begin to curve upward as if Dora's natural warmth had somehow thawed his ice-encased heart. When he spoke, Beth knew that she was mistaken. "I am sorry, but I do not take charity cases."

She recoiled as if she had been slapped. This man was her last hope, Dora's final chance to live a normal life, and he was going to refuse them the treatment the child needed so desperately. How could he?

Beth thought that she had outgrown the quick temper that had been the bane of her childhood, the temper that had gotten her into more than one scrape and earned her more than one beating. For years she had worked on controlling it, yet with only a few sentences this man's arrogant manner had destroyed all the progress she had made.

Clenching her fists in an effort to keep from shouting, she enunciated her words carefully. "I am not a charity case," she said. "I have already told you that I am willing to pay." Surely he could see that she would do anything—anything within her power—to help Dora. The one thing she would not do was to beg. She would pay for Dora's treatments. Beth opened her reticule and drew out two precious coins. "Here. Take this as your first payment." She extended her hand toward him. "I shall trust you to perform the treatment," she said, her voice low but trembling with anger.

Seemingly oblivious to her insult, the man kept his hands at his sides. "Madam, the answer is still no."

"Dora needs you."

He shook his head. His hair was golden blond, his eyes as blue as the summer sun. Were it not for the stern line of his lips, he could have been one of the angels she had seen pictured in the big church Bible. Unfortunately, his words were anything but heavenly. "She may need me, but so do my other patients, and they pay me well. Now I advise you to leave before I'm forced to call a policeman."

Beth stared at him, unwilling to believe he could be so cold, so cruel. When his expression remained as hard as his marble porch columns, she grabbed Dora's hand and pulled her into the vestibule. The child began to cry. "Hush, sweetheart," she said. "The nasty man will not hurt you." *But he also will not help you,* she added silently.

Sleet was falling and the pale afternoon sun had set, making the streets treacherous as Beth picked her way along holding Dora in her arms.

She had thought the nightmare would end when they reached the doctor, for his skill was legendary. Andrew Muller, miracle worker, people called him. What the legends had not revealed was that the good doctor worked miracles only for the wealthy. Why had no one mentioned that very important detail? She could have saved herself and Dora a difficult journey. Beth shook her head and cradled the girl closer. She still would have come to Buffalo, even facing likely rejection, for this precious child in her arms deserved a better life than her mother had had.

Beth shivered. She and Dora needed shelter for the night. Though it meant walking into the wind, Beth continued south. She had heard there were rooming houses near the canal where a woman could find safe, inexpensive lodging. They would stay there tonight. Then tomorrow she would find a way to earn the money for Dora's treatments. The doctor was mistaken if he thought he had seen the last of Elizabeth Anne Simmons.

The genteel neighborhood changed as she rounded another corner. This street boasted none of the expansive lawns and large houses that were common near the doctor's home. Here the buildings encroached on the street, and a woman sang bawdy lyrics accompanied by a poorly tuned piano. Two men smoked in a doorway, while across the street a trio placed bets on how long it would take a fourth to drink a flagon of beer.

Even wrapped in Beth's cloak, Dora began to shiver. "I know, honey. I'm cold, too." Beth looked around. There was no sign of a rooming house. Dora started to cry. Beth tightened her grip on the child and pressed her head close to her breast. Instinct honed by years of experience told Beth to attract as little attention as possible.

It was too late.

"Hey, Lou. The skirts is out." One of the men who had been smoking tossed his cheroot into the street.

His companion slapped his thighs. "Waddya say? It's our lucky night."

Beth continued walking. Perhaps if she ignored them, they would lose interest.

"Hey, doll, you're going the wrong way." The first man's voice echoed off the buildings. "Business is back here."

"First one to grab the skirt gets her." The second man shouted the challenge.

Beth started to run.

"So that's her game. C'mon, Jed. Let's show her what real men are made of." To Beth's ears his chuckle was pure evil, for she knew exactly what real men were made of.

She ran, terror lending her weary feet strength. But it was to no avail. Hampered by her long skirts and the child she carried, she had no chance of outrunning the men.

"I've got her." The first man slid into her, his weight knocking her forward.

"Dora," she cried, twisting her body in an attempt to protect the girl as she fell. And then the world went black.

Andrew Muller frowned as he drew back the heavy draperies. The last of his patients had left. Now it was time to prepare for the evening. The sleet that was falling, turning the piles of snow into mounds of ice and the roads into treacherous pathways, announced that winter had no intention of abdicating its rule to spring. That gentle season, Andrew had long since learned, came late to the city by the lake.

Andrew turned and began inserting his onyx shirt studs. While many deplored the long, bitter winters, he found them invigorating and more than a little advantageous, for as the cold weather lingered, many of the city's wealthiest citizens found an increasing number of reasons to seek his professional services. And if the price he had to pay was occasional attendance at charity balls like tonight's gala, so be it.

By the time he and Helen Pratt arrived at the Pierce mansion, the ballroom was crowded with the elite of Buffalo society. The scents of forced flowers, melted candle wax, and women's perfumes were far more pleasant than the rancid odors of illness and fear that he normally encountered, and the strains of music mingling with men's voices and women's murmurs soothed the ear, a welcome counterpoint to the cries and groans that accompanied his life's work.

"What a wonderful turnout!" Helen said as she and Andrew entered the large room. Though no one would call Helen beautiful, the petite blonde's ready smile and sweet disposition made her a popular member of the highest social echelon. Tonight she wore a gown of pink taffeta that displayed her softly rounded shoulders to advantage. Andrew frowned. Though there was no doubt the latest fashions were designed to entice a man, bare shoulders in a Buffalo winter were foolhardy. No wonder he had so many female patients complaining of fevers.

"Mrs. Pierce will be pleased that she was able to raise so much money," Helen continued.

"And, of course, the fact that she will establish her position as the city's premier hostess is of no account." Andrew muttered the words, more to himself than Helen. He had few illusions about the motive behind the charity ball. Though the organizers would claim it was designed to raise money for a mission, Andrew suspected that the primary allure was providing an opportunity for the wealthy to see and be seen.

In truth, he had no reason to be critical. It was not as though charity was why he himself had come.

"Shall we dance?" At least holding Helen in his arms would keep his more cynical thoughts at bay.

As their feet moved in the intricate steps of the quadrille, Andrew glanced around the room, his gaze moving from one woman to another. The color of their gowns varied, but their faces appeared to be poured from the same mold—round cheeks, full smiling lips—happy, well-fed faces, not like . . .

"Do you have any idea how annoying it is to be dancing with you and see you watching other women?" Helen's words were soft enough that they would not be overheard by others, but there was no mistaking their sharpness or the fact that her fingers, which appeared to rest lightly on his arm, dug in like a cat's claws.

"I wasn't doing that." Though he protested, it was a mere formality. Helen was right. He had been inexcusably rude to the one woman whose company he enjoyed, the one who made these obligatory social occasions bearable. When he should have been paying court to Helen—or at least listening to her—he had been wool-gathering, thinking of another woman. He had looked down at Helen and remembered how the redheaded woman had been taller than most and how proudly she had held herself despite her obvious poverty. For the first time he noticed Helen's nose. It was short and rounded, not slender with an intriguing tilt to its tip like the young widow's. Since Andrew could hardly tell Helen his thoughts, he shook his head again.

"Andrew, if you value our friendship at all, I beg you not to lie. You were staring at Lucinda Fields for a full thirty seconds."

Lucinda. He hadn't realized where his gaze had ended. At least now he had a plausible excuse. Andrew nodded, smiling at Helen as he twirled her around in time to the music. "If I was staring at her, it was simply because Miss Fields has made a most amazing recovery. She was in my office only this afternoon, complaining of a sore throat."

The steps of the dance separated them. When they were once again together, Helen continued speaking as though they had not been interrupted. Her ability to concentrate was one of the many things Andrew admired about her. "Undoubtedly Lucinda heard that you would be here and did not want to miss the opportunity to dance with you."

"Surely not!" Andrew raised a brow. He had not thought to ask Lucinda for a dance.

"Oh, Andrew." Helen's laugh was as cheerful as her smile. "Everyone knows that Lucinda Fields hopes to become Mrs. Doctor Andrew Muller."

Marriage! For the first time Andrew's steps faltered, and he nearly collided with the man next to him. Helen's arch smile and quick glance at his feet did nothing to improve his disposition.

"You know that I have no intention of marrying her or anyone else," he said, his voice tight with anger, though he kept a smile fixed on his face.

Helen's smile widened, and he saw genuine mirth in it. "Those are brave words, Andrew, but stronger men than you have rued pronouncing them." She twirled in time to the music, her face as placid as if they were discussing nothing more serious than the weather. "It will give me great pleasure to be here watching when you find the woman who can thaw that ice block you call a heart."

An ice block! What a joke! There was no ice in his chest, not a chunk, not even a tiny icicle. There was nothing at all, merely an empty cavern. It had been that way for a long, long time.

"Why is it that women think men should marry?" he asked Helen as they executed a particularly intricate step.

He felt Helen's hand tighten on his arm, as if the subject distressed her. "Perhaps it's because we long for children, and marriage is the normal route. Society tends to frown on other arrangements." Her voice was so light that Andrew realized he had imagined her discomfort.

"You're doing it again." Helen dug her nails into his arm once more.

This time his eyes focused on a tall redheaded woman who stood on the other side of the room, her back to him. Surely it was not the same woman who had come to his office this afternoon. Of course it was not. That woman's ghastly black clothing had proclaimed her mourning. The last place she would be this evening was at a party. Besides, she had looked as though she had never seen the inside of a ballroom, except perhaps to clean the floors. Poverty, albeit genteel poverty, had clung to her as tightly as little Mary had. Andrew shook his head slightly. The girl's name was not Mary. With her dark hair and eyes, she bore not the slightest resemblance to blond, blue-eyed Mary. As for her mother, it was foolish to think of her, to wish he could have given a different response to her plea. That was impossible.

"You're right, Helen. I am a brute."

She smiled sweetly, then curtsied as the dance ended. For the next hour, Andrew danced, smiled, paid empty compliments to his partners, and kept a sharp eye on the tall clock in the corner of the room.

Soon.

"Dr. Muller, if you could come with me." His hostess put her hand on Andrew's arm and led him off the dance floor, her silk skirts rustling as her hoops swayed.

"There's a man. . . ." Her expression left no doubt that she did not consider him a gentleman. "A man who says he must see you."

Andrew could feel his pulse begin to race. "It must be a patient, Mrs. Pierce." He had little doubt of the man's purpose, though he knew he would be a total stranger.

His hostess led him to a man who stood in the foyer, clearly ill at ease in the opulent surroundings. The stranger wore the rough clothing of a farmer and held a battered cap in his hand. Though the man kept his eyes downcast, Andrew could feel waves of tension emanating from him. "Mr. Smith needs you," the farmer said. "He's taken bad."

Andrew nodded solemnly as his hostess moved away, leaving him with the messenger. "Which Mr. Smith?"

"Mr. Floyd Smith."

It was the answer he had expected. Though his face remained impassive, the singing in his veins told Andrew his body was preparing for the night to come. Healing the Floyd

Smiths of the world was his life's mission, and, oh, how satisfying it could be!

"Hell and damnation!" The fire had gone out again.

The man strode to the stove, heedless of the snow his boots tracked onto the floor or the door that swung open, bringing a fresh gust of cold air into the already chilled cabin. Grabbing a handful of kindling, he swore loudly and fluently as he lit the fire. When the flames began to flicker, he stretched his hands toward the warmth.

Damn it all! This was woman's work. He shouldn't have to make fires or cook meals or keep this godforsaken cabin from looking like a horse's stall. That was why a man had a woman. That and to warm his bed. Lord knows Lenore hadn't been good for much, especially once she'd whelped the brat, but she had kept the fires burning. Now they were all gone: his wife, his child, and his fire.

He reached for the jug, which was never far away. Double damnation! It was empty. There was nothing to keep him warm.

Peter Girton stood up, shaking his fist at the powers that had taken his wife, his fire, and his whiskey. A man was not meant to live like this. A man had needs. Powerful needs. Needs that couldn't be satisfied by an occasional foray into town.

Thank God for the government of the good old U.S. of A. Those fancy lawmakers in Washington Town were the answer to his pleas. Thanks to them, he would soon have enough money to buy everything he needed; even better, he would be able to buy everything he *wanted*. All he had to do was a little hunting, and if there was one thing he was good at, it was hunting. In the meantime . . .

Peter spat on the floor in disgust. He wasn't going to spend another night with only an empty jug for company. Slamming the door behind him, he headed for town and a woman who would light a fire or two.

# Chapter Two

She was warm, blessedly, blessedly warm. Beth lay motionless for an instant, savoring the unexpected comfort. As she
turned on the pallet, waves of pain washed over her. Her arm
and leg throbbed, and her head! Gritting her teeth against the
agony she knew would come, she flexed each of her limbs,
then moved her fingers and toes. Nothing broken. She was
lucky this time. Perhaps he had passed out before he could
vent all of his fury; perhaps the cane had broken, for what
she felt was not the fire of the lash.

As Beth breathed shallowly, ever mindful of possible broken ribs, she stiffened. The sweet scent she inhaled was an
unfamiliar one, a combination of fresh air and dried heliotrope. How could that be? No place she had ever slept had
smelled like that. Her eyes flew open, and she saw a small
room with clean, whitewashed walls and crisp muslin curtains. Daylight spilled across the patchwork quilt and
streamed onto the scarred pine floor planks. It was a pretty
chamber and one that, despite her all too evident injuries,
somehow felt safe. Where was she?

She struggled to a sitting position, groaning as her muscles
protested the exertion. Memory flooded back. The long journey; the doctor's office; the evil men. Dora! *Please, God, let
her be safe*.

"Dora!" Beth's cry was instinctive, for her heart filled with
terror at the thought of what the men might have done to the
child. She was too young to have learned how to protect
herself.

The door opened, revealing a heavyset middle-aged
woman in the most outlandish clothing Beth had ever seen.
Her wrapper was festooned with rows of ruffles and ribbons
better suited to a woman half her age, while its bright pink

hue made Beth want to blink. "Dora? That the little girl's name?" The woman's light, lilting voice seemed at odds with her bulky body. "She wouldn't tell me." She shook her head slowly, as if mystified by the child's silence, and closed the door behind her.

Beth's panic began to subside as she realized Dora was somewhere in this peaceful house. "Who are you? Where am I? And where is Dora?" The questions came out in a stream, reminding Beth of the days she had stood in front of the schoolroom, posing questions to her pupils.

The other woman's friendly smile did not mask her own curiosity. Her gray eyes appeared to assess Beth, and she clucked softly at whatever it was she saw on Beth's face. "You got more questions than the policeman and the lawyer put together." She sighed and, pulling the room's only chair closer to the bed, settled herself onto it, seemingly oblivious to the creaking as the spindly legs protested her weight. "I reckon you won't answer mine if'n I don't start with yours. You can call me Silver." She touched the two wings of silver hair that framed her temples, as if indicating how she had gained the sobriquet. The rest of her hair was blacker than any Beth had seen, providing a startling contrast to her bright pink wrapper.

As a boarding teacher, Beth had stayed in her students' homes. She had once believed that experience had introduced her to the full gamut of personalities. She had been wrong. Nothing in her past had prepared her for this woman named Silver.

"Let's see, what was next?" Silver tilted her head slightly, and the unnaturally black curls bounced against her neck. "This here's my establishment. Reckon you know you're in Buffalo on Canal Street." Her smile softened as she glanced at the door. "Your little girl's safe now; I stuck her with the other children."

Beth swung her legs over the side of the bed. She had to go to Dora. Even if she were unharmed, only the Good Lord would know what the child was feeling, alone in a strange place, away from the one person she could trust, unable to communicate with the people around her.

As if she could read Beth's thoughts, Silver said, "Young'uns are stronger than you think. They bounce back from most everything."

But Beth, who could not remember either herself or her sister bouncing, was not convinced. She took a deep breath, then winced at the renewed pain. Experience had taught her that her ribs would hurt for weeks and that her only recourse was to take shallow breaths. Outside the door she heard the sound of women's voices and soft slippers on a wooden floor. Two strong perfumes that should never have been mingled wafted under the door and caused Beth to wrinkle her nose.

"How much do you recall of last night?" Silver asked, her gray eyes seeming to inquire as to what Beth found offensive.

"Not much," Beth admitted, being careful to breathe shallowly. "There were men chasing me. I don't know whether they pushed me or I fell. All I remember is running." And falling and then waking, certain that the nightmare she had thought gone forever had somehow come back.

"Reckon it don't matter." As Silver shrugged her large shoulders, the pink taffeta rustled. "My man heard cries and went out to investigate. Figured the ruffians was beating on one of our girls." She chuckled with obvious pride as she continued. "Those two men took one look at my Tom and run the other way. He brung you here."

Beth tried not to shudder at the thought of a strange man putting his hands on her. "Thank you, Silver," she managed to say. "Now I need to see Dora. She'll be frightened."

As Beth started to stand, Silver laid a restraining hand on her arm. "You stay right here. I'll bring your girl in."

Beth tried to quell her fears. Think of something pleasant, she admonished herself, for Dora seemed acutely aware of her moods. Searching for a happy thought, Beth looked out the small window. Only a few feet away a cherry tree grew, its twisted branches silhouetted against the sky. When it bloomed, the room would be filled with the sweet scent of its flowers and the songs of birds eagerly awaiting the fruit. Even today the tree was beautiful, for recent snow frosted its dark branches, and a few icicles hung like Christmas ornaments. Beth began to smile.

As she heard Silver's heavy footsteps, her smile broadened. Silver was bringing Dora, the one bright spot in her life, the sole good thing she had left. The older woman was obviously carrying the girl, for only one set of footsteps rang on the floor.

As she opened the door, Silver put Dora on her feet and pointed. "Mama," she said. Dora stood motionless, her fear palpable. Then the apprehension on her face turned to joy as she hurled herself onto the bed and into Beth's arms.

"There, there, sweetie. You're safe." Beth held the child close, reveling in her fresh scent and the warmth of her small body. She stroked Dora's head, then held her back a few inches so the little girl could see her smile.

The floor creaked as Silver walked to the foot of the bed, her arms crossed in front of her ample bosom. "She's a right pretty girl," she said, "but mighty quiet. Didn't say a single word when I bathed her. Just looked at me real serious like. I reckon she's scared of us."

Beth shook her head slowly. How simple it would be if fear were Dora's only problem. "Dora doesn't speak at all," she explained. "She's unable to hear."

A gust of wind rattled the windowpanes. Though Beth turned slightly at the sound, Dora continued to stare at the quilt, her slender fingers tracing the outlines of the brightly colored pieces.

Silver's gray eyes widened. "Oh." She opened her mouth, then closed it, apparently at a loss for words.

Beth continued to stroke Dora's hair, soothing the child in the only way she knew. "Dora's hearing is the reason we came to Buffalo," she said. "I want Dr. Muller to treat her."

The doctor's name appeared to restore Silver's voice. She harrumphed loudly, then demanded, "You sure about that? The man's colder than the river in January."

Beth managed a weak smile. "You must have met him." Dr. Andrew Muller of the glacial blue eyes and the gaze that could freeze hot coffee.

"Him . . . heck, no." Silver softened her words, presumably in deference to the child, even though Dora could not hear her. "A fine doctor like him don't deal with folks like us."

Beth nodded, realizing that although Silver's house was clean and neat, it was no match for the doctor's mansion. "He made it quite clear that he only treated the wealthy," Beth said.

"Money ain't the only thing keeping the doctor away from us." Silver gave Beth an appraising glance, then said in a matter-of-fact tone, "Honey, I reckon you know this is a whorehouse."

A whorehouse! Surely this warm, friendly, *safe* place could not be one where women let men . . . Beth felt her face flush with embarrassment. What would the school committees think if they learned she had spent the night in a house of ill repute? Everyone knew that a teacher's single most important responsibility—far more critical than teaching the three R's—was to instill high moral standards in her students. And to do that, it was expected that she herself would live an exemplary life.

Beth's embarrassment grew when she thought of this room and how it had *not* been used last night. She had slept here, unaware that her presence had deprived Silver of revenue. The woman had been kindness personified, literally saving her and Dora, and now Beth was even more deeply in her debt. "I'm sorry, Silver; we'll leave." She drew Dora closer, hoping the child would not sense her distress. Dora squirmed and scooted to the side of the bed, her bright eyes serious as she regarded Beth.

Silver shrugged an ample shoulder. "Where you gonna go, honey?"

Heavy footsteps, obviously belonging to a man, echoed outside the door. Beth shuddered at the realization that only a thin wall separated her and Dora from him.

"We'll go to a boardinghouse. That's where we were headed last night."

Tipping her head to one side, Silver asked, "What you gonna do for money? You weren't carrying no reticule when you came here. All I found was your Bible."

The flush that had colored Beth's cheeks fled as she recognized the gravity of her situation. The few precious coins she had been able to save for Dora's care were gone, stolen by the thugs, leaving her even fewer options than she had had a day ago, and those had been few enough.

"You and the little girl can stay here as long as you need." Silver shrugged. "This room's been empty for a long time. Might as well put it to use."

Beth closed her eyes, trying to marshal her emotions. The room was warm, clean, and she—despite everything—felt safe here. It would only be for a short while, and the school committees need never know. It was tempting to stay. If only she could pay Silver.

"Silver, you already know I have no money."

The madam shrugged again. "Don't matter."

But Beth, who remembered the doctor's disdain of charity cases and her mother's admonition to never be indebted, was uncomfortable with the offer. "I'll find a way to repay you." Somehow. Someday.

Dora, sensing Beth's distress, placed a small hand on her face, her fingers urging Beth's lips upwards.

"Just worry about your little girl," Silver said with a smile at the child's actions. "Get her well."

Slowly Beth nodded. Dora was what mattered, not her pride.

By the time Andrew arrived home, it was an hour before dawn. By all rights, he should be exhausted, and indeed he was. He was also well satisfied with his night's work. Mr. Smith was out of danger now, though the outcome had not always been certain. At times, as the night passed and he guided his patient on the perilous journey between life and death, Andrew had felt that the hounds of Hell were closing on them. Perhaps they were; perhaps the baying he had heard came from infernal canines, not mortal ones. If so, he had managed to elude them once more. And, thank God, tonight he had not had to be Charon, ferrying a man across the last river. How he hated that! It was both physically and mentally exhausting.

He released the horse's harness and led him into the barn, leaving the buggy outside the small carriage house. What he needed now was a couple hours' sleep; the cabriolet could wait.

Afterwards, Andrew could not have said what wakened him. It was not that his body no longer craved sleep, for he was far from that state. In all likelihood, the unwelcome sounds filtering through the windowpane and the thick draperies had roused him from his habitually light slumber.

As he parted the drapes, his fatigue was replaced by anger at the sight below. Idiot! Flinging open the window, he leaned out. "Stop!" But the man did not appear to hear him. Seconds later, Andrew stood in the yard, seemingly oblivious to the light snow that had begun to fall and the fact that he was clad only in his nightshirt.

"Roberts, what do you think you are doing?" he bellowed at the coachman, who even now was preparing to climb into the carriage. How far had the man gotten? Had he found . . . ? Andrew refused to complete the thought or consider the consequences.

The man turned, his face betraying surprise at seeing his employer. "Why, sir, I was putting the buggy into the carriage house." He gestured toward the building at the end of the cobblestone drive.

Andrew felt his anger grow. Damn the man, putting him in this position. From the corner of his eye, Andrew saw the kitchen curtains part. Within minutes, every servant would have heard the tale of his reaction to an apparently minor infraction. The last thing he needed was the speculation that would follow.

He turned back to his coachman. The man's face was almost as gray as his livery, and Andrew noted that he swallowed with difficulty. Fear would do that to a man.

"And, why, might I ask, were you moving the buggy?"

Roberts's eyes widened. "Because, sir, it has started to snow." He looked at the gray sky and the wet flakes that even now were beginning to cover the black cowhide.

As if he cared about the coach's exterior! "Did I, or did I not, tell you never to touch my buggy?" Though his blood boiled with anger, Andrew managed to infuse his words with his usual frigid tones. The damage was done, but perhaps he could mitigate it by feigning normalcy. "Did I, or did I not, explain to you and everyone else in this household that two things were never to be touched: my medical bag and this buggy?"

Roberts paled in the face of Andrew's anger. "You did, sir, but I thought . . ."

The sound of a window sliding told Andrew his fears were realized. At least part of his house staff was listening to this exchange.

"Thinking was your first mistake," he said coldly. "Your second was disregarding my instructions."

The man dropped his head. "It won't happen again, sir."

"If you value your employment, it had best not."

As the first of his patients arrived, Andrew tried to put the incident from his mind. The buggy was stowed inside the carriage house, ready for his next summons, and Roberts, suitably chastened, would henceforth follow instructions explicitly. In all likelihood, no damage had been done. His life's work could continue as planned.

"I'm leaving, sir." Andrew's housekeeper greeted him as he entered the dining room for his midday meal.

Andrew nodded and took his place at the head of the table, thinking—not for the first time—that a man who lived alone had little use for a table that could easily seat eighteen. "That's fine, Mrs. Fisher," he said as he picked up his soup spoon. "You don't need to tell me your itinerary."

Andrew waited, expecting her to leave as she did each day after the first course was served, but the gray-haired woman stood in the doorway, her hands fisted on her hips. "I'm leaving," she repeated. "I won't work here anymore."

"I beg your pardon."

Mrs. Fisher's voice was accusatory. "You had no call to talk to Roberts that way. No call at all." Andrew stared at the woman, astonished. She had worked for him for almost a year, and this was the first time he had heard her string more than three words together. Apparently she was the person who had opened the kitchen window while Andrew was berating the coachman. "My sister raised Roberts to be a good boy," Mrs. Fisher continued, further surprising Andrew. He had had no idea his housekeeper and his coachman were related. "You had no call at all to be rude," she announced.

Andrew's housekeeper took a deep breath. "You think you're so high-and-mighty, but let me tell you, Doctor, I don't care if your mother was a duchess. Even royalty needs to show some manners."

As she stormed from the room, Andrew frowned. A duchess! If only she knew.

It was afternoon by the time Beth was ready to leave. She had been surprised by how late she had slept, but exhaustion and the injuries she had sustained the previous evening had taken their toll, and even after she had wakened, she had moved more slowly than normal.

Though she was still uncomfortable with Silver's offer of free lodging, Beth realized she had few alternatives and had agreed to accept Silver's hospitality until she was able to secure work. She would start looking tomorrow. First she needed to see Dr. Muller again.

"Mama will be back soon," she told Dora, stroking the child's hair and pressing a kiss on her soft cheek. Though she hated to leave the girl, Beth knew the trip would take far less time if she was not carrying her. Then, too, there was another reason for confronting the doctor alone. Without Dora there to sense Beth's fear and anger, she would be free to discuss the child's case more openly. Surely when he realized how much Dora needed his care, he would agree. The man, though cold, must have some human feelings.

"Stay here and play with the children," she murmured to Dora, punctuating her words with gestures. As if she understood, Dora smiled and took the wooden block that the other little girl offered her. The three children, Dora, a girl of about three, and a boy whom Beth guessed to be six or seven, were playing in the corner of the kitchen. It was the first time Dora had played with other children, and—to Beth's delight—she seemed to have joined the group, apparently able to communicate without speech. Perhaps Silver was right. Perhaps children did bounce. Just because she and Lenore hadn't, that didn't mean no one did.

The morning snow had stopped, and the sun had emerged briefly from the heavy blanket of clouds. Beth felt her spirits rise. Though she knew better than to trust in omens, she couldn't help enjoying the sun's warmth and the way it made the fresh snow sparkle. All too soon, the snow would turn brown and melt into slush. In the meantime, she would take pleasure where she could find it.

She turned the final corner and stopped, her heart pounding at the sight of Andrew Muller's residence. It looked even more impressive in daylight than it had the day before. Then Beth had realized only that it was huge, its wide front porch anchored by six large columns. Today she saw that the columns were fluted with Corinthian capitals and that the window in the richly carved front door was leaded glass. That window had probably cost as much as her parents' farm. It was certainly more valuable than the house where Dora had been born.

Taking a breath to quell her nervous heart, Beth climbed the front steps. The waiting room was empty. After knocking on the inner door to announce her arrival, she sat in one of the thickly padded chairs. He had to agree to her proposal. He just had to. Her fingers gripped the chair arms, and she felt the soft leather flex. The man was wealthy; he lived surrounded by luxury; surely he could spare a few hours of his precious time to help a child.

At the sound of the door opening, she looked up, her heart beating the way it did when she carried Dora up a steep hill. Dr. Muller was taller than she remembered, probably a full six feet, wearing an impeccably tailored dark gray suit that only emphasized his broad shoulders and long legs. Other than being male, he bore little resemblance to her father or Peter or any of the other men she knew. Perhaps yesterday had been an anomaly. Perhaps he was compassionate. Perhaps he would have changed his mind.

"You again?" Andrew Muller raised one eyebrow as he stared at her, his expression leaving no doubt of his displeasure at finding Beth in his waiting room.

Her hopes fell, but she would not admit defeat. Beth rose and drew another deep breath. *Pretend he's a member of the school committee,* she admonished herself. *You were able to convince them to pay for your training at the Troy Female Seminary, though no one thought you could. Surely you will be able to persuade him.*

"Good afternoon, Doctor." While he might ignore the social niceties, she would not. "I have come to speak to you about Dora."

There was no response. As far as Beth could see, he did not move a muscle, and she wondered if he were indeed carved from a block of ice. The only sign that he was human were the deep circles under his eyes. The doctor, it appeared, had had little sleep last night.

When the silence grew oppressive, she said again, "Doctor." Beth gripped the chair back, her fingers digging into the soft leather as she strove to control her temper.

"I heard you the first time," he replied, "but I was under the impression that we had completed this discussion yesterday, Mrs. . . ."

"Simmons."

"Mrs. Simmons. What has changed?"

What had changed? She had been attacked and robbed by ruffians; she was living in a whorehouse; and Dora had gone another day without hearing the sound of birds singing, rain falling, or herself laughing.

"Nothing has changed. That's the problem, Doctor. There were no miracles overnight, so Dora is still deaf."

The expression flitted across his face so quickly that Beth thought she might have imagined the softening, the momentary look of pity. She must have imagined it, for when he spoke, his words were uncompromising, his tone frigid. "That is not my problem, madam."

"No, it's not," she agreed. By some miracle her voice remained calm, though she wanted to shout her frustration. "You're the solution to the problem. You're the only one who can help her. Please! I implore you." Oh, how it hurt to say those words. Years ago she had vowed she would never again beg a man for anything, never give one that satisfaction, that measure of control over her. She had kept her vow. Until today. But Dora was more important than any childhood vow. Beth would plead, grovel on her knees, do whatever it took to convince him to restore the little girl's hearing.

Andrew looked at the woman who stood before him, her back ramrod straight, her face so soft it seemed as if it would crumple from the weight of her emotions. She was a bundle of contradictions, apparently as stern as the schoolmistress who had drummed multiplication tables into his head, yet as vulnerable as Mary.

He would not think about Mary.

"Madam," he said in a voice that betrayed none of his momentary weakness, "the answer is still the same."

She stared at him for a moment, and he could see her lips tremble, although he did not know whether from anger or fear. "Have you no heart?" she demanded.

"There are those who say I do not," he admitted. "As a physician, I know that to be an impossibility."

She straightened her shoulders, and Andrew saw her breasts rise under the poorly fitting black dress. She ought to look like a scarecrow, all in black. Most women did. But the gown, though obviously cheap and designed for a larger woman, made her reddish-gold hair look like firelight.

Her voice was warmer than fire as she continued. "If you do have a heart, do you have any idea what it's like, seeing a child suffering, wanting desperately to help her, and not being able to?"

Did he? The pain he had fought so hard to suppress shot through him, and he closed his eyes for a second, trying to regain his composure. What was there about this woman that she managed to find spots that were still raw? Those wounds should have healed years ago.

When a thick cloud obscured the sun, Andrew lit one of the lamps, glad of the opportunity to turn away from the woman who asked such probing questions.

"If I did agree to treat the child," he said, keeping his voice devoid of emotion, "how would you propose to pay my fee?"

He named an amount that was half his normal fee, yet still enough to cause the woman's face to blanch.

"I will find a way," she insisted. "I'm a schoolteacher. I trained at Miss Willard's academy." Despite himself, Andrew was impressed. Emma Willard's Troy Female Seminary was the Harvard of teacher training. "I'm sure I can find a position in Buffalo," the young widow continued.

He nodded slightly, though he knew there was little chance that even with her credentials she could earn his fee. He ought to refuse unequivocally. After all, he could not afford to have this woman and her child nearby. And yet—though common sense told him otherwise—he could not destroy her last remnant of hope, for he knew all too well what life without hope was like. "When you do have the money, bring the child to me."

Sorrow clouded the woman's green eyes, and her lips began to quiver. "Dora can't wait. Each day that she goes without hearing means another day without speaking and without learning. She may never catch up." The tears that filled her eyes threatened to spill over. "Please, treat her now. I'll pay your fee as soon as I can."

"No, madam." He forced the words out, knowing they would hurt her but realizing he had no choice.

She was silent for a moment, and Andrew watched the play of emotions on her face. Incredulity, anger, and disappointment vied with sorrow. Finally, with apparent reluctance, she took a step forward. "I implore you, Doctor."

As she moved closer to the light, Andrew saw the dark stains of bruises along one cheek. They had not been there yesterday; he was certain of that.

"What happened to you?" He extended his hand to touch her face, to determine how serious the contusions were.

"No!" she cried, and jumped back as though he had struck her. "Nothing happened!" Moving so quickly that he had no time to anticipate her actions, she turned and fled, letting the door slam behind her.

Andrew stared at the empty room for a long moment. The woman was frightened. Lord knows he had seen enough of fear to recognize it. The question was, why?

# Chapter Three

The stitch in her side that reminded her all too vividly of her bruised ribs subsided, and she could breathe evenly now that she was blocks away from the doctor. Beth's pace returned to normal, but as she turned the corner and spotted Silver's house, she began to hurry. No matter how the building was used and how she might deplore its inhabitants' profession, this was her home, at least for the next few days. She and Dora would be safe here. No one would touch them, and the little girl, who for three weeks had been Beth's only living relative, would have playmates.

A whorehouse. Beth shuddered. Seen in daylight, it was a far cry from Andrew Muller's beautiful mansion. This building could only be described as garish, with its silver front door and bright pink shutters against the brown clapboards. Still, compared to some of the other establishments on Canal Street, it was conservative. The colors did not clash, and there were no tawdry paintings of half-clad women announcing the trade that was plied within. Silver, it appeared, believed her shiny front door was adequate advertisement.

The building was also in good repair. The shutters, bright though they might be, did not hang askew, and the roof had no visible holes, unlike the house across the street.

Beth hurried toward the front door, then stopped abruptly when she saw two men heading in the same direction. Their ribald comments left no doubt of their destination, and even from a distance Beth could see the eager expressions on their faces. Her mouth grew dry at the same time that she felt her palms dampen. Would they stop her? Would they think she worked there?

Bile rose in her throat. No! Though she had an almost irrational need to see Dora and hold the little girl in her arms again, she would not—could not—go near those men. There had to be another entrance. Beth's eyes moved quickly, looking for a path to a side or back door. There were none. Then she spotted a narrow alleyway three houses away. Perhaps that led to the back of Silver's building.

The stench that greeted her as she entered the alleyway told Beth that the local residents used it for disposing of garbage; in addition, several people appeared to call it their home, for she saw and smelled the remnants of open fires. She drew her muffler closer to her face in an attempt to block the noxious odors. Lenore had told her that her sense of smell was keener than most people's. At the time, her sister had insisted she was fortunate, for Beth enjoyed flowers' scents that Lenore could barely identify. Today, an overactive olfactory nerve seemed a curse rather than a blessing.

The alley wound between two houses, then made a right-hand turn to continue behind them. Beth took a deep breath as the path widened and the smells dissipated. There it was. There was no mistaking Silver's house, for the pink shutters continued even to the back.

The rear entrance opened into a small vestibule, leading to the kitchen, where two women sat at a long table.

"She's back." One of the women looked up from the vegetables she was peeling.

A moment later Silver burst into the room, bringing with her the scents of cheap perfume and face powder. "What did he say?" she demanded. Her high heels clattered on the floor as she led Beth toward the room she had designated as Beth and Dora's chamber. "Your little girl was plumb tuckered out," she called over her shoulder, reassuring Beth that Dora was napping in one of the other rooms.

Beth followed in Silver's wake, trailing behind her wide rustling skirts. It was obvious Silver had spent several hours dressing for the evening. Her face, now covered with a powder that was almost white, was framed by long sausage curls that bounced on her bare shoulders as she walked. Though the hairstyle was one more suited to a woman half Silver's age, Beth had to admit it was flattering. And the vivid pink dress that barely covered her ample bosom was testimony to

Silver's apparent fondness for that particular shade. With her own reddish-gold hair, pink was a color Beth would never have worn, even if there had been money for a ball gown.

"What did the doctor say?" Silver repeated.

As she hung her cloak on one of the wall pegs, Beth shrugged. She would not—absolutely would not—think about those final seconds in the doctor's office. "It was a little better than yesterday." She had convinced herself of that once her initial fear had subsided. "At least he didn't say no. What he told me was to come back when I had the money."

Silver consulted the small gold watch that she had pinned on her bodice, then muttered something that sounded like, "Almost time." She released the watch, letting it bounce gently against the pink taffeta, and asked, "How much?" When Beth named the amount, Silver flinched. "I heard the man was richer than any ten folks had a right to be. Reckon I know how he got that way. That's robbery."

"He would tell you his services are worth it." Beth grimaced at the thought that she was defending Dr. Andrew Muller when less than an hour earlier she had fled from him. "The fact is, it could be half that amount, and I would be in the same situation. Even if I taught school for another fifty years and saved every penny I was paid, I wouldn't earn that much."

She heard the front door slam and men's voices calling out greetings. The only good Beth could find in Dora's deafness was that her ears would not be subjected to such foul language.

Silver tipped her head, leaving Beth uncertain whether she was considering Beth's statement or listening to the men. Finally Silver asked, "Do you reckon he'd agree if you paid him part now and promised the rest?"

If only! "I suggested that, and he refused."

Her legs suddenly weak, Beth sat on the edge of the bed. Though she motioned Silver toward the chair, the older woman remained standing.

"Well, then, honey, there's only one thing to do." As Beth raised a questioning brow, Silver continued. "Keep asking.

Did you ever see what water does to rocks?" Without waiting for Beth's response, she said, "It wears them down. You can do that to Dr. Icicle."

Silver, it was clear, had never heard of mixed metaphors. Despite herself, Beth smiled at the image of the doctor melting under her persistence. Though unlikely, it was a beguiling thought. "How did you get to be so wise?" Beth asked.

The madam shrugged her dimpled shoulders and glanced at her watch again. With a quick nod, she started toward the door, then turned back to Beth. She was silent for a moment, and Beth sensed that Silver was trying to choose her words carefully. Since Silver normally appeared to blurt out her thoughts, Beth wondered what was causing the internal debate. "Look around, honey." Silver gestured expansively. "Reckon you can see I like the place clean. Fact is, this house is too much for Mavis. Her knees bother her something fierce when she scrubs the floors. Reckon you could help her?" When Beth hesitated, Silver continued. "Cain't pay much, but you and your little girl would have a place to stay."

It was a solution, and yet . . . Beth's face whitened as she remembered the men walking toward the front door. They had been big, and they looked as tough as the ruffians who had chased her last night.

"The house is closed to customers in the morning," Silver said, as casually as if she were discussing the weather. "You'd never see them."

Beth's eyes widened at the woman's perception. "How did you know?" She hadn't told Silver her fears.

"Honey, I don't need no fancy education to see that you're afeard of men. I don't need to know why." Silver's ringlets bounced as she shook her head. "I reckon it's enough that I know what you're feeling right now. Sooner or later, you'll figure out that not all men are bad."

The front door opened again, and two raucous male voices demanded their favorite girls and drinks delivered in that order. Beth revised her judgment. Silver was not as wise as she had thought. "Every man I've known has been," she said quietly.

Silver was silent for a moment, apparently digesting

Beth's statement. "Even your husband?" she asked.

Beth could not control her shudder or the feeling of revulsion that swept over her. "That's how Dora lost her hearing," she said when her teeth stopped chattering. "Her father hit her." She closed her eyes, trying to block out the painful images.

There was a long silence. Then Silver spoke. "You're safe now that he's gone."

Beth's head jerked up, and she stared at Silver, momentarily confused. *Gone. Of course.* She nodded.

"You and Dora will be safe here," Silver repeated. "We'll even put some meat on those bones of yours."

"I'm fine," Beth insisted, not wanting to hurt Silver's feelings by explaining that she did not aspire to the other woman's undeniably hefty frame.

"Honey, I can see you ain't been eating good," Silver announced. "Why, if you don't look out, that wedding ring's gonna slide right off your hand."

Beth lowered her eyes in confusion.

The woman was most definitely not ill. Her color was normal; she had no fever; and her throat, which she told him ached so much that she could not swallow even clear soup, was neither inflamed nor swollen. Coming here once was a waste of time. Three times in a week was outrageous.

Though he seethed internally, Andrew fixed a pleasant but serious expression on his face. He knew what his patients expected. "Your throat is fine, Mrs. Fields."

She raised an elegantly groomed hand to her throat and smiled, fluttering her lashes so rapidly that Andrew wondered if she had a foreign object in her eye. It seemed unlikely, for he doubted that even a dust mote was allowed to remain in the Fields mansion. The furniture, which he had been told half a dozen times was imported from Europe, was cleaned daily by two chambermaids, also imported from Europe.

"Oh, Doctor, I feel so much better now that you've looked at my poor little old throat. You don't know how much I appreciate your coming all this way to see poor little old me."

Andrew nodded stiffly. Mrs. Fields's penchant for exaggeration was as well known as her imaginary ailments. The "great distance" that he had traveled consisted of three blocks; however, the fee he intended to charge would compensate handsomely for any inconvenience he had incurred. He would don his gravest expression as he doubled his customary fee for house calls. To judge from his past experience with Mrs. Fields, she would be delighted. In all likelihood she would tell her friends that her condition was so serious it had required an extraordinary effort to cure, and that Dr. Muller's services were worth every dollar he charged.

At one time Andrew would have been ashamed to be so mercenary. No longer. It was all part of the plan. Patients like Mrs. Fields provided the money he so desperately needed.

Andrew gathered his instruments, placing them carefully in the black leather bag. With a final nod to Mrs. Fields, he closed the door behind him.

Thank God that was over!

As he stepped into the wide hallway, Andrew was careful to walk on the Persian carpet. If luck was with him, the rug would muffle his steps enough that he could escape without encountering his other patient.

Luck was not with him.

"Good morning, Doctor." Lucinda Fields emerged from the chamber opposite her mother's so quickly that Andrew suspected she had been waiting for him. Yet surely that couldn't be, for her dress was not completely fastened, its bodice dipping alarmingly. "I'm so happy to see you." Lucinda took another step toward Andrew and extended her hand to him. To avoid touching her, Andrew made a show of checking the contents of his bag.

"I'm certain you have put Mama's mind at ease, and now she will be able to eat again. Papa and I have been so worried."

There was nothing wrong with what Lucinda said. Indeed, a child should care about her mother. It was only her simpering tone that set Andrew's nerves on edge and told him there was no true feeling behind her words. He was certain that when Mrs. Simmons's daughter was Lucinda's age, she would do more than spout empty phrases. Andrew clenched his jaw. Damn it all! He would not think about the lovely widow and her child.

Fixing a pleasant smile on his face, he turned to Lucinda. "Your mother is quite healthy." *Her only ailment is hypochondria,* he added to himself, suspecting the pampered woman had nothing to occupy her time other than worry about imaginary illnesses.

"Still, it's such a blessing to have you here." Lucinda Fields put a hand on Andrew's arm and drew him toward the staircase. "Let me walk to the door with you." When they reached the landing, she turned and smiled. "Now, tell me, Doctor. Will you be going to Mrs. Wilton's ball?"

That, then, was the reason for her solicitous manner. Though he had thought Helen exaggerated when she claimed Lucinda attended parties in hopes of dancing with him, Andrew was forced to consider that his friend's perception might be accurate. It was not a pleasant prospect.

He nodded. "I received an invitation." There was no reason to tell Lucinda he had not yet decided whether to attend, that it would depend on many things, not the least of which was the weather. If the preceding nights were heavily overcast and the North Star was not visible, there would be little reason to endure an evening of forced gaiety.

"I do so hope you'll be able to stay for the whole party." Lucinda paused at the foot of the stairs and looked up at Andrew, her brown eyes liquid with emotion. Andrew wondered if it was only coincidence that she had stopped in a position where he would have an excellent view of her breasts. "I was so disappointed when you missed dinner at the Pierces' ball," she said with a deep sigh that brought those generously proportioned mammary glands closer to him. "Although a lady shouldn't admit it, I do declare that the food lost its savor when you weren't there to enjoy it."

Andrew repressed a smile. Lucinda Fields was a bit like a puppy. Though one might deplore its tendency to chew on slippers, there was something so engaging about its eagerness to please that any annoyance was short-lived. "There was an emergency," he said mildly. "Although regrettable, that is part of a doctor's life."

"Oh, Doctor, I would not call it regrettable. I would say that it was exciting."

If only she knew! It *had* been an exciting evening, following the summons to Mr. Smith's case. And, since the Wiltons' party was being held at the time of the new moon, there was every likelihood that he would receive a similar summons that night.

When he bade Lucinda farewell, Andrew drew a deep breath, then began to walk quickly down the street. His feet moved mechanically while his mind recalled Mr. Smith. That case had been a close one, far more perilous than normal. Andrew suppressed a shudder as he considered that future cases like Mr. Smith's might not have the same successful ending. Failure was unacceptable. Totally, completely unacceptable.

"Hello, Andrew. Calling on the Fieldses again?"

He turned, startled by the sound of Helen Pratt's voice. For a few moments he had been so lost in his thoughts that, though his feet moved mechanically, he had been unaware of his surroundings. He blinked rapidly to clear his mind and bring himself back to the reality of a snow-and-ice-covered Buffalo street. "I see you're out taking your constitutional," he said, referring to Helen's habit of walking whenever the weather permitted rather than answering her question directly.

Helen was not so easily distracted. "Let me guess." She tipped her blond head to one side. "You were treating Lucinda's sore throat."

Though the wind was damp, a harbinger of more spring snow, Andrew felt his spirits rise as he walked at Helen's side. If anyone could dispel his odd malaise, it would be Helen. "For once you are mistaken." He matched his pace to hers as they continued down Delaware Avenue. "I was called to cure Mrs. Fields's sore throat."

Placing a gloved hand on his forearm, Helen raised one brow. "A tendency toward sore throats must be a hereditary weakness." There was more than a hint of amusement in her voice.

Though the sun emerged from behind a cloud, Andrew's mood darkened. "Don't mock me, Helen. I know you may not be convinced, but there is such a thing as heredity." That, in addition to cases like Mr. Smith's, was one of Andrew's primary interests. Though he had gained fame treating hearing problems, few in the medical community knew that he was fascinated by the theory that physical traits were passed from one generation to another.

When he had told Helen of his research, she had listened intently, and if she was skeptical, she had hidden her disbelief well. Andrew wondered why she seemed so mocking today. "How else can you explain that your face is the same shape as your mother's, and you and your father have the same hair color? It's not chance." He guided Helen around a snow pile.

"I never said it was chance. I just find it interesting that both Lucinda and her mother claim to have the same ailment, when they look perfectly healthy." Helen tightened her grip on his arm as her boots began to slip on the ice. "Maybe it's a lack of imagination that's hereditary," she said when they were once more on firm ground. "Maybe the only excuse the Fields women can find to ensure that you call on them is a sore throat."

Despite himself, Andrew chuckled. "You really are a breath of fresh air."

"Translation: I say the things you're thinking but save you the embarrassment of putting them into words."

"Perhaps."

They crossed the street, turning onto Mohawk. As mutual acquaintances drove by, slowing their buggy to call greetings, Helen smiled and Andrew doffed his hat.

"So, tell me, Andrew-who-believes-in-heredity, which characteristics did you inherit from your parents?" Helen asked when the carriage was half a block away and the sound of wheels and hooves had subsided.

He shrugged. Though this was not a topic he wanted to discuss, he knew Helen would badger him until he made some response. "I'm not sure. They died when I was young." That much was true. The implication that he was too young to remember them was not true, but he had no intention of sharing that particular fact with Helen . . . or anyone.

Tilting her head again as if she were analyzing his features, Helen said, "I don't know about your father, but I can tell that you inherited both the Duchess's regal air and her money. No one would dispute that, especially after seeing her portrait."

An hour later, Andrew stood in his front parlor gazing at the painting of the blond-haired woman Buffalo society knew as the Duchess. With her high cheekbones, prominent nose, and strong chin, she was a formidable-looking woman, while the mass of jewels that hung from her neck and ears left no doubt as to her wealth.

What would Mrs. Fields, Mrs. Pierce, and the other matrons who reveled in his aristocratic background think if they knew the truth? How would they react if they knew that the haughty woman in the portrait was not his mother, was in fact no relation at all? How many doors would be slammed in his face, the way they were the night Mary . . . ?

Andrew clenched his fists, then relaxed them, expelling a long breath. He would not think about that night or the days leading up to it. That was the past. Though he could not change it, he could ensure that the future was different, far different. And, thanks to the very people who would scorn his origins, he was close to reaching his goal. Soon no one would close doors in his face; no one would refuse to help him. Soon he would have enough money to ensure that he could buy everything he needed.

The woman in the portrait looked down at him, her smile unchanging. Helen might be right, Andrew reflected. He might owe his regal air to the Duchess, for some things could be learned, even if they were not inherited, and he had learned much by studying the painting.

Unbidden, his mind conjured an image of the woman who had visited his office the previous afternoon. Had the Widow Simmons inherited that combination of vulnerability and confidence, or had she learned it from someone? And which of her parents bequeathed her those grass-green eyes and that hair that looked like sunset on the lake?

Andrew shook his head in disgust. Spring must be in the air, if he was harboring such poetic thoughts. They were frivolous, nonsensical, and had no place interfering with the important things in his life, things like the night to come.

The bitch! Peter Girton raised the buggy whip over his head and lashed at the horses, cursing when he missed their backs. He raised his arm again. That two-bit whore was lucky he hadn't knocked out her remaining teeth. Imagine! She had called him a pervert. Him! Just because he wanted her to pleasure him in a special way, a way that made him feel real good. The other whores did it, but that high-and-mighty bitch had said no.

He sure had showed her who was boss. Peter grinned, remembering. She wouldn't forget Peter Girton any time soon. The hell of it was, even after he knocked her around a bit, she still refused to do what he asked. Said he would have to pay more. Damn it all! He didn't have the amount of money she demanded. Not today.

Who did she think she was, anyway? Just a whore. Nothing special. But someday soon, when he had the money, he would be back. And then she wouldn't refuse him. No, sirree. She would do everything he asked and smile while she did it.

But first he had to get the money.

"I'm sorry, Mrs. Simmons." The woman's gray eyes radiated sincerity. "Your credentials are excellent. Quite honestly, we could use someone with your training here at Parson's." Her lips tightened. "Unfortunately, we cannot hire a married woman. Our founders believe that would be a bad influence on our pupils."

Beth bit the inside of her lip to keep from shouting her frustration. This was the third school she had visited and the third—and most unfair—rejection she had received. When she had left Silver's this morning, she had been optimistic that she would be able to find a teaching position. Her optimism, it appeared, was misplaced.

There had to be a way she could earn the money for Dora's treatment. There just had to be. Unfortunately, Beth had yet to find it.

"A, B . . . What comes next?" Beth kept her hand poised over the slate, waiting for the response she knew would come. As the little boy chewed his lower lip and scrunched his eyes closed, Beth smiled. No matter how often she saw children grimace and writhe as they sought an answer, then dance with glee when they found it, she never grew tired of guiding them on the path to learning.

The boy's eyes flew open, and a grin split his face. "C!"

"That's correct, Mark." She gave his shoulder a reassuring squeeze. "Now let's see how many C's you can find on this page." Opening Lenore's Bible, she placed it in front of him. The boy bent his head and began to study the page, making a mark on the slate each time he found the letter.

The feeling of warmth that swept over Beth reminded her why she had chosen to be a schoolteacher. It was not, as her father had once accused, because she wanted to leave his house, although that was an undeniable benefit. The real pleasure came from watching children like Mark absorb knowledge the way a thirsty plant did water. And like the plants, they grew and blossomed.

Each afternoon when she finished her cleaning, Beth would gather the children and read them a story. Though Dora could not hear, she would sit in Beth's lap and watch her lips, laughing when the other children did, almost as though she heard the words. But Mark had watched, not Beth's lips, but the printed page, and she had seen him trying to make sense of the strangely shaped characters. The child wanted to learn to read, and Beth—rejoicing in his curiosity—began to teach him.

When she heard about the tutoring, Silver had offered to pay Beth, but she had refused. Though this was a far cry from her dream of teaching in an exclusive school, Beth could not deny that it was satisfying. Watching Mark's progress, seeing how quickly he learned, provided rewards far beyond any gold that Silver could offer. For it gave her hope that once Dora could hear, she would be like Mark and learn quickly enough to overcome the handicap of two years without hearing.

Dr. Muller would help her. He had to.

Involuntarily, Beth touched her cheek. The bruises were almost healed. Though she had vowed to be persistent, to make daily visits to the doctor's office, she had not been back. She would not return until the bruises had disappeared.

It was cowardly to have fled the way she did. A strong woman would have stayed, would have knocked the doctor's hand away and demanded that he listen to her. But that day fear had overcome her common sense. It had been instinctive, fleeing an upraised hand.

So be it.

Though she could not change the past, she could—and would—control her future. One thing was certain. No man would ever again lay a hand on her.

# *Chapter Four*

She wasn't coming back.

Andrew yawned as he reached for a cravat. Though another man with his wealth would have had a valet to dress him, personal servants played no part in Andrew's life. At first, he could not afford one, and now he had no desire for any. Helen claimed it was another example of his eccentricity. Andrew knotted the cravat, frowning at his reflection in the cheval glass. If the good people of Buffalo chose to believe him eccentric, he would be the last to dispute their opinion. Not when that belief served his needs so well. A servant would have realized just how many nighttime forays the doctor made, and an intelligent man might have discerned the pattern. Andrew shuddered. That was something he couldn't allow.

He slipped his arms into his waistcoat, then closed the door to the massive wardrobe Helen had insisted he buy. At the time, he had thought it pure extravagance, far larger than he would ever need. Now he found the wardrobe's deep recesses useful hiding spots for clothes no prosperous physician would own.

It was better this way. No valet, no one close to him, no one who knew of the memories that haunted him. Andrew yawned again as he descended the stairs, pausing only briefly to admire the stained-glass window that had been the reason he had bought this particular house. Even on dismal rainy April mornings like this, the window provided welcome color.

Gripping the railing, Andrew stifled yet another yawn. One of these nights, he needed to sleep. As a physician he knew the danger of sleep deprivation; as a man, he knew he could not refuse those who needed him in the dark hours of the night. His own fatigue was of little importance compared to the dangers they faced.

Andrew entered the dining room, his fatigue forgotten when he saw the empty table and sideboard. Damn it all! This was the third day that Mrs. Kane had failed to have his breakfast ready. What was the woman doing? He had hired her to cook, hadn't he? Andrew strode across the hall, flung open the door to the kitchen, and bellowed for his coffee. When his highly paid servants were properly chastised, he returned to take his place at the head of the long mahogany table.

A maid whose dark hair gleamed in the lamplight scrambled to place china and flatware in front of him. Andrew leaned forward. Surely it was his imagination that the maid's hair held glints of red. It was improbable, for few women had red tresses. Yet when he closed his eyes, he pictured a tall woman with hair the color of sunset. Utter foolishness!

She wasn't coming back. Andrew's frown owed nothing to his cook's failure to provide coffee. What was there about that redheaded woman that she thrust her way into his thoughts at the most inopportune times? He would be consulting with a patient, driving to another's home, even doing such mundane tasks as tying his cravat, when her face would appear. It wasn't as though he had any desire to see her. Far from it! But, just as he had once been unable to prevent her from appearing in his office, he now failed to expunge her image from his thoughts.

Andrew pulled out his watch, wondering how much longer it would be before his food arrived. Though the redheaded woman and her daughter were slender, he imagined Mrs. Simmons saw to it that their meals were timely. Her again! Andrew snapped his watch shut. His life was too full for this sort of nonsense. Didn't he have an enviable number of patients, not to mention his research? And then there were his deliveries.

As a blond maid placed a cup of steaming coffee and a plate of bacon and eggs in front of him, Andrew began to smile. The food smelled delicious. Mrs. Kane's schedule might be unreliable, but there was no denying her culinary skills. She was a master of her trade, just as he was of his.

Andrew's smile broadened as he buttered a piece of toast. He had been successful again last night. Though he would pay a price in fatigue today, there was no denying the thrill that never seemed to diminish, no matter how many times he took someone on the journey between life and death. It wasn't simply the result of outsmarting his opponent, of surmounting dangers. No, the exultation came from the knowledge that what he did was right, even though some would call it illegal.

He was doing good things, important things. There was no reason his thoughts should stray to that woman. She wasn't coming back. He didn't want her to come back. Still, he would have thought Mrs. Simmons would have been more persistent.

Why hadn't she returned?

"You would like it here, Lenore." Beth smiled as she ran the feather duster over the gilded picture frame. It had become a habit, talking to her sister while she cleaned Silver's house.

At first, she had conducted the conversations silently, imagining the words. But today she felt the urge to speak the words aloud. Perhaps it was because the day was so dismal, and the sound of her voice helped drown out the noise of rain pelting against the window.

Lenore wasn't here, of course, but that didn't mean she couldn't hear her. Beth smiled again, imagining her sister's spirit hovering over her, listening. Though it wasn't difficult to conjure the image of Lenore in a flowing white gown like the night shifts they had both worn, Beth couldn't quite picture her with wings. Lenore had always been the mischievous, daring one, while Beth had chosen the relative safety of silence, preferring to remain in the background, hoping *he* would not notice her. Lenore, it seemed, had never learned from the painful lessons but had continued to rebel. Though Beth would have called her "vibrant" or "lively," "angelic" was not a word she would have applied to her sister.

"The furniture is beautiful," Beth continued as she dusted the deeply carved sofa legs. "Silver has one of the prettiest carpets I've ever seen. It's almost as nice as the one in the doctor's office." Beth's lips tightened. She did not want to think of the doctor. There was no reason—absolutely no reason—why she should dream about those blue eyes and the way they had softened when he looked at Dora. He was a man, and Beth knew what that meant.

Deliberately she forced her thoughts back to the present and continued her conversation with her sister. "This carpet begs you to take off your shoes and walk barefoot on it." Beth remembered the day Dora had done exactly that, and how her young companions had soon followed her example. Though Beth had thought Silver might be angry at the children's invasion of her parlor, the older woman had merely smiled, telling Beth that rooms were meant to be used, not simply admired.

Moving to the far side of the room, Beth began to dust the largest piece of furniture. "Oh, Lenore, you should see the piano!" Beth ran her hand over the intricately carved music stand, imagining her sister's pleasure. "I hope you have one where you are now."

Beth's eyes misted as she remembered how her sister had longed for a pianoforte of her own. From the time she had seen her first picture of one, Lenore had announced that she wanted to learn to play. That, of course, was not possible. Even if the family had been able to afford lessons, money would not have been squandered on something so foolish. But Lenore was determined. When old Mrs. Hastings gave her piano to the church, Lenore made her plans. Though Beth had pleaded with her, Lenore had snuck into the church to play. Beth remembered the joy on her sister's face as she described the sound of the magical instrument.

"Someday," Lenore had whispered from her side of the bed, "I'm going to have my own piano. I'm going to marry a rich man and have pretty clothes and a piano and we're going to have two boys and a girl, and they'll all learn to play the piano." Lenore giggled in pure delight, then stifled the sound with her pillow, for both girls knew the danger of having laughter overheard.

Dreams! Lenore had had more than her share of them. Unfortunately, they had not come true.

Somehow *he* learned about the clandestine visits to the church. And then . . . Beth clapped her hands over her ears and shut her eyes. But some scenes were indelibly etched on her memory. Her hands and eyelids provided no barrier to the memories of the whip, her sister's cries, and Lenore's bloodied back.

*I won't think about it!* Beth clenched the feather duster so tightly that the ribbed handle dented her palm. *I'll think about something else.* She strode from the parlor, heedless of the chairs she had yet to dust, and ran to her room. Thrusting aside the crisp white curtains, she stared at the cherry tree, trying to envision it covered with blossoms.

But memories could not be thrust aside so easily. Though her eyes focused on the gnarled branches and the raindrops that clung to the rough bark for an instant before they slid to the ground, she heard Rodney's voice and saw the concern in his dark eyes. "I brung some salve for her," he said, holding out a small jar that gleamed white against his brown hands. At the time, Beth was so thankful for the comforting cream that she had not asked how their neighbor had known of Lenore's wounds. Later she wondered. Surely Lenore's screams had not carried all the way to the next farm. When she recovered enough to speak, Lenore had managed a weak smile as she said, "Rodney always knows when I need help. I can't explain it, but he does."

Beth took a deep breath, willing her heart to stop pounding. Lenore was safe. No one would hurt her now. As Beth turned away from the window, her glance fell on the rag doll lying on Dora's trundle bed.

"Oh, Lenore," Beth cried as she sank onto the hard chair, "I wish your dreams had come true!" She leaned forward and touched the doll, smoothing its yarn hair. "I miss you so much, but I know you're in a better place now." Beth brushed a tear from her cheek. Rising, she straightened her shoulders. "I'll keep Dora safe. I promise." She took a step toward the door. "No one will ever hurt our little girl again."

"You want me to do *what?*"

Andrew leaned forward in his chair, surprised by his friend's vehemence. It wasn't as if his request was so unusual. "I want you to find me a housekeeper," he repeated.

David Coleman was silent for a long moment, a tactic Andrew had seen him use to quell angry witnesses, but one that had never before been directed at him. For some reason, it appeared David disapproved of his request.

"A housekeeper," David sputtered, his golden eyes filled with disgust. "For God's sake, Andrew, I'm a lawyer. My job is to draft contracts, settle disputes and try cases—not interview housekeepers." David scowled. "What you need is a wife."

Andrew clenched his fist. He and David had been friends since Andrew first moved to Buffalo. They had spent many an evening together, regaling each other with humorous tales and sharing each other's few defeats. Their friendship had been both personally and professionally beneficial, for each had used his contacts to help the other's career. Though they had disagreed on a number of issues, this was the first time

Andrew had felt the urge to smash his fist into his friend's face.

"Why on earth would I want a wife?" he demanded.

David smirked as he twirled his light brown moustache. "Besides the more obvious benefits, she could interview housekeepers for you. Hell, Andrew, she could be your housekeeper."

Andrew strode to the window, trying to control his urge to smash something: one of the marble bookends that decorated David's desk, the plate-glass window with its view of the courthouse across the street, David's nose.

"I have no intention of marrying." He ground the words out, one at a time.

"So you say." Andrew didn't have to turn to see the grin on David's face; he could hear it in his voice. "Helen Pratt might have other ideas."

"Helen is a friend." Andrew emphasized the last word. "Just like you're a friend."

"Then ask your *friend* to hire you a housekeeper." Andrew heard David sigh. "Look," the young attorney continued, "I'd help you if I could, but the simple fact is, I've got too many cases to worry about right now. That damned Fugitive Slave Act has given me more business than I would like."

Andrew walked slowly back to his chair. "More illegal searches?" Thank goodness his voice betrayed none of the interest he felt.

David nodded. "It's a fine line, distinguishing between reasonable cause for searching a man's home for a runaway and violating the Bill of Rights. I tell you, Andrew, I don't know why Fillmore signed that law. You'd think the man would have known better, considering Buffalo's role on the Railroad. As it is, the law's done nothing but cause trouble."

Andrew leaned back in his chair, the picture of a man at rest. "Does that mean you don't subscribe to the theory that the Act was made deliberately punitive to enrage Abolitionists and encourage them to flout it?"

"Who knows what those lawmakers think?" David picked up a glass paperweight and gazed at it as if it were a crystal ball. "All I know is that one thousand dollars and six months in jail is a pretty steep penalty to pay for harboring a fugitive or working on the Underground Railroad."

"Damn right about that."

*What a mess!* Andrew rifled through the papers on his desk, muttering soft imprecations as a pile slid to the floor. David was wrong. He did not need a wife; he most definitely did need a housekeeper. Mrs. Fisher had had her faults, but at least she had kept the household running smoothly. During her tenure, breakfast was ready when he wanted it, and the reams of paper that formed the heart of his research were never allowed to grow to such alarming heights that they tumbled onto the floor when a man did no more than breathe on them. Somehow, he would have to find a housekeeper, although the thought of interviewing a stream of candidates was almost as painful as the idea of losing a patient.

With a groan of frustration, Andrew gathered the pages from the floor. *Aha! There they are!* He settled back in his chair, and this time the lines that formed between his eyes were caused by concentration rather than frustration as he reviewed his notes and considered their implications.

It was not a coincidence. He knew that. Though Helen might scoff at his theories, he was certain they were valid. Physical characteristics were inherited. Look at Beth Simmons and her daughter. They shared the same almost perfectly oval-shaped face, that slim, long nose. Though their hair and eye colors differed, there was no doubt of their relationship. And the similarities were more than bone deep, for they both evidenced the same skittishness.

Andrew leaned back in his chair, considering. Could behaviors as well as physical characteristics be hereditary? Or had the little girl learned that wariness from watching her mother? *Stop it!* Andrew clenched his teeth. He would not think about the widow and her child again. It was senseless, utterly, completely foolish to waste his time in such a fashion. He would never see them again, and that was what he wanted. He would put her out of his mind, once and for all.

But Andrew had learned at an early age that Fate had an odd sense of humor, and what he wanted was rarely what he received. That woman, with her intriguing blend of innocence and those eyes that appeared to have seen far too much, was like a mosquito: annoying, impossible to ignore, difficult to catch, and capable of inflicting pain totally out of proportion to her size.

If only he knew where she was staying, he could see her once more. It would be like spreading salve on a mosquito bite. Surely that would lay his silly thoughts to rest. But he didn't know where Beth was lodging.

Andrew tapped his finger on the desk, his expression pensive. What would David say if Andrew asked him to hire a detective to find the Widow Simmons? It might be worth the resulting inquisition just to see the expression on David's face. With a shake of his head, Andrew turned his attention back to his research. This was what was important. He scribbled a few notes.

Someone knocked on the door.

"Dr. Muller."

Andrew frowned. It must be his imagination. He had been thinking about her, and now he was conjuring her voice. But the knocking continued, and this time there was no mistaking the impatience in her voice. "Dr. Muller. Are you there?"

Trying to ignore the sense of excitement that flooded his veins, he rose. Mosquito salve. Seeing her was mosquito salve, nothing more.

"Yes, Mrs. Simmons, I'm here." He opened the door. She stood alone in his waiting room, dressed in the ill-fitting widow's weeds that he had seen before, her head held high and her shoulders braced as if for a blow.

His imagination had not misled him. The woman was beautiful, despite the haunted expression in those deep green eyes. Andrew's gaze lingered on her face. Her skin was paler than he remembered, and today he noticed four freckles on that aristocratic nose. The bruise that had marred her cheek had faded. Had her skittishness also disappeared? Andrew took a step closer to her. She stood her ground, but he saw that, though she tried to camouflage her fear by pursing her lips, her eyes held the same wariness, the same apprehension he had seen before.

Andrew took another step. As his shoes resounded on the wood floor, her skirts swayed, and a small hand appeared, clutching the fabric. The child was with her!

"How can I help you?" Deliberately, he kept his voice low and calm. This was his opportunity to see her, to exorcise her from his thoughts. He must not alarm her or her daughter. Though Beth did not move, he caught a glimpse of the girl's dark curls, and a moment later somber eyes regarded him from the shelter of her mother's wide skirts.

Beth reached down and put a reassuring hand on the child's head. "I believe you know the answer to your question, Doctor," she said, and he noticed that once again her voice was firm, almost defiant. "My little girl needs your help."

Though he knew it was impossible, Dora raised her eyes toward his face, as if she heard Beth's words and was adding her own plea.

A gust of wind rattled the window. The morning's rain had stopped, but the sky was still gray and the strong breeze beat the forsythia branches against the glass. Though the buds were swollen, it would be another few days before they burst open, their vibrant color signaling the arrival of spring. The season of hope. Unfortunately, he could offer no hope.

"I believe you know my answer, Mrs. Simmons."

As Andrew watched, she bit her lip, and he had the oddest sensation that she was trying to control her temper. Another woman would have been battling tears, but Beth Simmons was not another woman.

"There must be a way."

Andrew began to shake his head. It was unthinkable. He could not allow her into his house. She had already destroyed his equilibrium, invading his thoughts after only two short encounters. What would it be like if he saw her more often? It would be bad enough having the woman close by, but the child . . . No, it was impossible. He would not risk reviving painful memories.

Despite his best intentions, Andrew's gaze moved to Dora. Apparently reassured by her mother's touch, she had moved from the shelter of her skirts and stood next to her. Her small face, so like her mother's, tilted up, and as Beth smiled at her, the girl turned toward Andrew. She gazed at him steadily for a moment; then a smile lit her face.

Mary. Her smile was like Mary's, so innocent, so trusting. Andrew swallowed deeply.

"Doctor, there must be a way," Beth repeated. "I've told you I will earn your fee." Thankful for the interruption, Andrew averted his eyes from the girl who raised unwanted memories.

He had to refuse. It was the only answer. The dangers of letting anyone—especially this disturbing woman and her daughter—come too close were real. He could not afford the risk. But Andrew found himself oddly reluctant to turn Beth and Dora away again.

He took a step closer, and as he did, he saw Beth flinch. Perhaps there was a way. Perhaps he need not refuse her plea. Perhaps *she* would refuse *him*.

The windowpane rattled again. This time Andrew did not glance away. Instead, he kept his eyes fixed on the young widow. He continued walking until he was only inches from her. Though the wariness in her eyes deepened, she did not move. She did, however, put her hand on Dora's shoulder, whether to comfort or protect her, Andrew did not know.

"There may be a way," he said slowly, hating himself when he saw hope leap into her eyes. She would never agree to his proposal. Never. "You need my services," he said, nodding toward the girl, "and I find that I need yours."

As Andrew forced his gaze to move slowly from the top of her head to the serviceable boots that peeked from beneath the shabby gown, he watched her flush, then turn pale.

"What do you mean?" she asked.

"I would expect you to live here for a year," he said smoothly.

Though her green eyes deepened with a fear so intense that it was almost palpable, she said nothing.

"A year," Andrew repeated. He paused for a long moment, then said, "As my housekeeper."

The color began to return to Beth's face. "Your house-keeper?" she asked weakly. Her grip on Dora's shoulder must have tightened, for the little girl squirmed.

Andrew nodded. "I need someone to direct the cook and the maids," he explained. "I expect my meals to be served on time and my house to be kept spotless." He gestured toward the dust that lay on top of a bookcase and the jumble of papers on his desk.

"And we would have to live here, both Dora and I?"

She would refuse. He was certain of it. Whatever the reason, she was clearly afraid of him. She would never agree to forced proximity.

Andrew nodded again. "Those are the terms." He looked at her again, then when he sensed that she was wavering, added another condition. "You will also wear more cheerful clothing."

Her back stiffened. "I am in mourning," she announced.

"You look like a crow," he said bluntly. "I deal with death every day, and I have no desire to be surrounded by a constant reminder of it."

Dora, apparently sensing her mother's distress, grabbed her hand. Beth lifted the little girl into her arms and held her close as if to protect her.

"It would not be proper."

Of course it wasn't proper. The whole arrangement was distinctly improper, which was why Andrew had proposed it. She would never agree to it.

Dora turned toward him, a sweet smile lighting her face. "Those are my terms," he said firmly, refusing to look at Dora, lest her smile weaken his resolve. "You may either accept or refuse, but I will not change them."

He watched Beth swallow, then take a deep breath, as if she were trying to calm herself. She would refuse; there was no doubt of it.

As she gripped her daughter so tightly that the little girl winced, Beth raised her gaze to meet his.

"I accept."

# Chapter Five

"You're out of mourning." Silver fisted her hands on her ample hips and stared at Beth, her eyes widening at the sight of Beth's new dress. She stood in the doorway of the small parlor where Beth had brought Dora and the other children. Simpler than the main parlor with its delicate chairs and piano, the furnishings here were sturdy, and no carpet covered the floor. Except for the china figurines that decorated one table, it was as child-proof as any room in Silver's house.

Beth's flush owed nothing to the bright May sun that had darkened the smattering of freckles on her nose. The navy poplin was the finest gown she had ever owned, and—though she would never admit it to Andrew—her first brand-new dress. Its deeply ruffled skirt and the short sleeves that let her enjoy the sensation of spring breezes on her bare arms made it a far cry from the patched black serge she had worn during her first weeks in the city.

"I had no choice," she told Silver softly. "The doctor said he wouldn't hire me if I wore black." She had assuaged her conscience by telling herself that Lenore wouldn't have minded. The grief she felt over her sister's death was real; it didn't require outward signs like black clothing. "You know there's nothing I wouldn't do for Dora. Shortened mourning seemed a small price to pay for Dora's chance to hear again."

On the other side of the room, Mark laughed as he pulled a building block from Dora's hand. To Beth's surprise, Dora squealed, almost as if she had heard Mark's laughter and wanted to imitate it.

Silver brushed her dark hair from her face as she settled onto the largest chair. "You look prettier this way," she said. "That black made you look like a scarecrow."

58

"That's what he said."

"What do you know? The doctor and I think alike." Silver clapped a hand over her mouth, her eyes widening in surprise. "Lordy, I never thought I'd say that. But, honey, it's good to see you back here, and the little one looks happy."

Beth gave Dora a fond glance, watching the way she had rejoined her former playmates as easily as if they had left the game only an hour ago, though it had been two weeks since they had visited Canal Street. Those weeks had been busy ones for Beth, getting settled in the doctor's house. She had refused the former housekeeper's room, choosing instead the empty room opposite it in the attic. It wasn't, as Mrs. Kane seemed to believe, that she was putting on airs. The reason was much simpler: the second room's window overlooked a crab-apple tree, a tree that had burst into bloom, filling the room with its sweet scent. Each morning Dora stood on her trundle bed, stretching her arms toward the window, until Beth carried her close enough to enjoy the tree's beauty.

"Dora seems happy," Beth told Silver. That was one of the undeniable advantages of living and working in Dr. Muller's house. Each day Dora seemed less frightened. Perhaps it was the luxurious surroundings that soothed her. Perhaps the fact that there were fewer strange faces. Beth wasn't sure of the cause. What mattered was the result: Dora's happiness.

When Dora squealed again, this time in pain, Beth walked to the corner where the children were playing and gently pried a lock of Dora's hair from Mark's fingers.

"You're hurting her," she explained.

"I just wanted to touch it. It's pretty. Not like mine." The boy fingered his straight blond hair.

"Yours is pretty, too," Beth told him. "It's just different from Dora's." She understood how Dora's curls would appeal to a child. Hadn't she herself wished for naturally curly hair? It would save so much time with the tongs and curling paper.

With a rueful smile, Beth returned to her seat and continued her conversation with Silver. "Dora seems content. Mrs. Kane, the cook, dotes on her, and I caught the coachman sneaking her candy one day. But I can tell that she misses the children." Beth swallowed. "I miss you, too, Silver." In the few days she had spent in Silver's house, the older woman had become a friend. And friends, Beth knew, were a precious commodity.

"Pshaw!" Silver harrumphed loudly, clearly uncomfortable with Beth's declaration. "You don't have time to miss me, what with running that grand household."

"It keeps me busy," Beth admitted. The servants had grown lax with no one to supervise them, and the dirt and clutter had seemed overwhelming at first. "I pretend I'm teaching again," she told Silver, "only I'm giving out work assignments instead of lessons."

"And the little one? What does she do all day?"

Beth sighed. That was the problem. There was little for Dora to do while Beth worked. "She plays with the rag doll you gave her, and sometimes she'll try to talk. Mostly I keep her away from the doctor."

"You mean the ice man don't like young 'uns?"

"I've never seen him treat a child, so I'm not sure. I tell you, Silver, I was so frightened the day Dora broke a vase. I didn't know how he'd react, but all he did was tell me to have someone sweep up the pieces." Perhaps he truly was an ice man, with no real emotions in his veins. It was certain that no other man she had known would have been so calm. Her father and Peter would have had far different reactions. Dora would have paid a high price for destroying something of theirs.

"I reckon the vase must not have been too valuable."

Mark and little Rebecca clapped their hands as the pile of blocks tottered, then tumbled to the floor. When Dora imitated them, Beth smiled, then turned her attention back to Silver. "I think it was valuable," she said. "There was a lot of gold on it, and it looked expensive."

Silver clucked softly, then gave Dora an appraising glance as she eyed the fragile figurines on the table. "If'n it was a nice piece, his family probably brung it from Germany."

Beth shook her head. "It looked too new. I haven't seen

anything in the house that's old enough to have been his parents'."

"Sure, Mavis," Silver said when the tall thin woman poked her head into the parlor. "The young 'uns can go outside."

Beth wondered if Silver sought to protect her china ornaments from Dora's curious hands. Breaking the vase had been an accident, but accidents did happen, especially with small children.

"Then what did the doctor's family bring from the old country?" Silver reminded Beth of a terrier, refusing to stop digging until it found the bone.

"As far as I can tell, just his mother's portrait. I've been in every room of the house, and that's the only thing that looks old."

Silver's sausage curls bounced against her heavily rouged cheeks as she shook her head. "Nothing else? No clocks or china or fancy furbelows? Folks usually bring stuff with them."

Beth considered Silver's statement. "Maybe they left in such a hurry that they didn't have time." She could certainly understand that. If there had been more time, she would have brought a few other things with her, but as it was, she had been thankful to escape with Dora and Lenore's Bible.

"Somethin' ain't right," Silver declared. "Folks find a way. Why, look at you, honey. You brung your Bible, didn't you?"

Beth nodded. "It's the only thing I have left from my sister. I couldn't leave that behind."

"See what I mean? The doctor should have somethin'." Silver opened the window, letting in the warm spring air. Beth wrinkled her nose. The air was heavy with the odors of rotting garbage and unwashed bodies. "Tell me 'bout your sister. I figured you was wearing black for your man. Did you lose your sister, too?"

Beth closed her eyes for a second. Though the pain had diminished, it had not disappeared, and she wasn't certain it ever would. "Lenore died of influenza," she told Silver, her voice catching at the thought that she would never again see her dearest childhood companion, the one person on earth who had been able to make her see the humorous side of life.

"Influenza's bad," Silver said with a sage nod. "Reminds me of those plagues the preacher's always talkin' about."

"It took our parents just a few months before." That had been a mixed blessing.

Silver made clucking sounds that Beth knew were designed to comfort her. "Reckon God showed some mercy, sparing you and the little one."

*If God were truly merciful, he would have taken Peter.*

"The house was built in '18." Mrs. Kane handed Beth a cup of tea and gestured toward the plate of small cakes. The two women were seated in the corner of the kitchen at the table that Beth used for her meetings with the household staff. When she and Mrs. Kane had finished their weekly review of menus, Beth had asked the cook about the house's history.

"This is delicious," she said as she tasted a cake. It had taken a while to win Mrs. Kane's confidence, but Beth believed the effort well spent, for the older woman was a masterful chef. Short and stout with gray hair and pale blue eyes, she clearly enjoyed her meals as much as Beth and Andrew did. And, Beth had discovered, she enjoyed gossiping equally well. Today, spurred by Silver's questions, Beth had decided to encourage Mrs. Kane's garrulity.

"The doctor is the second owner," the cook said in response to Beth's query. "The first one was a lawyer. He went to Washington when Mr. Fillmore was Vice President. I reckon you know that Mr. Fillmore used to practice law here, don't you? A bunch of his cronies went to the capital with him."

Beth nodded. The former President's history was not what intrigued her; Andrew Muller's house and its contents were.

"Surely those aren't the original furnishings," she said, gesturing toward the dining room.

Mrs. Kane shook her head and stirred another spoonful of sugar into her tea. "Oh, no. Miss Pratt picked them all out." She laid her hand on top of Beth's. "You know who she is, don't you? The Pratt family is one of Buffalo's finest. Of course, Helen Pratt is only a shirttail cousin, but she's still a Pratt. I reckon that's why the doctor plans to marry her."

Beth tried to mask her shudder. Why would anyone want to marry?

"Mrs. Simmons." Though he always addressed her formally when in the company of others, the words sounded strange to Andrew, for in his thoughts she was "Beth." Not "Mrs. Simmons," "the Widow Simmons," or even "Elizabeth Anne." Just "Beth."

She raised her eyes from the papers that she was sorting. She had brought a small table into his office and was arranging his research materials in neat piles. Though it pained him, Andrew had to admit that hiring Beth Simmons had been a wise move, in many ways. Not only was his household once again running smoothly, but she had also somehow managed to organize his desk. That was something her predecessor would not have been able to do, even if he had trusted her with his files.

"Yes, Doctor?" As Beth propped her chin on one hand, he noticed that her fingers were long and slender, their only decoration a plain gold band.

"Would you bring Dora in here? I want to examine her." Beth was fulfilling her half of their agreement, had even done more than he had asked. Now it was time for him to assume his share of the responsibility. He had to do his best to heal Beth's daughter.

Andrew knew from questioning Beth that Dora had suffered no high fevers or illnesses, the normal causes of hearing problems. There was no recourse; he would have to perform an examination. It was something he should have done the first day. Normally Andrew felt no reluctance to examine a patient, but this was not a normal case. The reason he had waited, Andrew tried to convince himself, was that Dora needed time to grow accustomed to him. The delay had nothing to do with the fact that the patient was a child or that, though he knew it was irrational, she reminded him of Mary.

It was foolish. Dora bore utterly no resemblance to Mary,

for whereas Mary had been a blue-eyed blonde, Dora had dark brown hair and eyes. Mary had been a sturdy little girl with large bones, while Dora was slender. There was no similarity. None. And yet, when Dora smiled at him, giving him the same sweet, trusting smile he had seen so often on Mary's face, Andrew felt himself transported back to a different time and place, one he had no desire to revisit.

He would not revisit it. He would treat Dora Simmons like every other patient, with his famed objectivity. And as soon as he had cured her, he would release her mother from that absurd agreement he had insisted on. Then they would both be gone from his life. That was what he wanted. Of course it was.

The soft rustle of a woman's skirts alerted him to their arrival. It was disconcerting, having two such silent females in the house. Andrew had noticed that, although Beth spoke to Dora, treating her as if she were a hearing child, she would stop abruptly when he was near.

She led Dora into the examining room, and though her head was held high, her shoulders squared in what appeared to be bravery, she could not hide the apprehension in her green eyes. Did she think he was a monster?

The child clutched her rag doll, and Andrew saw wariness in her eyes, too. Perhaps it was the strange room; perhaps it was her mother's nervousness communicating itself to the girl. In any case, she was clearly uneasy.

"Come, Dora," Andrew said, beckoning to the child who was unable to hear his words. When he started to reach for her, to boost her onto the table, Beth moved quickly and scooped the girl into her arms.

"It'll be all right, sweetie," she said, brushing her daughter's hair and holding her close for a moment before she placed her on the examining table. "The doctor won't hurt you."

She did think he was a monster! It was a sobering realization. Andrew made a conscious effort to soften his expression. There had been a time when he had comforted rather than frightened little girls.

Dora bent her head toward her doll, touching its hair in

the same gesture her mother had used. Slowly, lest any abrupt motion startle her, Andrew reached for the toy. When Dora regarded him with puzzled eyes, he managed a smile, then took the doll from her. Carefully, he brushed the yarn hair from the side of the doll's head and pressed his otoscope to it, making a show of peering into the instrument, then repeating the process on the other side. When he had concluded his examination, he handed the toy back to Dora and pointed at her ears. For a second she stared at him. Then as her eyes widened in comprehension, she pushed her curls back from one ear and tipped her head toward him.

He heard Beth's sigh, and realized she was standing only a few inches away. She must be truly frightened for her child to have come so close to him. Always in the past she had kept more than an arm's length between them, as if she feared his touch.

Andrew bent his head toward Dora to study first the right ear, then the left. There was no doubt about it. It was what he had feared. The ossicles in both ears were deformed.

"What did you find?" Beth asked when he had smiled at Dora and placed her back on the floor. The child sat cross-legged and was peering intently at her doll's ears, a bemused expression on her face. "Do you know why Dora can't hear?"

Andrew shook his head slightly. "I see symptoms," he told her, "but I'm not certain of the cause. I'd like to examine your ears." He took a step toward her. Perhaps now that she had observed his treatment of Dora, she would allow him to touch her.

She did not. Beth moved backwards, holding her hands in front of her as if to ward him off. "Why?" she asked, and her voice quavered. If he hadn't known it to be an impossibility, he would have said she was acting like a frightened virgin, afraid that he would ravish her. But Beth Simmons was no virgin; the child who looked anxiously at her was proof of that.

"I saw an abnormality in Dora's ears," he told her, "and I wanted to see if you have a similar one. That way I would know if the problem was hereditary."

Beth shook her head. "Dora wasn't born deaf," she said. "She was injured in a fall."

"A fall?" Though it was a possibility, Andrew doubted it. To sustain injuries of the magnitude he saw would require a fall from a substantial height, and he could not imagine Beth Simmons, who gave every appearance of being a doting parent, leaving her daughter in such a precarious situation. "A fall?" he repeated.

Beth nodded, though Andrew noted that she did not meet his gaze, and her shoulders tensed. He would learn no more from her now. The woman was a bundle of contradictions. Though she was outwardly confident, it was clear that she had deep-seated fears. Right now those fears seemed to be centered on him. Andrew wished he knew why.

Impulsively, he said, "I'd like you to join me for supper tonight."

Beth raised her eyes and stared at him, the new wariness in her gaze telling him how startled she was by his invitation. "That would not be proper," she said firmly.

Andrew shrugged and looked pointedly at the dark blue dress she wore. He had refrained from commenting on her new clothing, knowing she was self-conscious about the absence of black, but he would not deny the fact that the well-tailored blue dress made it abundantly clear there was a softly rounded female form beneath it. Beth Simmons was far more attractive than her predecessor. That wasn't the reason he had hired her. Of course not. And it most certainly was not the reason he had invited her to dine with him.

"As I told you on another occasion, I'm not particularly concerned about propriety. The simple facts are, you need to eat, and I would prefer not to dine alone this evening."

She regarded him steadily for a long moment, and Andrew could see the indecision on her face. Did she fear that he would refuse to treat Dora if she refused his invitation? At last, squaring her shoulders in a gesture he had come to recognize as the sign that she had made a decision she didn't particularly like, Beth nodded her agreement.

If Mrs. Kane was surprised by the instruction to set two places for supper, she said nothing. Andrew could not, however, ignore the curious glances that the servants cast at Beth as they carried dishes into the dining room. He hadn't thought that his impulsive invitation would place her in an awkward position. He hadn't thought. That was the problem. He had reacted, piqued by Beth's obvious reluctance to speak of Dora's accident and her own palpable fears. Now they would both pay for his uncharacteristic impetuosity.

But Beth, it appeared, was oblivious to the staff's curiosity. She displayed no uneasiness, merely took her seat opposite him as if she were accustomed to eating from china and fine silver. She greeted the same people that she normally supervised graciously, without the slightest hint of condescension. When the various courses were served, she chose the correct utensils with no hesitation. Though Andrew wasn't sure what he had expected, it hadn't been this apparent ease with the social graces. If she were wearing silks and jewels, Beth Simmons would not have looked out of place in the finest mansion. Though her poverty was obvious, somehow she had learned etiquette. Andrew only hoped her lessons had been less painful than his.

"You have a fine library," she said as she cut a bite-sized piece from the succulent roast beef. Though her fingers were long and slender, Andrew noticed that they were callused. She had, it appeared, done more than teach school. "May I borrow some of the books?"

"Certainly. What do you prefer?" he asked.

"I read almost anything," she admitted with a self-deprecating smile.

Of course. That was the answer. A schoolteacher would learn about etiquette from a book. She wouldn't hide behind bushes, peering into windows. Her leg wouldn't bear the scars from a German shepherd that disapproved of young boys staring into its master's home.

"What was the last book you read?"

Though Andrew expected her to cite one of the classics, Beth surprised him with her reply. *"Uncle Tom's Cabin."*

*Uncle Tom's Cabin!* Andrew coughed to cover his discomfort. That was one book she would not find in his library.

"And did you form an opinion from it?" He raised one

eyebrow, as if her answer was of only moderate interest to him.

Beth laid her fork down and regarded him before she spoke. "I suspect Mrs. Stowe's book will convert more people to Abolition than a hundred fiery speeches. She paints a terrible picture of slavery," Beth said, her green eyes filled with the same fervor she attributed to the author. "Even if her tale is an exaggeration, as I've heard some people claim, it's still a powerful indictment."

Indeed.

"Then you're an Abolitionist?" Andrew wasn't certain why he was encouraging this conversation, since it had veered in a dangerous direction. He was always careful to discuss neither politics nor slavery with his patients, for a doctor needed to remain neutral, lest he alienate his patients. Still, Beth was not a patient. She was a young, attractive woman who appeared to feel as strongly about strangers' rights as she did her own daughter's handicap. Though she might fear him for reasons that he still did not understand, she had no qualms about expressing her opinions.

Beth nodded to the servant, indicating that it was time to clear the table. Once again Andrew had the feeling that she had done this before, though given what he knew about her background, that seemed unlikely. Perhaps Emma Willard's seminary taught deportment.

"I believe no one has the right to own another human being," Beth said, continuing the discussion as the dinner plates were removed.

"Perhaps." Though this was the most stimulating conversation he had had in weeks, Andrew waited until dessert was served and the servants had left before he spoke again. There were some subjects that were best not overheard. "I suspect it's easy for us in the North to pass judgment on the Southern states. After all, we aren't dependent on slave labor for our livelihood." He poured cream on top of his pie, then looked up at Beth. She had a pensive expression on her face. "The question of slavery seems almost rhetorical, because we're so far removed from the South. Why, I venture to say most vehement Abolitionists have never met a slave."

"I have." Beth placed her fork carefully on the edge of the plate as if she had lost her appetite for the dried apple pie that only a moment ago she had been eating with apparent gusto. "Our neighbors were former slaves."

"When did they come to New York?" The Fugitive Slave Act that David decried so often had greatly reduced the number of former slaves settling in New York State. Now that they could be returned to their masters, few stopped south of the Canadian border. "Were they fugitives?" Andrew wondered why he was asking the questions, when he did not want to know the answers. It was like probing at a wound, keeping it open when a wise man would allow the scar to form.

Beth shook her head. "Their master freed them when he died, but Rodney—that's their son—said they would have fled if they were sold to another planter. He used to talk about the signs they followed—quilts hanging on clotheslines, candles in windows, but mostly the North Star."

To avoid replying, Andrew took a bite of pie.

Beth, it appeared, took his silence for ignorance. "I'm sure you know that slaves use the North Star for navigation," she continued.

"I have heard that." Somehow, his voice did not reflect the sense of irony he felt.

Beth moved slowly, almost languorously, as she unfastened the row of hooks on her skirt. Part of her reason was caution, lest the rustling of her crinolines disturb Dora's sleep. But the other part—the larger part, if she were to be honest—was that she wanted to prolong the evening.

Though she had not wanted to accept Andrew's invitation, for it was unseemly for a servant to dine with the doctor, she had been afraid to refuse. What if he then refused to treat Dora? She was as concerned about that as about why he had suddenly required her company. In the past, he had seemed as anxious as she to minimize contact between them. What had made today different?

Though she had tried her best to disguise it, Beth's legs had trembled as she approached the dining room. But her nervousness had disappeared before she had finished Mrs. Kane's clear mushroom broth.

The evening had been . . . "exhilarating" was the only word Beth could find to describe it. It was the first time since her sister's death that she had had a thought-provoking discussion on subjects ranging from literature to politics. That in itself made tonight noteworthy. What made it extraordinary was that tonight was the only time in her life that such a discussion had been with a man.

Beth moved to the window. The night was clear, the stars sparkling. As she had done ever since Rodney had told her and Lenore about the North Star, she looked for the Big Dipper. Slaves called that constellation the drinking gourd and followed its handle to Polaris, the North Star. How often she and Lenore had speculated, wondering if they could follow a star to escape the nightmare of their childhood. They had tried. Lenore's star led her to marriage and motherhood; Beth's took her to teaching and then brought her here to Buffalo and Andrew Muller.

Who was he?

Beth had seen the cold man, the famed Ice Doctor, who had refused to treat Dora. But today there had been another side to him, for the doctor who examined Dora's ears so carefully could not be called frozen. A man who cared nothing for his patients would not have had the sensitivity to allay Dora's fears with his pretend examination of her doll.

And tonight, had she not known otherwise, Beth might have believed him to be a scholar or a lawyer. There was no doubt that his debates had been argumentative, yet clearly founded on facts. Beth had heard men pontificate, announcing their opinions as if there were no doubt of their validity. Normally, the louder they declaimed, the less valuable their opinions.

Andrew was different. Not only was he well informed, but he listened. When he asked her opinion, he acted as if it mattered.

Cold or caring; calculating or thoughtful. Which was the real Andrew Muller?

# Chapter Six

"I know it's here. It's got to be here." Andrew was muttering under his breath, shuffling the papers that today, as every day, cluttered his desk. Beth sighed. She had come into his office to remind him that the butcher's and grocer's bills were due, but judging from the frown that deepened the cleft in his chin and the fact that his hair looked as if he'd raked it with his fingers, this was not the most auspicious time to introduce household concerns. Andrew Muller might be a brilliant doctor, but he was an extremely disorganized man.

"Where is Mr. Hastings's chart?" he demanded, and this time he met her gaze.

Beth saw annoyance and a flicker of something she could not identify in his eyes. Though it meant moving behind the desk, she went quickly to open the second file drawer. When a man's anger was on the verge of erupting, a wise woman tried to placate him. Beth had never seen the white heat of Andrew's fury, and she hoped she never would. If she got the file to him quickly, perhaps his anger would dissipate. "It's right here, under H." She pulled out Herbert Hastings's file and handed it to him, being careful not to approach too closely.

Andrew stared at the sheaf of papers for a moment before he fixed his eyes on her. The sparks she had seen before were brighter. "Am I to assume that, now you've gotten my household organized, you've decided to work on my office?"

Though his voice was low, he could not disguise the strong emotion that edged each word. The Ice Doctor's voice was anything but cold. Beth flinched. What a fool she was! He had seemed pleased with the way she had organized his research notes. Alphabetizing the patients' charts had seemed like a logical next step, even though he hadn't requested it.

71

Beth had thought he would appreciate her efforts. The truth was, she should have known better. Hadn't the lessons been drummed into her as a child? Men liked their world the way they ordered it, and women—if they valued their lives—would leave them alone. But, no, silly Beth Simmons had forgotten that Andrew was not just a doctor, he was a man. Now she would pay the price.

"I thought the room needed organizing," she said as calmly as she could. Somehow, she found the courage to meet his gaze. As she watched, he fixed his lips into a straight line, the effort not to frown clearly evident. Then, when it was obvious he could contain his anger no longer, he opened his mouth and let out . . . a peal of laughter. Beth could not have been more surprised if the forsythia outside the window had suddenly sprouted legs and marched into the room.

"You're right!" he declared, his lips curving into a mischievous grin. "The office needs help. *I* need help," he added, and tiny crinkles appeared at the corners of his eyes. "Now, let me look at Hastings's file. I need to get his medicine ready."

He wasn't angry! Beth's legs trembled from sheer relief, and she sank into a chair on the opposite side of the desk. Though the man had been battling a strong emotion, by some miracle, that emotion had been mirth, not fury.

"Is Mr. Hastings your first patient today?" she asked.

The doctor looked up from the chart that he'd been studying. "You mean you don't know?" he asked, and she could see the laughter shining from his deep blue eyes. "I thought you would have checked my appointment book." He was chiding her gently, treating the whole episode as a joke.

"I would have," she admitted as fear receded, leaving her slightly giddy in its wake. "Only I couldn't find the book."

Andrew looked puzzled. "It ought to be right here." Shrugging when a quick search of the desktop revealed no appointment book, he reached for his black leather bag. "Ah, here it is!" he said, pulling it out with a flourish. "I wonder how it got there."

His mirth was contagious. Beth laughed softly. "Your office might benefit from some organization." She wasn't normally so tentative in her suggestions, but normally she wasn't dealing with a man. When she worked with Mrs. Kane and the other servants, though she was careful to phrase her orders as requests, there was no doubt the women would comply. With Andrew, Beth had no such certainty. He was, after all, a man.

"Are you proposing to teach me?" the man in question asked.

"No!" She shook her head, appalled by the thought. Not only was it unlikely he would take kindly to her lessons, but she doubted he would change. One of the things she had learned early in her career as a teacher was that some students were incapable of mastering certain lessons, and—from what she had seen of Andrew—neatness was one of his impossible subjects.

"Then what are you suggesting?"

She was silent for a moment, wondering if he was truly as amenable as he appeared. "I was merely going to propose that I assume responsibility for keeping your office organized and for arranging your appointments. That would leave you more time to practice medicine."

Though the door to the waiting room no longer squeaked since she had asked one of the maids to oil its hinges, Beth heard it open and close. The doctor's first patient had arrived.

"Let's discuss this tonight over supper," Andrew said. "Now, if you would show Mr. Hastings in."

Beth shook her head again. He must have forgotten to make an entry in his appointment book. "It's Miss Fields who's in the waiting room."

A furrow appeared between Andrew's eyebrows. "What makes you think that? I wasn't expecting her."

"I smell her perfume. It's very distinctive." Lucinda Fields visited the doctor's office at least once a week, and each time it took hours for her scent to dissipate, despite the open windows. Beth was surprised Andrew hadn't noticed it.

"I don't smell anything."

Wrinkling her nose, Beth shrugged. "It's there." Strong and almost cloyingly sweet.

Andrew laid the Hastings file on his desk and looked at Beth, his eyes clearly assessing her. "Did either of your parents have a heightened sense of smell?" he asked.

For a moment, Beth didn't want to answer, didn't want to be reminded of her childhood. Then she said, "My father." His keen olfactory nerve had alerted him to the tiny orange kitten she and Lenore had brought into their room. Beth shut her eyes, trying to block out the memory of the kitten in her father's big hands, its pitiful cries and the long, last meow as its bones were crushed.

"What about Dora?" Andrew's question brought her back to the present.

Beth nodded, grateful for the reprieve from ugly memories. It was safe to think about Dora. "I don't know," she admitted. "I've never noticed any signs that she was especially sensitive, but—obviously—she can't tell me."

Andrew scribbled a few notes on a piece of paper, then nodded slowly. "Once Dora can hear again, she'll soon learn to speak."

And, oh, how sweet that would be!

"When do you think you'll be ready to perform Dora's surgery?"

Andrew heard the hesitation in Beth's voice. He had seen her blanch a week ago when he had explained that Dora's only hope of hearing was for him to attempt to move the small bones of the middle ear, the ossicles, back into their proper position. Beth's normally pale complexion had whitened further when he had told her that no one—himself included—had tried this procedure.

"It's a gamble," he had said, wanting—needing—to be honest with this woman who loved her child so deeply. "She could die." Andrew knew all about loving and losing a child, and he had to prepare Beth for the possibility.

Her knuckles had whitened as she gripped the chair. For a long moment, she had said nothing, obviously battling her emotions. "I need to think about it," she had said at last. Tonight the thinking had ended, and she had announced she was willing to take the risk.

"When?" she asked, and he saw her fingers tremble as they held a goblet.

When? That was the question. Though Beth might trust him, Andrew wasn't certain he trusted himself. Not yet. Not when the patient was a child.

"I'm going to a conference in Rochester next month," he told her, knowing he could not procrastinate forever. "I want to consult with a few of my colleagues there. When I return, I'll treat Dora."

As a songbird warbled to his mate and Beth turned to gaze out the window, Andrew was struck again by the purity of her profile. That fiery hair that was so different from her daughter's framed her face and highlighted full lips that begged to be kissed. Andrew blinked. What had caused that thought? Beth Simmons was not one to beg, and she most certainly would not beg to be kissed.

"Will you take the canal to Rochester?"

Andrew seized the innocuous question, grateful for the distraction from those nonsensical thoughts of pressing his lips to hers, of tasting . . . *Stop it!*

"Not a chance," he replied.

"Why? Is it too slow?"

Andrew shook his head. Though most boats on the Erie Canal traveled only one and a half miles an hour and stopped overnight, speed was not the reason he planned to ride the train. "I don't like boats," he told her.

Beth looked up from the piece of bread she was buttering. "I've never been on one, but I think it might be pleasant to glide through the water."

"It's very muddy water," Andrew pointed out. The few times he had been near the canal, the water's murky color was what had impressed him, that and the stench of the mules pulling the barges. He was surprised that Beth, with her keen sense of smell, would even consider canal travel.

"I imagine that if you actually saw or smelled it, you'd change your mind about the canal," he added.

"Oh, I've seen it," she replied as she broke another piece of bread. "Dora and I visit friends on Canal Street."

Andrew's hand froze, gripping the tiny salt spoon. "You

do what?" There was only one kind of establishment on Canal Street: disreputable. Why had this woman, who looked like innocence personified, gone to the seediest part of the city? "Why?" he demanded.

"That's where Dora and I stayed before you hired me." Beth's green eyes challenged him to dispute her.

"Why?"

"Where else would a woman with no money go?" she asked.

Andrew had no answer.

The knocking roused her. At first she wasn't certain what had caused her to waken from a deep sleep, but when she heard the repeated banging on the front door, Beth moved quickly, slipping into a wrapper and running down the stairs.

Andrew was gone. She had heard him leave earlier that evening in response to another visitor. Middle-of-the-night disturbances, Beth knew, were part of a physician's life, and so she wasn't surprised when she heard the sounds of footsteps on the rear staircase followed by horse's hooves and carriage wheels on the cobblestones. What did surprise her was that the house calls weren't as frequent as she might have expected, coming only once or twice a month. Perhaps that was because Andrew had few pregnant women as patients. Mrs. Bartlett, the midwife, handled all but the most difficult deliveries, and patients with other ailments usually waited until daylight to summon the doctor.

As she opened the front door, Beth noticed that the night was clear but moonless. Many of Andrew's house calls seemed to occur at the time of the new moon, and that puzzled her as much as the calls' infrequency. Though Beth had little experience with doctors, she recalled her mother and a neighbor commenting that the full moon appeared to affect people, for illnesses—particularly serious ones—were apt to worsen then.

The woman who stood at the door was tall and thin, her face lined with concern, her eyes filled with fear. Though she wore expensive clothing, her expression told Beth that riches provided no consolation in this time of need.

"How can I help you?" Beth asked as she ushered the woman into the house. Her bonnet was askew, the points of her shawl misaligned.

"I must see the doctor." The woman spoke haltingly, as if she had run a distance and was just now catching her breath. That seemed unlikely, for Beth had seen a handsome coach stopped in front of the house. The woman's shortness of breath was probably caused by fear.

Beth shook her head slowly. Though she wished she could reassure the woman, there was little she could say to comfort her. "Dr. Muller was called away on a house call," she explained, "and it may be a while before he returns." His night calls frequently took hours. Beth didn't know whether that was because he traveled a long distance to his patients' homes or because of the severity of the ailments. All she knew was that when Andrew left, he rarely returned within an hour.

The woman clasped her hands together tightly. "It's my husband," she said, her voice now trembling with emotion. "Mr. Hastings has taken worse."

Mr. Hastings. It had been only a little more than twelve hours since Beth had handed Andrew his file.

"The doctor expected to see him this morning."

Mrs. Hastings nodded, her eyes beseeching Beth to help her. "He thought he was better and didn't want to bother Dr. Muller." The woman turned her hands palm up, as if saying she knew how foolish her husband's behavior had been.

Beth was silent for a moment, considering. Her heart went out to Mrs. Hastings, for she knew how painful it was to watch a loved one suffer, how horrible it was to be powerless to relieve the pain. Remembering the medicine Andrew had decocted earlier that day, Beth hesitated. She wanted to help Mrs. Hastings, but could she? Should she? She could be taking a terrible risk. Beth wasn't a doctor, after all, and how could she know if she was making the right medical decision? Perhaps Mr. Hastings had developed new symptoms that needed different treatment. But, knowing that the man was in agony and that it might be hours before Andrew returned, how could she do nothing?

"Please sit down for a moment," Beth said, motioning Mrs. Hastings to one of the comfortable chairs. "The doctor prepared some medicine for your husband this morning. I'll bring it to you."

As she placed the vial in the older woman's hands, she saw tears in her eyes. "Thank you, ma'am. You're a saint."

Far from it. She was a thief and a liar. It was Mrs. Hastings who deserved to be canonized, for she endured the pain of marriage and somehow seemed to love her husband.

"I'll ask Dr. Muller to call on your husband as soon as he returns."

As Beth climbed the stairs, her mood turned pensive. It was odd. When she had heard Andrew leave, she had thought that he might be going to the Hastings'. Obviously, he had not. Where then had he gone?

The buggy moved slowly, and from a distance it appeared as if the driver were in no hurry to reach his destination. In truth, the horse plodded, his breathing strained from the additional weight he bore. The driver leaned back in his seat, feigning indolence, although all his senses were heightened, his ears attuned to distant sounds, his eyes searching the open roads for signs of other travelers.

The carriage and horse were unremarkable, both black with no distinguishing marks. As for the driver, tonight his hair appeared whitened with age, his shoulders slumped from either years or fatigue, while his coat bore signs of wear. From a distance, no one would connect this lackluster conveyance with the wealthy and notoriously exclusive Dr. Muller. Andrew knew the disguise would not bear close scrutiny, but he had no intention of allowing anyone close enough to perform that scrutiny. Far too much depended on the success of his masquerade.

"Follow the drinkin' gourd." He began to hum the song, then stopped abruptly. Even the trees had ears, and that was one song he had no business humming. If someone heard him . . .

"Okay, Nag," he said, "we're almost there. Just another mile and we'll reach the river." Though he addressed the words to the animal, they were meant to reassure his passengers, that precious cargo concealed in the false bottom of the carriage and tonight, because the train had brought more than expected, in his hollow seat back. "Soon you'll smell the water, and then we'll rest for a long drink." No matter how tired he was, the horse sensed the Niagara River long before he could see it and would quicken his pace. Perhaps he, like Beth, smelled things that Andrew could not.

What Andrew smelled tonight was the acrid odor of fear and the lighter, sweeter fragrance of hope. When they reached the river that his cargo called Jordan, the fear would dissipate, leaving only a faint residue that somehow clung to the wood and leather.

The sixth sense that had saved him so many times in the past alerted Andrew to the distant sound of hooves. A single rider, pushing the horse to its limits. It might be innocent, a man hurrying home. It might not. Andrew could take no chances. He turned the carriage toward a small copse.

"Someone's coming," he said, knowing his passengers would hear his words. "If we're in danger, I'm going to make three right turns. That'll put us in the middle of the trees. When I slow down, you need to jump. Run for the water; the man there will greet you as 'Pilgrims.'" While he was speaking, Andrew reached behind him to unlatch the back of his seat. He had already shown the men how to open the buggy's floor.

"Stop!" He heard the rider call. "I know what you've got! Stop, or I'll shoot!"

Andrew's heart plummeted as the rider's words destroyed his last shred of hope that this was an innocent traveler. Somehow the man knew about Andrew's cargo. Andrew clenched his teeth. The rider might have the law on his side, but he would not touch these men.

He heard the almost imperceptible sounds of his passengers moving and the ominous pounding of the pursuer's horse. It was close now, dangerously close. Andrew tugged on the reins. His only hope was that the other man was so unfamiliar with the forest that the moonless night would slow his progress, for a heavily laden carriage had no chance of outrunning a single man on horseback. As if Nag sensed the urgency, he began to trot, turning so abruptly that the buggy swayed. When they reached the center of the thicket, Andrew slowed the horse.

"Godspeed!" he said as the men fled.

"God bless you," came the reply, soft but fervent.

Andrew flicked the reins, and Nag began to trot again.

"Stop!" The rider was closer now. If he realized that Andrew had slowed momentarily in the thickest part of the trees, he gave no sign of it.

*Thank God. They're safe.*

Andrew turned again, then stopped the buggy and climbed out. Seconds later, the rider reined in his horse.

"Stop!" he demanded, and in the faint starlight Andrew saw the glint of a revolver. The man was of medium height with dark hair, a full beard, and unremarkable clothing. It was only the fanatical gleam in his eye and the way he waved his weapon that told Andrew this was no ordinary farmer.

Speaking slowly and slurring his words deliberately, Andrew walked to the side of the buggy. "Already stopped," he announced, and swayed, gripping Nag's harness for balance. "Say, what's that?" He gestured toward the gun.

"Where are they?" the man demanded. "Where are the slaves?"

"What you talkin' about?" Andrew kept his head averted. Though the rough cap shaded his face, he could not afford to have anyone—especially this man—recognize him. "Got no use for slaves," he muttered. "Ain't even got no whiskey left. Took all the kegs to Old Man Wilson. All 'ceptin' one." Andrew made a retching sound, as if to indicate the fate of the remaining keg. He bent over, then groused, "Can't a man puke in private?"

*Damn it all! His informants were wrong again.* Peter lashed the horse's flanks. Next time he saw that one-eyed bartender, he'd show him a thing or two. No one made a fool of Peter Girton, and if sending him on this damn wild-goose chase wasn't a foolish thing, he didn't know what was. There were plenty of other pleasurable things a man could be doing of an evening. A man didn't ride through this cursed country-side for his health. No, sirree. He went for one reason, and one reason only.

Money.

The bartender had been so sure. Delivery tonight, he had told Peter. He had sounded so convincing that Peter had given him the coin he'd demanded. He'd get that back, that's for sure. And more. Much more. The man wouldn't soon forget that he had messed with Peter Girton.

A delivery! The signals were all right. A buggy headed in the direction of the river. A diversion into the woods to throw him off the trail. A driver who wouldn't stop when ordered. It could have been what he sought. Those slaves should have been there. Instead, what did he find? Some simpleton who had drunk too much whiskey and got lost on his way home.

*Damn it all!* He was close, so close to everything he deserved—money, a big house, lots of fancy women. All it would take was ten of them. Ten of those runaways who were taking a ride on the invisible Railroad. He'd get them. *Damn them and their North Star!* He was smarter than any old slave. He would catch them, and when he did, he'd make them pay. They'd pay for tonight and every other night of fruitless hunting. Mostly, he'd make them pay for the one that got away.

# *Chapter Seven*

There was a pattern; he knew it. He also knew he was close to having the definitive proof. Another month or two should yield the results he needed. Unfortunately, he didn't have another month. The paper was to be delivered in three days.

Andrew leaned back in his chair and closed his eyes. The sweet scent of roses on the trellis perfumed the room. It was odd. Undoubtedly those roses had bloomed every June he had lived in the house, yet this was the first time he had noticed them. The fault was Beth's. With her sensitivity to odors, she had made him more aware of smells. Or was it that, since she had taken charge of his office, he'd had more time to sit and think and notice scents?

First she had organized his household, then this office; now she was even helping with the patients. Andrew tapped his fingers on the desk, remembering the first time Beth had dispensed medicine. He had had two close calls that night. Fortune had smiled on him, for he had managed to elude the slave catcher. Then, when he had returned home, he had found Beth's note telling him of Mrs. Hastings's call. Thank goodness Beth hadn't stayed up to talk to him! Andrew wasn't sure how he would have explained his coarse farmer's clothing. Beth Simmons was far more intelligent than the slave catcher. She wouldn't have believed his tale.

Since that night, she had taken on more of the routine work, and that had given Andrew free time. It wasn't bad, of course, having time to work on his research. He even enjoyed the scent of the roses. Make no mistake, though. The research was what was important, not a certain red-headed woman whose delicate scent seemed to linger far too long, distracting him from his work.

The paper. He needed to finish the paper. Andrew stared at the three sheets of paper spread before him. The first contained an outline of the speech he had agreed to deliver in Rochester, a scholarly dissertation on the treatment of hearing disorders, while the second and third were covered with scribbled notes, ink blots, and scratched-out formulas. When he looked at the scribbles, Andrew's pulse began to race, and he could feel his enthusiasm grow. These were the seeds of the speech he wanted to give. If only he dared. It was ironic, Andrew realized, that he felt less fear facing a slave catcher's revolver than presenting new theories to other physicians. If he presented his views on heredity, would his colleagues listen to his hypothesis, or would they close their ears, unwilling to have their traditional beliefs challenged? Physical courage was one thing; facing almost certain rejection and ridicule was another.

As he reached for a clean sheet of paper, Andrew heard the snick of the latch and a faint creak as the office door opened. He looked up, expecting to see Beth. But it was her daughter who stood in the doorway, a hesitant smile on her face, the rag doll that seemed to be her constant companion cradled in one arm.

"Come in, Dora," he said, donning a welcoming smile. She would understand that, even if she could not hear his words.

She walked toward him, her shoes making almost no noise on the polished floor. Not for the first time, Andrew marveled at how quiet this child was. It wasn't simply that she didn't speak; she made virtually no noise at all. Not like Mary. Mary had been a lively child, chattering even in her sleep, so filled with energy that she bounced from place to place, her boots clattering as she propelled herself at a whirlwind pace.

He would not think about Mary.

Though his smile was forced, Andrew kept it fixed on his face. "What brings you here this morning, little one?" he asked.

As if she could understand him, Dora pulled her doll from the crook of her arm and began to examine her ears. Then she handed the doll to Andrew.

"You want me to look at Sally's ears?" he asked. When he picked up his otoscope, she grinned. Andrew tried not to flinch at her smile. It wasn't her fault that it reminded him of Mary and all he had lost.

When he had finished a careful examination of the doll's ears, Andrew turned to Dora. She pointed to her own ears. "You're next," he agreed, and lifted her onto the table. With another of those heart wrenchingly sweet smiles, she tilted her head to one side.

Andrew peered into the ear canal, frowning when his examination confirmed what he had seen the last time. There was no doubt about it. Dora's ears had been damaged, and he would bet his professional reputation that the injury wasn't the result of a fall. Only a blow could have caused the broken stirpes that had healed so poorly that sounds no longer traveled toward the auditory nerve. Andrew had little doubt that his diagnosis was accurate; what he didn't know was how Dora had sustained the injury. It could have been accidental. Perhaps she was standing behind a door when it suddenly opened, slamming her into the wall. Lord knows the child was quiet enough that no one would have realized she was there. That must be what had happened.

Unwilling to consider the alternatives, Andrew lowered Dora to the floor and returned to his desk. "I have to write my speech," he told her, pointing to a blank sheet of paper. She nodded and climbed onto a chair on the other side of the desk, her anticipation evident.

Despite himself, Andrew smiled. The girl was a charmer, no doubt about it. Without uttering a sound, she was able to communicate and—even more remarkable—to bend even crusty old men like him to her will.

Rummaging in his bottom drawer, he found the slate he sometimes used to draw diagrams for patients. He handed it and a stick of chalk to Dora. For a few minutes, the only sounds in the room were the soft scratching of Andrew's quill and the squeak of Dora's chalk. Then, he felt a tug on his sleeve.

She stood next to him, her face bearing an expectant smile. He had forgotten how short a child's attention span could be.

"What's next?" he asked.

Holding her doll by the arms, she began to swing her. When Andrew smiled, she held out her own arms, clearly inviting him to play with her.

He ought to be working. That was what he wanted to do. He most certainly did not want to swing a little girl the way he had once swung Mary. But as Dora smiled, Andrew knew he was lost. Somehow, though it was the last thing he wanted, this too-silent child had started to worm her way into the frozen space where a heart had once beat. And somehow her guileless smile had begun to thaw the glacier.

"All right," he said with another smile. Reaching for her hands, he swung her back and forth, and when she shook her head violently, as if to tell him not to stop, he swung her even higher.

Andrew was so intent on watching Dora that he didn't hear the door open, didn't sense Beth's presence until he heard her scream, "Stop that!"

The room was once more silent. It was only in Andrew's imagination that her cry reverberated. But it was not his imagination that Beth stood motionless, as if petrified with fear. Abruptly, he lowered Dora to the ground, giving the child a quick smile before he turned his attention back to her mother. She opened her arms and Dora ran into them, her face wreathed in a smile.

Beth did not smile. Even from the other side of the room, Andrew could see that she was unnaturally pale, and her emerald eyes glistened as if with unshed tears. She stroked Dora's hair, her hand trembling. Beth was clearly frightened.

"What's wrong?" Andrew asked, once again puzzled by the woman who had made such dramatic changes in his household. Though not completely gone, her skittishness had diminished, and when they dined together, she seemed totally relaxed, as if she enjoyed their conversation. Andrew knew he did. Her quick repartee added more spice to his meals than any of Mrs. Kane's succulent dishes. But now, normally calm Beth was making a visible effort to control her fear.

"What's wrong?" he repeated.

"Nothing." She shook her head, but did not meet his gaze. Instead she kept her eyes on Dora and continued to stroke the child's hair. It was a gesture Andrew knew Beth used to calm Dora. Today it appeared she sought to calm herself. "I'm sorry that Dora was bothering you. I'll keep her away from your office in the future." Beth's voice was flat, as emotionless as if she were reciting a lesson. Outside the window a bird chirped madly. Normally Beth would have peered outside, looking for the avian songmeister. Today she seemed as oblivious to the sweet sounds as Dora.

"Dora was no bother." The words were out of Andrew's mouth before he realized he was going to utter them. Another man might have said the same thing, merely to be polite, but Andrew had little use for social niceties. He made the statement because, odd though it was, he meant it. Dora *was* no bother. The minutes he had spent with her had brought unexpected pleasure.

Beth nodded, though it was apparent that she didn't believe him. Gripping Dora's hand, she started toward the door. Then, when the girl did not move quickly enough, she gathered her into her arms and hurried into the hallway.

The woman was a puzzle. Her fear was palpable, and yet Andrew could not fathom the cause. What could possibly have caused that stark terror? All he had been doing was swinging the girl. Surely that wasn't cause for alarm. Surely Beth didn't believe he would hurt Dora.

As the wind wafted the roses' perfume toward him, Andrew paused, appalled by the thought. Perhaps Beth did believe he would harm her daughter. Perhaps someone had hurt Dora previously. It was a horrible thought, and yet if it were true, it would explain so much: Beth's fear, her extreme protectiveness toward Dora, her reluctance to speak of the injury that had caused the child's deafness, his own belief that no fall could have damaged the ossicles.

Andrew shuddered. Had Beth been swinging her daughter, playing an innocent child's game, when somehow she dropped her? Was that how Dora lost her hearing?

What a burden for a mother to bear!

Beth shuddered. She had to leave. There was no other answer. She simply could not afford the risk any longer. She walked slowly across the lawn, scarcely noticing the pungent smell of wet grass and the dampness that seeped through her slippers.

What would she have done if Andrew had dropped Dora? He wasn't a deliberately cruel man like Beth's father or Peter, but he was still a man—strong enough to hurt a woman, able to crush a child almost as easily as her father had killed the orange kitten.

Beth gripped the crab apple's trunk and laid her face against the bark. Closing her eyes, she willed herself to think of nothing but the soft rustle of leaves. Gradually her heartbeat returned to normal, and as it did, Beth knew what she would do.

She could not leave, not until after Dora's surgery, but she could keep Dora away from Andrew. Beth sighed. That would not be easy, for ever since the day that Andrew had first examined her ears, Dora had developed a fascination with the doctor, eluding Mrs. Kane's watchful eyes to run toward the office several times a day. Always in the past, someone had intercepted her, but today she had somehow escaped undetected. That could not happen again.

Beth doubted Dora remembered her father's cruelty and the angry blows that had destroyed her hearing. She had been too young then. But if Andrew were to harm her now, the memories might haunt Dora for the rest of her life. Beth would not allow that to happen. She had promised her sister to keep Dora safe, to ensure that she was raised with love instead of fear. No matter what it cost her, that was one promise Beth would keep.

Though it wrenched her heart, Beth knew what she must do. Once Dora could hear again, she would find her a safe place to live while Beth finished her year in Buffalo. Although it would be horribly painful being parted from the little girl she loved so dearly, Beth knew she could not risk Dora's health and happiness. She straightened her shoulders and walked back to the house. Emma Willard would know of an all-female school where she could send Dora.

Andrew yawned. It wasn't that he was bored with *The Tempest* or even with Helen's company, but when a man had as little sleep as he had had the past four nights, a darkened room provided an almost irresistible invitation to doze. The cushioned seats and the audience's whispers only added to the soporific atmosphere in Buffalo's newest and most beautiful theater.

Helen dug her fingers into Andrew's forearm and hissed, "That's the seventh yawn! Wake up!"

Andrew drew a deep breath. Perhaps if he concentrated on something, he would be able to stay awake until intermission. Then, at least, he could stand up.

He turned his head slightly, grinning when he saw the other occupants of the Pratts' box. Though the actors on the stage displayed admirable oratorical skills, their voices reaching to every corner of the theater, Helen's father's chin rested on his chest, and her mother's eyes were closed. Unlike their daughter, they did not appear to appreciate Shakespeare's witty dialogue, and unlike him, Andrew doubted they had the excuse of four consecutive deliveries.

The audience's laughter reminded him of the soft smiles last night's passengers had given him as they ran toward the rowboat. There had been three, a husband and a wife who had taken turns carrying their small child on the perilous journey toward Canada and freedom. Though his eyes were focused on the Metropolitan's stage, Andrew's mind saw the wonder on the woman's face when she spotted the river. "Jordan," she had murmured. The tears that had spilled from her eyes were tears of joy, relief, and—Andrew suspected—incredulity that the Railroad's terminus was in sight. Physically the woman bore no resemblance to Phoebe, and yet the expression of almost unbearable happiness he saw in her eyes reminded Andrew of his first passenger.

As the curtain fell, Andrew rose and offered his arm to Helen. "Shall we go outside?" he suggested. With enough activity and fresh air, he might be able to stay awake for the rest of the play.

Helen nodded and touched her mother's shoulder to rouse her. "What's wrong, Andrew? You were half asleep for that entire act," she said as they made their way through the crowd, nodding at acquaintances, greeting friends.

What was wrong? Andrew took another deep breath, noting that the mild June air felt refreshingly cool. Had it been only this morning that he had asked Beth the same question? He had been annoyed that she had denied anything was amiss when she had been so clearly frightened. Now he was going to tell his own lie.

"I've been working late." It wasn't exactly a falsehood; still, Andrew fixed his eyes on the elegant brickwork of the theater's exterior rather than risk Helen's all-too-shrewd gaze.

Helen tightened her grip on Andrew's arm, then raised one perfectly groomed brow when he turned his attention back to her. "I thought your housekeeper was helping with that."

"Did I hear rightly?" David Coleman appeared at Helen's side. Like Andrew, David wore formal evening clothes, the black long-tailed coat and breeches, the white waistcoat and ruffled linen shirt, and the cravat that Andrew so hated to tie. Unlike Andrew, David had acquired a new cane, its gold head so large and elaborately carved that Andrew wondered how a man could carry it comfortably. David appeared to have no problem. He tucked the cane beneath his arm, bowed, and kissed Helen's hand.

Though he kept his gaze on Helen, David's words were directed at Andrew. "Can I assume from this beautiful lady's words that she was able to find you a housekeeper?"

Andrew glared at his friend. Why had he been so misguided as to ask the attorney for help? "I hired the housekeeper," he said firmly.

"And by all accounts, he chose a good one, a veritable paragon." Helen tapped Andrew's arm with her fan in a mildly scolding gesture.

Andrew had no intention of discussing Beth Simmons with either Helen or David. He raised one brow, imitating Helen's gesture, as he asked David, "What did you think of tonight's performance?" He couldn't resist needling his friend, for David had made no secret of his dislike for Shakespeare and rarely attended one of the Bard's plays.

"Not as bad as I expected," David confessed, "but not as entertaining as I expect *Uncle Tom's Cabin* to be." He paused, then asked, "Will I see you there?" His eyes moved between Andrew and Helen.

Andrew shook his head. What was in the air tonight that it made his friends continue to introduce subjects he did not want to discuss? Just as he had never admitted to having read Mrs. Stowe's book, he had no intention of attending the traveling show that was garnering high praise and sellout crowds at each stop.

"You know that I can't afford to alienate any of my patients."

David hooted and winked at Helen. "You can afford to do anything you please. Hell, Andrew, you're as rich as Croesus."

"Not quite." *Not yet.* Andrew doubted he would ever have enough money to banish his fears.

"I'm leaving for Rochester tomorrow." He made a show of sipping the clear consommé, while casting glances at Beth. Since the day she had found him playing with Dora, she had seemed different, quieter and more pensive than before, as if she were trying to reach a difficult decision. Though she continued to deny anything was amiss, Andrew did not believe her. The problem was, he had no inkling of what the dilemma could be.

"Is this the physicians' meeting where you're presenting the paper about ear diseases?" Beth asked. She wore a green dress today. Like the blue one, the shade was so dark it was almost black. Almost but not quite. Their agreement had been that she would wear no black and Beth, Andrew had learned, took promises seriously. If she wasn't clad in the spring pastels he had envisioned, Andrew could only blame himself for his lack of specificity. Beth had kept her part of the pact. Just as he would probably keep the unspoken pact with his colleagues and deliver the speech they expected.

Andrew nodded. "That's what I'm supposed to be doing," he admitted. "But I'm considering another topic."

Beth took a sip of water from one of the gold-rimmed goblets, and when her gaze met his, he saw genuine interest reflected in her eyes. "What is the other subject?"

Beth's smile told him they were on more comfortable ground now. Andrew wasn't surprised. She enjoyed discussing ideas. It was only when the conversation turned to personal topics that she retreated, shuttering her eyes and erecting an invisible wall between them.

"I've been studying the effects of heredity," he told her as he finished the soup and waited for Beth to ring for the main course. "I correspond with several other doctors and scientists. We all think there's a pattern."

"What kind of pattern?"

A dark cloud blocked the sunlight. Moments later a clap of thunder rattled the window glass, followed by the spattering of raindrops.

"We believe that physical characteristics like height, body shape, hair, and eye color are all passed from generation to generation." He paused as the maid cleared their soup bowls, replacing them with dinner plates. Would Beth react as Helen had, with skepticism? When they were once again alone in the room, he continued. "That's why I asked you about Dora's sense of smell the other day. I wondered if it might be inherited, too."

Beth appeared intrigued by the concept. Though Andrew knew the pot roast was one of her favorite dishes, she made no move to cut a piece, but kept her gaze fixed on him.

"Look at you and Dora," Andrew said. "There are many differences, but you have some marked similarities, too. For one thing, your faces have the same shape, and Dora's nose has the same tilt that yours does."

Beth stiffened, and if he hadn't known it to be absurd, Andrew would have said that he saw fear flickering in her eyes. But that *was* absurd, for there was no reason she should be frightened by her daughter's resemblance to her. Perhaps thunderstorms made her apprehensive.

"Of course, your coloring is different," Andrew continued. "Dora must have inherited that from her father. I assume he had brown hair."

Beth nodded. Lowering her eyes, she picked up her knife and fork, her motions as stiff as a wooden toy's. It was surely the weather that bothered her. Either that or the reminder of her widowhood.

"He must have had brown eyes like Dora's."

Beth's own eyes widened. "You're mistaken. Her father's eyes are blue." She shuddered slightly, as if a chill had swept down her neck.

Andrew shook his head. "They must have been brown," he insisted. "All our research shows that two parents with blue eyes cannot produce a child with brown eyes."

Beth gripped her fork so tightly that her knuckles whitened. "I'm afraid your theory is wrong, because Peter's eyes are definitely blue." Apparently relaxing, she speared a piece of cauliflower, then looked up at Andrew, frown lines appearing between her eyes. "Perhaps eye color is not inherited. My father had brown eyes. My mother's were blue, and so were my sister's. But mine, as you can see, are green. If your theory is correct, shouldn't they all be the same?"

"Not necessarily."

Andrew chewed his meat thoughtfully. Did Beth realize that when she had referred to her husband, she used the present tense—not once but twice? She must have felt his death so deeply that even now she could not admit he was gone.

What would it be like to be loved so well?

"The little ones are learning fast." Silver leaned back in the chair, seemingly unaware of its ominous creaking. Today, though she wore less pink than normal, her dress was trimmed with ribbons of her favorite hue.

Beth smiled and took a sip of the buttermilk that Silver offered her each time she visited, insisting it would keep Beth healthy.

"Mark is so quick that it's a pleasure to teach him," Beth said. Though she was unable to give the children daily lessons as she would have liked, she had arranged to come to Silver's twice a week. On those days, once lessons were over, Dora played with the other children, while Beth enjoyed a few minutes with Silver. Today they were sitting in the kitchen, a large pitcher of buttermilk on the table between them. The air was crisp and fresh, the sky a faultless blue as so often happened after a storm. Beth only wished her thoughts were as clear as the sky. Instead, they seemed muddier than the canal.

"I'm happy I can help Mark," she told Silver. And she was. It was deeply rewarding, watching a child learn, helping to nurture his love for books. When she was here, she had no ambivalence, no fears.

"How can I thank you?" After refilling Beth's glass, Silver took a deep swallow from her own. "I know you won't take no money, but I'm beholden to you."

Beth shook her head. "You're wrong, Silver. The debt is

all on my side. I owe you more than I can ever repay for rescuing Dora and me. Without your help . . ." She stopped, unwilling to consider what might have happened if Silver's man Tom hadn't found them.

Silver shrugged one of her ample shoulders. "Shucks, honey, Tom's a good man. He don't expect to be paid for doing what's right."

Beth managed a weak smile as she took another sip of milk. There had been a time when the distinction between right and wrong had seemed so clear. Lies were wrong; truth was right. Hatred was wrong; forgiveness was right. Now the lines were badly blurred.

On the opposite side of the table, Silver narrowed her eyes. "Is somethin' wrong?" she asked. "You look perturbed."

Beth started to shake her head, then nodded. It was futile to try to dissemble before Silver. The older woman might not be able to read books, but she was a master at reading human nature.

"I can't fool you, can I, Silver? You always did see too much." She set the glass back on the table, lest her suddenly weak fingers drop it. "I'm scared," she said.

Silver's eyes widened, and she studied Beth's face carefully. "The doctor ain't hurt you, has he?"

Beth was quick to reassure her. "He's never touched me, and he never will. Even when we're in the same room, I keep my distance from him." She shook her head slightly. "It's not that. I'm afraid he'll learn the truth."

An involuntary blink was the only sign Silver gave that she was startled by Beth's words. "What truth, honey?" she asked.

Beth took a deep breath, trying to calm her nerves. She hadn't planned to tell Silver—or anyone—her secret. When she had left home, she had vowed that no one—not even Dora—would know the truth. That was before the doctor had told her about his studies, before he'd started asking questions about Dora's parents. Now the urge to confide in a friend and ask for advice was too strong to ignore.

She moistened her lips and fixed her eyes on Silver's face.

What would she say when she knew? Would she condemn Beth's actions?

Beth swallowed again, then blurted out the words that haunted her.

"Dora's not my child."

# *Chapter Eight*

"Did I hear you right? Did you say that sweet little girl ain't yours?" Silver's eyes widened in disbelief, and she raised both hands to touch the silver wings in her hair. It was a gesture Beth had noticed she made whenever she was disturbed by something, and heaven only knows that Beth's announcement was a disturbing one.

Beth kept her fingers wrapped around her glass, trying to still their trembling. She met Silver's wide-eyed gaze and nodded. "Dora's my niece." Though she had thought that pronouncing the words would be difficult, they came out easily, and the sense of relief she felt when they were in the open made Beth realize how much she had missed having a confidant.

Silver reached for Beth's hand and clasped it tightly, her warmth helping to quell Beth's jitters. The kitchen door opened and two women entered.

"C'mon, honey. Let's go to my room." Matching her actions to her words, Silver rose and led the way to her own bedchamber. With its shocking pink draperies and coverlet and the silver-framed mirror, there was no doubt of its owner.

"Sit down, honey." Silver pushed Beth into a large stuffed chair. "Now tell me about Dora. I reckon she's your sister's daughter."

Beth leaned forward, clasping her hands together. So far

Silver did not seem disapproving, but what would she say when she learned everything?

"When Lenore was so sick, I promised her I'd care for Dora. Then after she died, it seemed the best thing for Dora for me to pretend to be her mother." Beth shuddered, remembering the child cowering in the corner of the cabin that day, seeming to sense the moment her mother died, though she was unable to hear her final tortured breaths. Lenore had not wanted Dora to approach her, for fear that she might catch the dreaded disease, and yet neither woman had had the heart to insist that the child be taken to a neighbor's house, where she would be deprived of everything familiar. It had been early afternoon when Beth had closed her sister's eyes and slid the gold band from Lenore's hand onto her own.

"The poor child had suffered so much," Beth continued. "First, her deafness, then losing her mother. I thought there would be fewer explanations if everyone believed she was my daughter." And if Peter believed his daughter was dead. Heaven only knows what he would have done if he'd known Dora hadn't succumbed to influenza and wasn't buried with her mother, but was living with the sister-in-law he had always hated.

"I reckon it was good for you, too," Silver said as she laid a comforting hand on Beth's arm. "After losing your man and all, seems like Dora gave you a reason to keep on living."

It was a lovely thought. It was also a lie.

"Silver, I've never been married. I only pretended to be a widow for Dora's sake."

"I see." But the puzzled expression on Silver's face contradicted her words. Beth couldn't blame her friend for being confused by the deception Beth had woven. How could she, when she'd had to remind herself on so many occasions of the role she was playing?

"I can never replace Lenore," she told Silver, "but I promised her that her daughter would grow up surrounded by love."

Silver patted Beth's arm. "You're doin' a mighty fine job of that. Your sister would be proud of you."

Beth hoped that was true. She couldn't bear the thought of Dora enduring the cruelty that had marred her childhood and Lenore's. That horrible, destructive pattern of a loveless marriage and undeserved brutality had to stop.

"What about Dora's father?" Silver made a moue. "I reckon he don't want her, 'cause you said he done caused her deafness."

Beth closed her eyes for a second as she tried to block out the memories of Dora's father, but the sight of Peter's handsome face contorted with rage would not be banished. "He was gone when Lenore died." That was true. There was no need to burden Silver with the full extent of her lies.

"An orphan." As Silver squeezed her hand, Beth felt a surge of relief. Silver had assumed that Peter was gone permanently, not merely on one of his frequent hunting trips.

"Poor little girl." Silver gave Beth a reassuring smile. "You done right. Don't you ever doubt it."

Beth shook her head, thinking of the fears—many of them irrational—that wakened her in the middle of the night and the doubts that seemed to be her constant companions. "I thought it would be easier pretending to be a widow," she told Silver, "but now I'm not so sure. I never counted on working for the doctor and living in his house."

She shuddered. Was there no end to Fate's irony? Lenore, who had dreamed of riches and a fairy-tale husband, had married a brute and died in poverty, while Beth, who sought a life without men, now was living in a mansion with a man who disturbed her days and her nights. Lenore might have laughed. Beth did not.

She raised her gaze to Silver's, seeking her friend's counsel. "What would Andrew do if he knew that I was an unmarried woman? You know it's not proper for us to live in the same household without an older, married woman."

Silver shrugged her plump shoulders as if to tell Beth that thoughts of propriety rarely gave her sleepless nights. "You got no cause to tell him," she said. "Honey, you're only going to be in that fancy house a few more months. Once he cures Dora, you'll leave. The Ice Doctor won't hold you to your bargain."

Silver's words should have reassured Beth. They were meant to, and yet all they did was raise new doubts. When she had left the farm, Beth had not thought beyond her immediate goal. She would go to Buffalo to restore Dora's hearing, and then she would forge a new life. Somehow. She hadn't worked out the details. At the time it had seemed simple. Perhaps it was merely that she hadn't wanted to consider the obstacles she might encounter. Now that she was here, reality was anything but simple, and the future she had so blithely predicted would be full of promise looked bleaker each day. As Lenore would have said, her star appeared to be setting.

What would she and Dora do?

Andrew wrinkled his nose as he entered the room. He had been to this hotel half a dozen times before, for the Western New York Physicians' Association preferred this to Rochester's other hotels. He had even been in this particular assembly room. He recognized the wooden chairs whose wide arms let a man relax or, if he chose, balance paper and a quill to record his colleagues' hypotheses. He even recognized the dent in the brass spittoon that appeared to have been made by a cane. Why, then, had he never noticed the way the scent of stale tobacco hung in the air, causing his nostrils to flare and his throat to burn? Surely it wasn't only because his conversations with Beth had sensitized him to odors.

Andrew forced a smile onto his face as he greeted the man who was to introduce him. "Good to see you, Barclay." The man's hair oil gleamed in the light and gave off a faintly rancid odor that would have made Beth grimace.

Damn it all! Andrew gripped his papers so tightly that they crinkled. There was no reason, no reason at all, to be thinking of her. He was Andrew Muller, one of the region's preeminent physicians, a man who had been invited to present a scholarly paper to his colleagues. Beth Simmons was merely his new housekeeper. It was absurd to remember the way that patrician nose of hers twitched when she smelled something distasteful or how the corners of her mouth would turn up ever so slightly when the scent was a pleasant one.

He would not think about her. Instead he concentrated on the introduction Barclay was delivering. This was what mattered, this and his work on the Underground Railroad. The one brought him the money he needed, and the other rewards of a very different kind. They were the important parts of his life, not an all too beautiful housekeeper whose image would not disappear.

"Gentlemen, friends, colleagues." Andrew took his place at the podium and began to address the audience. "My topic for today is three causes of deafness and the methods I have found most efficacious in treating them."

Two men in the front row nodded, then pulled out sheets of paper, preparing to take notes. This was the speech they were expecting. What would they have done if he had announced that he was going to discuss the role heredity played in physical characteristics? Would they have been as disbelieving as Helen had been, or would they have evinced Beth's keen interest?

Andrew had paced the floor of his office, trying to decide which speech to deliver. He wasn't certain whether he was being cowardly by hesitating to share his theories, or prudent. Andrew preferred to believe it was the latter, that he needed more time to confirm his hypotheses. It was true that Beth's revelations had confounded him. Until they had discussed Dora's eye color, Andrew had been convinced of the pattern he had found. Now he wasn't so sure. How could Dora have brown eyes if her parents had blue and green? The theory was correct. He believed that. And yet . . . until he had an explanation for Dora's eyes, he was unwilling to make his ideas known. A good scientist resolved all questions before he published his findings.

"And the third cause," he told his audience an hour later, "is injuries. These can be sustained either through an accident or the deliberate infliction of a blow." And which, he wondered, had caused Dora's deafness? "In the event of such an injury, the bones of the middle ear . . ."

"Muller, have you ever seen a case like that?" George Nailor rose to ask his question. A tall, thin man, Nailor had a reputation for attempting to disprove other physicians' hypotheses.

Andrew took a deep breath, thankful that he had not presented his other paper. He could defend this one easily; the other would have been more controversial, particularly with Nailor here to shoot it down.

"As a matter of fact, I have one in my care at the present time." The murmurs that greeted his announcement told Andrew the audience's flagging interest had been renewed.

"And do you postulate that your patient's deafness can be cured?" Nailor demanded in his typically argumentative tone.

Andrew smiled. Though he doubted it was his colleague's intention, he had ensured that the audience, some of whom had been dozing, would remember Andrew's paper. "I do, indeed," he said confidently.

There was a moment of silence, then a low murmur as the other physicians considered the import of Andrew's words.

Refusing to take his seat, Nailor raised one eyebrow, as if to say that he doubted Andrew's claim. "Are you willing to share your proposed technique with this esteemed body?"

Andrew nodded. Nailor was in rare form, being more obstreperous than normal. Fortunately, Andrew was comfortable with his theory. "Surgical intervention will restore the bones to their proper positions."

"Indeed, Doctor." The other physician made no attempt to hide his skepticism. "Are you aware that no one has achieved the goal you seek?"

Andrew shrugged and gave the audience a deprecating smile. "There is always a first time." *And,* he told himself, *I will succeed. Dora will hear again.*

He finished his speech, accepted the audience's polite applause, then took his seat in the middle of the room. As the next speaker walked to the podium, Andrew glanced at the program. As usual, Nailor was not one of the men presenting papers. His mission in life appeared to be attacking others' credibility.

Andrew leaned back in his chair. This speech held little

interest for him, and so he spent the time reviewing his own work, picturing the bones inside Dora's ear and the technique he would use to restore them to their former positions. He was so lost in thought that he missed the speaker's apparently joking reference. All he saw was a man two rows in front of him who flinched when his neighbor clapped him on the shoulder.

*She was sitting in one of the low-backed chairs in his library, apparently so engrossed in her book that she did not hear him approach. "Beth," he said gently. She did not answer. Andrew laid his hand on her shoulder. "Beth," he repeated.*

*Through the thin fabric of her dress he felt the warmth and softness of her shoulder, and for the briefest of moments he forgot why he was here and what he wanted to ask her. His only thought was that she was a woman, a warm, soft, desirable woman.*

*The moment was shattered as Beth jumped to her feet. She turned toward him, her hands balled into fists, her face flushed. It must be anger that animated her; surely it could not be fear. She had no reason to fear him. Surely the weeks that she had spent in his house had shown her there was nothing to fear here. Though there had been no denying her initial wariness, Andrew had believed it had disappeared.*

*"Don't you ever do that again!" She took a step backward, as if to distance herself from him. Her voice was low, but seething with anger.*

*"I'm sorry I startled you."*

*She shook her head, and that glorious strawberry-blond hair bounced against her cheeks. "Don't you ever touch me!" She pointed her index finger at him to emphasize her command. For Andrew had no doubt that this was a command, and it confirmed his opinion that she was angry rather than afraid. A woman who feared him would never order him to her bidding the way Beth did. When it came to regal behavior, the mythical Duchess could take lessons from Beth Simmons.*

As he settled back in his chair and returned to the present, Andrew reflected on that afternoon. She had been angry at being touched. Andrew knew that. What he didn't know was why. The only thing that made any sense was that he had somehow affronted her sensibilities. But how? His touch had been friendly and impersonal, even if his own reaction had been unexpectedly sensual. All he had done was touch her shoulder. That was certainly less intimate than dancing, and if Helen—the ultimate arbiter of good breeding—had never opposed his touch when they danced, why would Beth? It made no sense.

It was ridiculous to care. He had more important things to occupy his thoughts. Even this speech, boring though it might be, was more significant than the megrims of his housekeeper. And yet, a small voice reminded him, Beth had quickly become more than a housekeeper. He wouldn't think of the way her image popped into his mind at the most inappropriate times. Instead, he would remember how she had simplified his life. Not only had she organized his household and his office, but she had also helped with his practice. Ever since the night she had given Mrs. Hastings the medication that had eased her husband's heart palpitations, Mr. and Mrs. Hastings had taken every opportunity to tell him what a good decision he had made, letting Mrs. Simmons work in his office. Other patients who had turned to her for assistance when he had been called away had been equally complimentary.

Satisfied patients told others; his practice would continue to grow, and he would reach his goal. That was the reason he worried about Beth Simmons.

The only reason.

It was mid-afternoon by the time Beth and Dora left for Silver's house. With Andrew in Rochester, Beth had thought she would be able to leave his house early, but she had reckoned without the number of patients who had come to the office, unaware that the doctor wasn't home. She had helped those that she could, made appointments for those whose complaints were less serious, and referred the others to Dr. Wallace. Now, at last, she and Dora were on their way. The sky was leaden gray, the damp wind off the lake promising rain at any moment, and yet Beth could not repress a smile. For the afternoon at least, she and Dora were free. Dora could play with her young friends, and she would have time to talk to Silver. For she needed Silver's advice.

"Silver!" Beth called, opening the door to the small room where one of the women had told her Silver was waiting. It was, Beth had learned, Silver's custom to spend a few hours each day in one of the rooms where customers were entertained. She would inspect each piece of furniture, then spend at least an hour in the room, trying to view it through a stranger's eyes.

"I want to . . ." Beth stopped abruptly, her mind refusing to register what her eyes saw. For today Silver was not sitting on a comfortable chair or reclining on the bed. She was standing near the window, embracing a man. Her arms were clasped around his neck; his hands stroked her back as they kissed. Their bodies were pressed together intimately, the musky scent of desire filling the room. In the distance Beth heard a bird chirping; then the roar of blood in her ears drowned all other sounds.

Beth gasped. Her face flamed, and for a second she thought she would faint. Away! She had to get away! She was too late. Silver and the man must have heard her, for they drew apart.

"Come in, honey," Silver said. Though she turned to face Beth, she remained in the circle of the man's arms, and she tipped her head back so that she could smile up at him. Beth recognized the man as Tom, Silver's protector, who had rescued Beth and Dora from the hooligans. Though Beth knew that Tom lived in the house and that he and Silver shared a bed, she had never seen them touch, much less embrace.

"Come right on in." Tom echoed Silver's invitation. His smile was as wide as Silver's, his brown eyes sparkling with happiness. "You can celebrate with us."

Beth gripped the chair back and tried to steady herself. Though she forced herself to take deep breaths, her heart continued to race. "Celebrate?" As far as she knew, the kind of celebration they had been engaged in involved only two people.

"Sure enough, we're celebrating." Tom grinned and pressed a kiss on Silver's head. "Silver here promised to make an honest man of me."

Beth's expression must have revealed her confusion, for Tom continued. "She's agreed to marry me."

Marriage! Beth's heart began to pound again, and the gray mist threatened her. Marriage! Why would a savvy woman like Silver do something so foolish? Surely a woman who ran a whorehouse knew enough of the ways of men not to be caught in that trap.

Silver and Tom continued to smile, and Beth realized that they were waiting for her to speak. Silver was her friend. Tom had saved her and Dora. She couldn't disappoint them, no matter what she felt.

Beth swallowed deeply, then said, "I'm happy for you." That was the expected response, wasn't it?

It must have been, for Silver grinned that silly smile that Beth had never seen before. She kissed Tom again, then said to Beth, "The preacher's comin' tomorrow. I hope you'll be here."

Tomorrow. There wouldn't be time to talk Silver out of this folly. Once again, Beth made the expected reply. "Of course." As Tom released Silver, Beth hugged her. She ought to touch Tom's hand. Good breeding required that, but there were some things Beth simply could not do, and touch a man was one of them. She managed a small smile.

"Bring the little one with you," Tom admonished her, apparently oblivious to Beth's less than enthusiastic reaction.

Silver chuckled. "I'm lucky Dora's so young. If she were a few years older, Tom might have asked her to marry him instead of me."

Tom's response was a rude snort. "Ain't no one but you, Silver, and you know it."

The two of them smiled at each other, and once again Beth had the feeling that they were in their own world. Though Beth had seen Silver on many different occasions, she had never seen her look this way. Even the heavy makeup couldn't conceal the fact that her cheeks bore a natural glow, and her eyes sparkled. For his part, Tom seemed more relaxed than Beth had ever seen him. And both of them looked happy.

Was this how a marriage started? Were there a few moments of joy that lulled a woman into thinking she was making the right decision? Beth couldn't remember her mother ever looking happy. She and Lenore had speculated on why their parents had married. They understood what their father got out of the relationship—a clean house, meals on the table, a woman to warm his bed, three targets for his anger. But their mother? That was the mystery.

From early childhood, Beth had vowed she would never marry, for a woman's fate was clear. If she was lucky, all she endured were shouts and threats. Those were the good days. On the bad days, the threats turned into blows. And on the really bad days, those blows resulted in more than bruises.

Lenore had known all that, and yet she had married Peter. Not even Beth's most fervent entreaties had swayed her. When Beth had asked her sister why she had finally acceded to their father's demands and agreed to marry Peter, Lenore had said only that it was the right thing to do. She had not glowed with happiness the way Silver did. Instead Lenore had been a pale, somber bride whose red-rimmed eyes betrayed a night of weeping. The wedding had reminded Beth of a wake, only a wake marked an end. Lenore's wedding had been the beginning of a nightmare, for her marriage had been no better than her mother's. That much Beth knew. Although Lenore was stalwart in her denials, Beth was certain that Peter had caused the bruises she saw so often on her sister's face, just as she knew Peter's blows had caused Dora's deafness.

Tom gave Silver a final kiss, then left the room.

"Oh, honey," Silver said with another fatuous smile, "how I love that man!"

Love. That was a word Beth's mother had never used when she spoke of her marriage. And yet, as she was dying, Lenore had whispered that she loved Dora's father. How could she? How could anyone love Peter?

# Chapter Nine

"A wedding—how wonderful!" Mrs. Kane leaned her fore-arms on the kitchen table and smiled as she said, "I do so love weddings."

Beth tried not to shudder at the thought. She had to admit that Silver had seemed happy the afternoon she had become Tom's wife. She and Tom had both smiled constantly, and Silver had giggled like a girl. It wasn't just the perfect weather or the fact that she'd been dressed in her favorite pink, a taffeta gown with six ruffles and a skirt so wide it barely fit through the doorway. There had to be something else that had given Silver that smile that threatened to crack her face.

Beth managed a small smile of her own as Mrs. Kane handed her a cup of coffee. The beverage, like all of the cook's creations, smelled delicious. It was only the thought of weddings that made Beth's stomach turn. She couldn't understand it. How could Silver or any woman be happy when she was on the verge of surrendering her freedom? It wasn't only that she was giving a man the legal right to touch her body, to do whatever he wished with her, but she was also promising to obey him. How could anyone be so fool-ish?

Picking up her cup with hands that somehow did not be-tray her distress, Beth took a sip of the steaming beverage. Foolish. That's what brides were. But Silver had looked as if she knew exactly what she was doing, as if she liked the prospect. When she had walked into the parlor where Tom and all her girls were waiting, she and her husband-to-be had exchanged private smiles. Beth had never seen her parents or Lenore and Peter look like that, and yet Silver's smile tugged at the back of her memory. She knew she had once seen someone with that radiant look.

"Was your friend a beautiful bride?" Mrs. Kane appeared so anxious to hear the details of Silver's wedding that she pushed her coffee aside. That was not a typical act, for there were few things she enjoyed more than heavily sugared coffee.

Beth stirred her own beverage thoughtfully. "Beautiful" was not a word she would have used to describe Silver, and yet that afternoon her face had been so suffused with happiness that she had seemed beautiful.

"Yes, she was."

Mrs. Kane blinked her eyes. Beth wasn't sure whether it was due to the inexplicable emotion that seemed to affect some women when weddings were mentioned, or whether the cause was simply the ray of sunshine that spilled onto Mrs. Kane's face. "I thought so," the cook said. "Brides are supposed to be beautiful. Why, I imagine Mr. Simmons could hardly take his eyes off you the day you two were wed."

Mr. Simmons. Beth lowered her eyes to cover her confusion. Why was Mrs. Kane asking about her father? Then, remembering her alleged widowhood, she nodded and reached for one of the sweet rolls that Mrs. Kane had just taken from the oven. This was her morning for making sweet breads; tomorrow would be dinner rolls in addition to the two loaves of plain bread that she baked each day.

"I reckon the doctor will be marrying soon," Mrs. Kane continued.

Beth tried not to frown, though she had no desire to discuss weddings, and especially not Andrew Muller's. "These rolls are delicious," she said.

But Mrs. Kane would not be stopped. "He's been courting Miss Pratt for a long time, you know. Maybe when he gets back from this trip, he'll ask her." The older woman took a sip of her coffee and smiled. "It sure would be nice to have a wedding here."

The morning was warm, even for June, and the heat from the oven made the kitchen uncomfortable. Beth rose and opened the window, letting in the scent of roses and the lazy drone of bees. Though she knew it was cowardly, she closed her eyes for a second, trying to banish the thoughts of weddings. The clop of a horse's hooves on cobblestones and the faint creak as someone opened the stable door drifted through the window.

Unbidden, a memory returned. It had been late afternoon when Beth saw Lenore sneaking out of the barn. She had come into the kitchen, her lips swollen, her eyes filled with a strange expression, and had started paring potatoes as if her life depended on each peel being the same thickness. Rebuffing Beth's attempts at conversation, Lenore had continued to prepare the vegetables, her head jerking up and her gaze turning to the window at the slightest sound.

Several minutes later Rodney had emerged from the barn, whistling a tune, his brown face more relaxed than Beth had ever seen it. Beth heard her sister's sharp intake of breath, and when she looked, Lenore wore the same awestruck expression Beth had seen on Silver's face the day of her wedding.

Andrew grabbed his bags and looked around for Roberts. Where was the man? He'd sent a telegram advising Beth which train he would take so that the coachman could meet it. The train had been on time. There was no excuse, no excuse at all, for Roberts's tardiness.

Andrew raised his hat in greeting to a colleague whose wife had met him. He at least would soon be home, while Andrew . . . He frowned and forced himself to stop pacing. There was no reason for him to be so anxious to reach his house. It wasn't as if he had any emergencies waiting. Beth's last telegram had told him he had no patients scheduled until tomorrow morning, and though it was likely he would have to make a delivery tonight, it would be hours until the sun set and he could consider taking the buggy on its dangerous route.

Aha! There was Roberts. Andrew surrendered his valise to the coachman and climbed into the small barouche. He soon found himself tapping his foot impatiently as they made their way through the uncharacteristically crowded streets. Had everyone in the city decided to take advantage of the sunny day by going for a drive?

As they turned onto Delaware Avenue, Andrew began to relax. Soon. He'd be home soon. And then . . . He stopped as a doubt assailed him. Why *was* he so eager to be home again? He attended meetings frequently, and never before had he felt such anticipation. That was supposed to happen at the start of the trip. At that point he should be eager to reach his destination, to see his colleagues, and to present his paper. There was no reason to long for home, and yet that was exactly what he felt, an unexplained yearning to be back on Niagara Square. It must be because he would soon perform Dora's surgery. That must be the reason his pulse raced as if he were a young man courting his first girl. Courting! What a ridiculous thought. What strange brain fever had made him think of that? Andrew placed both feet firmly on the floor and forced himself to think of the questions his paper had generated.

"Yes, the speech was well received," he told Beth when they were seated at the dining room table. Andrew spread butter on a roll. His imagination had not exaggerated. She was beautiful. Her hair was as gloriously vibrant as he had remembered, while her eyes were as cool as a pond. Beth Simmons was a beautiful woman. She was not, however, the reason he was so glad to be home. Of course she wasn't. He took a bite of the roll.

"Which one did you deliver?" she asked.

Deliver? Andrew's hand, which had been reaching for his water goblet, faltered. What did Beth know about his deliveries? He stared at her for a moment before he realized she was asking about his speech, then took a sip of water to cover his momentary confusion. How foolish a man could be, thinking about the way a woman's lips curved when he should have been listening to the words that were coming out of that delectable mouth.

"The one on deafness," he said. "My colleagues were intrigued when I explained how I plan to cure Dora."

The smile she awarded his announcement was far different

from the one she had worn when she greeted him. That one was cool and friendly. This one was warm and maternal. Andrew knew she was thinking of her daughter. He also knew it was foolish to wish he'd seen the same emotion animate her face when he had arrived home.

After all, Beth was here to help her daughter, not to fuel his ridiculous fantasies.

She sprinkled salt on her potatoes, then looked up at him. "When do you think you'll be ready?" Andrew saw apprehension war with anticipation in her eyes. That was natural. He, too, felt the same ambivalence. Though his rational mind wanted to perform the surgery, to prove that his theory would work, another side of him feared failure. What if . . . ? He would not consider that possibility.

"In three days," he told Beth. When Roberts had driven past the front of his house, Andrew had seen the sign. As he had anticipated, he would have a delivery tonight. And, because the moon was new, in all likelihood, there would be another tomorrow. After that he would give himself a night of uninterrupted sleep before he performed the delicate operation.

Beth's eyes widened, and he knew that for the moment her fears outweighed her hope. Slowly, she nodded. "I'm glad."


"So, when will it be?" David tossed the crystal paperweight from one hand to another.

Andrew couldn't say what had brought him here. He had work to do before the sun set, and even more to accomplish afterwards, but he had found himself strangely restless and had decided to pay his friend a visit. He had found David in his office, surrounded by the piles of paper that were an integral part of an attorney's life.

"Three days."

David's hands stilled and he looked up, surprise evident in his tawny brown eyes. "So soon?" He raised a brow and when he spoke, his voice was mildly accusing. "You could have given me some warning."

Andrew leaned back in his chair, crossing his legs before

him. "It's not as though I'm sending out invitations." Both Nailor and Barclay had asked if they could observe, but Andrew had refused. Dora's operation would be difficult enough without having people watching his every movement.

"Why on earth not?" David demanded as he plunked the paperweight back onto the desk. "I would have thought the Pratts would insist."

Andrew narrowed his eyes, considering. The sun shone brightly on the courthouse dome, and on days like today, it cast almost painful light into David's office. Had the reflection somehow disturbed his brain?

"What do the Pratts have to do with it?" Andrew asked. He gave David a careful look. His friend did not appear feverish, and there was no sign that he had drunk too much whiskey. Perhaps it was just a passing madness. Something was wrong, though, for David's face bore an odd expression, as if it were Andrew and not David himself who was speaking nonsense.

"She's their daughter." David pronounced each word carefully, almost as if he doubted Andrew's ability to comprehend such a simple concept.

"Helen?" David was definitely suffering from some strange malady. Andrew would have to find an excuse to examine him. He only hoped the condition was not permanent.

"I believe Helen is the only daughter they have." David's expression changed from puzzled to concerned.

"That may be true," Andrew said as agreeably as he could, "but I fail to see the relevance."

David slapped his hand on the desk and began to laugh. "Oh, Andrew, my friend, you're priceless! Only you would find it odd that the bride and her parents should be involved in planning the wedding."

The man was mad. Stark, raving mad.

"What wedding?"

"The one that's going to take place in three days." As Andrew fixed a stern look on his face, David's grin faded. "Weren't we talking about weddings?"

"Hell, no!"

"Helen!" Andrew could not conceal his surprise at seeing her in his waiting room. In all the time he had known Helen Pratt, she had never consulted him for medical problems. She had been to his office before, but only when accompanying one of her parents or when she had assisted him in decorating the house. "Is something wrong? Is one of your parents ill?" Though the elder Pratts were in apparently good health, Andrew knew all too well that illness could strike with no warning.

The weather had turned cold and damp overnight, and that had brought more patients than normal to his office. Andrew wasn't complaining. Not only did the extra patients keep him from worrying about the surgery that was now only two days away, but the inclement weather also made his deliveries less dangerous. Fewer people ventured outdoors in the rain, and that decreased his chances of being observed.

Helen smiled as she shook her head. "No, Andrew, nothing's wrong. I simply wanted to ask a favor of you."

That was almost as unusual as the sight of Helen in his office. "And what is this favor that's brought you out on a rainy day?" He ushered Helen into his examining room. Though there were no other patients in the waiting room, he didn't wish Helen's request—whatever it was—to be overheard.

But, rather than reply, Helen tipped her head to one side, her eyes narrowing slightly as she apparently considered something.

"Your office looks different," she announced. "The furniture in here is arranged differently, and I don't recall seeing that potted plant in the waiting room before."

Andrew looked at the room, trying to see it through Helen's eyes. Yes, the desk did appear to be at a different angle, and he didn't remember having two chairs in front of it a week ago. In truth, the only change he had noticed was that he could now find files on his desk. That had been such a novelty that any other differences had paled in comparison. Women, it appeared, noticed different things.

"Do you think it looks better?" he asked.

"Indeed it does." Helen's reply was instantaneous. "Your office is far more welcoming now."

Welcoming. Andrew opened the door and looked at the waiting room again. The furniture and rug were the same, but something—he couldn't quite pinpoint it—was different. Though he wasn't sure a physician's office needed to be welcoming, he also saw no reason to resist change, especially if Helen felt this was an improvement. Over the years, Helen had given him good advice. It was thanks to her that his house was filled with furnishings that Buffalo society considered elegant and worthy of his station. If Helen liked the changes, they could stay.

"I'm afraid I can't take any credit," he told Helen. "Whatever's different must be Mrs. Simmons's doing."

Helen raised one eyebrow as her fingertips traced the carving on a small clock Andrew couldn't remember seeing before. "Mrs. Simmons? Your paragon of a housekeeper?"

"She's my housekeeper," Andrew said shortly. *Although I'd be more likely to describe her as a gadfly than a paragon,* he mused. It was odd. Though she was quiet—almost timid on occasion—Beth had managed to exert her will on the household and, if he were willing to admit the truth, on himself. She had organized his life and his practice, and she must have cast some sort of spell. How else could he explain the fact that he found himself thinking of her at the strangest times?

"I must meet her," said Helen.

This time it was Andrew who raised a questioning brow. "Why on earth would you want to do that?" He could not picture Helen Pratt, herself the paragon of Buffalo society, having anything in common with Beth other than the fact that they were both female.

"Why?" Helen laughed softly. "I should think the answer would be apparent. I want to see the woman who's changed you."

"Changed *me?* What an absurd thought!" Yes, the office furniture might have been rearranged, and there might be doodads in the waiting room, but he hadn't changed. Not one iota. Those ridiculous thoughts he kept having were of no significance. They must be caused by the phases of the moon or the tides, just like David's absurd fixation on weddings.

"It's not absurd," Helen insisted. "You have changed, Andrew. You're gentler and more considerate of others."

She was wrong. He was no different than he'd been three months ago before a lovely redheaded woman and her engaging daughter had come into his life. "I was always considerate."

"Of course you were." The tone of Helen's voice made mockery of her apparently conciliatory words. "As I was saying, you've changed. Why, the next thing you know, you'll decide to marry."

"Never!"

"Oh, yes, you will." Helen's smile could only be described as smug. "I've discovered your secret."

The blood drained from Andrew's face. How could she have guessed? He swallowed deeply. She couldn't have. It was only a bluff.

"And what secret would that be?" he asked as lightly as he could.

"You're not cold-hearted at all."

*He was hot, so hot. His head felt as if it were on fire; every inch of his body ached; and his throat seemed to be swollen to twice its size. "Ma, water," he managed to croak. Even a sip would ease the pain. "Ma," he begged. There was no answer, no sign that she heard his plea. "Ma!" The silence that followed his cry wrenched him into full consciousness. Ma was dead; she would never again sing Mary a lullaby or bring him a glass of water.*

*Andrew closed his eyes, refusing to let the tears fall. An eight-year-old boy was too old to cry. Besides, crying would do no good. It would not bring Ma back or make food and water suddenly appear. It would not give him and Mary a home. Though it was simple to close his eyes, shutting his ears was impossible. He heard the soft whimpers from the pallet next to his.*

*"It's okay, Mary." He whispered the words, as much from*

*fear of being discovered as from the need to protect his throat.* "I'm here."

The small form slid closer to him. "I'm hungry," she whispered, and touched his face with her hand.

As if in response, Andrew's stomach rumbled. How long had it been since they had eaten? Andrew could not recall how many days he had lain in the dark closet, his head burning with fever. Mary had been stricken first, and he had been afraid to leave her alone, lest someone overhear her cries and discover their hiding place. And then his own agony had begun, the bone-wrenching chills followed by raging fever. How long had it been? How long since his little sister, already weakened by the grippe, had eaten?

"I'll find something," he promised. It took every ounce of strength he could muster to raise himself to a sitting position. "Don't make a sound while I'm gone," he admonished her. "I'll be back soon."

His head throbbed and his legs threatened to buckle under him, but Andrew refused to let weakness defeat him. Mary needed food, and he was the only one who could help her. He had promised their mother that he would take care of his sister. He would. Somehow, he would.

The big house was quiet in the early twilight. Moving silently, Andrew crept down the stairs and turned the knob on the kitchen door. That was where he had found bread and a few pieces of meat the last time. Today the door was locked. Andrew bit his lip to keep from crying. Big boys didn't cry. They helped their little sisters.

Andrew swallowed, then winced from the pain. Straightening his shoulders, he slipped out the back door and made his way to Mr. Wilson's shop. Mr. Wilson would help. He would give him food. But the store was closed. It was too late. By the time Andrew reached the next shop, his entire body was trembling with fatigue.

"What do you want?" The shopkeeper's bellows hurt his ears.

"Food." The word came out as a croak. The cheese smelled so good. Mary liked cheese.

This shopkeeper was bigger than Mr. Wilson, and he wore

*a frown instead of a smile.* "Show me your money."

Andrew shook his head. He had no money. The few precious coins that he had found in his mother's cloak were gone. "Please." It hurt just to pronounce the word.

The big man took a step toward him, his florid face darkening. "No money, no food. I've told you that before." As he leaned forward, Andrew could smell garlic on his breath. "Get out of here, you vermin. Go back to your country. You damned foreigners don't belong here."

Before the man could strike him, Andrew ran from the shop. The last of his energy spent, he crept into the alley and slumped to the ground. Tears of pain and frustration leaked from his eyes. Where was he going to find food? Mary needed it. He couldn't go back without something. How much longer could he walk? His head was so hot, and his legs felt like rubber.

Please, God.

As if in answer to his prayer, Andrew spotted a chunk of moldy bread next to an overflowing garbage bin. He lurched forward, grasping the bread, then dragged himself to his feet.

"Mary," he whispered as he opened the door. The hallway light spilled into the small closet. His sister was lying motionless and silent on her pallet. Andrew nodded. She had done what he'd told her. If a stranger opened the door, he would have seen a pile of rags, nothing more.

"Look, Mary," Andrew said as he closed the door. "I brought you food."

She made no reply. Andrew knelt next to his sister and touched her shoulder. "It's okay, Mary. It's me, Andrew." Still, she did not move. Slowly, fearfully, he touched her face. It was cold.

"No!"

He woke, his limbs trembling as they had that night so many years ago. It was only a nightmare, Andrew told himself. It would never happen again. He had enough money now that no one would ever deny him food or shelter. More importantly, he had made certain that he let no one take Mary's place in his heart. He would never again endure the agony of losing someone he loved.

A nightmare. That was all. But why, oh, why, did it come so often? Was there no way to escape his past?

What a godforsaken place! It was cold and damp and, oh, the wind. Peter frowned as he felt the wind blowing through his clothing. It had been warm when he'd left the farm, but then that damned rain had come. Why would anyone want to live here? If it weren't for those cursed runaways, he would find himself a nice, warm place to live. Trouble was, a man had to go where the money was. And, sure as snow in January, this was where the money was. The sun might not shine all year long here, but those slaves just kept coming.

He tugged on the reins, slowing the horse. If there was going to be a delivery tonight—and he was sure there would be—it would be near here. This deserted stretch of road near the river was the perfect place to drop the slaves. Men with rowboats would be waiting to take them to Canada. Only, tonight they wouldn't get there, because he'd be waiting.

You'd think those darkies could have found a better place to go. Course, if they had any brains, they wouldn't have left those nice, warm plantations. They had everything there: food, clothing, a place to live, and masters to take care of them. Why would they leave all that for this?

Peter had to admit he was mighty glad they were dumb enough to head north. If there hadn't been any runaways, their masters wouldn't need him to find them. It might be cold work, but the money was good. Damned good.

As another blast of wind hit him, Peter shivered. He needed dry clothes and some whiskey, but most of all, he needed a woman to warm him. Not just any woman, but one with hair the color of flames.

He looked around. There was no sign of the slaves. They ought to be here by now. Peter narrowed his eyes, searching the road. Where were they? He wanted to catch them and then get himself a woman.

It was a damned shame Lenore died when she did. He didn't have to pay her, and she was prettier than a whore . . . except when she was breeding. She looked like a cow then, big and clumsy, with that same dumb expression a cow had when it was chewing its cud. Nope, Peter sure hadn't liked those months. At first she had tried to refuse him his manly rights. He'd put her straight about that. But then, when she had gotten so big that she took up the whole bed, he had found himself another woman, one who knew better than to get herself into that predicament.

As the rivulets of rain began to run down his neck, Peter cursed. He'd wait five more minutes, and then he was going to town. A man had needs. Especially on a cold, wet night.

Thank God the brat was dead. It served no earthly use, and it sure would have been hard, having it around when Lenore was gone. Wayne didn't hold much store in God, but Peter knew He was looking after him. Look how He got rid of the brat. If that wasn't the answer to his prayers, Peter didn't know what was. Yes, indeed, God was favoring him. And He would do it again, because Peter was doing His work, returning property to its rightful owners.

Peter spurred the horse. He was going to Canal Street. To hell with the slaves. There'd be more. Tonight he needed a woman. Wayne had said Silver had a redheaded one. He said she was young and pretty, too. Just the way Peter liked them.

It was good for the young ones, having a man like Peter teach them a thing or two. Trouble was, Silver was one tough bitch. She charged more than most of the madams, and she had rules about what her girls could do. Took a lot of the fun out of it. It was wrong that a man had to pay for what ought to be free. Still, a man had needs and tonight those needs had to be satisfied.

Soon it would be different. Soon he would collect the money, and then he could find himself a wife. A pretty, red-headed wife who would do just what he wanted whenever he wanted it. A wife like Lenore.

Peter spurred the horse again. The woman could wait. Unless his ears deceived him, that was a wagon approaching.

# Chapter Ten

The moans wakened her. For an instant Beth lay paralyzed. Lenore! He had hurt Lenore again. Then her heart began to pound with anxiety and her throat constricted as her eyes flew open. Lenore was safe now. Something must have happened to Dora. Beth leaped from her bed and ran the few feet across the polished floor, her arms ready to enfold the child. But Dora was asleep in the trundle bed, her breathing soft and regular.

Beth stood for a moment, watching her beloved charge sleep, listening to the sound of raindrops on the roof. Normally rain soothed her so that she rarely woke on a rainy night. Perhaps Andrew had moaned in his sleep. She had heard him cry out more than once, though it had been days since his last nightmare. The sound was not repeated; nothing was wrong. Beth returned to her bed and pulled the sheet to her shoulders. Perhaps her worries over Dora's operation were what had wakened her. Though she tried not to dwell on the possibility of failure, it haunted her. What would she do if Dora's hearing wasn't restored, or if . . . ? Beth refused to complete the sentence.

She turned onto one side, determined to fall asleep again. Morning would come quickly, and if she wasn't rested, the day's tasks would be difficult. But as she plumped the pillow in an unsuccessful attempt to relax, she heard the moans again. It wasn't a dream. The sound had come from someone in the house, and that person was in pain. Sliding her feet into slippers and grabbing a wrapper, Beth hurried into the hallway. The sounds were coming from the back of the house. The front door was never locked. Had a patient come into the office and, not finding the doctor, made his way into the living quarters?

Where was Andrew? His bedroom was below hers. Surely he would have heard the cries. But Andrew, Beth remembered, had gone on a house call this evening. He must not have returned. Beth lit a candle and descended the stairs, listening carefully. The sound was not repeated, and for a moment she believed she had imagined it. Then she heard it again, a low cry that sounded as if the man—for she now realized it was a male voice—was trying desperately to make no sound. As a horrible fear assailed her, she ran down the remaining stairs.

"Andrew!" she cried. He lay crumpled on the floor, one leg bent under him while his left hand clutched his right shoulder. Dear God! He was bleeding. The dark stains on his hand and sleeve were blood, not rain. Bile rose to her throat.

"What happened?" Beth knelt next to him, trying to control her fear. *Please, Lord, not again! No more blood!*

"I was wounded." He took a shallow breath between each of the words, and Beth saw that the simple effort of speaking was exhausting him. His face was gray with lines of fatigue bracketing his mouth.

"What happened?" She repeated the question as she tried to assess the damage. There was so much blood! Had he fallen and somehow cut his arm? As the image of her mother's face, blood flowing from her cheek and lips, rose before her, Beth felt the room darken and begin to spin. No! She could not faint. Andrew needed her. She heard the rain dripping from the eaves, and for a moment she thought she was hearing Andrew's lifeblood seeping away. *Dear God, no! Please don't let him die.*

"Gunshot." His voice was weaker now. "Shoulder." Andrew winced as another spasm of pain swept through him. "Help me . . . office." He placed his left hand on the floor and attempted to rise.

Beth closed her eyes, trying to fight the painful images. It wasn't an accident. Someone had done this to him. But who, and why? As the memory of her father's face, contorted with anger, appeared, Beth bit her lip. Pa was dead. He couldn't hurt Ma or Lenore or anyone ever again. She wouldn't think about him. What mattered now was getting help for Andrew.

Beth brought the candle closer. Andrew's blue eyes were clouded, and his color had worsened. She didn't need a degree in medicine to tell her that the man was seriously wounded.

"I'll summon another doctor," she said. By some miracle, her voice was as steady as if she were in a classroom instead of crouched on the floor next to a man who badly needed medical care. Dr. Wallace was a colleague; surely he would help.

"No." Andrew struggled to a sitting position and shook his head for emphasis as he spoke the word. "No one must know." He took another breath, wincing at the effort. "Help me get to my examining room."

It was a reasonable request. He would be more comfortable there, waiting while she brought Dr. Wallace, for surely Andrew wasn't serious about refusing to call a colleague. The pain must have affected his judgment. Beth stood and extended her hand.

"You need a doctor," she said as they moved slowly along the hallway toward his office, his uninjured arm draped over her shoulders. He lurched as if unable to put weight on one foot, and though Beth knew he was trying not to lean on her, her shoulders ached from the extra burden. Her breath came in short gasps. That, she was well aware, had more to do with the fact that a man was touching her than with the effort she was expending. *He won't hurt me,* she told herself. Aloud, she said, "The bullet has to come out."

Andrew stopped, his fingers digging into her shoulder. "You'll have to remove it."

Beth felt the blood drain from her face. He expected her to pull a bullet out of his flesh! "I'm not a doctor." This time there was no disguising the tremor in her voice.

"I am," he answered. "I'll talk you through the steps."

"I can't." It was unthinkable. He had no way of knowing how sick the sight, the very smell of blood, made her. It was all she could do to keep walking, supporting his weight, when she could feel the sticky substance. She had wrapped her right arm around his waist to steady him, and the cloying scent of blood from his injured shoulder made her stomach roil.

"You must," he repeated. As they stumbled into the examining room, he paused, resting against the door frame for a moment. "Please, Beth."

The agony she heard in his voice and saw reflected on his face made her forget that he was a man. For the moment, he was only a fellow human who needed her. She guided him across the room, helping him hoist himself onto the table. "What happened?" she asked. "How were you shot?" It made no sense. Beth couldn't imagine who would shoot a doctor making a house call. It wasn't as if he had patients who would have summoned him to the seedier parts of the city. The only possibility was that he had gotten into a fight. But Andrew didn't seem like a man who would fight, and she could smell no liquor on him. Still, Beth knew that men were unpredictable, and brutality was a fact of life where the male of the species was concerned.

"Can't tell you." He leaned back on the table, catching his breath. "Too much risk."

Beth busied herself lighting another lamp, then turned back to him. "I won't help you unless you tell me how you were injured." Somehow, although she could find no reason for it, it seemed vitally important that she understand why Andrew had been shot.

His eyes widened, and she saw his lips tighten, as if in response to a new wave of pain. He glared, and she knew he expected her to back down. Beth refused to drop her gaze. She needed—oh, how she needed—to feel some measure of control over this impossible situation. Perhaps only a few seconds passed while she waited, but to Beth it seemed like an hour before Andrew nodded. "All right," he agreed, his reluctance evident. "I was making a delivery."

"I don't understand." Beth was certain Andrew had no pregnant patients. "Wasn't the midwife available?"

Andrew shook his head. "Not that kind of delivery."

It made no sense. "Someone shot you while you were delivering medicine?" What kind of crazy person would do that?

"Not medicine." As his lips twisted, she sensed that his pain was both physical and mental. "Slaves."

Slaves! It couldn't be true.

"You're part of the Underground Railroad?" Beth heard her voice rise in disbelief. Andrew Muller, the man who refused to treat anyone except the socially elite, was a conductor? This oh-so-proper man was engaged in a highly illegal activity? And yet, as her mind reeled at his revelation, Beth realized that the pieces of the puzzle fit. The frequent house calls at night, most of which occurred during the new moon, his reluctance to discuss almost any aspect of slavery, even his aloof attitude.

"Yes." He winced again. "Now you know, so get that bullet out." Andrew told Beth where to find the scalpel she would need. While her back was turned, he struggled out of his coat, the effort etching new lines onto his face.

"No more," he gasped. "Cut the shirt."

Beth's eyes widened at the thought of what was to come. How could she do this? She had no choice. Even if she cared nothing for Andrew, Dora needed him.

Beth took a deep breath and gripped the scalpel. Carefully she slit the fine cotton, trying not to touch Andrew's skin. She wouldn't think about the muscles underneath or the pain they could inflict on a woman or a child. But when she had removed his shirt, Beth gasped. Andrew's chest was broad and firm, the taut muscles covered with pale golden hair. Though there was no ignoring the latent power of his arms, he looked nothing like her father or Peter.

A clock chimed the half hour. Beth's hand paused. The sound was so normal that it startled her, for nothing else had been normal from the moment she had wakened.

"You're not going to swoon, are you?"

Beth shook her head and studied Andrew's shoulder. She had dealt with cuts and bruises, but never a gunshot. The wound was ugly, a gaping hole with rough edges that marred the perfection of Andrew's body.

"Look at the back," he told her. "Is there an exit hole?"

Biting her lips to calm her trembling nerves, Beth studied the other side of Andrew's shoulder. When she shook her head, he said, "I thought not. The bullet's still in there. You'll have to remove it." He lay back on the table, extending his arm to give Beth better access.

"Where's the laudanum?" Her mother had hoarded pennies to buy a bottle. Though she had refused to drink it herself, no matter how badly she'd been beaten, she had given Beth and Lenore sips when their pain was the worst.

"No laudanum," Andrew insisted. "I need to talk you through the steps."

Beth shuddered. This wasn't a nightmare. She wouldn't waken and discover it had been nothing more than a bad dream. He expected her—he needed her—to remove a bullet. How would she do it?

She closed her eyes for a second, trying to gain the strength to proceed. When she opened them, she knew what she would do. She would pretend. Hadn't Lenore told her she was gifted with imagination? She would use it tonight as she had so often in the past, to transport her to a better place.

Beth followed Andrew's instructions, reaching inside the gaping hole, searching for the instrument of his pain, wresting it from his shoulder, then pouring whiskey on the wound before she carefully stitched it closed. Andrew need never know that she had removed herself from the examining room. In her mind, she was kneeling in her mother's peony bed. Instead of extracting a bullet, she was pulling a marble out of the heavy, clay-ridden soil where Lenore had buried it. Then she poured water on the bed so no one would know she had disturbed the soil. And when she threaded the needle, she pictured herself sewing Dora's rag doll, taking tiny stitches to secure the arms.

"Done," she said at last. The dressing was amateur, and she feared it might become dislodged, but at least the wound was closed and his blood had stopped dripping.

"Thank you." Though Beth knew the pain must have been fierce, Andrew had made no sound while she operated, and now his face seemed relaxed. "I need you to help me again," he said. "Take me to my room."

Though Beth tried to protest, he would not listen. "I must

be upstairs," he insisted. "No one must know that this happened." Dawn was only an hour away, and with it Mrs. Kane would return to the house to prepare breakfast. Though Beth feared the exertion would be too great for him, she understood Andrew's desire for secrecy. The success of the invisible Railroad that had taken so many slaves from living hell to freedom depended on its stationmasters' and conductors' anonymity. No one in the household must know that Andrew was involved.

Slowly, pausing on each step, they made their way up the front staircase. This time Andrew did not lean on Beth, but gripped the railing tightly and used it to hoist himself from one step to the next. When they reached the top, Andrew stopped and leaned against the wall, clearly mustering strength for the walk down the hallway. Beth left him there and hurried toward his room. Pushing open the door, she lit a lamp and pulled back the bedspread.

She had been in the room dozens of times, ensuring that the maids had cleaned it thoroughly. She knew the carving of the heavy mahogany furniture as well as she did the feel of her hairbrush, for she had touched the ornate legs and bedposts numerous times to be certain no dust remained. It was a large room, dominated by the massive bed and chest of drawers. Though the wood was warm to the touch, Beth had always considered it a cold room, a proper lair for Dr. Icicle. But tonight the room felt warm . . . oppressively so. Was it her imagination, or simply the thought of being in the same intimate chamber as Andrew?

He sank onto the edge of the bed, clearly exhausted by his trauma and the difficult climb up the stairs. "One more favor," he said when he caught his breath. "I need you to help me undress."

Had she thought the room was warm? Beth could feel her skin chill, and her hands grew clammy at the prospect of removing his clothes, of seeing . . . Her mind balked at the thought.

As if he sensed her uneasiness and was amused by it, one corner of Andrew's mouth turned upward. "Surely you assisted your husband many times."

Her husband. Of course. Her husband.

Beth nodded. Now was not the time for explanations. Instead, she knelt next to the bed and reached for one of his boots. With a tug, she released it and found herself looking at a stocking-clad foot, one toe protruding from a hole that Mrs. Chandler had obviously missed the last time she laundered it. Beth started to remove the sock, then changed her mind. She would take off the other boot first. Perhaps he could sleep in his socks. Perhaps if she was careful, she would not have to see or touch any more flesh.

She could feel her pulse begin to pound at the very thought. *Think of something else,* she admonished herself. *Anything else.*

And so she said, "I'm surprised by your involvement with the Railroad."

"Why would that be?" Andrew shifted his weight as she helped him slide his arm into a loose robe. "Do you think me incapable of conducting people to safety?"

"Not incapable." The man could do anything he chose; of that Beth had no doubt. What surprised her was that he chose to help fugitives. "It seems out of character," she explained, trying not to think of the next garment she would have to remove.

A spasm of pain crossed Andrew's face, and Beth willed her fingers to move more quickly. She had to prepare him for sleep, for he needed its healing properties desperately.

"Why do you say that?" he asked.

She spoke slowly, though her fingers hurried to unbutton his trousers, working carefully lest she inadvertently touch him. "You claim you don't care about people, but you must. You would not risk your reputation otherwise."

The law, ever since the Fugitive Slave Act had been passed, was clearly on the side of the slave owners. Not only was anyone convicted of aiding and abetting runaways subject to a substantial penalty and imprisonment, but he risked becoming a social outcast, for many wealthy Northern landowners sympathized with the plantation owners, demanding that property be respected. Beth imagined that if Andrew's patients knew of his illegal activities, many would be appalled enough to seek another physician.

"You misunderstand." Though Andrew's blue eyes were glazed with pain, his voice was stronger than Beth had heard it since she had first found him. "This is not a crusade. It's a game. I can't resist the challenge, pitting myself against the slave catchers and their dogs."

He spoke firmly, and his voice sounded sincere. He wanted her to be convinced; she knew that. And yet, she did not believe him, for the words—despite his earnest tone—did not ring true.

He fell asleep. Beth stared at him for a moment, seeing the lines of strain still etched in his face. No matter what he said, she would no longer believe that he cared for nothing but money.

Andrew turned, and as he did, the pain radiated down his arm, waking him from his fitful sleep. Oh, how his shoulder hurt! He had learned in medical school that bullet wounds were painful, for they penetrated deep into the flesh, destroying tissue and muscle along their path. He had seen the damage inflicted on others, watched the way they flinched from even the lightest of touches, never dreaming that one day he would have personal experience.

He shifted his weight, moving so that his shoulder was exposed to the cooling night air. It hurt like hell, but it could have been worse. He could have lost a hand and been unable to continue his practice. That would have been even worse than Phoebe's foot.

Phoebe.

It was natural that he would think of her tonight, for she was the reason he had become involved.

*"What's the problem, Nag?"* There was no apparent reason for the horse's skittishness. The sun was still high as they returned from his rounds; there was no sign of snakes or other animals that might spook Nag, and yet the horse moved restlessly, ignoring Andrew's commands and continuing along the path toward the creek.

*"Thirsty, old boy?"* That must be the reason for the

horse's uneasiness and the single-minded way he moved toward water.

But when they approached the banks of the creek, Nag stopped three feet away and refused to move. Whatever he sought, it wasn't a drink.

"What now?" Andrew tugged on the reins. This wasn't like Nag. Andrew looked around, trying to see what had drawn the horse to this part of the creek. It was an idyllic spot, with large willow trees lining a portion of the bank. The water moved slowly, and the fronds of one tree swayed slightly in the breeze. There was no breeze. Andrew's eyes widened at the realization. Something was making that motion, and it wasn't the wind. It was, he was willing to wager, whatever had brought Nag here. The swaying stopped, but not before Andrew saw a small, dark form standing in the water.

Though the scene could have been innocent, nothing more than a child fishing, something about the boy's posture disturbed Andrew. Quickly he dismounted and ran toward the creek. There was no point in trying to move quietly, for he knew the child had seen him. Instinctively, like a frightened animal, the boy began to run. He succeeded in taking only two steps in the shallow water before he fell on a slippery rock, landing with a splash and a cry of dismay.

"I won't hurt you," Andrew said as softly as he could, trying to allay the child's fear while he pulled him out of the water. He judged the boy to be no more than eight years of age. The reason for the boy's fear was evident. His brown skin, tattered clothing, and the manacle on one ankle betrayed his status. As long as he was on this side of the river, he could be recaptured and returned to his master.

"I won't hurt you," Andrew repeated. "You're safe. Now, tell me your name."

The child kept his eyes on his feet, and Andrew sensed that he was seeking an opportunity to flee again. Though he was dripping wet, he made no effort to shake himself dry. "Jonah," he muttered, his Southern origins evident in the liquid sound of his voice.

"Where's your family, Jonah?" Andrew knew it was unlikely that a child had made the long journey north alone.

"Ain't got no family."

Andrew didn't believe him. "Tell the truth," he said sternly.

The boy hung his head. When he spoke, his voice was filled with pain, reminding Andrew of another boy. "My ma's hurt real bad. The hounds got her."

No wonder young Jonah was standing in the creek. He was attempting to confuse the dogs by breaking the trail of his scent. In all likelihood, the dogs were long gone, but Jonah had no way of knowing that. Trying to mask his horror at the image that rose before him, Andrew said only, "Take me to your mother. I'm a doctor, and I can help her." Though Andrew had heard tales of the vicious bloodhounds that the slave catchers used, he had never seen the result of their attacks. He had, however, treated enough animal bites to know that Jonah's mother needed him.

Jonah shook his head, his fear palpable. How was Andrew to convince him? Every slave knew better than to believe a white man, simply because he murmured kind words. False promises were the first trick slave catchers used.

"You'll just have to trust me," Andrew said. "I can help your mother."

She was hidden beneath another willow tree, sitting in the shallow creek, her foot so badly mangled from the hound's jaws that she could not walk. At one time she might have been a pretty woman. Today pain, worry, and the undeniable torments of the journey north had leached her former beauty, leaving a dangerously thin female whose huge brown eyes reflected more agony than anyone should ever know. Andrew felt the heart that he thought had died along with Mary flutter.

"He's a doctor, Ma," Jonah told her. "Gonna help us."

Andrew helped her onto the bank and examined her leg. As he had feared, the gashes were deep, the flesh was mutilated, and some of the sinews were cut. "I need to suture your foot," he told Jonah's mother. "You'll be able to walk in a week or so."

She shook her head. "Me and Jonah gotta get to Canada."

Knowing the futility of trying to convince her, Andrew simply lifted her into his arms and carried her to the buggy, motioning Jonah to follow them. "You won't get to Canada unless you can walk." And unless she and the child ate. They were both suffering from malnutrition.

Andrew cleaned and stitched the wound, marveling at the stoicism of Phoebe—for she had admitted that was her name. Though he longed to feed both of them, Andrew recognized the need for secrecy, and so he waited until the sun had set before he took Jonah and his mother home. When he was certain that his house was empty, Andrew led them into the wine cellar. No one would have any reason to go there during the next week, and by then Phoebe and Jonah would be well enough to travel again.

For a week, Andrew made surreptitious trips to the cellar each night, bringing food and water to the fugitives and changing the poultices on Phoebe's foot. Gradually Phoebe's trust grew, and she told him of her master's threat to sell Jonah to another plantation.

"I couldn't lose him," she said simply.

And so she had done what countless other slaves had, leaving the only home she knew on a moonless night, following the North Star as she traveled the perilous route to freedom, hiding in abandoned buildings and under shrubs during the day, foraging for food, learning to ignore hunger.

That was the beginning, the first step. He had never turned back.

# Chapter Eleven

The touch was as soft as a butterfly's wing, flitting from one eyelid to another, then lighting on her nose. Beth smiled and started to turn onto her side. As she did, her hand encountered a small, unmovable object. Instantly, the last vestiges of sleep fled and her eyes flew open. Why was Dora on her bed?

Careful not to alarm the little girl, she continued smiling as she moved into a sitting position. The sun streamed through the window, and even without consulting a clock, Beth knew that it was far later than she normally woke. She looked at Dora's trundle. Her rag doll lay discarded at one end, and the chair that normally stood next to the bureau had been moved to the foot of Beth's bed. Apparently Dora had tired of playing with Sally and had decided it was time to waken her mother.

"Yes, sweetie, I'm going to get up," she told the child, and swung her legs off the bed. Sweeping Dora into her arms, she spun her around once in their morning routine, then deposited her on her trundle. "You're going to wear the dress that matches Sally's," she announced, pulling the red plaid frock from the chest. Dora's smile of delight was worth the extra effort of washing a second dress next week. After all, she owed the child something for playing so patiently while Beth slept.

Beth pulled the nightgown over Dora's head. Tomorrow was the day Andrew would operate. Andrew! As memory flooded back, Beth couldn't stop herself from frowning. He would not be operating tomorrow or any day soon. Though Beth felt a pang of disappointment that Dora's silent world would continue, her heart lurched at the thought of Andrew's wound. He might deny it, but she knew it was a serious one that deserved a doctor's care. She also knew that he would not agree to that. Beth shook her head slightly as she realized that she was still dazed by last night's revelations. Andrew Muller, the Ice Doctor, was part of the Underground Railroad. Who said there were no miracles?

"It's all right, Dora," she said, once more smiling as the child tugged at her hand. When she finished buttoning the back of her pinafore, she handed Dora her doll. "I'll be back in a couple minutes," she told the child, and settled her on her trundle. Then, moving as quietly as she could, she descended the stairs to Andrew's room.

*    *    *

130

She was coming. Andrew heard the sound of her footsteps, though he could tell that she was trying to walk silently. Thank goodness she had not forgotten the need for secrecy. He had lain here as quietly as he could, considering the seriousness of his situation, weighing alternatives. There were damned few of those.

Groaning with the effort, Andrew raised himself to a sitting position. Beth must not guess how ill he was, or she would never agree to his plan. She would continue to insist on calling Wallace. The man was a dyed-in-the-wool Copperhead, the last person Andrew would let treat him.

A fresh wave of pain made Andrew close his eyes. When he heard the rustle of Beth's skirts, he snapped his eyes open and tried to appear alert. Today she wore a maroon dress. Though it was almost black, at least it wasn't those ugly widow's weeds she had worn at first. Andrew had no desire to be reminded of death, especially this morning when he had come far too close to it himself. A few inches lower and the fiend would have killed him.

"How are you feeling?" Beth's voice was low, filled with concern and yet somehow sweet.

*Like a man who's been shot,* he thought. Aloud, he said, "As well as can be expected." Damn it! Even to his ears, his voice sounded weak. Maybe she wouldn't notice. "I need your help," he said. She stood just inside the door, obviously reluctant to come closer. "You can't let anyone know I'm here."

"You need a doctor, don't you?"

Andrew shook his head, immediately regretting the action. Fever addled a man's brains. He knew that. Why, then, was he exacerbating the situation by shaking those brains?

"I just need time to heal." A gunshot wound did not cure itself overnight.

She moved closer, as if to assess his condition for herself, and he heard her sharp intake of breath. It didn't take a genius to figure out that he probably looked as bad as he felt. "You really do need a doctor, Andrew." Though her voice had that schoolmarmy tone to it, he saw her hands tremble. "I'm not qualified to help you."

But she was. She had to be.

Sunlight filled the room. When he had wakened to see that the rain had ended, Andrew had considered it a good omen. The third one. The first had been that the slaves he'd been transporting had managed to escape before that maniac on horseback reached them. The man had been demented, so angered by his failure to find the runaways that Andrew suspected he had shot him out of pure frustration. But at least the wound, though serious, wasn't fatal. That had been the second good portent. Then the sunshine. If Beth helped him, there would be four.

"You need to keep everyone away," he told her. In his most lucid moments, he had tried to concoct a plausible reason for his wound. He had failed. If people knew that he'd been shot, speculation would begin, and speculation was one thing he could not afford.

With visible reluctance Beth laid her hand on his forehead, checking for fever. Damn it! Now there would be no way of convincing her that he wasn't ill, for she would surely realize that her fingers were much cooler than his head.

Though she frowned, she did not refuse to help him. "I understand," she said slowly. Her green eyes were serious, and he could see that she was wrestling with something. "We need to move you to the attic," she said. "If you stay in this room, the staff will know that you're in the house. No one goes into the front attic." Beth and Dora's room and the one the previous housekeeper had used were in the back attic, reached by the steep service stairs, while the house's main storage was in the front.

One more thing had gone right this morning. Beth had agreed to help him, and her brain was operating more clearly than his, for she had anticipated a problem that had not occurred to him.

"Good thinking," he said. Though he would not have expected it, a flush colored her cheeks. His housekeeper, it appeared, was unaccustomed to praise, even as minimal as his had been.

She reached for the robe that had slid onto the floor during one of his bouts of fevered thrashing.

"No." She had been here too long. Each minute that she remained away from her normal morning routine increased the likelihood that someone would discover him. "You keep everyone downstairs. I'll get myself to the attic."

He had no idea how he was going to manage that feat.

"The doctor was called to New York," Beth told the assembled servants. She and Dora had eaten a hasty breakfast, then gone into the kitchen, where Beth normally instructed the staff on the day's tasks. Though she excused her tardiness by saying she was feeling poorly, she was not certain anyone believed her. Perhaps when they heard the rest of her tale, they would believe she was merely taking advantage of Andrew's absence to shirk her responsibilities. Let them think that. It was certainly preferable to their learning the truth.

"He received a message in the middle of the night," Beth explained, continuing the fabrication. "It begged him to consult on a difficult case." That wasn't exactly a lie. Oh, the New York part was pure fiction, but he had received a message, and his delivery of passengers could be construed as a difficult case. If he did more than consult on this case, why quibble?

"He didn't know how long he would be away." That much at least was pure truth. "I thought we would take advantage of his absence to clean his office. A thorough cleaning," she added, wanting to maximize the time the maids were on the first floor. "We won't need to do normal cleaning until the office is completed."

"The doctor's room?" Sylvia, the chambermaid, raised the question.

"That can wait. He won't be needing it for a while." And that was truly no lie. Before Sylvia came upstairs, Beth would ensure that Andrew's room bore no signs of his injury. The last thing they needed was to have telltale bloodstains on the sheets.

Leaving Dora in the kitchen with Mrs. Kane, Beth entered Andrew's bedchamber. Good. No drops of blood on the floor. The bed looked slept in, but that was to be expected, for—according to Beth's tale—Andrew had been roused from his sleep. Now, if only the sheets were still snowy. She pulled back the coverlet, searching the linens for stains. None! The angels must be looking after Andrew Muller.

Of course, Beth thought with a wry smile, if in truth he had a guardian angel, surely he would not have been shot.

She climbed the stairs to the back attic, ostensibly to rest for a few minutes. Beth closed the door to her room, making it appear that she was still in it, napping. Though she did not expect any of the servants to venture to the attic, she would take no chances. Moving as silently as she could, she entered the small storage area that held the doctor's trunks. She slid one aside, then pushed on the center panel behind it. As she knew it would, it swung easily, opening into the main attic.

Beth had discovered the concealed passage one day when she had been searching for a chest to store Andrew's research papers. Though she couldn't have said why, she had never mentioned the small door to anyone, and she doubted the others were aware of its existence. Thank goodness! Her chances of keeping Andrew's presence a secret increased if no one suspected there was a passage between the two sections of the attic.

Ducking her head, she crept into the front attic. There she found Andrew, sprawled on the floor. His ragged breathing told her he had collapsed of exhaustion.

"Oh, no!" she cried. The poor man could not lie on the bare floor. Beth pulled three heavy woolen blankets from one of the storage chests. After arranging two of them at his left side, she knelt next to Andrew. "Come," she said softly. "You need to roll onto the blanket."

Though he tried, it appeared he was incapable of moving even the small distance to the makeshift bed. Beth frowned. The only way to get him onto the pallet was to help him, but that meant touching him . . . again. She closed her eyes for a second. He couldn't hurt her, she told herself. Not in his current condition. Trying not to grimace at the thought of touching a man, she slipped one arm under him and gently pulled him toward her. There! He would rest more easily now. When she had covered him with the remaining blanket, Beth leaned back on her heels.

"How do you feel?" she asked. His face was flushed with fever, and she saw the way he winced when the blanket touched his shoulder.

"Better," he said in a tone that belied his optimism.

Beth shook her head. "Those are brave words, Andrew, but you ought to know better. You're a doctor; you know you have a fever."

And fevers, Beth knew, rarely cured themselves in a few hours. Most took days of constant nursing before the patient recovered. If he recovered. Refusing to consider that possibility, Beth realized that she could not care for both Dora and Andrew at the same time. Though she hated the thought of being parted from the child, Beth knew that while only she could nurse Andrew, someone else could watch Dora.

"I'll be back as soon as I take Dora to Silver's," she told Andrew. "She can stay there until you're well."

Andrew shook his head, then closed his eyes as a spasm of pain crossed his face. "That's not an appropriate place for the child," he said when the color had returned to his cheeks.

"She's my daughter. I'll do what's best for her."

The words came out more sharply than Beth had intended, and for a moment she expected Andrew to remind her that he was her employer. But, as if too exhausted to argue, he nodded slowly, then closed his eyes.


"Thanks, Silver," Beth said an hour later when she had seen Dora settled with the other children. "I'll sleep better knowing she's here."

It was early afternoon, and although few customers would arrive for several hours, Silver had started to prepare her toilette. She had directed Beth to a comfortable chair in one corner of the room she shared with Tom.

"Imagine that," Silver said as she dusted powder over her face. "That high-and-mighty doctor asked you to take care of his patients while he's off in the big city. I never thought I'd see the day."

Beth pushed back her guilt. Though she wanted to confide in Silver, she knew she could not afford to tell the truth to anyone, even someone she trusted as much as the older woman. If the wrong people learned of Andrew's activities, he could be jailed. Just as importantly, a vital link on the Railroad would be broken.

"I'm not really caring for the patients," she told Silver. "I just need to be there if they come. And, you know, sometimes they come in the middle of the night."

As Silver nodded, Beth forced a smile onto her face. What would Lenore think if she could hear the web of lies her sister had spun? No one in the doctor's household had questioned Beth when she had said that she was feeling so poorly that she feared she was sickening with the ague and wanted Dora far away. That excuse, Beth had reasoned, would explain why she spent so much time in the attic and why she might have to make forays into Andrew's office for medicine. But Silver would clearly realize that Beth was not ill, and so she had concocted another tale for her.

Beth wrinkled her nose as she opened the door to the hallway. Now that she had brought Dora here, she was anxious to return home. "What's that smell?"

Silver shrugged one of her ample shoulders. "I don't smell nothing."

"Cloves, cheroots, and something else ... something I don't recognize."

As Silver took one last look in the cheval glass and patted her hair, she said, "Must be the new customers. We had a couple real rough ones last night." She gave Beth an appraising glance. "Close the door again, honey." When Beth complied, she said, "One of 'em wanted a redhead. Afterward, Libby said he tried to knock her around."

Beth shuddered, her body recoiling from the thought of men and their brutality. Though Libby was a large woman, Beth knew that even a strong female was rarely a match for a man, particularly an angry one. She stared at the ruffled counterpane on Silver's bed, willing herself to focus on the pink floral design instead of the ugly images that Silver's words evoked.

But Silver was not finished. "You gotta be careful, Beth." She laid a plump hand on Beth's arm. "I reckon you shouldn't come here no more. Men could get the wrong idea and think you was one of the girls."

That possibility had never been far from Beth's mind, and it had so frightened her that not only did she time her visits for the hours the brothel was least busy, but she never, ever entered by the front door.

"You're my friend, Silver. I want to see you and teach the children." Unspoken was the knowledge that Silver would never be welcome in Andrew's mansion.

"Honey, you know I'd miss you powerful like if you didn't come no more, but you gotta protect yourself." When Beth nodded slowly, Silver continued. "I mean it. Let me show you what I teach my girls. Here's how you hurt a man real bad."

As she demonstrated, Beth shuddered. "I don't know if I could do that to someone." For her whole life, she had tried to avoid pain. She had run from it and tried to protect those she loved. How could she deliberately inflict pain on another?

Silver shook her head. "Honey, if he's gonna hurt you, you gotta be ready to protect yourself. But, just you wait a minute." She opened one of her bureau drawers and pulled out a brown bottle, then poured a clear liquid from it into a small vial. "I give my girls this," she told Beth. "If you're smart, you'll keep it with you all the time. Put it in your reticule, or better yet, in your pocket."

Beth stared at the vial in Silver's hand. "What is it?"

"A mighty powerful drug. A man gives you trouble, you put it in his drink. It only takes a minute or two."

"Silver, I can't kill a man."

The older woman shook her head, setting the corkscrew curls to bouncing against her cheeks. "Won't kill 'em." Silver muttered something that sounded suspiciously like, "More's the pity." "Just puts 'em to sleep. That's all. Now, take it."

Reluctantly, Beth slid the vial into her reticule.

"I hope I never have to use it," she told Silver.

"Me, too, honey. Me, too."

*     *     *

By the time Beth returned home, the other servants had departed for the day. When she had first moved into Andrew's mansion, Beth had wondered why only the housekeeper lived in. Now that she knew of Andrew's involvement on the Railroad, Beth understood his motives. Today the unusual arrangement served her well, for now there would be no one to question her actions and she had no need to feign illness. She climbed the attic stairs, her heart pounding with fear of what she might find. Unless a miracle had occurred, she worried that Andrew's fever would have worsened.

It had. She could tell by the heightened color in his face and the glassy look she saw in his eyes.

"You're right," he said in a surprisingly strong voice. "I have a fever."

Beth managed a small smile. While he was ill, she would think of Andrew as a small child, no different from Dora or Mark. She would not—she absolutely would not—think of the broad expanse of chest she had seen last night, or of the powerful arms and shoulders that were attached to that chest.

"I didn't need years of training to tell that you were sick," she said. "Dora looks the same way when she has a fever." It wasn't true. Andrew looked nothing at all like Dora, but maybe if she repeated it often enough, she would start believing there was a similarity.

Placing a rag in the basin, Beth poured cool water from the ewer over it, then laid the compress on Andrew's forehead. He closed his eyes for a second, and she saw the lines at the corner of his mouth relax. Perhaps he would sleep now. But Andrew's eyes opened, and he regarded her steadily.

"Uncover the wound," he told her. "You need to check for infection."

Following Andrew's instructions, she inspected the wound. Thank goodness, there were none of the red streaks that he feared.

Andrew sank back on the pallet, apparently exhausted by the effort of lifting his head and shoulders enough for Beth to perform her examination.

"Is Dora all right?" he asked.

Beth nodded. "She's usually happy with the other children

at Silver's. It's difficult for me, though, guessing how much she understands. I tried to tell her that this was temporary and I would come every day, but I don't know if she comprehended it all."

Dust motes danced in the afternoon sun. Though the room was warm, Andrew shivered. Beth brought another blanket from the trunk and placed it over him.

"I hadn't considered that aspect of deafness," he admitted. "That fiend's bullet means that Dora's surgery will be delayed."

Shaking her head, Beth dragged an old rocking chair from the far corner of the attic closer to Andrew's pallet. If, as she feared, she was going to spend hours here, she needed a place to sit.

"What matters now is letting your shoulder heal," she said firmly.

The cleft in Andrew's chin deepened as he frowned. "Damned slave catcher. I hope he rots in Hell."

It was a sentiment Beth could second. Though she had never taken an active role on the Railroad, she shared many Northerners' abhorrence for the peculiar institution of slavery, and especially for the men who tracked fugitives like animals.

Andrew was silent for a moment, and Beth hoped he was sleeping. When he grimaced and opened his eyes, she knew he was still awake and in great pain. Rising to refresh the compress, Beth passed by the window. Though it was late afternoon, the summer sun would not set for hours. To Beth's surprise, an elegant carriage stopped in front of the house and a woman descended from it.

"You have a patient," Beth told Andrew. "I'll be back as soon as I've seen her." It appeared her story of caring for patients had become reality, after all.

A flicker of interest crossed Andrew's face. "Who is it?"

"Miss Fields."

He managed a wry smile. "I doubt she is ill."

Beth stopped in the doorway and turned toward Andrew. "That's fortunate, isn't it, since her doctor is in New York City, consulting on a critical case."

Andrew's smile broadened, though he could not mask his pain. "It's a great tale," he said.

Flushing with pleasure at the unexpected praise, Beth descended the front stairs and intercepted Lucinda Fields. Though the beautiful brunette was obviously disappointed by the doctor's absence, she left as soon as she had seen Beth write her message in Andrew's appointment book.

When Beth returned to the attic, she found Andrew asleep but restless. Knowing he would need food when he wakened, she prepared a tray with a light broth and some of Mrs. Kane's fresh bread. Then she settled herself into the rocking chair and waited for him to waken.

"You can't go!" His voice, harsh and muddled with sleep, startled her. Beth jumped to her feet and ran the few steps to his pallet. He was still asleep, but clearly in the throes of a nightmare. She placed a comforting hand on his head, then freshened the compress. The fever was higher now, his lips parched.

"You need to drink," she said softly, trying to waken him. That was the advice the doctor had given Lenore when Dora was fevered: make her drink. "Wake up, Andrew." When he opened his eyes, Beth held a glass to his lips and helped him take a few swallows. He stared at her, his eyes clouded with confusion.

"Who are you?" he demanded.

Beth's spirits plummeted. She knew little about delirium, other than that it was a bad sign. Now she could not ask Andrew which medicine she should give him, for in his current state, he might tell her the wrong one. She could do nothing but watch, wait, and pray.

As he lay back and closed his eyes, Beth slipped through the small door to the other side of the attic. Retrieving her sister's Bible, she returned to Andrew's bedside. When the sun set, she would cover the window with a thick quilt so that no passersby would note the unusual light in the front of the house. In the meantime, she would read to Andrew. Though he might not understand the words, perhaps the sound of her voice would soothe him.

She opened the book to Psalms and began to read. "The Lord is my shepherd." Perhaps it was only her imagination, but Andrew did seem calmer. Beth continued to read, choosing the passages that had comforted her over the years, and Andrew continued to sleep. When her throat grew parched, she laid the Bible facedown on the floor to mark her place and poured herself a glass of water. Refreshed by the cool liquid, she picked up the book to resume her reading. As she did, a lock of hair fell to the floor. Beth's eyes widened in surprise. She had found a few flowers that Lenore had pressed between the pages. Those had brought back memories of early morning walks to school when they had stopped to pick flowers. This was unexpected. Even without touching it, Beth knew whose hair it was, for of all their acquaintances, only one had dark brown, almost black, curly hair.

Why had Lenore saved something of Rodney's? They were friends, but friendship didn't explain this memento. Beth realized she would never be certain, for her sister was dead and no one knew where Rodney was. A few weeks before Lenore's wedding, Rodney had left his parents' farm. At first Lenore had been puzzled; then she had grown distraught. Hoping to ease her sister's mind, Beth had made inquiries. Unfortunately, no one seemed to know where Rodney was. At last Peter told them that he had seen the young black man carrying a satchel. Rodney, Peter announced, had claimed he was taking the Erie Canal to New York to find better work. Though the story sounded plausible, Lenore had refused to believe it. Rodney wouldn't leave without saying good-bye, she insisted. But he had.

"Mary!" Andrew's tortured cry broke Beth's reverie. "Don't leave me! No, Mary, no!"

The anguish in his voice tore at her heartstrings, making her wish there were some way she could comfort him. The Ice Doctor was not as heartless as he claimed. If only in his dreams, this man cared deeply, passionately about another. A tiny seed of something—surely it was doubt and not jealousy—lodged within Beth's heart. Who was Mary?

# Chapter Twelve

It had been three days. For three days Beth had watched while Andrew's fever raged, rising so high that nothing she did—not the cool compresses, nor the warm broth, not even the fervent prayers she had said on his behalf—helped. When in the throes of his delirium, he would grimace, his face contorted into a gruesome mask. Though Beth had expected him to shout from the pain, his voice lowered to a whisper.

"Mary!" he cried. "Don't leave me, Mary!"

Her heart wrenched by his agony, Beth tried to comfort him. "I'm here," she would reply when he called to the mysterious Mary, but her words appeared to bring him no comfort, and she soon ceased her responses, remaining with him in a silent vigil.

There was no outward sign of infection in his wound. She had checked that during one of his calmer periods, when she could approach his pallet and not worry about flailing arms. The gunshot might be healing, but something else was wrong. Beth had no need of medical school to make that diagnosis. What worried her was that she had no way of knowing what had caused Andrew's illness or—even more importantly—how to help him.

How much longer could he withstand the force of whatever it was that plagued him? Each day she could see him weaken. Surely the fever would break. It must, for the alternative was unthinkable.

At last, exhausted by the hours she had spent at his bedside, Beth fell into a restless sleep. When she wakened, the mourning doves' soft cooing announced the advent of dawn. She blinked and tried to clear the sleep from her eyes. Something was different. At first she was not sure what had changed. There was no rain, and the wind's soft soughing seemed unchanged from yesterday. Beth tipped her head to one side, listening intently. That was it, she thought as a smile lit her face. Andrew's breathing had changed. The labored breaths that had terrified her were gone, replaced by the deep, even respiration of normal sleep.

Straightening her skirts as she moved, she hurried to his side and placed her hand on his forehead. Thank God! The fever was gone. He would live. He would heal. Her touch must have wakened him, for he opened his eyes. A wave of pure joy swept through Beth. Andrew's eyes were clear as the summer sky, no longer fogged by pain.

"Welcome back," she said softly.

He smiled, and her heart turned over. For a moment, nothing mattered but this man and the fact that he was still alive. Though he appeared confused by his surroundings, so different from his luxurious bed one floor below, she could see memory rush back.

"How long?" he asked. His fever might have broken, but his voice was weak and hoarse with disuse.

Beth poured a tumbler of water. "Three days," she said, supporting his shoulders so that he could sip from the glass. "I was so worried!"

The words slipped out, unbidden. She hadn't wanted to admit the toll those three days had taken. It had been horrible, sitting here, watching and waiting, not knowing whether he would live, sure of only thing: that she was unable to help him. How she hated feeling helpless!

Her vigil with Andrew reminded Beth of those terrible days when Lenore had been dying. Though she had told Lenore she was recovering, the tears in her sister's eyes when she had held Dora told Beth she had not believed her lies. Still, they had pretended, neither of them wanting to voice the thought that they would be separated.

The sun was climbing, replacing dawn's rosy hue with golden light. Songbirds had joined the doves' serenade, and the strong scent of marigolds drifted through the window. It was a morning like many others in July, and yet the sight of Andrew's blue eyes and the smile she had feared would be lost forever transformed it into a magical moment.

Andrew managed another smile. "I'm strong," he asserted. "A hard man to kill."

As if to demonstrate, he tried to push himself to his feet, then fell back onto the pallet. He looked so disgusted that Beth decided to make light of his weakness. "Not as strong as you think," she said softly. "Either that, or you like these luxurious accommodations and want to stay here."

His smile was self-deprecating. "Do these luxurious accommodations include meals?" He put his hand on his stomach, which growled as if on command. "Can you bring me some food? I know Mrs. Kane must be here by now, but you can invent some excuse."

Beth shook her head. "No need for excuses. I have some bread and milk up here." She reached for the jug of milk that she had kept in cool water in the darkest part of the attic. She wouldn't tell Andrew how each day she had prayed that he'd be well enough to drink it. What mattered was that today at last her prayers had been answered.

"Bread and milk!" Andrew's lips turned down in distaste. "I'm not a child."

Indeed he wasn't. Beth feared that the game she had played, trying to convince herself that Andrew was as little threat to her as Dora, would become impossible to continue now that he was awake and alert.

"You may not be a child, but you are as weak as one," she retorted. "Now, let me help you." Beth broke the bread into pieces in a bowl and poured milk over them. When they were softened, she raised Andrew to a sitting position and began to feed him.

"I can do that," he protested as he swallowed the first bite.

Beth smiled and refilled the spoon. "You're right-handed, Andrew. If you want to be stubborn, I suppose you could try, but it seems to make more sense to let your shoulder heal."

Though she didn't want to be this close to him, the important thing was for him to recover so that he could cure Dora. Then, perhaps, Silver would be proven right. Perhaps he would release Beth from their agreement. She and Dora would leave Buffalo and start a new life somewhere else. That was what she wanted. Wasn't it?

"Where did you learn to be such a good nurse?" Andrew asked when he had eaten half of the bread but could swallow no more.

Though he looked exhausted, Beth sensed that his question was more than idle curiosity and that he would not rest until she had answered. He had no way of knowing that his words opened half-healed wounds. Beth tried to keep her voice even. Perhaps if she feigned normalcy, he'd be satisfied with a simple answer. "I cared for my sister when she was ill," she said. *Please, don't ask any more,* she begged him silently. *It's bad enough that I thought about Lenore's suffering all the time I was watching you. I couldn't bear to speak of it.*

Andrew nodded. "And your husband, too?"

"No," Beth said quickly, hoping her voice didn't betray the panic that thoughts of her mythical husband always raised. "I wasn't with him at the end." How she hated to lie! Though her words weren't precisely false, the entire premise was. She should never have pretended to be Dora's mother, but now that the lies had been spun, she could not retract them. What would Andrew think if he knew the truth? Would he condemn her for lying, not only to him but to Dora's father? Even more importantly, what would he do? Would he insist that she leave before he cured Dora? The day, which had seemed so bright only a few minutes before, darkened.

Andrew leaned back on the pallet, resting his head on the pillow she laid beneath him. From this position, he could look at her, and she sensed that he was studying her.

"You never speak of your past," he said thoughtfully. "Is it too painful to remember?"

Whatever she had imagined him asking, it was not that. Beth stared at him, uncertain how to answer. Painful? "Yes. No." She shook her head. Surely it was only fatigue and the strain of the past three days that confused her.

"Not the past, then," he said, his voice low and oddly

comforting. "Let's speak of the future. What will you do after Dora's surgery?"

That was the question, wasn't it? "You know I used to teach," she told him. Let him think she had left the classroom when Dora was born; that was safer than telling him the truth. "My dream has always been to teach in a girls' boarding school." It was the closest she would ever come to having children of her own.

"There are several good ones here." Andrew's eyelids closed briefly, as if fatigue was winning the battle with his will.

"I know." Beth tried to hide her bitterness. "They won't consider me."

His eyes widened, though he said nothing for a few moments. "You're very good with Dora," he said softly, and she sensed that he was watching for her reaction. When she nodded, he opened his mouth as if to speak, then closed it, and she could see the indecision on his face. "Have you ever thought of teaching other deaf children? Buffalo could use a school like that."

Beth stared at him as she considered the idea. It was a good one. An excellent one, in fact. But how could she even contemplate it? Establishing a school required a great deal of money, and as Andrew had cause to know, she had none.

Though he normally woke quickly, Andrew found himself easing into wakefulness as slowly as Nag waded into the river. He heard the sound of a woman's footsteps and caught the sweet scent of powder and something else—perhaps flowers. Beth. She had stayed with him while the fever raged. Though he had only fragmentary memories of those days, he remembered a woman's soothing voice and the soft touch of a hand on his forehead. In his few lucid moments, he recalled a faint breeze coming through the window, bringing with it the smells of grass and horses and roses.

Roses!

The last remnant of drowsiness vanished.

"What day is it?" Andrew forced himself into a sitting

position. If what he thought was true, he would need to do far more than sit today.

"Why, it's Tuesday," Beth answered, her tone saying more clearly than words that she found his greeting strange. "Tuesday afternoon," she continued, consulting her watch. "Ten minutes after three."

Perhaps there would be no problem. Perhaps. "Can you see the front light post from that window?"

Beth walked toward the window. "Yes, I can. Why do you ask?"

"There are flowers hanging in a pot. What color are they?"

Her skirts swayed as she leaned forward slightly to peer out the window. She was wearing a medium-blue dress today, and the sunlight that spilled onto her hair gave it a fiery glow. "There's one yellow; the rest are bluish purple." Beth turned, a smile on her face. "If you expect me to identify them, I have to tell you that I'm not a horticulturist."

Andrew frowned. This was what he had feared. Not that she could not name flowers, but that there were colored ones there.

"It's odd," Beth said, her tone pensive as she glanced outside again. "I thought the flowers were white yesterday."

"They were." Normally, the flowers were either white or pale yellow. When a brighter color appeared—placed there by an unseen messenger in the middle of the night—it was a signal that passengers were expected. Under normal circumstances, Andrew would pretend to have a house call the same evening. Unfortunately, this week nothing was normal. He had been shot in the shoulder, rendering one arm useless, and he'd wrenched his left ankle so badly that he could put no weight on it. Andrew was still unclear how he'd gotten up two long flights of stairs, but he knew there was no chance he could navigate them again. How would he make his delivery when he could not stand, much less drive a buggy?

He had never ignored a summons, and he hated the thought that men and women whose lives depended on him tonight would be forced to wait. When the messenger returned before dawn tomorrow, he would know Andrew had failed to make the delivery, for the flowers would be unchanged. Another conductor would be alerted. It was only a day's delay, but with the waxing moon, each day increased the danger.

Andrew closed his eyes and searched for an answer. Though he was not supposed to know the identities of other conductors, he had learned that Frank Saylor also made deliveries. Perhaps Beth could get a message to him. The question was, should he trust her with that much knowledge? It was bad enough that she knew of his involvement. How could he endanger her with the details of deliveries?

"What's wrong?" Beth asked. Furrows appeared between her eyes. "Why do the blue flowers bother you? And," she added, "don't deny that you're troubled by them, because I know you are."

She saw too much. Andrew sighed as he made his decision. He had trusted her with his life. He could trust her with this. "You're right, Beth; I am disturbed. The flowers are a signal that passengers are waiting."

"Passengers on the Underground Railroad?"

He nodded.

Her eyes widened as the significance of his words registered, and he saw her lips thin with disapproval. "You can't be thinking of going out tonight! Andrew, you're much too ill. Why, your fever broke only a few hours ago."

If the situation hadn't been so serious, he would have been amused by the combination of her outrage and her protective air. She reminded him of a mother goose he'd once seen defending her goslings. Was that how Beth saw him, as a child? Though the thought was disturbing, Andrew felt a rush of warmth. How long had it been since a woman—since anyone, for that matter—had worried about his health and well being?

There she stood, her hands fisted on her hips, her attitude announcing that anyone who disagreed with her did so at his peril. Andrew would have been amused if it were simply his own health that was at risk. But the stakes were much higher.

"I know I can't go." Andrew clenched his good fist in frustration. "That's the problem." How he hated being helpless! He had spent the majority of his life ensuring that he was in control, that he would never again feel the way he had the night Mary died—helpless, alone, deserted by the one person on earth who loved him. Yet here he was, once again unable to help people who needed him.

Beth nodded, and when her green eyes met his, he had the strangest sensation that she understood his fears. She pulled the chair close to his pallet. "Perhaps I could go in your stead."

Andrew heard a gasp, and was startled to realize it had come from his mouth. Once again this remarkable woman had surprised him. Could he let her go? It would be the answer to his problem, and yet how could he ask her to take on his responsibility? Andrew was silent for a long moment, considering. Should he? No! It was too dangerous. He couldn't let an inexperienced woman take such chances. He started to shake his head when he caught the glimmer of excitement in her eyes and something else . . . fear. It was the apprehension that convinced him. Without a word being said, she recognized the danger and had worries about it. This was not an adventure for her, but a mission.

"Do you know how to drive a buggy?" he asked. Though she might be willing, that was not enough.

Beth shrugged. "I doubt it can be much different from plowing, and I've done that."

She plowed. Was there anything this woman hadn't done? One hurdle crossed. Only one left.

"You'd be taking an enormous risk," he cautioned her, and looked down at his wounded shoulder. The man who had shot him would be back. If not tonight, someday soon.

Though Beth's face paled, her voice was calm. "Perhaps the risk would be less than you fear," she countered. "I doubt anyone would suspect a woman—a widow—of being part of the Railroad."

It was a valid point, and yet Andrew still hesitated. No matter what she said, she would be in danger. How could he let her take that risk? How would he live through the hours while she was gone, wondering what was happening? As a feeling of anguish that had nothing to do with his bullet wound raced through him, Andrew closed his eyes. What was happening? It must be weakness caused by his injury that made him feel so vulnerable. It wasn't that he cared about Beth Simmons. He didn't care about anyone. Anyone.

"Are you certain you want to do this?" He had to ask the question once more.

Beth nodded, her face solemn but her eyes glistening with anticipation. "Yes," she said. "I want to help them." She paused for a second, then added so softly that he had to strain to hear the words, "I want to help you."

That same unfamiliar warmth that had swept through him when he realized she had stayed with him during his delirium began to course through Andrew's veins again.

"All right," he agreed slowly. "Here's what you need to know. There's a false bottom to the buggy." He explained how to release it. "The passengers hide there. When you approach the river, stop and let them out. Don't wait. As soon as they're out of the buggy, come home. And when you get here, take the flowers out of the pot."

In the hours that remained before sunset, he coached her through the steps, having her repeat the route so often that she accused him of wanting to be a schoolteacher. At last, when the sky began to darken, Beth slipped a shawl around her shoulders and left.

Andrew lay back. A wise man would sleep. A wise man would not allow images of a redheaded widow to flit through his mind, haunting him with the thought that she might be captured or hurt. A wise man would not worry. Andrew was a wise man. Why, then, was he unable to relax? Why did he force his eyes to remain open, lest the chimeras of his fear return to plague him?

The hours passed, the tiny sliver of moon continued its journey across the sky, and still she did not return. Cold dread clenched his heart. Something had happened. He knew it, just as he knew he should never have allowed Beth to make the delivery. But she had insisted, this feisty woman who had turned his household upside down, this woman who had—despite his deepest resolve—touched his heart.

He didn't want to care. God knows he had tried his best not to care. Yet somehow she had insinuated her way into his life and his heart. And now . . . now it hurt so terribly much, knowing she was risking her life for him.

It seemed like days passed before he heard the sound of soft footsteps on the stairs. She was back! Andrew struggled to sit, though his shoulder throbbed horribly. She was back! Beth held a candle to light her way, and in its flickering, he could see both lines of fatigue and a joyous smile on her face.

"They're on their way!" she cried, her voice filled with the elation he remembered all too well. It was always that way for him, total exhaustion mingled with an almost inexpressible happiness.

"Was there trouble?" The words tumbled out instead of a greeting. "You were gone so long." Did he sound annoyed? Was that why she stepped back a pace? Beth straightened her shoulders and stared at him.

"I waited until they were safely in the boat," she said, and he heard something—could it be disappointment?—in her voice.

He felt a cold fear invade his body at the thought of the unnecessary risk she had taken. "I told you not to do that." Her head jerked up, and he watched a flicker of anger light her eyes. What a fool he was—chastising her, when she had performed a herculean feat. "How many were there?" he asked, hoping she would take his softer tone as a sign that he wasn't angry.

Beth pulled the chair closer to his bed and sat down. She clasped her hands tightly in her lap, the nervous gesture telling Andrew more clearly than words what she had gone through. "There were two men," she said. "Oh, Andrew, my heart ached for them. They were so thin, I thought they hadn't eaten in weeks. Their clothes were tattered, and everything else they owned was tied up in knapsacks so small that they couldn't have held more than a loaf of bread. It was so sad!" She slumped back in the chair, and Andrew knew that the excitement that had guided her through the long night was dissipating, leaving her drained and exhausted.

"What happened to them was tragic," he agreed, "but that's over now. You can't undo the wrongs of the past, Beth.

All you can do is help make the future better. That's what you did tonight."

Beth woke with a smile on her face. She had done it! She had made a delivery last night, and it had felt so very, very good. No wonder Andrew had joined the Railroad. It was a heady feeling, knowing that you could help someone who needed aid so desperately.

When she ducked her head going through the small door into Andrew's part of the attic, she found him struggling to his feet. The man was impossible! He knew he had hurt his ankle badly enough that it would be days before he could walk.

"Careful," Beth cautioned. "Someone might hear the noises." Especially if he fell.

Andrew frowned, his irritation evident. "I need to get out of here. I hate being cooped up in one room. I hate not seeing my patients. I hate this beard." He ran his hand across his stubbly cheek, his disgust evident.

Beth knew how frustrating Andrew found his confinement, and she had seen his disappointment when he had realized that he would be unable to make the delivery last night, so she let him vent his anger and frustration. There was nothing else she could do. Or was there? Though she couldn't cure everything, she could resolve one of his complaints. The question was, did she want to? It would mean touching him again.

She looked at him, considering. Andrew had gone through so much. Surely she could do this one small thing to make him more comfortable. It couldn't be that difficult.

Before she lost her courage, Beth asked, "Would you like me to shave you? I've never done it, but I think I could." Between removing the bullet from Andrew's shoulder and making the delivery last night, Beth realized there were few things she could not do. It was ironic. She had come to Buffalo for Dora's sake, but—so far at least—Beth had been the one who had benefited. She was stronger now, more confident of her abilities.

Andrew raised one brow. "You mean your husband never asked you to shave him?"

"No!" The word came out more forcefully than Beth had expected. How she wished he would stop asking about her husband! Her mythical marriage was one thing she did not want to discuss. "Do you want me to try?" she asked again.

"Yes." He grinned.

When she returned with warm water and his shaving gear, Beth realized that her hands were shaking. It was one thing to tell herself that she was brave enough to do anything, another to actually translate those thoughts into actions. How was she going to do this? She hadn't counted on his removing his nightshirt!

Andrew was seated on the chair where she had spent so many hours, his shirt hung over the back. It was sensible, of course. Beth knew that shaving could be a messy process, even when an experienced man wielded the razor. But, still . . . she hadn't expected to be confronted with such a broad expanse of very male skin. Oh, she had seen it when she had removed the bullet, but that night fear and shock had kept her from thinking about anything other than the need to help a wounded person. Today, he was not wounded and he was no longer just a person. He was a man. A man who threatened her in ways that none had ever done before.

She couldn't do it. She had to. She would.

As she lathered the soap, Beth remembered how she had coped with the horrors of extracting the bullet. That technique might work again. She would concentrate on something else. She would pretend she was washing Dora's face. Beth began to spread the thick lather on Andrew's face and neck. The pretense was more difficult than she had expected. His skin was so different from Dora's, more like a sturdy, woven cloth than the soft, velvety cheek of a young child. It must be that difference that made her fingers tingle.

"Who's Mary?" she asked. Perhaps if she and Andrew spoke of something, she would be able to ignore the strange warmth that had begun to make its way up her arms.

If she hadn't been so close, Beth would have thought she had imagined Andrew's reaction, but there was no denying the way his head jerked, as if her question surprised him.

"Mary?" His voice sounded innocent. "Why do you ask?"

Beth held the razor in her hand, wondering where to start. His cheeks, she decided. She stroked carefully, removing soap and whiskers, flicking the mixture into a second bowl. His skin was once more smooth, and her fingers felt the oddest desire to trace the path the razor had made.

*Think of something else,* she admonished herself. "You called Mary's name when you were delirious. Many times," she added. "She must be important to you." A sweetheart, perhaps. The thought caused Beth's stomach to clench. Perhaps the cherries she had eaten last night were overripe. There was no other reason her insides should roil.

She finished one side of his face. Though pale from the fever, he looked much better without the stubble.

Andrew appeared reluctant to answer. At last he said, "Mary was my sister."

"You have a sister!" Beth was glad she had been between strokes, for her hand jerked in surprise. Somehow, she had never imagined Andrew with any family. Even the Duchess seemed so remote that it was difficult to picture her bouncing Andrew on her knee. He seemed so independent, so self-sufficient that—had Beth not known it to be an impossibility—she might have imagined him appearing on earth one day, fully grown, with no parents.

"I *had* a sister," he corrected her. "She died when we were children."

Beth's hand stopped its even strokes. "Oh, Andrew, I'm sorry." Sorrow welled inside her. Poor Andrew! "I know how it hurts to lose a sister."

Beth shook her head to clear the tears that had risen to her eyes. She would have felt this way about anyone, she told herself. Andrew was no one special. No, indeed.

# Chapter Thirteen

It wasn't working. Though it had seemed like a good idea, she simply wasn't succeeding in thinking of Andrew as a child in her care. Oh, he was almost as dependent on her as Dora was, but the similarity ended there. Andrew was a man, a grown man, and every day that she spent in his company reinforced that realization. He was at times cranky and demanding, at others surprisingly acquiescent and sensitive to her needs. At all times, he was undeniably male.

The attic, which had once seemed cavernous, grew smaller each day. When she came through the low door, Beth saw that Andrew had pulled the chair near to the window. Thank goodness he had taken care to place it so that no passersby would see him, although on this rainy morning, it was unlikely that anyone would be looking into attic windows.

"You're earlier than usual." As Andrew's smile lit the dark room, Beth's heart skipped a beat. Though there were days when she knew he regarded her as his jailer, today at least he seemed to welcome her presence. It was foolish, of course, to care, but she did.

"I thought you must be tired of this room," she said as calmly as she could.

Andrew raised one brow, and this time his smile was mocking. "Indeed! It feels like a prison, and I have no hope of parole."

Beth laughed. "As odd as it seems, you're both the prisoner and the jailer. Only you can release yourself."

For a moment the only sound was the steady patter of rain on the roof. When Andrew nodded, Beth continued. "How long do you think it will be before your wound is healed?" Each day it grew more difficult to conceal Andrew's presence from the others.

"Too long." He shrugged, then winced at the pain the motion caused his right shoulder. "Probably only another week. I'll have some residual soreness at that point, but I can pretend that I strained my arm in New York. Now," he said when Beth refused his offer of the chair, "tell me why you are so early."

"It's Sunday," she told Andrew. "The servants usually have a half day, but I gave them the whole day off, since you weren't here." As she had hoped, Andrew chuckled. "Anyway, if you feel you're able, I thought you might want to go downstairs."

Andrew's eyes shone with anticipation. "I've been reprieved! It doesn't matter if I have to crawl. I'm going downstairs."

Though he did not resort to crawling, their progress was slow, for Andrew was still weakened by the fever and the injury to his ankle. Gripping the banister tightly, he descended one stair at a time, resting slightly before he attempted the next. But when they reached the parlor and he was seated on one of the horsehair settees that flanked the stove, his grin was as triumphant as if he had just run a mile.

"I'll bring us some coffee," Beth said when she was certain he was comfortable. Even more than the nourishment, she needed a few minutes to regain her equilibrium. Though it was Andrew who had struggled with the stairs, her heart was pounding as fiercely as if she had climbed them, two at a time. It was foolish, of course, to feel that something as simple as descending two flights of stairs was an accomplishment. Even more foolish to believe she had shared in that accomplishment. And yet Beth could not deny that her heart had been in her throat until they had reached the parlor. What if he had fallen? What would she have done? It would have been her stupid idea that had injured him again. But he had not stumbled, and the idea—judging from the proud grin on his face—had been anything but stupid.

"Do you play chess?" Andrew asked when she set the tray on the table between them. She had chosen the heavy silver coffee service and the delicate Meissen china cups that she had admired so many times. It seemed a shame to keep such beautiful pieces locked in a china cabinet rather than using them. Though Mrs. Kane had told her they were brought out only for the rare dinner parties Andrew hosted, Beth decided that today qualified as a special occasion.

"Chess?" She shook her head and took a sip of coffee. The teacup felt so fragile, and yet she knew that bone china was far stronger than it appeared. Unlike her, it was in little danger of shattering, while she felt that the slightest provocation would destroy her carefully constructed calm facade. "No," she repeated, "I don't play chess."

Andrew's raised brow gave him a quizzical look that was soon replaced with a grin. "At last!" he crowed. "I've finally found something the paragon doesn't do." He made it sound as big a triumph as descending the stairs.

"The paragon?"

Andrew laid his cup back on the table and smiled at Beth. "Helen Pratt called you that one day." Beth knew her face must have reflected her puzzlement, for he continued. "It appears I spoke too highly of you. There is one thing on earth you cannot do."

Beth could feel the flush of pleasure color her cheeks. Even delivered indirectly, praise was welcome. And praise from this man who had once been so disapproving was, oh, so very sweet.

To cover her confusion, she said only, "Will you teach me to play chess?"

At Andrew's direction, she brought the board from the corner cabinet and arranged the pieces. "I'll handicap myself," he told her as they started the first game. Even without his queen, Andrew had no difficulty winning, but as the morning progressed, Beth could feel her skill increase. How Lenore would have loved this game! Her quick mind would have relished the variety of pieces and the need for strategy, while her competitive nature would have insisted that she win each game.

Beth leaned back in her chair, surprised by the emotions that roiled through her. Though she missed Lenore and always would, today her thoughts were bittersweet, filled with sorrow that there were so many things Lenore would never experience, but no longer colored by the deep sadness that had characterized the first weeks after her death. Perhaps the healing that the minister had promised Beth was at last beginning.

The day was damp and gray, with raindrops sliding down the windowpanes; the house was unnaturally silent; and yet Beth felt content. It was an unexpected but welcome sensation.

She fingered one of her rooks, planning her next move. "I'm going to bring Dora home tomorrow," she told Andrew. "I can't pretend that I'm ill any longer, and besides, I miss her terribly." It had been difficult trying to convince the servants that she was ill enough to send Dora away but not so ill that she needed their assistance. Even worse had been Dora's enforced absence, for Beth had been unable to visit her as often as she had planned.

If she had expected Andrew to protest, he did not. "Good idea," he said, quickly capturing the rook that she had just moved. "I'll enjoy her laughter."

Beth frowned. Why hadn't she noticed that knight? Because she had forgotten the sideways moves knights made, she had lost her second rook. "But you won't see Dora. I can't let her know that you're here. Even though she doesn't speak, we can't run that risk."

Andrew nodded. "I know, but I'll hear her. Have you noticed how she laughs now?"

Beth was puzzled by the question. "She always made some sounds."

"True, but there've been more in the last few weeks."

Perhaps the change had been so gradual that Beth hadn't noticed it. As she thought of her last few visits to Silver's, she realized that Dora had appeared to be quieter than normal.

"Maybe she feels at home here." Though the words were hers, they surprised her. When had she started thinking of this house as home? It was an oddly disturbing thought, for she knew this was only a temporary residence, a place to stay until Dora could hear again.

As if he somehow sensed her uneasiness, Andrew changed

the subject, giving Beth her next lesson in chess strategy. The hours passed quickly, and it was only the rumbling of her stomach that reminded Beth she should prepare dinner for them.

As she sliced meat and warmed a gravy to pour over the potatoes she was boiling, Beth found herself humming, and realized that her heart was singing along. This had been the most enjoyable morning she could remember in years. It had been so pleasant, sitting in the elegant parlor, learning to play chess. *Be honest, Beth,* she chided herself. *What made the morning enjoyable was being with Andrew.* It had felt a bit like the times she and Lenore had retreated to one of their play spots and shared secrets. And yet it was different. Lenore was her sister, while Andrew was . . . Beth searched for the proper word. Andrew was her friend, she concluded. That must be why it felt so different. After all, she had no experience with men as friends.

Lenore had had Rodney. Beth hadn't understood why they had shared secrets, for it made no sense that Lenore would voluntarily spend time with a man. Her sister was smart; she should have realized that men brought only one thing, and that was pain. At the time, Beth had tried to tell Lenore that she was foolish, but her sister had only smiled and said, in that arch older-sister tone that never failed to irritate Beth, that one day she would understand. Beth smiled at the memory. Lenore was right. Today she understood what her sister had tried to tell her: It was good to have a friend.

The rain stopped in the early afternoon, the warm July sun quickly drying the ground. Beth looked outside, calculating. Yes, it would work.

"I have one more surprise," she told Andrew when they had eaten supper and the sun had begun to set.

"Is it a good one?" he asked. Though he had protested when she had insisted he rest during the afternoon—reminding Beth of Dora on a cranky day—she could see that today had been good for him. His color was stronger, and he appeared happier. They still had to face the hurdle of climbing the stairs, but if they were careful and conserved his strength, he might enjoy the last part of her plan.

"I think it's a good surprise," she told him. Then, because she could see the impatience on his face, she said quickly, "If we go out the side door, no one will see us. You can be outside."

Andrew's grin told her he more than approved.

They walked slowly, Andrew leaning heavily on Beth, but soon they were outdoors. Beth led the way to the two wrought-iron chairs she had placed under one of the cherry trees. She had chosen the spot carefully. On this side of the yard, a row of tall forsythia bushes blocked the neighbors' view, and they were far enough back from the street that no one could see them. Arranging her skirts as she sat, Beth leaned forward slightly to watch Andrew. She hoped the extra effort would not harm him.

"It feels so good to be outside," he said. Though his face was pale, some of the strained lines seemed to have vanished. "I will never again take fresh air for granted." Andrew breathed in deeply and smiled. Beth's heart skipped again. How wonderful to be able to bring a friend pleasure!

The evening was perfect, a warm breeze keeping the insects at bay at the same time that it wafted the sweet scents of night-blooming flowers toward them. The grass was soft and fragrant under their feet, while overhead a half-moon added mystery to the dark sky.

"I'm glad you wanted to come outside," Beth confessed, "because I love summer evenings. Sometimes Lenore and I used to sneak out our bedroom window so we could lie on the grass and watch the stars." They had spun dreams on those magical evenings, dreams of happily ever after.

"You miss her, don't you?" Beth heard the sympathy in Andrew's voice, and knew he was remembering his own sister.

Perhaps it was the darkness that broke down her fears; perhaps it was the realization that Andrew had somehow become her friend. Beth wasn't sure which. All she knew was that she felt able to talk to Andrew and to share her feelings with him.

# Thrill to the most sensual, adventure-filled Historical Romances on the market today...

## FROM  LEISURE BOOKS

As a home subscriber to the Leisure Historical Romance Book Club, you'll enjoy the best in today's BRAND-NEW Historical Romance fiction. For over twenty-five years, Leisure Books has brought you the award-winning, high-quality authors you know and love to read. Each Leisure Historical Romance will sweep you away to a world of high adventure...and intimate romance. Discover for yourself all the passion and excitement millions of readers thrill to each and every month.

## SAVE AT LEAST *$5.00* EACH TIME YOU BUY!

Each month, the Leisure Historical Romance Book Club brings you four brand-new titles from Leisure Books, America's foremost publisher of Historical Romances. EACH PACKAGE WILL SAVE YOU AT LEAST $5.00 FROM THE BOOKSTORE PRICE! And you'll never miss a new title with our convenient home delivery service.

Here's how we do it. Each package will carry a 10-DAY EXAMINATION privilege. At the end of that time, if you decide to keep your books, simply pay the low invoice price of $16.96 ($17.75 US in Canada), no shipping or handling charges added*. HOME DELIVERY IS ALWAYS FREE*. With today's top Historical Romance novels selling for $5.99 and higher, our price SAVES YOU AT LEAST $5.00 with each shipment.

## AND YOUR FIRST FOUR-BOOK SHIPMENT IS TOTALLY FREE!*

*IT'S A BARGAIN YOU CAN'T BEAT! A Super $21.96 Value!*

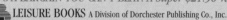

# GET YOUR 4 FREE\* BOOKS NOW—
## A $21.96 VALUE!

### Mail the Free\* Book
### Certificate
### Today!

## 4 FREE\* BOOKS 🌹 A $21.96 VALUE

## *Free \* Books Certificate*

**YES!** I want to subscribe to the Leisure Historical Romance Book Club. Please send me my **4 FREE\* BOOKS.** Then each month I'll receive the four newest Leisure Historical Romance selections to Preview for 10 days. If I decide to keep them, I will pay the Special Member's Only discounted price of just $4.24 each, a total of $16.96 ($17.75 US in Canada). This is a SAVINGS OF AT LEAST $5.00 off the bookstore price. There are no shipping, handling, or other charges\*. There is no minimum number of books I must buy and I may cancel the program at any time. In any case, the 4 FREE\* BOOKS are mine to keep—A BIG $21.96 Value!

\*In Canada, add $5.00 shipping and handling per order for first shipment. For all subsequent shipments to Canada, the cost of membership is $17.75 US, which includes $7.75 shipping and handling per month.[All payments must be made in US dollars]

*Name* _____

*Address* _____

*City* _____

*State* _____ *Country* _____ *Zip* _____

*Telephone* _____

*Signature* _____

If under 18, Parent or Guardian must sign. Terms, prices and conditions subject to change. Subscription subject to acceptance. Leisure Books reserves the right to reject any order or cancel any subscription.

# Get Four Books Totally
# F R E E\* —
# A $21.96 Value!

(Tear Here and Mail Your FREE\* Book Card Today!)

PLEASE RUSH
MY FOUR FREE\*
BOOKS TO ME
RIGHT AWAY!

*Leisure Historical Romance Book Club*

P.O. Box 6613
Edison, NJ 08818-6613

"It's getting easier now. I know Lenore's happy where she is." *And safe,* she added silently. Though death had robbed Beth of her sister, it had freed Lenore of fear, and for that Beth gave thanks.

"Look, Beth. There's the North Star." Andrew reached across the short distance that separated them and laid his hand on Beth's. Yesterday she would have drawn away. Today his touch seemed warm and comforting, not threatening, and so she left her hand beneath his.

"I always used to think it was a beautiful star," she said softly. Though he touched only her hand, tendrils of warmth had spread up her arm, and her fingers tingled pleasantly. "I can understand why the slaves follow it. It gives such a strong, bright light." Beth swallowed deeply. "Now that I've made a delivery, I don't think I'll ever look at the North Star in the same way." She kept her gaze fixed on Andrew, hoping he would understand what she meant. "Now it's more than a star to me. It's a symbol of hope."

Hope for the slaves and for herself, for when she looked at the star Beth could believe that somehow, someday she would find happiness.

"Good-bye, Silver." Beth adjusted her hat as she prepared to leave the house on Canal Street. Three days had passed since she had brought Dora home, and this was the first opportunity Beth had had to visit Silver. "I hope Dora will come with me next time."

As Silver patted Beth's arm in a reassuring gesture, her gray eyes were solemn. "I reckon she's afraid you'll leave her here again and that's why she don't want to come." Beth's hands stilled as she considered the possibility. Dora had certainly seemed skittish since she had returned to Niagara Square, and Beth had been surprised by the child's refusal to go outside the house with her. At first she had thought Dora had developed a fear of the outdoors, but that seemed unlikely, since she willingly accompanied Mrs. Kane to the market.

"That child missed her ma something powerful," Silver continued.

Silver was probably correct. Not for the first time, Beth marveled at the older woman's understanding of human nature. Though she had no children of her own, Silver appeared able to grasp the sometimes convoluted way their minds worked.

"Thanks, Silver." Impulsively, Beth hugged her friend, and was rewarded with a wide smile.

"Go on home now," Silver admonished. "The young 'un needs you." She shooed Beth outside as if she were a "young 'un."

Beth blinked at the bright sunlight. Silver's hypothesis seemed accurate. Since she had returned, Dora had not wanted to leave Beth's side, and each morning she would waken and find the child sitting motionless, staring at her as if afraid she would disappear. The poor girl! She had had so much uncertainty in her life. Beth hated the thought that she had added to it.

Rounding the corner of the alley and stepping onto Canal Street, Beth was so lost in thought that she did not hear the man approach.

"Well, well! If it ain't the little schoolmarm." A big hand grasped her arm and yanked her toward him.

Beth felt the blood drain from her face as she stared at the man she had thought she would never see again. How could *he* be here? Had he somehow learned the truth? Though fear rushed through her veins, somehow she managed to keep her voice steady as she said in her haughtiest tone, "Take your hand off my arm."

Peter Girton tightened his grip. "Oh, no," he said, his grin expelling whiskey-scented breath. "I ain't gonna take my hands off you. Fact is, I'm gonna put them all over you. All over that purty white skin." Before she knew what he intended, he grasped her other arm, dragging both arms behind her and imprisoning her wrists with one hand.

He chuckled, an evil laugh that made a shiver of pure dread ripple through Beth's body. She looked around. Where were the people who normally frequented the street? The three women walking slowly in her direction were too far away to hear her screams. Besides, they might pay no attention to her cries. On the surface, Peter was a handsome man, and most people, Beth had discovered, believed that a pretty exterior meant a wholesome interior. Peter's rotten core would not be visible to a casual passerby.

Beth tugged, trying to pull away from him, but she was no match for Peter's strength.

"I been wantin' a redheaded woman ever since your bitch of a sister died," Beth's erstwhile brother-in-law announced with a sneer. "Looks to me like I done found one."

The women turned in to a house half a block away, extinguishing Beth's last hope of an easy escape. "Let me go." Beth kept her eyes fixed on his, refusing to let him see her fear. Surely he could do nothing to her in broad daylight, even on Canal Street. All she had to do was face him down. Bullies retreated in the face of resistance, didn't they?

"No, sirree. I ain't letting you go." His blue eyes were cold, holding more than a hint of cruelty, and Beth wondered, as she had so often, how Lenore could have married this man.

Peter's gaze darted in both directions. When he saw that the street was empty, he drew Beth closer. Her nostrils twitched. His smell was both unpleasant and familiar. Where had she smelled it before?

"This looks to be my lucky day." Peter made no attempt to hide his gloating. "I heard Silver had a new redheaded whore. Never thought it was you. What happened?" He moved his face closer, his fetid breath almost making Beth gag. "Bet you got tired of teaching those brats and thought you'd give a new kind of lesson."

The man believed she was a prostitute! For a second, the mere thought paralyzed Beth. "I am not a whore," she told him, willing her voice to retain its coolness while her mind raced. Somehow she had to get away from him. Beth took a deep breath, regretting it the instant his sour odor assailed her. Silver's. That was where she had smelled the stench. Beth had no doubt Peter was one of the rough customers Silver had mentioned.

"I am not a whore," Beth repeated. She looked around. There was no one to help her.

"So you say." While one hand kept her pinned close to him, the other reached for her neck. "Mighty lucky for me. This way, I won't have to pay for you. You'll warm my bed for free." His hand moved lower, grasping her breast.

No! She would not allow him to touch her. She would not be a victim. Never, ever again.

*Hit him where it hurts,* Silver had told her. With her hands locked behind her back, Beth could not hit, but she could kick. She knew she had only one chance. If she missed, she would face Peter's wrath. Marshaling every ounce of strength she possessed, Beth drew back her foot, aimed, and kicked Peter's shin.

"Damn it!"

As he bent down to rub his leg, Peter released his hold on Beth. It was all she needed. She fled, her shoes clattering on the cobblestones.

"Come back, bitch!" She heard him just a few steps behind her.

Where could she go? Not Silver's. He would look for her there.

Beth ran blindly, heading for the alleys. They were narrow, malodorous, and treacherous underfoot, but she knew them well, for this was the route she took each time she visited Silver.

"I'm gonna get you," Peter yelled. His voice sounded closer. Though she had the advantage of familiarity, he was stronger, his legs longer and unencumbered by skirts and petticoats. She would never outrun him. Her only chance was to outsmart him.

She gasped for breath. Her legs ached, and her heart pounded with exertion. She had to stop soon. Her body could not continue to run. But she could not . . . could not . . . could not . . . let him catch her. Her eyes darted from side to side, searching for a place to hide. It had to be close. There! She rounded a corner and saw it. Thank God! There were two twisting side alleys just before it. If she was lucky, he would think she had turned and would follow one of them.

Fear gave her a final burst of strength, and she slid into the dark alcove. It was so low that she had to crouch, drawing her skirts close around her, praying he would not notice her ragged breathing.

"Where are you, you little whore?" Beth heard Peter's cry as he ran by her, his boots pounding. She could see his hands clenched in fists, and she shuddered at the thought of those fists pummeling her. She closed her eyes and prayed that he would not turn around.

Beth was not sure how long she remained in her hiding place. Though it felt like hours, it might have been only minutes. Gradually, her breathing returned to normal, and her legs began to cramp. She had to go home. Dora would be worried when she didn't return.

Thank goodness Dora hadn't been with her. Beth's heart began to pound as dread filled her once more. What would Peter do if he learned his daughter was alive? Beth knew he didn't love the child, but there was no telling what a crazed man might do. That was why she had pretended that Dora had died and was buried with her mother. At the time, when Peter had shown no sorrow at the news, Beth had known that her decision was the right one. She would protect Dora by keeping her away from her father. Though Beth had thought she and Dora would be safe in Buffalo, for Lenore had told her that Peter had no use for cities, it appeared something had drawn him to the city by the lake.

Though she was anxious to return home and hold Dora in her arms, Beth forced herself to slow her pace once she was away from Canal Street. She didn't want to attract any attention, and a woman who was obviously fleeing would cause comment in the nicer sections of town.

As she walked up Franklin, Beth kept her steps even. She nodded greetings to the people she passed, fixing a smile on her face as if this were an ordinary day and she were taking a simple afternoon stroll.

Her expression was placid; her thoughts were turbulent. That glorious moment of contentment that she had experienced the day Andrew had taught her chess had vanished, destroyed by Peter's threats. She was no longer safe. In truth, safety had been nothing more than an illusion.

# *Chapter Fourteen*

He was a bad patient, and he knew it. Andrew pummeled the pillow as he attempted to find a more comfortable position. The problem wasn't the lumpy pillow or the thin pallet. He had slept on worse in the past and probably would again. No, the problem was himself. He hated the forced inactivity. It was bad enough being confined to this small space, but what he truly hated was the fact that there was time to think, when that was the last thing he wanted to do.

He lay back and closed his eyes, willing sleep to come. Instead of blessed oblivion, images paraded through his consciousness, reminding him of all the things he was missing: his patients, his work on the Railroad, Dora's sweet smile, Dora's mother. Damn it all! He did not want to think about them, especially Dora's mother.

With a sigh of resignation, Andrew opened his eyes. Sleep, it appeared, would not come soon. A clear night followed the sunny day, and a star-spangled sky hung outside his window. Where was the North Star? Andrew clenched his fist. He did not want to think about the North Star or the expression he had seen on Beth's face when she had spoken of it as her symbol of hope.

Though it had been years since Andrew had hoped for anything, recently he found himself wishing his life were different. That was absurd. He did not want his life to change. It was fine just the way it was.

He stared at the stars, picking out the familiar constellations. Though their position in the sky changed with the seasons, the patterns never varied. It was Beth who had seemed different tonight. She was more nervous than Andrew had ever seen her, worse even than those first few days when she had acted as if he were a monster, ready to pounce on her with no reason or warning. Tonight her normally graceful hands had been clumsy. She had dropped a spoon and spilled water when she attempted to pour it into a glass, but when he had asked her what was wrong, she had denied that anything was out of the ordinary. That was a blatant lie, and the way Beth had avoided his gaze had told him she knew it. Something was most definitely wrong, but for some reason, she did not want to confide in him.

Why not?

Andrew turned onto his other side as a wry smile creased his face. He was a fine one to talk. He certainly hadn't confided in her. Even when he had spoken of Mary, he had told only a portion of the truth. No one needed to know what his childhood had been like. He didn't need people's disdain or—even worse—their pity. That was why he had resorted to a fable. The tale he had concocted was what he wished his youth had been.

He closed his eyes, deliberately relaxing his muscles. He was almost asleep when he heard muffled sobs. At first, he thought it was his imagination continuing to play tricks with his mind. But when he sat up and listened carefully, he heard it again. Beth was crying. Andrew's heart began to pound. Something was wrong! He had not been mistaken. The nervousness she had displayed at supper was not coincidental. Andrew fought back the bile that threatened to rise in his throat. Something must be terribly wrong, for he had never heard Beth cry. Though he had attended patients in hours of great distress and sorrow, he had never heard anyone cry with such desperation. There was only one reason Andrew could imagine: Dora. His heart thudded.

Crouching to make his way through the low doorway, Andrew listened, then moved quickly, following the sobs. For some reason Beth was not in the room she shared with Dora. He found her in the spare bedroom, huddled in one corner, her arms wrapped around her body as if to protect herself from some danger. Andrew's heart lurched.

"What's wrong?" She looked so alone that he ached to hold her. Deliberately he kept his arms at his sides. He dared not give Beth the comfort she so clearly needed, for she would push him away. Andrew was still surprised that she had let him touch her hand the other night in the garden. Normally, she retreated like a frightened virgin if he came too close.

"Is Dora sick?" Andrew asked. Even without waiting for Beth's response, he knew that was unlikely. If her daughter were in any danger, Beth would have remained with her. Instead, she was here in an empty room. She had lit the lamp, perhaps in the hope that light would dispel some of her pain, but she sat as far away from the window as possible. That surprised Andrew almost as much as her sobs, for normally Beth liked to gaze outside.

"Is anything wrong with Dora?"

When Beth shook her head, Andrew continued. "Are you in pain?" Another shake of her head. Though her sobs had subsided, her eyes were red-rimmed from weeping. "Beth, I can see that something is wrong. What is it?"

The room was silent save for the faint sounds of nocturnal insects. At last Beth shook her head again, more emphatically this time. "Nothing is amiss."

Once again, she had refused to meet his gaze. "I don't believe you." Andrew tried to keep his voice low and calm. He had no desire to worsen the situation by frightening or antagonizing her. "Remember, I saw how upset you were earlier this evening."

Her arms tightened, and she rocked slowly back and forth. It was a gesture Andrew had observed in several of his most seriously ill patients. When he had questioned them, they had said simply that rocking helped reduce the pain. He clenched his good fist as he realized how desperately he wanted to know what could have caused Beth such anguish.

At length, she raised her eyes to his. "There's nothing you can do to help me," she said simply. Though Andrew tried not to gasp, the pain he saw in her eyes stunned him. Something had happened, something of monumental proportions that had leached the life from her face, replacing it with an expression that could only be called haunted.

"Please, Andrew. I need to be alone."

She was wrong. He knew that as well as he knew that she

would not believe him. And so he left the room, closing the door softly behind him.

How he hated feeling helpless! Cursing the lingering weakness that made his legs feel no more stable than the tomato aspic Mrs. Kane liked to serve during the summer, he descended the stairs. It was time to take matters into his own hands. He would be helpless no more. He would no longer ask Beth to do his job for him. When it was time for the next delivery, he would make it. And then he would return to his practice and his normal life. If his shoulder was still stiff . . . surely the man who had invented the Duchess could concoct a plausible explanation. In the meantime, he would check the buggy to be certain everything was ready.

The first flight of stairs was easy. Perhaps it was his anger or simply his determination that propelled him, but he descended the steep service staircase almost as quickly as he had before his injuries. He should have done this before. Activity was what his body needed, not rest. He was halfway down the second flight when his left ankle buckled. Damnation! Andrew reached for the railing, desperate to break his fall, but his injured right arm refused to obey his command. Double damnation!

He landed at the bottom of the stairs.

Seconds later, Beth crouched at his side.

"Andrew! What happened? Why are you here?" Though her face was tear-stained, that horrible haunted expression had left her eyes.

"I was on my way to the carriage house," Andrew said with as much dignity as he could muster. He ran his hands over his arms and legs, assessing the damage. If he believed in guardian angels, Andrew would have said that his had been on duty, for he had sustained nothing more than bruises.

"Why were you doing that?" Beth's tart tone left no doubt that she regarded his attempt as nothing short of lunacy.

He struggled to his feet, then gripped the banister. He would take no more chances with weak legs tonight. "I wanted to make sure everything was ready for the next delivery," he explained. "I expect one in a day or two."

He climbed a step, then rested. As if she sensed how much

energy he had depleted, Beth stood next to him and put her arm around his waist. Her hair smelled fresh and sweet, like lemons and sunshine, and he could feel the softness of her body beneath her wrapper.

"I can make the delivery," she told him when they had reached the first landing.

"You're not strong enough," she added. Her body might be soft and desirable, reminding Andrew how long it had been since he had held a woman, but her voice was acerbic, leaving no doubt that she had been a strict schoolteacher.

"I don't need you to tell me that," he retorted, his own voice harsh with anger. "Don't you know how much I hate being useless?"

In the candlelight, he saw her face soften. "You're not useless," she said, her voice once more filled with compassion. "You're an injured man, Andrew. You're also a doctor, and you know healing takes time."

As they climbed the final flight of stairs, neither of them spoke. Andrew's shoulder throbbed from the fall, and both legs ached. Thanks to his foolish plan, the healing that he knew all too well could not be hurried would now take even longer. Clenching his teeth against the waves of pain that radiated upwards with each step, he forced himself to concentrate on happier thoughts. Like the woman who walked so close to him.

*I wonder what her marriage was like,* he mused. She never spoke of it, not even a passing reference. Andrew realized he didn't even know her husband's name. Andrew gritted his teeth. Six more steps. He could make it. It was odd, he reflected. Though at first grief might have kept Beth from speaking of her loss, surely a widow would mention her husband's name at least once. Beth had not.

Four steps. The pain from his ankle radiated up his leg. *Don't think of it. Think of Beth.* She was unlike any woman he had ever met. She was beautiful, but that did not make her unique, for Andrew knew other beautiful women. She was intelligent, but so was Helen. Though, honesty forced Andrew to admit, Beth was more widely read and more opinionated than Helen. But what set Beth apart from the other women of his acquaintance was her determination. Nothing and no one would stop Beth Simmons from reaching her goal. Just as nothing and no one would stop him from reaching his own goals.

One more step. Then he could rest. Andrew took a deep breath and raised his leg. If he were to marry, Beth was the type of woman he would choose. He stumbled. What a thought! Where on earth had that come from? He had no intention of marrying.

The office was immaculate. Beth smiled at the gleaming wood and the polished brass candle sconces. Andrew would probably never notice how much work his staff had done during his absence, but Beth was pleased with the newly restored order. Though the day was dark and damp, with rain imminent, the room's cleanliness brightened Beth's spirits.

She opened the bottom file drawer and pulled out the small sheaf of papers that Andrew had requested. The closely written sheets contained his notes on Dora's case along with information he had gathered about similar conditions. Beth smiled again. This morning was the first time Andrew had asked to review any of his files. Beth considered it a double blessing. First of all, studying his notes would distract Andrew, if only briefly, and might relieve some of his boredom. That was good, for if he was less bored, perhaps he would attempt no more foolish forays downstairs, risking his health.

The second blessing was that this newly revived interest must mean that Andrew thought he was close to being ready to operate on Dora, and that was truly wonderful news. The sooner he cured Dora, the sooner they would be able to leave. That was what Beth wanted more than anything: to have Dora's hearing restored and to take her away from Buffalo and Peter. Of course it was what she wanted. There was no reason why the second prospect should fill her with such dread.

Beth's smile faded. As she placed the papers on Andrew's desk and reached for the book he had requested, she heard the front door open. She walked into the waiting room.

"Good morning, Miss Pratt," Beth said when she recognized the blonde. Had the woman come to ask Andrew for another contribution to the church's stained-glass fund? Andrew had groused about Helen Pratt's request, stating emphatically that he thought the money could be spent on better things. At the time Beth had wondered what Andrew viewed as "better." Now she suspected he would use the money on the Railroad.

The other woman smiled as she brushed raindrops from her gloves, and—to Beth's surprise—it appeared to be a genuine smile, unlike the patronizing smirks many of the other female patients gave her.

"Call me Helen," she said. Beth raised an eyebrow. She needed no lessons in social etiquette to know how inappropriate that greeting would be. Helen was a member of the gentry. As far as anyone in Buffalo knew, Beth was only a servant. "Has Andrew returned?" Helen asked.

Beth shook her head. "He was delayed again, Miss Pratt." Though Helen frowned slightly, Beth knew her place. "It appears to be a difficult case." She and Andrew had rehearsed their story.

Helen took a seat in one of the comfortable waiting room chairs, apparently in no hurry to leave, and motioned Beth to the other padded chair. Beth lit a second wall sconce to dispel the room's shadows, then sat on one of the plain wooden chairs across from Helen.

The other woman's lips twitched slightly, as if she found Beth's actions amusing, but she said only, "I'm puzzled by several things."

The hair on the back of Beth's neck began to prickle. Had Helen somehow guessed that Andrew had never left Buffalo? That seemed improbable. She and Andrew had been so careful.

Beth laid her hands in her lap and willed them to relax. She must not betray her anxiety. "What things might those be?" Though she would not encourage gossip, Beth wanted to know how much Helen knew or suspected. The fact that Helen had come out in the rain disturbed Beth. If her purpose was nothing more than a social visit, she would have waited for better weather. But if she sought to have suspicions confirmed, she might not have wanted to delay.

As Helen shrugged her shoulders, the soft fabric of her dress rustled. "I'm surprised Andrew was willing to be gone from Buffalo for such a long time."

So far they were on safe ground. "I don't believe he expected the consultation to be this lengthy," Beth said. "Fortunately, there have been no serious illnesses among his patients. Unless you or your parents . . ."

"No, Beth." Though Beth might refuse to use her first name, Helen obviously had no such compunction. "I've come to see Andrew as a friend, not a patient. Still, I'm confused." She moved her hand in a restless gesture, wafting her perfume toward Beth. It was lighter and sweeter than the scent Lucinda Fields wore. Helen's expression was pensive. "I believe you said Andrew was summoned to New York."

Beth nodded. That was the story she had concocted, and she knew she had been consistent. Why was Helen puzzled?

"I doubted any force on earth could persuade Andrew to return to New York."

The rain, which had been a light drizzle only moments before, turned into a downpour. Beth tried not to frown at either the weather or Helen's statement. Still, she couldn't help asking, "Return?"

Helen's blue eyes appeared guileless as she nodded. "His family lived there when he was a child. Though he says very little, I gather that his mother died there."

*Bad idea,* Beth chided herself silently. If she had known, she would have invented another destination for Andrew. Perhaps Rochester or Syracuse. But the damage, if indeed it was damage, could not be undone. All she could do was continue to bluff. Perhaps Helen had told the truth. Perhaps her curiosity was due to nothing more than her friendship with Andrew. Perhaps loneliness was the sole reason she had come today. Perhaps she did not suspect that Andrew was only two floors away from her.

"Is there anything else I can do for you?" Though Beth knew it was rude, she rose.

Helen shook her head and said sweetly, "Please tell Andrew I called."

As Helen reached for her gloves, Beth could feel herself relax. The visit was almost over. She glanced outside. The cloudburst appeared to have ended. Though the rain continued, it was only a drizzle. Helen Pratt would have no difficulty going home.

Beth moved toward the door, planning to open it for Helen, but before she reached it, the door was flung open and Dora rushed in. Her braids flew sideways as she skidded to a stop and grabbed Beth's skirts, clutching them as if something had frightened her. *Peter!* Beth felt the blood drain from her face. She swallowed deeply, forcing herself to remain calm, and laid a comforting hand on Dora's head. Peter couldn't have discovered where she and Dora were living.

"Is this your little girl?"

In her moment of terror, Beth had forgotten the other woman's presence. She nodded and stroked the child's hair. "This is Dora."

Helen's eyes moved between them. "She doesn't look much like you," she said at last.

This, it appeared, was Helen Pratt's day to make disturbing pronouncements.

Though Beth smiled reassuringly at Dora, when she answered Helen, her voice was cool. "Her hair and eyes may be a different color, but most people say she has my face."

Helen's laughter tinkled. "Oh, my dear, I didn't mean to insult you. Please take no offense at my hasty words. The dark hair surprised me, but she's a lovely child. I see why Andrew is so taken with her. And now, I shall leave you two in peace."

Seconds later, only Helen's perfume and the faintly disturbing memory of her visit remained. Though Andrew had alluded to it once, Beth frowned at the thought that he had discussed not only her but also Dora with the other woman. Why would he have done that? Surely he was not in the habit of mentioning his household staff to his friends. But what if Helen were more than a friend? Beth's frown deepened. Perhaps Mrs. Kane was right and Andrew planned to marry Helen. That would explain why he had confided in her. He would want to share many aspects of his life with his future bride.

Beth didn't care. Andrew was nothing more than her daughter's doctor and her own temporary employer. It was true that they had taken the first steps toward friendship. But even if they were friends, Beth didn't care whether he married Helen Pratt or any other woman. She didn't care. Not one whit.

But as she climbed the stairs to the attic, Beth found herself clenching her fists. Surely there was no reason to be angry.

"There are red flowers by the light post," she told Andrew as she entered the room, the sheaf of papers he had requested clenched tightly in one hand.

Andrew had pulled the chair near the window. When he saw Beth, he rose, wincing slightly as he put weight on his ankle. If he was surprised by Beth's abruptness and the sharp note in her voice, he said nothing. "I know," he told her. "I saw them, too." It must be something about the weather. Maybe the rain had affected them both, for Andrew seemed as disagreeable as she.

She handed him the papers and the book, taking care not to let their fingers touch. She didn't want to think about how good his hand had felt on hers or how tingles had spread along her arm when she had guided him up the stairs the night he'd fallen.

"I'll make the delivery," she said, forcing herself to think about the signal that passengers waited. She wouldn't think about the fact that this far too disturbing man needed to be shaved again.

Andrew stood so close that she could feel the heat from his body. He shook his head slowly. "It's too risky. I don't want you to do it."

They were ordinary words. What caused Beth's pulse to race was the concern she heard in Andrew's voice. His tone told her that his disagreeable mood was not caused by her, but by his own inability to make the delivery. That knowledge melted Beth's anger and sent a flush of warmth to her face. Since Lenore had died, there had been no one who worried about her. It was odd that she hadn't realized how much she missed having someone who cared.

"I'll be careful," she said when Andrew finally accepted her decision.

The rain continued throughout the day. By the time Beth left, the roads were muddy, slowing the horse's pace. It was a dismal night to be out. Though she had no doubt that what she was doing was right, Beth felt none of the excitement that had characterized her first delivery. Perhaps it was the weather, perhaps the tumult of emotions she had felt over the past few days. All she knew was that she wanted to be home again. The horse plodded; Beth tried to dismiss her sense of unease.

When she reached the clump of shrubs where the passengers were to wait, the horse slowed, as if he recognized the spot. Tonight only one man emerged from the hiding place. As she greeted him, Beth saw that though he looked nothing like her first passengers, his eyes held the same combination of despair and hope that had wrenched her heart the last time. How could she have even considered turning around?

Within seconds, she had stowed the man beneath the false floor and was on her way again. Last time it had taken half an hour to reach the drop-off point. Today, because of the muddy roads, it would be closer to an hour. Beth frowned as the rain continued. The only good thing she could say about rain was that it kept others home and off the roads. That meant there was less chance of encountering someone who might wonder why a woman was out alone on such an unpleasant night.

Beth spoke aloud, as if to the horse, commenting on the farms they were passing, talking about the weather, promising that they were close to their destination. Though Andrew had said nothing about talking to the runaways, Beth knew that if she were confined in a small, dark space, she would want to hear a human voice and know where she was headed.

They were still a long distance from the river when Beth heard the sound of a horse approaching. She listened carefully. Even though the rain and mud muffled sounds, she could tell that it was a single horse, not a buggy, and it was moving quickly. Beth's feeling of unease grew. Though this might be someone on an urgent errand, she could not forget the slave catcher who had wounded Andrew.

"Stop!" The rider shouted his command as he approached, and Beth's heart began to pound. A man on his own mission would not be concerned with others on the road; a slave catcher would.

Beth pretended not to hear the command. Her only hope was to feign innocence.

"Stop!" he called again. His voice was closer now. Beth gripped the buggy whip and pulled it to her side. As the rider drew next to Beth, he reined in his horse and peered into the buggy.

"You!" The word burst from him.

*Dear Lord, no!* A jolt of pure terror swept through Beth. How could Peter have found her? She bit her lip to keep from crying out, and gripped the whip handle fiercely as the memory of his hands on her body made bile rise in her throat. She would not, absolutely would not, allow Peter to touch her again.

"Well, well. If it ain't the little schoolmarm again."

The slight motion as the slave shifted his position reminded Beth of why she was here. How could she have forgotten, even for a second, that a man's life depended on her? Though Peter was evil, Beth could not follow her instincts to flee from him, for that would jeopardize her passenger's life. It was horrible, horrible luck that Peter had happened to be on this road tonight. Somehow, though she wasn't sure how, she had to persuade him to leave so that she could complete her journey.

"What are you doing?" he demanded. His breath was as foul as she had remembered, and a scowl disfigured his face. "Out lookin' for customers?" Peter spat in the road. "I'd be mighty happy to oblige you. A man sure could use some warmth on a night like this." Beth drew her shawl closer, more to protect herself from Peter's gaze than from the weather.

He spat again. "Don't you go thinking that I'm gonna pay you. No, sirree. You owe me for what you done the other day. You coulda broke my leg." He leered at her, then leaned forward as if to seize the reins.

He was a bully, Beth reminded herself, and there was only one way to deal with bullies. "If you come one inch closer," she said firmly, "I'll hurt more than your leg. I won't hesitate to use this." She raised the whip slightly and fixed her eyes on his face.

As she had expected, the threat to his looks cowed him and he backed away from the buggy. *Thank God!* "I need to be on my way."

"Could be we're going the same place. The friends I was supposed to meet are up this road a piece." A sly grin crossed Peter's face. "Reckon you could be neighborly and offer me a ride, being as it's raining."

Not likely!

Beth shook her head. "I'm afraid I can delay no longer." She flicked the reins, and the horse began to plod forward.

Another drop of rain tumbled from Peter's hat onto his nose. "Where are you going?" When Beth refused to answer, he spurred his horse, blocking the road. "How'd you get the buggy?" he demanded.

Beth kept her expression even. She had to get Peter to leave. If he followed her, she would not be able to release her passenger. She thought quickly. Fortunately, Peter wasn't overly bright. If she was lucky, he would believe her story.

"I'm delivering medicine to a very sick woman," she told him. "The doctor warned me that it could be dangerous if any of the medicine spilled near a man. He said it had bad effects on men. Something about family jewels." Beth dropped her eyelids, as if in embarrassment. From the corner of her eyes, she saw Peter give the buggy a wary glance, then stare at his crotch.

"Reckon I'd better go see my friends," he said, and whipped his horse's flanks.

Beth waited until he was out of sight before she flicked the reins, urging her horse to hurry. Peter was gone, but until she reached the river, she could not relax. At last she stopped the buggy and raised the floor.

"Thank you, ma'am," her passenger said as he climbed out. "I sure do hope that man don't come back for you. He was a bad one."

He was, indeed.

Beth's hands were still shaking when she returned home. It was foolish to think Peter had known she would be on the road tonight, she told herself as she unharnessed the horse. He had been as surprised as she. But Beth knew that Peter harbored grudges, and now he had two reasons to want to settle them with her. She shuddered, remembering Lenore's face the times Peter had vented his anger on her. Somehow Beth had to ensure that he did not see her again, and—more importantly—that he never learned his daughter was alive and in Buffalo.

Forcing a smile onto her face, Beth climbed the stairs to Andrew's room. "Success," she said. "One passenger delivered safely."

And if there had been an unexpected stop, if she had trembled with fear, Andrew had no need to know that.

What mattered most was getting him well enough that he could treat Dora. Then they could leave Buffalo and forge a new life. A life without Peter. A life without Andrew.

# *Chapter Fifteen*

"I hope I never again see a buggy from that perspective."

Beth smiled as she watched Andrew stretch his legs and arms and roll his head from side to side. You would have thought the man had been confined for hours, not mere minutes.

Though the morning was overcast, there was no rain. Beth knew it was irrational, but the thought of driving the buggy in the rain made her stomach knot with dread. Logic said that if Peter was going to find her, he would do it regardless of the weather. But her heart refused to listen to her mind, and she knew it would be a long time before she could divorce the thought of rain from her fear of Peter.

Today's delivery, thank goodness, was as different from that last one as possible.

"It appears that compartment wasn't meant for someone your size," Beth said with a glance at the floor. She and Andrew had agreed that after his long unplanned absence, he had to make a public return, and so he had hidden in the buggy's secret compartment for the drive from Niagara Square to the train station. Taking advantage of the pandemonium that always accompanied a train, he had emerged at the same time that a train arrived, and had taken his place among the disembarking passengers, returning to the carriage and greeting Beth as if he had not seen her for weeks.

Andrew nodded a greeting to one of his patients. As he and Beth left the station, his face was once again sober. "The amazing fact is that even though I felt like I barely fit, I have carried three men in that compartment, and not one of them complained."

"It was probably the easiest part of their journey." Beth could only imagine the horrors that the fleeing slaves encountered. Even reading *Uncle Tom's Cabin* had not prepared her for the sight of the men who had traveled hundreds of miles on foot, sleeping under hedges and scavenging for food.

"When I think about them, my problems seem trivial in comparison. Still," Andrew said, "I won't deny that it feels good to be back."

The news of the doctor's return spread quickly, and within an hour the first patients arrived at the office. Beth escorted them into the consulting room and remained to assist Andrew, for he had admitted that he was unable to raise his arm above his shoulder and might have difficulty removing medicines from the cupboard. The story, they had agreed, was that Beth was helping in the office so that Andrew would be able to treat more patients.

The majority of the patients, many of whom had met Beth during Andrew's absence, greeted her with a smile. The next, she feared, would be different, for a waft of cloying perfume told Beth that Lucinda Fields had arrived. Dressed in a frock of sprigged muslin and a frivolous hat whose price had shocked Beth when she had seen it in a shop window, Lucinda smiled at Andrew and ignored Beth when she opened the door for her.

"Oh, Doctor," Lucinda gushed, "I'm so glad you've returned. It's been dreadful since you were gone." Though Andrew nodded toward the chairs in front of his desk, she did not sit, but instead took another step toward him and laid her hand on his arm. "You know how poorly my mother has been and what a trial that has been to my father and me. Why, the very day that you left, she suffered a relapse. I tell you, Doctor, I was at my wit's end. I simply did not know what to do. Why, I was so worried, I could not eat or sleep."

As Lucinda took a breath, Beth studied her. Despite her protestations, she did not appear to be suffering from either hunger or fatigue. Her dress fit perfectly, and no circles ringed her eyes. Beth wondered what the obviously pampered young woman would do if she saw one of the runaway slaves, men and women who knew all too well the privations Lucinda so blithely claimed as her own.

"I beg you, Doctor." Lucinda turned beseeching eyes on Andrew. His calm glance that neither encouraged nor discouraged Lucinda made Beth wonder how often this scene had been repeated. "My mother needs you," Lucinda continued. "I pray that you will call on her."

Andrew nodded slightly, only the tightening of his lips betraying the fact that he was trying not to smile. He displayed no other sign of mirth. "Certainly, Miss Fields," he agreed.

Lucinda fluttered her eyelids. "This afternoon?" she asked.

But Andrew was unwilling to commit himself. "I need to consult with Mrs. Simmons to see what other cases may need my immediate attention." The stiff words and blatant lies—for Andrew knew exactly which patients were ill—told Beth her assumption that Lucinda Fields had made the same plea many times before was accurate.

When Andrew gestured in Beth's direction, Lucinda gave her a look of pure disdain. "Her? She's your housekeeper." And that, her tone said as plainly as words, meant that Beth was beneath contempt.

The faint amusement Beth had seen on Andrew's face disappeared. He withdrew his arm from Lucinda's grip and said sternly, "Mrs. Simmons has also cared for my practice while I was in New York."

The lovely brunette flushed. She was not, it appeared, accustomed to even mild censure. "Don't be angry, Doctor." She clasped her hands together in a supplicating gesture. "It is simply that I've been so worried about my mother. I'm sure you understand."

What Beth understood was that Lucinda's tone did not match her words. Perhaps it was uncharitable of her, for Lucinda could indeed be concerned about her mother's health, but Beth had the impression that Lucinda Fields's primary—and probably only—interest was herself.

The stream of patients continued through the morning, and although Beth could see that Andrew was tiring, there was no doubt that he was happy. This was where he wanted to be. Watching him work, Beth realized what a talented physician he was. She smiled at the realization that the legends surrounding Andrew Muller were founded on reality. He listened to his patients' complaints carefully, then asked probing questions before he prescribed a treatment. And always he made the patient feel that his health was vitally important to Andrew. Beth had brought Dora to the right man.

"You need to rest," she said after she had ushered a patient out of the office.

Andrew nodded reluctantly. "One more. Then we'll have dinner. Would you tell Mrs. Kane we'll be ready in half an hour?"

By some stroke of luck, there was only one person waiting when Beth returned.

"Come in, Miss Pratt. The doctor is ready."

Helen raised an eyebrow, as if to remind Beth that she had

asked to be addressed by her first name, but said nothing until she reached Andrew's examining room.

"Welcome home!" The smile that lit Helen's face was matched by the one Andrew gave her, and Beth couldn't help contrasting it with the polite but cool reception he had given Lucinda.

"It's good to be here." This time when Andrew motioned toward the chairs, his patient took a seat. Beth remained standing, ready to assist Andrew. "Mrs. Simmons said you called while I was gone. Is one of your parents ill?"

Helen shook her head, and her laughter trilled. She wasn't beautiful like Lucinda Fields, but Beth found her more attractive. Perhaps it was because Helen seemed genuine.

"No, thank goodness," Helen said with a quick smile for Andrew and another for Beth. "They are both in good health. It's simply that they missed your company and asked me to inquire when you would be able to join them for an evening."

Andrew took his seat behind the desk and motioned Beth to sit. This, it appeared, was not going to be a professional visit.

"Dare I hope that you missed me?" he asked Helen.

She leaned forward and tapped a finger on the desk. "Foolish man, you know that I pine away when you're gone." She turned to Beth and laughed again. "Didn't I come here expressly to see him?"

Beth smiled and nodded. It was impossible to resist Helen's charm. She had been pleasant the day she had come during Andrew's absence, but today she seemed radiant, as if someone had turned up the wick in a lantern. Beth watched, bemused, as Helen and Andrew bantered. Helen glowed with animation, and Andrew's fatigue seemed to have disappeared. It was odd. Somehow their playful joking and quick smiles reminded Beth of her childhood with Lenore. That made little sense, for Helen and Andrew were not siblings. This must be something else.

Beth and Lenore had always claimed that they were friends as well as sisters. Though what Helen and Andrew shared might be friendship, Beth doubted it. The past few weeks had shown her what friendship between a man and a woman could be like. It wasn't this. Even though she and Andrew were becoming friends, they didn't laugh the way he and Helen did. The differences were even deeper. Andrew and Helen seemed at ease with each other, while "ease" was not a word Beth would use to describe her relationship with Andrew. When she was with him, she was constantly aware of the current that flowed between them. That current heightened her senses and sent shivers up her spine. It was neither easy nor relaxed. It was also nothing like the way she had felt with Lenore or the way Helen and Andrew seemed to feel about each other.

Beth knew that what she felt for Andrew was friendship. That must mean that what Helen and Andrew shared was something else. It must be love.

As the clock chimed, Andrew rose. "Will you stay for dinner?" he asked Helen.

To Beth's surprise, the petite blonde shook her head. "It would not be proper," she said. Beth suppressed a smile, wondering what Helen would think of the impropriety of an unmarried woman living in Andrew's home. Fortunately, neither she nor Andrew would ever know that Beth was not a widow.

Andrew raised one brow. "We'll be chaperoned," he told Helen. "Mrs. Simmons will join us."

Helen gave Beth an appraising glance, her eyes betraying their interest in Andrew's revelation. It was, after all, unconventional for a member of the staff to dine with the family. "Well, then," she said slowly, "I accept with pleasure."

Beth excused herself and went to the kitchen.

"I told you so," Mrs. Kane crowed when Beth asked her to set a third place at the table. "Didn't I tell you that he was courting her? Mark my words. There'll be a wedding before the leaves fall."

"Helen, have you finished the book I gave you?"

Andrew cut another piece of the succulent pork roast that Mrs. Kane had made to celebrate his homecoming. Though he had never particularly liked the heavy mahogany dining room furniture Helen had helped him select, today he was so happy to have resumed his normal life that the room seemed warm and welcoming. Even the crystal chandelier seemed to sparkle more brightly, as if someone had spent hours polishing it. It was only his imagination, of course. Nothing had changed while he'd been imprisoned in the attic.

Andrew knew that was a lie. His house might not have changed, but *he* had changed. Somehow, the protective shield he'd erected around his heart had cracked. Cracked? It had shattered so badly that Andrew wasn't sure he could find any of the pieces. That was part of the reason he had invited Helen to dine with him: He could use her as a shield against the lovely redheaded woman who had destroyed his defenses.

Helen shook her head as she reached for one of Mrs. Kane's flaky biscuits. "I must confess that I am not enjoying it."

"What are you reading?" Beth asked. Today she sat at his left, having given her customary spot to Helen as the guest of honor.

The two women were as different as any Andrew knew: one petite and blond, the other tall and redheaded; one dressed in costly silks, the other in serviceable muslin; one a member of society, the other his housekeeper. And yet, despite the exterior differences, no one watching them would believe there was any social distinction, for both spoke with carefully modulated voices, both had impeccable manners, and both were able to converse easily on a variety of subjects.

Helen wrinkled her nose, her distaste for the book apparent. "The *Iliad*." She broke the biscuit and buttered it. "It doesn't make sense."

Andrew had enjoyed the epic poem, which was why he had given Helen a copy. Before he could speak, Beth leaned forward and nodded as if she understood and sympathized with Helen. "I find it helps to read it aloud," she said in that clear voice that reverberated in Andrew's mind, keeping him awake at night and haunting his thoughts during the day. "Greek poetry was meant to be recited, and dactylic hexameter is particularly beautiful when read."

Andrew tried not to smile at the look of awe that crossed Helen's face.

"You've read Homer?" she asked. The biscuit fell from her fingers.

Beth shrugged as if it were insignificant. "Not in the Greek, of course, but I used to teach school, and Homer was part of the syllabus."

Though Helen simply stared, the expression Andrew saw in her eyes told him he would hear about this later. It would be amusing to see Helen's reaction to his well-educated housekeeper.

Andrew decided to ask the question he suspected Helen would not. "So, tell me," he said, "what is dactylic whatever?"

Beth's green eyes sparkled with an enthusiasm that reminded him of himself the times he had found new proof of his theories of heredity. "It's dactylic hexameter," she said. "That's a pattern of verse—one long syllable and two short ones."

Listening to her, he had no doubt that she had been a teacher and a good one. She was a good housekeeper, a good mother. Andrew wondered whether she had also been a good wife. As the image of Beth in another man's bed rose before Andrew, he gritted his teeth. *Stop it!* Of course Beth had been in a man's bed. Dora was proof of that. He didn't care. It wasn't as though he had any interest in Beth other than her ability to keep his household running smoothly. Andrew sawed his meat with far more force than necessary.

Oblivious to the tortuous path his thoughts were taking, Beth continued. " *'Sing, goddess, the anger of Peleus' son Achilles'* is the beginning of the *Iliad*. That's what dactylic hexameter sounds like," she said.

Helen applauded softly. "Didn't I tell you she was a paragon?" she asked Andrew. Helen's question was meant to be rhetorical, for without giving Andrew a chance to reply, she turned to Beth and asked, "Will you go back to teaching when Dora is cured?"

Beth nodded. "I'd like to."

Helen laid her fork on her plate and turned her gaze on Andrew. "When will you operate?"

"Soon." He had told Beth that he would be ready to perform the surgery in two or three weeks. Andrew knew he ought to be filled with anticipation. After all, this was a chance to prove his theories, to demonstrate his skills as a surgeon. If he succeeded, he would make medical history. But what if he did not? That was the question that haunted him, that caused him to delay the operation. What would he do if Dora still could not hear afterwards? How would he tell Beth that he had failed? Andrew pushed his plate aside. Suddenly Mrs. Kane's succulent meal had lost its flavor.

He took a drink of water, trying to wash the fear from his throat. There were times, Andrew knew, when a patient did not respond to treatment. In the past, he had accepted that knowledge philosophically, but this time he was unable to conjure the same impartiality. This was not simply "a patient." This was Dora. He shouldn't care. He never had before. But, try though he might to deny it, he cared about Dora as a person, not simply a patient. And Beth was far more to him than Dora's mother and his housekeeper.

How on earth had that happened?


As often happened, the sky cleared before sunset, banishing the humidity and leaving in its wake crisp, dry air and a light breeze. Andrew didn't care. There could have been torrential rain and he would still have agreed to meet David. The man's instincts were uncanny. How did he know that Andrew needed desperately to escape the house and spend an evening away from two distracting females? When the messenger had brought David's note, asking Andrew to meet him at the Eagle Street Tavern, he accepted with alacrity. That was just what he needed to clear his head, a night drinking good whiskey and talking to his friend.

"Good to see you!"

Andrew tried not to wince when David clapped him on the shoulder. After the elaborate charade he and Beth had enacted over the past weeks, and the grand finale at the train station this morning, he could hardly tell David to be careful of that shoulder because he had been shot by a slave catcher. Though Andrew suspected David was an Abolitionist at heart, he couldn't take any chances.

The two men made their way to their favorite table near the back of the establishment. It was, to Andrew's surprise, a slow process. At almost every table they passed, they were stopped by patients and acquaintances, all wanting to welcome Andrew back to Buffalo.

"I've got to hand it to you," David said when they were finally seated and had ordered their drinks. "You sure know how to drum up business. I would never have thought of disappearing for a couple weeks just so my clients would discover how much they needed me."

Andrew leaned back in his chair, careful not to bump his shoulder. "You lawyers are afraid to go away. I always figured you were worried people would discover they *didn't* need you."

"Touché!" David twirled his moustache. "Still, that little holiday you took doesn't seem to have helped you. You look like you need to relax."

David was right about that, although the cause had nothing to do with his alleged holiday and everything to do with one delightful little girl and her far too beautiful mother.

"It wasn't exactly a holiday." Andrew took a swallow of his whiskey. This was what a man needed, not that soggy bread and milk Beth had insisted on feeding him.

"Obviously not." David waited until another patient had greeted Andrew before he continued. "You're wound up tighter than my grandfather's watch. Whatever that case was in New York, you need to forget it. I've got just the way to help you."

Andrew laughed. It was obvious why David was such a successful attorney, with his flare for dramatic declamations. Andrew could picture him in front of a jury, persuading them that his client, who had been caught with a bloody knife in her hand, had planned to cut a loaf of bread, not her husband's throat.

"And just what would this marvelous cure be?" he asked.

As the waiter approached, Andrew nodded to him to bring another round.

David feigned innocence. "Why, sailing, of course."

"And I thought you were my friend."

"I am." Though David sounded earnest, Andrew thought he saw his lips twitch. That damned moustache made it difficult to read a man's expression.

"Perhaps you need my professional services," Andrew said smoothly. "It appears you're hard of hearing, for I know I've told you a dozen times that I don't like sailing."

"And I've told you just as often that sailing with me isn't an ocean voyage. We'd go out on the lake for no more than an hour."

Andrew had heard that argument before. "It's still a boat." This was one case the esteemed counselor would not win.

"I can't deny that, but a boat is not a death sentence."

It had been for his father, although that was another thing Andrew had no intention of telling David.

"Let's drop the subject; agreed?"

David nodded. "Certainly." Again, Andrew had the feeling that his friend was smiling behind his moustache. "If you don't want to go sailing, you can at least tell me about Helen."

Andrew took another swig of his drink. Was it only a few hours ago that he had thought an evening with David would be a good idea? How wrong he had been!

"You really should let me check your hearing, David. I know we had that discussion, too."

"Not exactly." David straightened his shoulders in a gesture that Andrew knew meant he was going to argue a legal technicality. "We discussed Helen; that much is true. But new evidence has come to light." When Andrew refused to respond, David continued. "I have it on good authority that Miss Pratt dined with you today."

Andrew shrugged. "News spreads quickly. I trust that your witness"—Andrew used the word deliberately—"informed you that we were properly chaperoned."

"Indeed." David nodded. Then he leaned forward, dropping his court mannerisms. "The truth is, everyone likes Helen. They all want to see her married."

Andrew wondered if David realized he had used the third person rather than the second. Didn't he want to see Helen married?

"We're friends, David. Just friends. Now, are you going to finish that whiskey or should I help you?"

"This place is worse than a pigsty."

Peter looked around. What was Wayne grousing about? So what if the cabin smelled a bit and if the roof had a hole the size of a man's fist. It gave them a mostly warm and dry place to sleep. More importantly, it was so far back in the woods that no one would find them. That was what they needed. Some of those damned Abolitionists were starting to look for honest men like him and Wayne, and the tales of what they did when they found them made a man glad he had a place to disappear when things got too hot.

Peter figured his good friend Lady Fortune had been looking after him the day he got lost. He'd been wandering around for what felt like hours, and then he'd spotted it—some farmer's old abandoned icehouse. It might not be a palace, but it sure beat sleeping out in the open on cold and rainy nights. You'd think Wayne would have figured that out. Course old Wayne always was a bit slow on the uptake.

Peter grabbed the bottle of whiskey from Wayne and took a long swallow. "You wanna waste money on a hotel, go right ahead. Far as I'm concerned, this place is fine." The whiskey was fine, too.

"You know I ain't got no money." Leave it to Wayne to start whining like a woman. Times like this, Peter wasn't sure why he'd hooked up with Wayne. Sure, he needed a partner to help him get those slaves back to their rightful owners, but he didn't need a whiner.

"It ain't my fault you got no money."

When Wayne reached for the bottle, Peter took another long swallow. The old fool didn't deserve good liquor.

"Sure is your fault," Wayne said. He kicked one of the apples that had been lying on the floor, laughing when it squished against the wall. "You promised me it would be easy work. Most anybody can find slaves, you said."

"Should be easy. Everybody knows they ain't got no brains." Why didn't Wayne shut up? Peter didn't want to talk about the trouble they'd been having. Though it pained him to give Wayne whiskey he'd paid for, Peter handed him the bottle. Maybe a little firewater would stop his moaning.

Wayne took a long drink, then smirked. " 'Pears them slaves ain't so dumb if'n they manage to get themselves all the way to Canada without us finding them."

Peter shook his head and grabbed the bottle back. At the rate he was going, he'd need more than one jug to figure this one out. "It don't make no sense. We know the way they come. Don't know why we can't catch them."

Wayne looked like he was thinking. Peter wasn't sure that was a good sign. "Maybe that railroad really is underground. We ain't found no tunnels."

"Wayne, you are one dumb farmer." Peter spat in disgust. "It ain't a real railroad."

"Says who?"

"Says me."

Wayne reached for the whiskey. "If'n you know so much, how come you ain't been catching any of them darkies?"

Peter shrugged as if it wasn't important. He wasn't going to let Wayne know how angry he was that it was taking so long to collect the bounty. There were some things whining Wayne had no business knowing. "I'll get one tomorrow. Tonight I'm gonna get me a woman."

Though he kept a tight grip on the bottle, Wayne slapped one thigh and chuckled. "A redheaded one?"

"Nah!" Peter spat again. "I'm tired of them. Had years of red with the bitch I married. I want a change now—maybe blond, maybe a young one." He stretched out his hand. "Now, gimme the whiskey."

As Peter tried to quench his thirst, Wayne rubbed his hands in anticipation. "Few years, you can put your daughter out to work. I hear some places pay good money for young 'uns."

Peter plunked the bottle on the floor and stared at Wayne.

He hadn't thought about the possibility of selling the whelp. When he'd come home from one of his hunting trips and found Lenore dead and buried, he'd been so glad to hear that the brat was gone, too, that he hadn't considered the future. "Damned shame the brat died." Money was money, and Peter would take it any way he could get it.

"That's not the way I heard it." Wayne grabbed the bottle and tipped it toward his mouth. When the stream missed and ran down his neck, he swore fluently. "I heard she didn't die."

The man had fewer brains than a slug. "You don't know nothing," Peter told him. "The brat died of influenza same time as her ma." At least that useless sister-in-law of his had had the good sense not to waste his money on a separate grave or casket. That was the first smart thing that prissy schoolteacher had done, as far as he knew. Lucky for her, or he'd have had to take the money out of her hide.

"That's not the way I heard it," Wayne repeated.

Old Wayne was more annoying than usual. Peter was gonna have to find himself another helper. "So, what did you hear?"

Wayne smirked. "I heard your wife's hoity-toity sister is in Buffalo."

"Gimme that whiskey. That ain't news. I seen the bitch myself."

Wayne smirked again. The fool better look out, or Peter would smack him. "Reckon you don't know she's got the brat with her."

Peter stared at Wayne. The man's brains were more addled than normal. "Can't be true." Beth had been alone the two times he had seen her. Besides, the brat was dead. She had told him that, and no one would lie about death.

"Don't know, Peter." Wayne's face was just begging for Peter's fist to rearrange it. "It 'pears to me that you're not real good at catchin' people. Bad enough you can't find a runaway, but your own whelp? What's wrong with you?"

Peter swung his arm at Wayne. "Nothin's wrong with me!"

Damn it all! The man ducked before Peter could teach him

a lesson. To hell with Wayne. What Peter needed was a woman. He stormed out of the cabin.

Wayne was wrong. The brat couldn't be alive. The image of his prissy sister-in-law's face rose before him. If Dora was alive and that conniving bitch had made a fool of him, it would be the last thing she ever did.

# Chapter Sixteen

They were sitting next to each other on the horsehair settee in the parlor, their heads bent in concentration, their hands almost touching. As Andrew watched, Beth transferred what appeared to be a mass of string from her hands to Dora's tiny ones. The child stared at her fingers in apparent wonder, then looked up at her mother. For an instant Andrew's heart stopped beating. Beth's smile was breathtaking in its intensity, a look of pure love blended with something else, something Andrew couldn't quite identify. It might have been sorrow; perhaps it was nothing more than awe at the miracle that created children.

Clearing his throat in an attempt to remove the lump that had somehow settled there, Andrew took another step into the room and asked, "What are you playing?" At first he had thought they were winding yarn, but it appeared to be some sort of a game. Though Andrew didn't really care what they were playing, perhaps he would be able to regain his equilibrium while Beth answered the prosaic question.

She looked up, her green eyes sparkling with happiness, and smiled at him. The lump that refused to dissolve, no matter how often he swallowed, seemed to double in size. If he hadn't seen the smile she had given Dora, Andrew would not have been disappointed by her greeting. But he had seen her smile, and this seemed a pale imitation. It was ridiculous. He was a successful man who was close to having everything he had dreamed of. Andrew didn't want the pain that love brought. That was why he had so carefully constructed a wall around his heart.

It was just bad luck that the wall had collapsed. Bad luck, but not the end. He could rebuild it, and this time he would add extra fortifications. He would be protected once again. That was what was important. There was no reason, no reason at all, to wonder if Beth would ever smile at him with such pure, unconditional love.

"It's called cat's cradle," Beth said as she showed Dora how to move her hands. "Do you want to play?"

"I don't know how."

Dora, who had been staring intently at her hands, apparently so engrossed in learning the game that she wasn't aware of Andrew's presence, looked up. A smile lit her face. Shaking the string from her fingers, she slid from the settee and ran to him, throwing her arms around his legs.

Andrew blinked in surprise. Though Dora frequently smiled at him, this was the first time she had been so open in her affection. Without thinking of the consequences, he lifted her into his arms and hugged her. It was a mistake. A big one. For Dora hugged him back, and as she did, Andrew could feel his heart begin to thud. She was so precious, this little one who had somehow burrowed her way into his life, his thoughts, and, yes, his heart. It wasn't supposed to have happened. He had thought it impossible, yet—call it a miracle, call it a curse—it had. Now he cared. Oh, how he cared! And that was one of the worst things that could have happened, for now it would be difficult, maybe even impossible, to rebuild his protective wall.

"Didn't your mother play cat's cradle with you and Mary?" Beth's words brought him back to the present.

"No." Andrew shook his head. Though he had no desire to speak of his childhood, anything was preferable to the realization that he cared too much. He didn't want to even consider what his life would be like when Beth and Dora left.

For a second Beth looked puzzled by his response. Then she said, "Maybe it's not a German game."

Andrew did not want to admit that he could not remember any of his childhood pastimes, so he said only, "Perhaps not." The reality was, his mother had had no time to play. His earliest memories were of her toiling in the fields, working with his father and uncles to plant and harvest crops. He could not remember either of his parents playing. What he did remember was his father telling them that life would be easier in America. Perhaps it might have been, had his father lived. When the family had finally arrived, Andrew's newly widowed mother had struggled to find enough work just to provide food and the rudest of lodging. She had been too tired to play cat's cradle or any other games with him and Mary. But Andrew had no intention of telling Beth of his mother's short, pain-filled life. As far as Beth knew, his mother had been the wealthy, privileged Duchess.

Dora laid her cheek on his, her soft skin and sweet scent wrenching Andrew's heart with memories of Mary. Had she lived, Mary would be a young woman now, perhaps Beth's age. Would she have been as beautiful as Beth?

"Dora and I can teach you," Beth offered. For a second Andrew wasn't sure what Beth meant. *The child's game. That's right.* They had been speaking of pastimes. Of course he would refuse, for if he accepted Beth's offer, he would have to spend even more time with these two females who had already taken too great a hold on his heart.

"Perhaps another day." Andrew swallowed again, suddenly unwilling to give Beth what by all rights ought to be welcome news. "Tomorrow," he said. "I'll operate on Dora tomorrow." He loosened the child's arms from around his neck and placed her back on the floor. She smiled, that eager smile that wrenched his heart, then climbed onto the settee next to her mother.

"So soon?" Beth put her arm around Dora and drew her close. When she looked up at Andrew, he saw that her eyes glistened with moisture.

This was not the response Andrew had expected. "Aren't you ready?"

Beth nodded, though her face was unnaturally pale and tears threatened to tumble from those vividly green eyes. "I am. It's just . . ." She pressed a kiss on Dora's head, then raised her face to meet Andrew's gaze again. "I'm afraid," she said simply. "I love Dora so much that I want everything to be perfect." She blinked furiously. "Oh, Andrew, I know that if anyone can help Dora, it's you, but I'm afraid something might go wrong."

Her eyes beseeched him to reassure her. Andrew wished he could. Like Beth, he wanted everything to be perfect. The problem was, he knew all about her fear, for he faced it daily. Unfortunately, it had never been so strong.

"Nothing will go wrong," Andrew said firmly, as much to convince himself as to reassure Beth. "God willing," he added.

"I'm worried." Beth shook her head, refusing the glass of lemonade Silver offered her. From the moment Andrew had told her that he would operate the following morning, her stomach had felt as if it were tied in knots, and she had had difficulty eating. Though she knew she was taking a risk, bringing Dora back to a place where Peter had seen Beth, she wanted Silver to see her one more time. Just in case. When they had arrived, Silver had taken one look at Beth's face and had shooed Dora off to play with the other children while she propelled Beth into the small parlor.

"Now, honey." Silver shrugged her ample shoulders as Beth explained that the long-awaited surgery would take place tomorrow. "The man may be an icicle, but he's a good doctor."

"I know that, Silver. It's just . . ." She balked at vocalizing her thoughts.

Silver took a long swallow of lemonade, then fixed her eyes on Beth. "You gotta have faith, Beth. Isn't that what you told me when Mark was so sick?" When Beth nodded slowly, Silver placed her glass on the table and hoisted herself to her feet. "C'mon. The children are waiting for their lessons."

Beth managed a smile. Perhaps Mark's thirst for knowledge and his insatiable questions would help distract her. When they reached the small room that Beth used as a schoolroom, they found Mark sitting on the floor, the two girls facing him.

"And then," he said, his voice low and dramatic, "the big, bad man jumped out of the bush and grabbed the little girl." He leaned forward, as if to pounce on his audience. Not understanding his words, Dora smiled. The other girl cringed. Beth shared little Rebecca's reaction. Though she hated to discourage Mark's creativity, she did not find anything related to aggressive men entertaining. Far from it.

"It's good to make up stories," Beth said gently, "but you shouldn't scare the girls." She stroked Rebecca's head to reassure her.

Mark raised his eyes to meet Beth's gaze. "It's not a story," he told her. "I saw it. It was the same man who hurt Libby. I saw it, Mrs. Simmons. I did."

A jolt of pure fear swept through Beth. Had Peter come back? She bit the inside of her lips, trying not to cry out. Somehow she had to get Dora home without Peter finding her.

Beth forced herself to breathe evenly before she shot a questioning look at Silver. The older woman would know if a child had been abducted or accosted in the neighborhood. When Silver shook her head, Beth said, "You must have had a nightmare, Mark."

But what if his story was true?

"Wake up, sleepyhead." Beth put her arms around Dora and brushed the hair from her face. Dora blinked, giving Beth a puzzled look. It was a rare morning when Dora slept later than Beth. The fact was, today *was* a rare day. "Today's the day." Beth continued her conversation. If all went well, in a few weeks Dora would hear her words. "Let's get you ready for the doctor." She slipped the nightdress over Dora's head, forcing herself to keep a smile fixed on her face.

Andrew had told Beth he wanted to operate early in the morning when both he and Dora were well rested. He was, Beth knew, doing everything possible to improve Dora's chances. Beth only hoped that he had slept better than she had, for she felt anything but rested this morning. "Of course you can take Sally with you," she told Dora when the child reached for her doll.

"How is she?" Andrew asked when Beth brought Dora and her doll into the office. If he was experiencing any of the fear that knotted Beth's stomach, his face did not betray it. He looked so calm that she thought perhaps the stories were true; perhaps he did have ice water in his veins. Today, that seemed preferable to Beth's own anxiety.

She managed a small smile. "Dora seems a lot calmer than me," she confessed.

"It'll be all right, Beth," he said. Had she thought him cold? Andrew's eyes were warm and reassuring when they met hers. Beth's smile widened and became natural. It was hard to be afraid when Andrew looked so confident. He stretched out his hand. As Beth shifted her weight so he could touch Dora, Andrew shook his head and reached for her. Slowly, tentatively she put her hand in his. His palm was warm and firm, as reassuring as his smile. A surge of warmth swept through Beth. Everything would be all right. Andrew had promised.

As Beth nodded, Andrew released her hand and held out his arms to Dora. "Upsie daisy." He lifted her onto the examining table. With a solemn face, he took the doll from her and examined its ears carefully. Then he laid Sally on the table, as if she were sleeping. When Dora nodded her understanding, Andrew took a strip of cloth and began to bandage the doll's ears. Though Dora's eyes widened, she made no sound. But when Andrew tied the end of the bandage in a big bow, she grinned and touched her ears, signaling that she wanted the same treatment.

Beth smiled as she admired Andrew's technique. Just as his touch had reassured her, his pantomime had allayed any fears Dora might have had.

"You're next," he told Dora, "but first you need to sleep." Andrew turned to Beth. "Would you hold her while I get the laudanum?"

The room seemed unnaturally quiet, the only sounds Andrew's firm footsteps and Dora's breathing. It was foolish, Beth knew, to believe that the world was holding its breath, waiting for Dora to regain her hearing before it resumed normal noises.

Beth kept her arms around Dora and gently stroked her head as Andrew laid the soaked cloth over her nose and mouth. "Do you want me to stay?" she asked when the child was sedated. Now that the moment she had longed for for so long had arrived, Beth found that her legs were trembling as if they were weaker than a pansy's stem.

Andrew nodded. As his solemn mien appeared to deepen the cleft in his chin, Beth noted a stray whisker, as if he had been preoccupied when he shaved. "You can hold Dora's hand," he said. "That may comfort her. All I ask is that you not speak. I need to concentrate." Andrew's voice was matter-of-fact, almost as cold as it had been the day she had first met him. Oddly enough, the faint chill reassured Beth. Andrew Muller, the famous Ice Doctor, was back. That was good, for everyone knew that he could work miracles.

Beth pulled a chair next to the table and sat, clasping one of Dora's hands between both of hers. She couldn't watch what Andrew was doing. Though Beth knew that Dora would feel no pain, the mere thought of anyone placing instruments in her darling's ears made Beth's stomach turn. She tried staring at the wall, the floor, the other wooden chair. Nothing worked. Though her eyes looked elsewhere, her mind kept visualizing what Andrew was doing. Finally, she focused on his face.

At first, his expression showed nothing other than concentration. His eyes narrowed as he did something, then the tiny creases between his brows eased. *Good!* But then, a few minutes—or was it an hour?—later, he frowned, and the cleft in his chin seemed to deepen. *Something was wrong!* Beth bit back her cry of anguish. She could only hurt Dora if she broke Andrew's concentration. One of those dangerous instruments, the same ones she had used to remove the bullet from Andrew's shoulder, could slip. Still, Beth had to know what he was doing and why he looked so formidable. She risked a glance at Dora, then recoiled. How could anyone survive this procedure?

Beth closed her eyes in a silent prayer. When she opened

them again, she saw Andrew's face relax. He let out a long sigh, then looked at Beth. For the first time, she saw lines of fatigue etching his face. No wonder he had insisted on early morning, if the surgery drained this much of his energy.

"You can breathe again." he said as he walked to the window and threw it open. Though the August day would soon be warm, Andrew had kept the window closed lest a sudden sound—a shout, a cat's cry, even a gust of wind—disturb his concentration.

"What did you find?" Andrew had told Beth that he could not be certain of the cure until he operated. Only then would he know the full extent of Dora's injuries.

"The damage was worse than I expected." His voice was cool, almost emotionless. Beth heard fatigue but not the sudden, wrenching despair she felt. As her spirits plummeted, Andrew continued. "I was able to repair most of it."

*Most.* She took a deep breath, willing her pulse to return to normal. Would "most" be enough? Beth turned her gaze toward Dora. Though a bulky bandage circled her head, covering her ears, otherwise she appeared to be sleeping.

"Will she be able to hear?" A blue jay's raucous call underscored Beth's question. Would Dora ever hear a bird's song or the soughing of the wind?

Andrew pulled a sheet up to Dora's chin and listened to her breathing. When he said nothing, Beth gripped the side of the chair, trying to keep her limbs from shaking. Andrew touched the bandages, as if reassuring himself, then said, "We won't know until everything heals." His voice was low and even, betraying neither hope nor despair. The Ice Doctor was still in control. "Dora may never hear perfectly—the bones were too badly broken to repair completely—but she should be able to live a normal life."

The clock ticked; a bird flapped its wings; a woman's laughter spilled out of a window. Ordinary sounds on this extraordinary day. As the import of Andrew's words hit her, the tears Beth had felt welling in her eyes began to spill down her cheeks. Dora would hear! The miracle Beth had prayed for had happened.

"I'm sorry, Beth." Andrew walked to the far side of the

room and rested his forehead against the wall. His shoulders slumped as if with dejection.

Beth dashed the tears from her face, shocked by his reaction. Something was wrong. Andrew should be as elated as she; yet there he was, looking as if someone had died. "Why are you sorry?" It made no sense. He had just performed the most incredible act, giving Dora her only chance at hearing, and he was apologizing.

As Andrew turned, Beth saw the regret in his eyes. "I wish it had been perfect. I did everything I could."

And then she understood. He thought she was unhappy. Beth moved to his side. "Oh, Andrew, these aren't sad tears." She brushed the last drops from her cheeks and managed a tremulous smile. "I'm just so relieved that it's over and that you think Dora has a chance of hearing." How could he ever question the magic he had wrought? When Andrew's blue eyes remained clouded with doubt, Beth continued. "Please don't think I'm disappointed. I knew it would take a miracle for Dora to hear again. That's why I brought her to you. You're the miracle."

"I don't know how you do it, David, but you make it look easy. It's not." Andrew gripped the mainsheet, willing the small sailboat to turn back toward the shore. It was a perfect August day, with deep blue skies, a few puffy clouds, and enough wind—or so David said—to sail. The problem was, try though he might, Andrew could not find that wind. The mainsail hung limp, and the boat drifted in lazy circles.

David's grin told Andrew how much he enjoyed watching his friend's discomfort. "It is easy," David asserted, "once you get the knack." He stared pointedly at the sail, which was clearly catching no wind.

"The wind keeps shifting," Andrew said. What a stupid idea this had been, agreeing to go sailing with David. Andrew should have continued to refuse the way he had all those other times. The truth was, he'd been feeling so good after Dora's surgery that he had decided to slay another demon. Andrew doubted he would ever forget the expression on Beth's face, the trust, admiration, and something else—

something Andrew was afraid to name—that he saw when she looked at him. Though her face was tear-stained, those lovely green eyes had told him he could do anything, even get into a boat.

Right now Andrew doubted the wisdom of that particular move. David had told him how much he would enjoy sailing, promising Andrew that it was the most relaxing of sports. Relaxing, indeed! Andrew hadn't been this unrelaxed in weeks.

There were a few other pleasure boats on the lake. Most of them had headed briskly away from the shore. David had kept his close in, for which Andrew was grateful. If they capsized, he wanted to believe they had a chance of survival.

"I don't think there's any wind at all," he announced in frustration.

"You'll learn to read it," David said mildly. "Now, watch."

David grabbed the mainsheet from Andrew, and within seconds the boat was tacking, then skimming over the water.

"How did you do that?" Andrew demanded. Hadn't he been holding the same rope, and the boat had refused to move? David must have invoked some kind of magic. David handed the mainsheet back to Andrew, showing him how to hold it and when to tighten it. Soon they were sailing. Truly sailing. Andrew took a deep breath, expelling it slowly. It was wonderful, moving with the wind. This was nothing at all like the voyage from Europe. David had been right.

"How's the little girl?" David asked when they reached the shore and docked the boat.

Andrew grinned at the realization that for the entire time he and David had been on the lake, he had not thought about his practice. All that had mattered was catching the wind and keeping the boat upright. Was that single-mindedness the reason David enjoyed sailing so much?

"It's too soon to be sure," he told his friend, "but there's a good chance she'll regain her hearing." From the moment she had wakened, Dora had made it clear that she hated having her ears bandaged, and Andrew knew it was only the fact that her doll wore similar linen wrapped around her head that kept her from pulling it off.

"You really took an interest in . . . what's her name, Laura?"

Andrew gathered the sail in his arms, then handed one end to David when they had secured the boat. "Her name is Dora."

"Fold it in half lengthwise." As they shook, then folded the canvas, David nodded sagely. "Next thing you know, you'll find yourself a wife and have children of your own."

Andrew handed the sail back to his friend. "I doubt it." Just as he doubted that David would ever stop needling him about marriage.

David nodded again, and this time his smile turned to a smirk. "That's what I thought."

Two men approached, the deck creaking slightly beneath their weight. Andrew waited until they were gone before he turned back to David. "What do you mean?" he demanded.

David fingered his moustache and chuckled. "Every other time I've mentioned marriage, you've refused categorically. This is the first time you've admitted there's a possibility."

"There isn't." But even as he said the words, Andrew realized that the thought of marriage no longer evoked immediate denial. He no longer felt the need to hide his heart behind a barricade. Perhaps there was a chance for him. Perhaps caring about others wasn't necessarily the road to heartbreak.

"I'm afraid."

There had been a time when Beth had lived with fear, when each day she had been afraid she or Lenore would do something to incur their father's wrath. That had been terrible, but today Beth realized there was a worse fear. Today her fear was not for herself but for Dora. Somehow that made it more intense. Even worse was the knowledge that she could do nothing to influence the outcome. It wasn't a matter of being good or keeping quiet the way she and Lenore had. What happened to Dora was beyond Beth's control.

She lifted the child onto the examining table, then averted her face so that Dora could not see the distress she knew was etched on it. Now that the moment had come to remove the bandages, Beth was reluctant. Until today, she had lived with hope and the possibility that Dora would hear. Today she would know if that possibility was reality.

"Don't you have faith in me?"

Beth saw a flash of pain in Andrew's eyes, and realized that her doubt had caused it. How selfish of her, to let her fears hurt Dora and Andrew. "I know you did everything you could," she said as Andrew reached for the scissors. "But you told me the operation might not work."

Beth managed a smile for Dora. She had to be strong for the little girl. "It'll be all right, sweetie," she said with a bright smile. "Watch what Andrew's doing."

Once again it was early morning. Today, unlike the day he had operated, Andrew had left the window open. Beth wondered whether Dora would soon hear the birds' serenade or the muted clop of horses' hooves.

As he had before, Andrew demonstrated the procedure on Dora's doll. He picked up Sally and carefully snipped the miniature bandage. As Dora grinned and touched her own bandages, Beth asked, "What will happen if it's not successful?"

Andrew paused and met her gaze. Though the birds continued to sing, Beth could hardly hear them over the pounding of her heart. Andrew's expression was solemn as he said, "She'll be no worse than before."

That was small consolation.

When he had removed Dora's bandages, Andrew stood back for a second. To Beth's untutored eyes, Dora's ears looked normal. That proved nothing, she knew, for they had appeared normal before. She waited anxiously while Andrew used the otoscope to inspect first the doll's, then Dora's ears. Through it all Dora sat quietly, her expression giving no indication that she heard anything.

When he finished, Andrew gave Beth a reassuring smile. "Don't expect too much," he cautioned. "The healing is not yet complete. When her hearing returns, it will be gradual." He had told her that before. Though impatience would gain her nothing, Beth wished there were some way to know that the operation had been successful. Andrew nodded, as if he could read Beth's thoughts. "I want to try something. Would you keep Dora looking at you?"

Beth stood in front of Dora. "How does it feel to have your ears back, sweetie?" she asked. Though Dora's eyes followed her lips, she gave no sign of hearing. Somehow, Beth kept a smile fixed on her face, when what she wanted was to cry in despair. Surely if the surgery had been successful, Dora would have heard *something*. Surely she would have blinked her eyes or touched her ears or done *something*.

"Sally's happy, too, isn't she?" Still no response.

Beth reached forward to touch Dora's hand, and as she did, she heard a loud noise. Dora turned.

For a second Beth was speechless. Then tears of joy filled her eyes. It couldn't be coincidence. "Oh, Andrew!" Beth stared in amazement as Dora gave him a puzzled look. "She heard you!"

He clapped the books together again. There was no doubt about it. The confusion on Dora's face could have only one cause. Beth drew the child into her arms and hugged her. "It's a miracle, Andrew!" she cried. "You're a miracle worker."

# *Chapter Seventeen*

Damn the bitch! Peter kicked open the door to the cabin and strode inside. She had disappeared. He dumped his bag on the table and reached for a loaf of bread. It sure wasn't much of a meal, but it would have to do until Wayne got there with the real victuals.

Where was that conniving bitch? Peter knew she used to go to Canal Street two or three times a week. One of the whores had told Wayne she taught the brats. Figured. Peter would bet she'd tried earning her living on her back and couldn't. She was probably like her sister. Lenore had sure needed to learn how to please a real man. It had taken months to teach her. Course, it didn't hurt that Lenore had been afraid of him. A little fear added to a man's enjoyment.

Peter tore a chunk of bread and stuffed it into his mouth. Damn it all! It was stale. A man like him shouldn't be eating stale bread, and he sure as hell shouldn't be living in a tumbledown shack like this one. No, sirree, he ought to be sleeping in one of those fancy mansions with pretty women at his beck and call.

Peter reached for the jug. The bread might be stale, but the whiskey was first-rate. He wouldn't steal anything but the best. That was what he deserved: the best food, drink, and women. That sister-in-law of his would be a tasty morsel. He reckoned she was like Lenore and would need him to give her a few lessons. Peter would teach her. Oh, yes, he would. With pleasure. Once he found her.

The trouble was, he didn't know where she was hiding out. Silver did. Peter was sure of that, but he couldn't come close enough to the old whore to get the information out of her. That big bruiser wouldn't let him in the house anymore. Said he damaged the merchandise. Hell, the whore asked for it. All that moaning was part of the game. She knew that. Just as Peter knew that the only way he would find Beth was to get Silver to tell him where she lived.

He leaned back in the chair and propped his feet on the table. There was more than one way to catch a whore. He might not be able to get inside her house, but Silver had to come out. And when she did . . .

"Oh, my God, Silver. What happened?" Feeling the bile rise in her throat, Beth clamped a hand over her mouth. This was the first time she had come to Silver's since Andrew had removed Dora's bandages. Though the weather was perfect, Beth had acceded to Andrew's request that she no longer walk to Canal Street and had allowed Roberts to drive her. In truth, she had been glad of the escort. Her own encounters with Peter and the tale Mark had related of a stalking man had worried her enough that she had no desire to come here alone.

Beth had been happy on the short ride, thinking of how pleased Silver would be when she learned that Dora could hear. It might only be loud sounds, but that was a beginning. There was another reason Beth had been eager to visit Silver. She wanted to ask her advice. Silver was wise. She would know why Beth's pulse began to race whenever she was with Andrew. She would know why Beth blushed so easily these days, and why she would waken in the middle of the night, only half remembering the dream, but filled with a nameless longing that was somehow connected to Andrew. Silver would know.

But something horrible had happened to her friend. Beth tried not to cringe. Not even the heavy makeup Silver normally wore could disguise the fact that her face was badly bruised. Her left eye was swollen almost shut, and an angry red streak beneath her other eye told Beth the tender skin had been cut.

Beth closed her eyes and gripped the door frame for strength. Not again! Her mother and Lenore had looked like this, but not Silver. Silver was strong. Silver was wise. She would never let a man do this to her.

"Oh, Silver!" Beth opened her arms to embrace her friend, then drew back. If Silver's ribs were broken, she wouldn't want to be touched. "What happened?"

"It was my fault." As she spoke, Beth saw that Silver's upper lip was split. Her fault? How often had her mother and Lenore claimed the same thing? It was *not* her fault!

"Did Tom do this?" she demanded.

Silver's eyes widened in horror. "How could you ask that?" She rose from the chaise lounge where she had been resting and faced Beth, her eyes fierce as she defended her husband. "Tom loves me," she declared. "He would never hurt me. How could you think that?"

Now was not the time to tell Silver that every man Beth had been close to—every man except Andrew, that is—had hurt women. Her friend needed comfort, not the tale of other women's pain. Beth stretched her hand toward Silver, hoping that a gentle touch would tell her how much she cared.

"Not Tom." Silver repeated the words, her voice so firm

that Beth believed her. Was Tom like Andrew? It could be true. Though Silver's husband was a big man who would not hesitate to throw a rowdy customer out the front door, kicking his backside to give him an extra incentive not to return, Beth had never seen him be anything but gentle with women. He had been more than gentle with Silver, always treating her as if she were fragile porcelain. Beth wondered if that was love. That was one of the things she had wanted to discuss with Silver today. But now was clearly not the right time.

Silver's boudoir contained more shades of pink than Beth had seen assembled in one room. Today, though, the only colors she saw were the unnatural ones that marred Silver's face.

"Someone hurt you. Who was it?"

Silver shrugged, and as she did, Beth saw the finger marks on her throat. Apparently not satisfied to pummel her face, Silver's assailant had attempted to throttle her. Beth bit her lip in an attempt not to cry.

"He was a big man," Silver said. "Brown hair, bright blue eyes. Good-lookin' if you like that type." She tipped her head to one side. "Remember I told you about the tough customer who wanted a redhead? It was him."

Beth shuddered and started to sway. "Peter." The room began to darken. Why had he done this? Beth knew the man was a monster, but even that didn't explain why he had hurt Silver.

Silver closed the door, then pushed Beth into a chair. "Sit down, honey, and take a deep breath." As if following her own advice, Silver reclined on her chaise.

Beth closed her eyes until the dizziness passed. When she opened them again, she saw Silver watching her. "I don't know his name," the older woman told Beth. "We weren't introduced proper-like."

Beth stared at Silver, almost as shocked by her hoarse laugh as she was by her bruises. "How can you joke about this? It's not funny."

"No, it ain't," Silver agreed. "But, honey, it's about time

you learned, laughter helps ease the pain." That was a remedy Beth had never tried.

"I'm sure it was Peter." *Just as I'm sure that, no matter what she says, no amount of mirth will lessen Silver's suffering.* "He's about four inches taller than me, and he smells like cloves and tobacco."

As Silver tipped her head to one side the way she always did when pondering something, Beth wondered if it was only her imagination that the gray wings at Silver's temples seemed larger than before. At length Silver nodded. "That's him, all right. How come you know him?"

"He was my sister's husband." *And I will never understand why Lenore married him.*

Her mouth gaping, Silver appeared to be struggling for words. "The one who . . ." Rather than complete her thought, she hoisted herself to her feet and crossed the short distance to Beth. "Honey, you gotta leave now, and don't you ever come back. Not ever." The fervency in Silver's voice frightened Beth almost as much as her words.

"Why?"

" 'Cause he was looking for you. He wanted to know where you and the little one were."

As Beth felt the room begin to darken, she blinked rapidly, trying to clear her head. "Dora?" The word came out as little more than a croak. "He knows she's alive?" The nightmare she had tried so hard to vanquish was back, stronger and more dreadful than ever. Somehow, some way, Peter had learned that Beth had lied about his daughter's death. She had no illusions about what he would do next. The man did not like being thwarted in even the smallest matter.

" 'Pears that way. Now, honey, you let Tom take you home. It ain't safe for you to be walking."

Beth shook her head. "There's no need. Roberts brought me." Silver's room was at the front of the house, where she could watch Canal Street, and so she had not seen Roberts bring the coach to the back entrance.

Beth shuddered. Peter had hurt Silver! The knowledge haunted her. "Why did he hurt you, Silver?" Beth had no doubt what Peter would do if he found her and Dora. But

Silver? It made no sense, unless . . . Was Silver like the orange cat her father had crushed simply because it was there?

Silver's gray eyes were solemn when they met Beth's gaze. "It was 'cause I wouldn't tell him where you live. He done heard you come here. Course, after he beat up Libby, Tom wouldn't let him put one foot inside the front door." Silver's face beamed with pride in her husband's abilities, then darkened with memories of Peter. "He waited till I went outside." She shook her head, her expression grim. "Honey, it was my fault. I was thinkin' about the new gown I was gonna have made and how Tom would like it, and that man caught me by surprise. I should'a known better."

"Oh, Silver, it's *my* fault." Beth tried to control her trembling. Her friend had already suffered enough on her account. She didn't want to add to her worries by letting her see how badly shaken she was. "You gave me shelter and friendship, and look what you've gotten in return."

"Now, you hush." Silver leaned forward and put a hand over Beth's. "Friends take care of their friends, and you're my friend. Besides," she added, "I hurt him real bad."

Once again Silver was trying to comfort her, when Beth ought to be the one providing consolation. "Not as badly as he hurt you."

"I wouldn't be so sure about that, sugar. He's gonna walk funny for a few days and"—Silver's grin was triumphant—"he didn't get what he wanted. He still don't know where you and Dora live."

Beth took a deep breath. "Oh, Silver, you've given us so much. I can never repay you."

Silver squeezed her hand. "Sure you can. Just keep that girl safe." Shaking her head, she said, "That pa of hers is pure evil. I surely don't know how he sired a little angel like Dora."

The moon had risen, a huge lemon-yellow orb that lit the sky. Beth frowned. No wonder the slaves preferred to travel under the new moon. With this much light, there were fewer hiding places and pursuit was simpler. If the situation were less serious, Beth would have waited until the moon was dark. But she could not afford a fortnight's delay.

She folded Dora's frock and laid it in the bag on top of her own clothes. She would stop in the kitchen, pick up some bread and cheese and a few of the dried apples that Mrs. Kane had brought from the root cellar. And then she would be ready. All that would remain would be to carry Dora downstairs.

Beth removed her shoes as she descended the back stairs. Andrew, she knew, was a light sleeper, and she must not rouse him. Avoiding the two squeaky steps, she made her way to the kitchen. Though the full moon might make travel hazardous, it kept her from having to carry a lamp. She moved soundlessly around the kitchen, packing a loaf of the bread Dora preferred and a few biscuits.

"Going somewhere?"

Beth dropped one of the apples. As if from a distance, she heard it bounce on the floor. Her heart thudded with shock and apprehension. What was Andrew doing here? She had been so careful. Beth knew she had made no sound as she passed the second-floor landing.

"I was hungry," she said, improvising. Even to her ears, the excuse sounded feeble.

As the moonlight streamed through the window, Beth saw Andrew's raised eyebrow and knew he didn't believe her. "If that's true," he said firmly, "you'll be happy to show me what's inside that bag, won't you?"

Beth gripped the handles. She had to think of a good story; unfortunately, her imagination refused to cooperate. The only images she could conjure were Silver's battered face and the possibility that Peter would inflict the same—or worse—pain on Dora. Beth wouldn't think about Andrew and the vast empty hole that would remain in her heart if she left here and never saw him again.

"Does this unexplained hunger and what appears to be a satchel have something to do with the fact that you were nervous this afternoon?"

"I wasn't nervous."

Andrew shook his head. "You're not a very good liar, Beth." He took the bag from her hand and opened it. "Food.

Clothes. If I didn't know better, I would say that you were planning to leave." Beth didn't need a lot of light to see the frown on Andrew's face. The cleft in his chin deepened as he scowled at her. "I don't suppose you were going to tell me."

Though his sarcasm flayed her already raw nerves, Beth tried not to wince. "I wrote you a note."

"What a nice personal touch!" She couldn't help it; she flinched at the anger she heard in his voice. It wasn't supposed to be this way. She was leaving because it was the best thing for him and Dora. Andrew would know that if he read the letter. Lord knows she had agonized over the wording, trying desperately to tell him enough that he would understand but not so much that he would be in danger.

"I thought we had an agreement," Andrew continued. "You would work for a year in return for my treating Dora. Unless you're operating on a different calendar, I feel obliged to tell you that you have not been here for twelve months."

Though his voice was as frigid as it had been the first day she had come to Buffalo, his eyes were not cold. They burned with anger and something else, something that looked oddly akin to the pain she was feeling. Beth wouldn't consider that. She had made her decision to protect him from pain, not cause it.

"Everything has changed."

Andrew shook his head again. "Not as far as I know." He gripped her arm and led her out of the kitchen. Though there was no gentleness in his touch, a sense of wonder filled Beth as she realized that she felt no fear. Andrew was angry. More than that, he was angry at her. He had her under his control, yet she was not afraid of him. He would not hurt her. Beth knew that as surely as she knew that he would be in danger if she didn't leave.

When they reached the parlor, Andrew led her toward the settee. "Tell me what happened."

Refusing to sit, Beth tried to pull her arm away. Andrew might not harm her, but she still needed to put distance between them. As she tugged, he tightened his grip. "I can't tell you," Beth said, hoping that somehow he would under-stand. "It's too dangerous."

Moonlight spilled into the room, turning Andrew's blond hair to white. He stood silently for a moment, his eyes study-ing Beth's face as if he thought it would reveal something her words had not. "You're making no sense, Beth." This time she heard concern rather than anger in his voice. "What is dangerous? Why are you leaving?"

Beth clenched her fists. Did he think she wanted to flee, to once again be a fugitive in the night? Did he think she wanted to leave the only place that Dora felt comfortable? Did he think she wanted to leave him?

"Because I have to!" Beth fairly spat the words at Andrew. "Don't you see? If we stay, he'll hurt you, too."

Andrew's blue eyes mirrored skepticism. "Who will hurt me?" he asked in a surprisingly gentle voice.

"Dora's father."

Andrew stared at Beth, trying to understand. She was obvi-ously distraught. That much was clear from the fact that she had tried to run away. But what did she mean, Dora's father would hurt him? Beth was a widow; her husband was dead.

"He's dead." Andrew stated the obvious. "A dead man can't hurt anyone."

Beth shook her head. Those lovely eyes that normally sparkled with enthusiasm were dulled by fear. Whether the cause was real or not, there was no denying the power of Beth's terror. As she started to tremble, Andrew led her to the settee. This time she did not resist. Sensing that she needed distance between them, he waited until she was seated. Then he lighted one of the oil lamps and drew a chair close to her. "Tell me, Beth. Why are you afraid?"

"He's not dead."

Andrew gasped, feeling as if he'd sustained a blow to the solar plexus. Beth's husband was still alive. *Good Lord, no!* Andrew clenched his teeth as he thought of the hopes he had begun to entertain. How foolish he had been, to covet another man's wife. The undeniable attraction he felt for Beth was wrong, one of those ten very basic thou-shalt-nots. Andrew thrust those thoughts firmly aside. What mattered now was Beth and assuaging her fears.

"Tell me," he said.

The mantel clock chimed the quarter hour, reminding Andrew that it was the middle of the night.

"It's a long story," she said.

"I have all night."

Beth took a deep breath, and he sensed that she was fortifying herself. What revelations could possibly require the amount of courage she seemed to think she needed? He would hardly condemn her for deserting her husband. Beth wouldn't be the first woman who had left an unhappy marriage. Andrew sat back in the chair, hoping that if he appeared relaxed, she would be more at ease.

She swallowed again, and he could see her nervousness. Did she think he would insist she return to her husband? Divorce wasn't common, but if she wanted one, David could help her obtain it. Andrew prepared to reassure her.

Before he could speak, Beth leaned forward. She took another deep breath, then blurted out, "Dora's not my child."

Andrew felt his jaw drop. This was not what he had expected. Not at all. If Dora wasn't Beth's daughter, who was she?

"She's my niece."

As the tale of deception and lies unfolded, Andrew's shock turned to wonder. Hadn't he once thought that Beth was filled with determination? How right he had been! She had surmounted obstacles that would have crushed a lesser woman, and she had let nothing—nothing at all—stop her from keeping her promise to her sister.

"So," he said at last, "you hid Dora and told Peter she had died and you were going back to your school." It had been, as Beth had promised, a long story. Once he had recovered from his initial shock, Andrew had been fascinated by Beth's resourcefulness. Like him, she had invented a past that opened doors to the future she wanted. There was only one point that was still unclear. "I understand why you wanted to get Dora away from Peter and why you came here. But why did you pretend to be her mother?"

Though Beth had appeared to relax under his quiet questioning, she now gripped the settee arm so tightly that Andrew saw her knuckles whiten. She was silent for a moment. When at last she spoke, her words had the ring of truth. "I thought it would be the simplest way to protect Dora. There would be fewer explanations, and it would be easier for me to go places as a widow than as an unmarried woman."

Her logic was faultless. Andrew had to admit that he would never have considered hiring her if he had known she was not a widow. And now that he knew it . . . First things first. He had yet to learn why Beth wanted to leave him.

"What happened today?" he asked as gently as he could. His face still burned when he thought of the sarcasm he had flung at her earlier. She hadn't deserved that, but he had been so worried when he realized she was fleeing that he had lashed out at her.

Beth swallowed nervously. "Wait right here," Andrew said. He strode to the mahogany cabinet and brought out a bottle of whiskey. They both could use a drink. He poured Beth a small serving and himself a much larger one. Though Beth protested, he insisted she drink it, and was rewarded by the color that returned to her face.

"About today," he prompted.

The liquor had relaxed her.

"First you need to know what happened a few weeks ago," she told him. A sense of foreboding swept through Andrew. Though the minister had taught him it was wrong to hate, Andrew hated Peter Girton, and he suspected whatever Beth was going to say would only intensify his hatred. It did.

"Peter saw me leaving Silver's one day. He tried to stop me." As Beth struggled to keep her voice even, the shudder that shook her body told Andrew that her loathsome brother-in-law had laid hands on her. He would kill the bastard.

"I escaped from him that day," she said. "I hid in one of the alleys until he was gone." Andrew wondered whether that was the day he had noticed how nervous Beth was. At the time, she had denied anything was wrong.

"There's more," she said. "I never thought I'd see him again. He didn't know where I lived, and Buffalo's a big city. But I was wrong, Andrew." Beth shuddered again. "Peter stopped me the night I made the second Railroad delivery. I don't know why he was on that road, but he was."

Andrew stared at her for a moment. "You never told me about that."

She clenched her hands together, and he sensed that she was trying to stop their trembling. "I wanted to, but I was too caught up in my lies. How could I tell you about Peter without explaining everything? I couldn't do that." Beth took another sip of whiskey.

"There was another reason, wasn't there?" he asked.

She nodded. "You were still recovering from the bullet wound. I didn't want to worry you."

She had been accosted by one of the most despicable creatures on earth. She had been deeply frightened, and yet she had worried about him. A feeling of humility swept through Andrew. What had he done to deserve a woman like Beth in his life? He wanted to hold her close and protect her from Peter, but first he had to discover why she thought she had to leave him.

"Today," he prompted. "What happened today?"

Though Beth bit her lip, probably to keep from crying, she could not disguise the tears in her eyes. "Somehow Peter learned that Dora's still alive. I don't know how, but he did, and now he wants to find her."

"We won't let him." There was no way that man was going to come within a mile of either Beth or Dora.

"Andrew, he's not going to stop. I know Peter, and when he decides he wants something, he gets it." Beth's voice trembled, and the tears spilled down her cheeks. Peter Girton would pay for every one of those tears. "He wants Dora. That's what happened today. I found out that he beat Silver to make her tell him where we were living."

Andrew revised his opinion. Killing the man was far too kind. He would make sure he suffered a slow and exceedingly painful death.

Beth gripped her glass with the same force she had used on the chair arm. "If he finds Dora, he'll hurt her." Beth closed her eyes, and Andrew knew she was trying to block out the image of Peter beating Dora. When she spoke, it was so softly that Andrew had to strain to hear her. "He's done it before, Andrew. He'll do it again."

"What do you mean, he's done it before?"

Beth's eyes were filled with pain when they met his gaze. "That's how Dora lost her hearing. Her father kicked her in the head."

Andrew reviewed the poisons he knew. One of them would be right for Dora's father. By the time Andrew was finished with him, he would beg to die.

"Don't you see, Andrew? We have to leave."

What Andrew saw was that they couldn't possibly leave. "What will you do if Peter follows you?"

Her expression said she hadn't considered that possibility. Andrew continued. "If he's as determined as you say—and I have no reason to doubt that—he'll keep looking. Eventually he'll find you." And that could not be allowed to happen.

Beth shuddered and wrapped her arms around herself. Though Andrew longed to enfold her in his embrace, he could not. Not yet.

"Stay here, Beth. Together we'll keep Dora safe." Alone Beth had few defenses against a bully like Peter Girton, but Andrew doubted the man would threaten another adult male. Bullies preferred to prey on the weak. The solution was simple: Beth had to stay. It was the only answer . . . to so many questions.

But Beth did not agree. As tears streamed down her face, she said, "I can't do that. I can't put you in danger."

Andrew had no fear of physical danger. It was emotional entanglements that he had always avoided. "What if I accept the risk?"

She stared at him, those beautiful green eyes brimming with tears. "I can't let you do that, even though I know why you want to help us."

It was a night for surprises. He hadn't realized that Beth had guessed the turmoil her revelations had caused. For, while there was no denying the horror he felt at the brutality her sister and Dora had endured, Andrew felt as if a burden had been lifted from his soul. Oddly enough, it was a burden he hadn't realized he had been bearing. Now the knowledge that she wasn't a widow, that she had never been married, set his blood to singing with hope for the future. Tonight was not the time to tell her. Beth was not yet ready, and so he asked only, "Why do you think I want to help you?"

Beth's face remained solemn, although her tears had dried. "I know that sometimes Dora reminds you of Mary. It's only natural that you would want to protect her."

Was that the reason? Perhaps it had been at one time, but it was no longer Andrew's primary motivation. He loved Dora. That was true. But the hope that filled him was that Beth would return his love. Andrew could deny it no longer. He loved Beth Simmons with all his heart.

Andrew met her clear gaze and shook his head slightly. The time was not yet right. It was clear that Beth wasn't ready for him to admit that he found her attractive, that he saw her as a woman, not just his housekeeper and assistant. Now that he knew about Lenore, Andrew understood why Beth had often seemed skittish. With her sister's example of an abusive marriage, it was no wonder she feared men. Andrew knew he would have to be patient. He needed to woo Beth slowly and gently, to overcome her fears. Teaching Beth to love would take time and patience. Fortunately, patience was a lesson Andrew had learned many years ago.

"I do care about Dora," he said with a gentle smile. Leaning closer to Beth, he continued. "It's not just Dora, though. I want to keep both of you safe."

And then, moving as slowly as he would if he were approaching a wounded animal, he raised his hand to her cheek.

# Chapter Eighteen

He touched her!

Beth stood under the apple tree, her face raised to the sky. The full moon cast long shadows on the grass, reminding her that this was not a night for fugitives. Was it only a few hours ago that she had planned to flee with Dora? How much had changed!

He touched her!

Beth raised her hand to her cheek. Not even the westerly breeze could cool her face or draw away the blood that still heated her cheeks. How could it be that Andrew's touch, as gentle as a mother's caress, as soft as a piece of down, could have branded her as surely as Peter's fists had marked Silver's jaw? Andrew had done no more than place his hand on her cheek, stroking it with his fingertips the way Beth had once stroked a piece of velvet. But velvet was an inanimate object, unable to react, while her skin had given an immediate response. She had felt the blood rush to her face, and even now, her cheeks tingled.

Beth leaned against the tree, savoring the feel of rough bark beneath her fingertips. Andrew's fingertips, firmer and rougher than hers, had wrought the most exquisite pleasure as they traced the contours of her face. And the pleasure he ignited had not been confined to her cheeks. As his fingers moved, the blood they heated coursed through her body, sending a warm glow all the way to the tips of her toes.

What would happen if he touched other parts of her body? Beth felt a flush of embarrassment color her cheeks. How could she be so wanton? Ladies didn't harbor thoughts like that! She never had before, and she most certainly never would again. It was simply that today's extraordinary events had temporarily destroyed her common sense. This odd feeling and that unprecedented curiosity were aberrations. They would vanish with the dawn. But the magic would not. Oh, how she hoped it would not.

Though she could not forget the horror of Silver's suffering, Beth felt as if a heavy burden had been lifted from her. Like the slaves who traveled the invisible Railroad, she could now breathe the sweet smell of freedom. The chains her lies had forged were sundered, replaced by a heady sense of liberation. Her fears remained, but they no longer weighed on her like a yoke.

It helped, oh, yes it helped, to share those fears with Andrew. Until tonight Beth had not realized the power of confiding in a friend. Though she and Lenore had shared their dreams, they had never spoken of the horrors that marred their childhood. Would their lives have been different if they had? Beth wasn't sure whether Lenore would have chosen a different path if she had confided in her. All she knew was that her own worries were greatly diminished since she had shared them with Andrew. How she wished she could have given Lenore that same wondrous feeling that she was not alone! Beth raised her eyes to the sky again and smiled, hoping her sister was looking down at her. *I love you, Lenore,* she thought.

"You should be sleeping."

Beth gasped. The soft grass had muffled Andrew's footsteps, and she had been so lost in her thoughts that she had not heard even the rustle of his clothing.

"I'm not tired. So much has happened today. There was so much to think about that I knew I wouldn't sleep. I couldn't stay indoors." The words poured forth, almost without her volition. She was babbling, trying but failing to mask her confusion. Why, oh, why, was her heart beating so quickly?

Andrew was standing close enough that he could touch her. Would he touch her? *Oh, please!* Beth's face burned in anticipation. Surely he couldn't see that. She lowered her gaze, lest Andrew read the longing in her eyes. The expression she had seen in his made her pulse race. Never before had a man looked at her with such warmth and tenderness.

The leaves rustled; an owl hooted; Andrew said nothing. At last Beth, unable to bear the silence any longer, said, "It's such a beautiful night."

"You're beautiful." Andrew's voice was low but fervent, sending a shiver down Beth's spine and more heat to her face. She turned, hoping the tree would shade her blush.

"No one ever called me beautiful before," she confessed.

In the moonlight, she saw Andrew shake his head slightly. "I find that difficult to believe. Some women are beautiful on the inside; others are beautiful on the outside. But you, Beth, are beautiful everywhere."

Her face burned, and she raised both hands to her cheeks to cool them and cover her embarrassment. "Oh, Andrew!" she cried. His words touched her soul and brought the same wondrous warmth to her heart that his fingers had wrought on her skin. It was magic.

Slowly, as if he had all the time in the world, Andrew reached for her hands and drew them away from her face. "Beautiful," he said softly. The evening breeze wafted Andrew's faint citrus scent toward her. Beth inhaled deeply, savoring the moment. Tomorrow, when reality returned, she wanted to remember every detail.

Slowly, Andrew raised his hands and cupped her face, his fingers resting motionless against her cheeks for a long moment, a moment when she dared not breathe. When his hands began to trace the outline of her jaw, she shuddered from sheer pleasure. Who would have thought that a man's touch could be so gentle, so tender?

Slowly, he closed the distance between them, his gaze holding hers while the corners of his mouth tilted upwards. He was only an inch away, so close that she could feel the warmth of his breath on her face. Beth's heart began to pound. He moved closer still.

"Beautiful," he said as his lips touched hers. It was the softest of kisses, a gentle exploration as his mouth moved to learn the shape of hers. It lasted mere seconds, and yet when his lips relinquished hers, leaving cool air in their place, Beth felt bereft. Never in her wildest flights of imagination or her most fanciful dreams had she conjured anything so wonderful.

"Oh, Andrew!"

"What's so urgent?" As soon as Andrew entered his office, David closed the door.

Andrew sank into one of the chairs and stretched his legs in front of him. Lord, he was tired! A physician was supposed to be able to survive on little sleep, and he'd done so for years, but last night had been more exhausting than any house call or even his Railroad deliveries. He was more than physically tired this afternoon; he was emotionally drained. Andrew had spent the night thinking about Beth's revelations, alternately rejoicing that she was not mourning a beloved husband and railing at the horrible deeds Peter had committed.

The day was warm and sunny, the perfect weather seeming to mock his turmoil. As the morning had passed, Andrew had found it difficult to concentrate on his patients, and so he'd sent David a message. He needed his friend's advice.

Andrew nodded when David offered him a drink. Though whiskey solved no problems, it might dull the edge of his fears. That was why he had insisted Beth drink it last night.

"I've got a problem," he said bluntly when the young attorney handed him a glass. Something in his voice must have told David how serious Andrew considered his problem for instead of sitting across the desk from him, David took the chair next to Andrew. Somehow controlling his normal fidgetiness, David sat quietly, not even fingering his moustache.

As he explained the threat Peter Girton presented, Andrew watched David's expression change from mild interest to fury. How well he understood his friend's anger! "I want to make sure the bastard can't hurt either of them," Andrew concluded.

David took a long swallow of his drink before he replied. "It sounds like the man's a bully," he said, his voice suffused with the barely controlled fury Andrew had seen reflected on his face. "I've met enough of them to know you can't stop their violence. They take pleasure in tormenting anyone who's weaker."

Andrew shook his head. That wasn't the primary problem. "I'm not worried about Beth and Dora's physical safety. I can take care of that." He clenched his glass so tightly that the ridges scored his fingers. "I need you to make sure I have the law behind me . . . whatever I do." He wouldn't tell David the fantasies he had entertained about torturing Peter Girton or how he planned to break his Hippocratic oath to cause no harm the very instant he set eyes on the man.

"He's the girl's father." The sound of David's glass being plunked onto the desk belied the lawyer's calm voice. "As such he has legal rights. I'd like to tell you otherwise, but there's not much you can do unless he relinquishes them."

"Then he'll relinquish them." Andrew rose to his feet. "Draw up the papers and find the bastard."

"What the . . ." Wayne's eyes widened. If he hadn't been so angry, Peter might have laughed at the shock he saw on the man's face. As it was, he had no patience for his whining accomplice.

"What do you think it looks like?" he demanded. "I shaved off my whiskers." And managed to cut his cheek in the process.

Wayne stared, his light blue eyes filled with a curiosity that annoyed Peter even more than his stinging cheek. "Why'd you do a fool thing like that? You had fine whiskers."

Damn right he had. Peter's beard had been thick and dark, not like that miserable excuse for a goatee that Wayne sported. He hadn't wanted to sacrifice it, but Peter's instincts had told him he needed to be less conspicuous. It had felt good—powerful good—to teach that old whore a lesson. Still, he had to be careful now. Silver's man had fists Peter didn't want to meet again.

"Why do you think I shaved it?" When Wayne had no answer, Peter said, "Hell, man, it's summer. Reckon you wouldn't know it, but a beard like mine gets mighty hot."

Wayne nodded. The man was dumber than his shotgun

and of less use. "So when we gonna catch ourselves some runaways?" he asked in that whining tone that Peter hated.

Peter glanced at his reflection in the cracked mirror. He sure looked different without those whiskers. "I been thinkin', Wayne, that maybe we oughta change our plans. Looks to me like we ain't never gonna get rich finding darkies."

Wayne nodded. Of course he would. The man couldn't find a slave if he was standing in front of him. "So what're we gonna do?" he whined.

"I figure we'll find ourselves some rich man and help ourselves to some of his gold. What d'you think, Wayne?"

Wayne smacked his lips. "I think it's a fine plan. A mighty fine plan."

Andrew knew his feet were dragging as he entered the house. It had taken David a week to locate Peter and set up the meeting. For Andrew, it had been one of the strangest weeks of his life. His mood had been like a pendulum, swinging from the undeniable joy of being with Beth and watching her trust unfold like the petals of a spring flower to the fear that he would be unable to stop Peter from somehow finding Beth and Dora. Those fears would waken Andrew in the middle of the night, filling him with terror that only the memory of Beth's smile and the growing warmth he had seen in her eyes could banish.

When he had left the house today, not even the steady rain could quench his optimism. Peter would agree. Any rational man would. Two hours later, Andrew had to admit that his hopes had been ill-founded.

He shook his umbrella fiercely, wishing he could shake off his fears as easily as he did the raindrops. How could he tell Beth that he had failed? He had promised her that he would protect her and Dora. Unfortunately, so far he had been a dismal failure. Andrew thrust the umbrella into the brass stand. He could take the coward's way and go straight to his office without seeing her, but Andrew was no coward. Besides, that would only postpone the inevitable. Somehow, he would have to tell her. He marched toward the library, where he knew she would be with Dora.

Beth rose to greet him. Though she smiled, Andrew noticed that her face was paler than usual and that she kept her hand on Dora's shoulder as if to comfort her.

"He refused, didn't he?" Beth's question told him she had read his hesitation and interpreted it correctly.

"Yes." There was no point in denying it. Andrew bent down to give Dora a quick hug, then nodded when Beth suggested she leave Dora with Mrs. Kane. "I tell you, Beth," he said when she returned and they'd seated themselves in the deep leather chairs, "I don't understand it. He doesn't have the slightest love for Dora. That much was obvious." Peter Girton's lips had been curved into a sneer the entire time that David had spoken of Dora, and the few times he had referred to his daughter, Girton had called her "the brat."

Beth nodded as if Andrew's revelation came as no surprise. Though her face was outwardly calm, she gripped the chair arm. Andrew laid his hand on top of hers, smiling when she turned it over so that he could hold it.

"Peter's horrible," she said softly.

The man himself had been a surprise. Beth had given him no physical description, but from his behavior, Andrew had expected a monster. Though he had no doubt that the man was indeed a beastly creature, on the surface he appeared to be a normal human being. Even one many women would consider attractive, for his features could have graced a statue, and the combination of his dark brown hair and blue eyes was striking. It was only when he opened his mouth that his true character was apparent. When Girton had launched into his diatribe about the uselessness of females in general and his wife and daughter in particular, Andrew had suppressed a shudder. Thank God Beth hadn't overheard some of her brother-in-law's accusations!

"Yes, he is horrible," Andrew agreed. He squeezed Beth's hand, hoping that she would find some measure of comfort in his touch. If only he could promise her and Dora protection!

When Beth's eyes sparkled with tears, Andrew wasn't certain whether they were tears of sorrow for the love Dora had never known, or anger over Girton's evil nature. She swallowed deeply, then said, "Peter never did love Dora. Lenore said he was furious when she was born. He told her he had no use for a daughter, and didn't Lenore know that she was supposed to bear him a son?"

Having met the man, Andrew could visualize the scene. "I thought he would be glad to be rid of the burden of a child. David outlined his responsibilities as a parent, thinking that would convince him, but all he did was laugh. He said he knew how to take care of a child."

Beth shuddered, and Andrew suspected her imagination had conjured the same pictures his had. "Now you understand why I'm so worried about Dora's safety," she said.

Though the door was closed, they heard Dora's laughter. Andrew tightened his grip on Beth's hand. Nothing must ever be allowed to turn that laughter into tears.

"I wish I knew why Peter seemed so familiar," Andrew said. He rose and began to pace, as if that would jog his memory. "It's odd. There's something about him that seems so familiar, but I know I've never seen him before." Girton's was not a face one would forget.

Beth looked up, a thoughtful expression in those lovely green eyes. How Andrew wished they weren't having this conversation! If only Peter had agreed. Better yet, if only Peter did not exist.

"It's probably Dora's resemblance to him that makes him seem familiar," Beth suggested.

Andrew shook his head vehemently. "Absolutely not! I saw nothing in him that reminded me of Dora. It's something else, something that keeps eluding me." He frowned. "For some reason, whatever it is, it seems important. I just wish I could remember what it was."

Andrew stared out the window at the raindrops that dripped from the apple tree's leaves. Had it been only a week since he had stood with Beth under that tree and felt the sweetness of her lips beneath his? His pulse raced at the memory, then slowed again. He wasn't worthy of Beth. Thus far he had not kept his promise, and Peter's menace remained an ever-present threat.

Andrew heard Beth's footsteps as she approached the window. When she laid her hand on his arm, he turned, trying not to gasp. Beth's face was colorless, and her eyes . . . her eyes. Not even on the night when she had told him about Silver's beating had he seen such anguish.

"What's wrong, Beth?" He laid his hand over hers. Though he wanted to take her into his arms and hold her close, something in Beth's expression told him she wasn't ready.

"Andrew, don't you see?" Her voice trembled with emotion, and tears threatened to tumble from her eyes. "It's the only way. Dora and I have to leave."

Andrew tried to swallow but could not, for fear gripped him, holding his throat in a vise and squeezing his chest so tightly he could hardly breathe. Beth leave? It was unthinkable. It would be as bad as the night Mary died—worse, because this time he would be losing two people he loved. Even worse, he would have to live with the constant fear that they had not run far enough or fast enough to elude Peter.

"Don't you trust me?" Andrew asked, fear making his voice harsh. "I promised I would keep you safe, and I will."

If only he knew how.


"It's supposed to be a fine evening."

Beth looked up, startled. This was the first time Andrew had come into the kitchen, where she and Dora normally played between supper and Dora's bedtime.

"Would you care to take a stroll with me?" he asked when he had given Dora her ritual hug. Each day it seemed that Dora was aware of new sounds. Though Beth doubted she had any memory of the operation that had restored her hearing, she appeared even more devoted to Andrew, making Beth wonder whether somehow she knew that the doctor was responsible for the miracle. Tonight Andrew set Dora back on her feet and turned his attention to Beth.

"A stroll?" she asked.

As Andrew smiled and nodded, Beth felt the oddest urge

to touch the cleft in his chin. She lowered her head to hide her confusion. Why was Andrew inviting her to spend the evening with him? They had never done that before. Beth knew it was unlikely he would have any Railroad deliveries for the next few days, since the moon was still too bright to make them safely, but surely it wasn't simply boredom that had precipitated his invitation. Though she had tried not to assign too much importance to it, Beth knew Andrew had treated her differently since *that* night. The day had a date, but in Beth's mind it was always *that* night, the night she had told Andrew the truth, the night he had kissed her.

Would he kiss her again? She felt her cheeks flame. Did she want him to?

"Yes," she said, not sure which question she was answering.

An hour later, they descended the front steps, Beth's hand resting in the crook of Andrew's elbow, where he had placed it. The sun was setting, casting a rosy glow over the horizon, and the breeze from the lake stirred the leaves on the elms. Tonight Delaware Avenue was deserted. Though families occasionally strolled, and a few carriages would pass by on a normal evening, Andrew appeared to have chosen a quiet time for their walk. Beth was glad, for the deserted street made her feel that she and Andrew were in a world of their own.

Beth marveled at the difference that a few months had made. The first time she had walked on Delaware, it had been winter. She had been exhausted from carrying Dora through the snow; she'd been apprehensive over meeting the doctor; and she had been more than a little awed by the beautiful houses. Today the city by the lake sparkled; the breeze was warm; and though she admired the homes, she was no longer intimidated by their grandeur.

"This wind would be good for sailing," Andrew told her. His words were commonplace. There was no reason her pulse should race, and yet it did, for the very fact that they were walking and speaking of ordinary things like two . . . two friends . . . was a novel and exciting experience.

"I didn't know you sailed." There was so much she did

not know about this man. As the breeze stirred his hair, Beth reflected how unusual it was that Andrew did not use Macassar. Most men preferred to oil their hair, but Andrew did not. Though she wondered why, Beth knew it would be a long time—if ever—before she felt comfortable enough with Andrew to ask him such a personal question.

Andrew chuckled. "I don't sail yet, although not for lack of trying. David's teaching me." As Andrew stopped, Beth saw the twinkle in his blue eyes. "I give the man a lot of credit for only wincing when I grounded his boat on a sandbar. But I'm improving enough that maybe you and Dora would like to go out with me."

They crossed Mohawk. Though Beth thought Andrew might turn left toward the lake, they continued north on Delaware.

"That sounds enjoyable." Beth wasn't sure which thought she found more appealing, sailing or being with Andrew. The combination promised to be wonderful. "I've never been on a boat," she admitted. "The neighbors' pond was big enough for a rowboat, but they didn't have one." Not to mention that there had been no time for frivolities like sailing.

Beth heard the steady clip-clop of a horse's hooves and the faint squeak that told her a carriage had turned the corner. Though she kept smiling, she felt a sense of loss that their private kingdom had been invaded.

Andrew's grin was warm and conspiratorial. He was, it appeared, unfazed by the approaching coach. "To tell you the truth, I never thought I'd enjoy a boat. Until David convinced me to go out on his, the only one I had been on was to cross the ocean—and that was an experience I had no desire to repeat."

Though he laughed, Beth could feel the muscles of his arm tighten. The crossing must have been terrible if he was still reacting to it so many years later. She had read that steerage was a horrible way to travel. Andrew, of course, had not endured that misery. The problem must have been the weather. "I've heard that even the nicest cabins are unpleasant in a storm," she said.

"And we had two." The carriage rolled closer.

"Oh, Andrew!" Beth tried to imagine how dreadful a storm-filled voyage must have seemed to a small child.

He placed his hand on top of hers and drew her to the side of the street so that the coach could pass. "I preferred the way you said that the last time."

The blood rushed to Beth's face as she realized that the last time had been when he had kissed her. "Oh, Andrew!" she said, mortified that he would remind her of what must have seemed a juvenile reaction to his embrace.

He laughed, his unhappy memories seemingly banished. "Those are just two words, but you've found so many ways to say them. I wonder." He paused, considering. "If I tease you, will you find another?"

Beth was spared the need to reply, for the carriage slowed, then stopped next to them. Andrew raised his hat in greeting, while Beth nodded and smiled at the passenger in the back of the buggy.

"Oh, Doctor, it's so good to see you!" The beautifully dressed woman leaned over the side of the carriage. Beth told herself it was uncharitable to think that Lucinda Fields chose that particular pose to give Andrew a better view of the expanse of creamy flesh that rose from her bodice. The woman's lilac silk frock was exquisitely cut. In comparison, Beth's muslin, which had seemed so attractive an hour ago, felt dowdy.

"Good evening, Miss Fields." Andrew's greeting was polite, but devoid of the warmth that his patient put into hers.

"Good . . ."

As Beth started to speak, Lucinda cut her short, saying, "I do hope you'll pay us a call, Doctor." She directed her words to Andrew, as if Beth were invisible. And in Lucinda's world, she would be invisible, a servant whose role was to blend into the background, to be seen and heard only when her employer demanded a service.

Seemingly unaware of the snub, Andrew raised one eyebrow. "Is your mother ill?"

Lucinda waved her hand, releasing the heavy scent that she preferred. "Oh, dear me, no. I meant a *social* call. We do so enjoy your company." She smiled and fluttered her eyelashes, then glared at Beth's hand, which remained on Andrew's arm.

Beth could not remember when she had been in such an awkward situation. She tried to pull her hand away, but Andrew placed his on top of hers in an oddly proprietary gesture.

"I believe you've met Mrs. Simmons, haven't you?" His voice was smooth, with an underlying hint of steel.

Lucinda nodded briefly. "I do hope we'll see you soon," she said, her smile a little less bright than before. Once again Beth had no doubt that the words were directed only at Andrew.

As the coach rattled down the street toward the Fields residence, Beth said softly, "You should have let me leave."

"Why?"

"Because Miss Fields will tell everyone you were seen walking with me."

"And is that a crime?"

"Oh, Andrew, you know I'm not part of your social circle. It's one thing for me to work in your office. This is different. Your patients will be horrified at the thought that you were observed in public with a servant."

The muscles in his arm tightened again, as they had when he had spoken of the voyage from Europe.

"Let me worry about my patients. Don't you know that I'd rather be with you than any other woman I know?"

He took her hand in his and raised it to his lips. Slowly, in full view of anyone who might be passing by, he pressed a kiss on the palm of her hand.

"Oh, Beth," he said with a soft laugh.

"Is that Mrs. Simmons?" David's brown eyes sparkled with interest as he slouched on one of the chairs in Andrew's examining room. As she did most days, Beth had greeted Andrew's patients and ushered them into the examining room, retrieving their files for him. She stayed while he treated some patients, but something in David's expression made Andrew shake his head slightly in a signal that Beth should leave them alone.

When the door closed, David grinned. "You didn't tell me she was such a beauty. It's too bad she's still in mourning."

"What does Mrs. Simmons's mourning have to do with you?" Andrew made a conscious effort not to clench his fists.

David studied his knuckles for a moment before he raised apparently guileless eyes to meet Andrew's gaze. "It's simple," he said. "If I could find a woman like that, I'd marry her."

Andrew felt his jaw tighten. "I assume you had a reason for coming here." *And it probably wasn't to have me punch your face,* he added silently.

"Sure did." David's grin said he knew how much he had annoyed Andrew and that he had enjoyed doing it. He sobered quickly as he continued. "I tried to find Peter Girton to offer him the money. Trouble is, he hasn't been back to his farm in weeks, and his cronies say he hasn't been seen in his favorite taverns, either."

This was not what Andrew wanted to hear. He would not rest easily until the threat to Beth and Dora was gone. "Damn! I had hoped we'd have everything settled by now." Andrew was certain that he could use Girton's obvious greed to his advantage. Surely a generous financial settlement would convince the man to entrust Dora to her aunt's care.

"They think he hides out somewhere in the area, but if anyone knows where, they're not saying. All they'll tell me is that he's got a reputation for being mean."

Andrew nodded. "That's the reason I want to get him away from Dora."

He and David talked for a few minutes longer, discussing ways to find Peter. Then David rose and walked toward the door. "Don't underestimate the danger," he said as he opened the door.

That was one mistake Andrew had no intention of making. "I know. I'd do anything to keep her safe."

# *Chapter Nineteen*

It was going to be another scorching day. Beth leaned her arm out the small window, searching for the breeze that normally made mornings pleasant, even in the midst of summer's heat. But this dawn was still, the air so thick with moisture, that she was surprised she couldn't wring it out like a dishrag. On the other side of the room, Dora turned restlessly on her pallet, the loose tendrils of her hair curled as tightly as a spring. For the past three nights while the heat raged, the child had slept fitfully, waking Beth with frequent demands for a cool drink. Then when the temperatures dropped just before dawn, Dora would fall back to sleep, waking several hours later, apparently refreshed.

Beth wished she herself was so resilient. Although Dora greeted each day with enthusiasm, once wakened, Beth would remember the letter she had received and wonder how she should reply to it. It seemed like years since she had written to Emma Willard, asking for her assistance in finding Dora a safe haven. Miss Willard had promised to help Beth, and she had. Indeed, her former teacher had done even more than Beth had asked. That was part of the problem. Now Beth was faced with a dilemma. Should she do what her mind told her was right, or should she follow her heart? A month ago the decision might have been easy; today it was proving to be anything but.

The sleepless nights were taking their toll on her, leaving Beth's eyes ringed with deep circles. If nights were difficult, days were worse. Fatigue and worry frazzled her, while the heat exacerbated the situation, for everyone was short-tempered, ready to snap at the slightest provocation. Even normally placid Mrs. Kane had ordered Dora out of the kitchen when she spilled a glass of milk.

Beth poured water into the basin and began her morning ablutions. Today would be different, or so she hoped, for today was the day Andrew had arranged for their sailing excursion. She brushed her hair, parting it neatly in the middle and securing the chignon at the nape of her neck. Her black snood would keep the errant locks from flying into her face.

Beth smiled. Andrew was so thoughtful. Not only had he offered her and Dora a special experience, but he had also given the servants the day off. Mrs. Kane had prepared a picnic for them last night, and Andrew had assured Roberts that he would care for the horse when they returned. Everyone would enjoy the holiday.

When she finished her own toilette, Beth wakened Dora.

"We're going to the lake," Beth said as she dressed her. Though she doubted the child understood her, Dora seemed to sense her excitement, for she wiggled more than normal and refused to let Beth lace her boots. It was only when they reached the first floor and Andrew frowned slightly at Dora's feet that she stood still long enough for Beth to fasten her boots.

To Beth's surprise, Andrew had harnessed the horse to the buckboard rather than the barouche that he used for house calls and his Railroad deliveries. "I thought Dora would enjoy being outside," he explained as he lifted her onto the front seat of the open carriage and helped Beth mount. For once the child sat calmly, her eyes wide with curiosity as Andrew flicked the reins. It was, Beth realized, probably the first time Dora had been in a vehicle. When the wagon began to move, Dora giggled, then slid closer to Andrew, wedging herself between his arm and his body.

"Come to Mama," Beth said, but as she reached for the little girl, Dora snuggled closer to Andrew. He settled Dora into the crook of his elbow and gave Beth a reassuring smile as if to remind her that Dora had nothing to fear from him. Beth returned the smile. God willing, Dora would never fear a man. If that happened, Beth would know that she had fulfilled her promise to Lenore.

Andrew kept the horse moving at a slow but steady pace,

and Beth assumed he was trying to both prolong Dora's enjoyment of the ride and avoid startling her with speed. The child stared at the horse, smiling when he tossed his head to dislodge a swarm of flies, clapping her hands when he swished his tail. Beth found herself grinning as she watched the world through Dora's eyes. How wondrous to be young and innocent!

Beth had considered that their route might take them near Canal Street. Though she had heeded Silver's admonition not to return until they were sure Peter would not harm her, the enforced absence saddened Beth. She missed Silver's advice and her friendship. Now more than ever, she wanted to talk to Silver about Andrew and the strange feelings his smile and his touch evoked.

They were traveling south when Andrew turned onto Erie, a route that would bypass Canal. Knowing it was the safer direction, Beth told herself she was being foolish to long for a glimpse of Silver. She would see her friend again when the danger was gone. Meanwhile, she would enjoy the outing.

Andrew flicked the reins again, and Dora giggled. In the distance Beth heard another carriage, the horse's rapid steps announcing that this driver was in a hurry. As the wagon began to overtake them, Dora turned and grinned. Beth's heart skipped a beat at the realization of what Dora's actions meant.

"She heard the horses!" There was no mistaking the pride in Andrew's voice or the smile that lit his face.

Beth swallowed deeply, wondering if she would ever take Dora's restored hearing for granted. "Every day she seems to hear more sounds." The carriage was in front of them now, and Dora stared raptly, her head moving in apparent time with the horse's steps. "It's a miracle, Andrew."

He tightened his grip on the reins, drawing Dora closer to him. "The success we've had with Dora makes me realize why I became a doctor," he admitted.

Beth raised one brow at the surprise she heard in his voice. "I thought you told me your purpose was to become wealthy." It had been a long time since Beth had believed that to be true. The question was, had Andrew ever believed it, or was it part of the role he played to camouflage his Railroad activities? She had thought the latter. Now she wasn't sure.

"Making a lot of money was the reason I studied medicine," he insisted. "Now, I'm not so certain it's the reason I continue. Having you and Dora here has made me view things differently."

Beth understood why he would feel that way about Dora. The girl's case had been challenging, and it had given Andrew a way to demonstrate his skill. But Beth had no idea why he had included her in his statement. Though she longed to know how her presence had changed Andrew's perspective, she was unwilling to pry. If he wanted to tell her, he would.

When they arrived at the lake, Dora's eyes widened again as she gave Beth a questioning look. Beth had seen Lake Erie before, but she never failed to be thrilled by the sight of the seemingly endless water and the waves that crested and broke on the shore. This was not like the neighbors' pond.

"It's water," Beth told Dora. "Like your bath." Though she was still uncertain how much Dora heard and understood, she continued to speak to her as if she had full hearing.

While Andrew hitched the horse, Beth and Dora walked slowly toward the shore. Dora stopped occasionally to touch the sand, and once she took a handful, letting the grains sift through her fingers. When her hand was once more empty, she looked up at Beth, a wide grin lighting her face. But when they reached the water's edge, she stopped, burying her face in Beth's skirts.

"It's okay, honey," Beth said, stroking the top of Dora's head. "Those are just waves." Beth knelt on the sand and extended her hand, letting the tide lap over it. A few birds walked through the water, thrusting their long beaks into the wet sand as they searched for food. For a long moment, Dora did nothing more than watch. Then, her lips pursed in obvious concentration, she stretched her hand onto the sand and waited. The first time the water touched it, she recoiled, but then she moved her hand back.

"The next thing you know, she'll be a water nymph."

Beth turned, then gasped as she confronted a pair of very bare, very masculine legs. Andrew had removed his boots and rolled up his trousers so that he could wade into the water. It was sensible, of course. He didn't mean to shock her. But he had. Though she had seen his limbs when he had been wounded and burning with fever, that was different. He had been a patient then. Today he was a man. Beth darted another look at him. His legs were shaped like hers, and yet they were different. They were larger, more heavily muscled, and covered with pale blond hair. Would that hair feel crisp and wiry like the mat on his chest?

Swallowing deeply to cover her confusion, Beth reached for Dora and drew the child to her feet as she herself rose. At least now she could smile at Andrew's face and ignore the exposed flesh.

"Ready?" he asked.

*Ready for what?* For a second Beth had no idea what Andrew was asking. *The sailboat. That's what he meant.* She nodded.

"I'll take her first." Andrew reached for Dora, gathering her into his arms and carrying her to the small boat that was now only a few yards from the shore. Beth watched as he moved, wading slowly but confidently toward the sailboat. Though she saw only his back, there was something about the set of his shoulders that told Beth he considered Dora precious. When he had placed the child in the bow, he returned, his smile jaunty, his face relaxed. Before Beth knew what he intended, Andrew had scooped her into his arms and was striding toward the boat.

"I can wade," she protested, trying to ignore the strange sensations that were coursing through her. Strong arms cradled her so close to him that she could hear his heart beat, smell the faint aroma of coffee on his breath, and feel the ripple of his muscles. She hated it when men touched her. Hadn't she spent her whole life willing herself to show no feeling, to freeze when a man came too close? Why, then, did Andrew's arms engender a warmth that exceeded the sun's blaze, a warmth that was so unexpected, so pleasant, that she wanted it to continue forever?

This was like the night he had kissed her. The feelings were so wonderful that Beth thought she was dreaming. It wasn't a dream, though, for no dream she had ever experienced had felt this good.

When they reached the boat and he released her, setting her carefully on one of the seats, Beth felt a sense of loss just as she had when their kiss had ended. For the few moments it had taken to wade through the water, the outside world had disappeared and she had felt safe. Now she was back to reality.

"Mama." Beth wondered if she would ever get used to hearing Dora call her that. In the days following her surgery, the little girl had started making new noises, trying to imitate adult speech. Though most of it had been incomprehensible, the day she had first said "Ma," Beth had thought her heart would burst with joy. If only Lenore had been there to share the moment!

As the child stretched her arms toward Beth, she reached for her. Judging from her wary expression, Dora was puzzled and more than a little frightened by the boat's rocking.

"Boat," Beth said, pointing to the two sides and the sail that flapped in the breeze. Though the boat rocked with the waves, Beth wasn't sure how they were going to travel any distance. The sail appeared to be useless.

"Bo." A grin lit Dora's face when Beth smiled.

"Close enough for today," she told Andrew, who was tugging on a rope.

And then they were sailing. By some magic, the sail filled with wind and the boat began to gather speed. Dora giggled and squirmed; Beth simply sighed. She had never dreamt that the simple act of moving over the water could be so wonderful. Was this how birds felt when they flew?

"You misled me," she announced as she watched the shore, amazed at how quickly they were moving away from it. "You told me you were a poor sailor. The evidence, as one of my teachers at the seminary used to say, suggests otherwise."

Andrew tightened one rope, watching the sail slacken, then fill with wind. When the boat turned and they were sailing parallel to the shore, he said, "I'm still learning. It's fairly easy in a light breeze like this one, but I wouldn't have risked bringing you and Dora out if it were windy. Everything happens so much faster then."

Though Beth knew little about boats, she surmised this was one of the smallest. Designed for pleasure excursions rather than extended voyages, it reminded her of a rowboat with a mast and sails attached. Beth and Dora sat on the back bench facing Andrew. Her initial fears overcome, Dora slid out of Beth's arms and clambered to the other bench.

"Come to Mama." Beth held out her arms. Though Andrew hadn't repulsed Dora, she didn't want the child to distract him.

"I don't mind," he said. He gave Dora a bright smile and settled her close enough to the center of the bench that Beth could reach her. It was a thoughtful gesture, and one that set Beth's heart to pounding again. Why had she ever believed Andrew to be like her father and Peter? He was not a brute. No, indeed. He was kind and affectionate toward Dora, behaving the way Beth believed fathers should. He was warm and caring, not the Ice Doctor she had once believed him to be. Had he changed, Beth wondered, or had he always been this way? It was possible she had been too blinded by her own past to see Andrew's true character. She had viewed him as a man and had thought all men were like her father and Peter. Was that why she had thought Andrew cold? Had he changed, or had she? Beth wished she knew.

By the time they returned to the shore, Dora's eyelids were beginning to droop. The day had been more exciting than normal; no wonder the child was tired.

"Shall we go back now?" Andrew asked.

Beth shook her head, unwilling to let their excursion end. "We still have dinner," she said. She spread the carriage robe on the sand and opened the picnic hamper. Mrs. Kane had outdone herself, with Beth's favorite fried chicken, the soft rolls that Dora preferred to ordinary bread, and a peach pie for dessert. Though it was delicious and the three of them ate more than their normal portions, Beth suspected she would have enjoyed stale bread and milk. Had it been just this morning that she had felt out of sorts? Not once while they had been in the boat had she thought about the letter from Mrs. Wilcox. She wouldn't think of it now and let the decision she faced spoil her happiness.

"It's been a perfect day," Beth told Andrew when they had repacked the hamper and Dora had fallen asleep, curled on one corner of the carriage robe. Beth and Andrew sat facing the lake, watching the waves continue to curl and break, then recede in an endless pattern. The faint tang of seaweed mingled with the aroma of fried chicken and peaches, while the drone of a few lazy insects was punctuated by the waves' lapping. Beth was certain she had never seen or smelled or heard anything so wonderful.

"Dora looked so happy."

"She's a lovable little girl," Andrew said with a soft smile for the sleeping child. "I don't understand why . . . No!" He broke off his words and frowned. "We won't talk about him today."

But the specter of Peter had been raised, and with that, Beth's impending decision loomed heavily over her. She needed to tell Andrew. This time she would not flee in the darkness of night. "We owe you so much," Beth said, remembering the day she had overheard Andrew tell David that he would do anything to keep Dora safe. He had kept his promise . . . so far. But, though she wanted to believe she and Dora were safe, Beth was not as confident as Andrew that Peter no longer posed a threat.

Andrew had been leaning on one elbow, apparently as relaxed as Dora. As Beth's words registered, he sat up, raised one brow, and gave Beth a long, appraising look. "That sounds like the preface to an announcement that you're leaving." The lump that formed in Beth's stomach owed nothing to Mrs. Kane's chicken. "Does this have something to do with the letter you received from Mrs. Wilcox's Academy?"

There were, it appeared, no secrets.

Beth nodded. Though this was not the time or place she would have chosen, Andrew had to know what she was considering. "I was looking for a safe place for Dora to live. Emma Willard suggested Mrs. Wilcox's school." Though the thought of sending Dora to Rochester had wrenched Beth's heart, it was better than living in constant fear for her. "Now it seems they have an unexpected opening for a teacher. One of their instructors eloped this summer and won't be returning, so Mrs. Wilcox has offered me her position."

And that was the dilemma. Mrs. Wilcox's Academy was precisely the type of school where Beth had dreamed of teaching. Accepting this position would mean that not only would she not face a separation from Dora, but that also one of her dreams could come true.

"I see." Andrew's blue eyes were solemn, though his voice remained as calm as if they were discussing the weather. The lump in Beth's stomach grew. Perhaps her decision meant as little to him as the direction of the wind. "What have you decided?"

"I haven't made a decision." When he was being so cool, how could she explain the torment the letter had given her, the hours she had spent in mental debates, never able to resolve the dilemma?

Andrew turned away from her and stared at the waves. "Go there, if that's what you want." She wished she could see his eyes. His lips were set in a straight line, neither approving nor disapproving. If only she could see his eyes, she would know if her decision was as insignificant as he made it appear.

"The year isn't over," she reminded him. That had been part of her dilemma, the fact that she had not fulfilled her half of the bargain, but it was only part—a small part.

Andrew shrugged in a gesture of apparent nonchalance. "I'll call the debt paid, if that's what you want."

Was it? That was the question that caused her to pace the floor at night and that haunted her during the day. A few weeks ago, she would have answered the question easily. Yes, she wanted to teach; yes, she wanted to leave. Now, she was not so certain. Though she longed for the challenge of the schoolroom, her heart was filled with another, far more disturbing, longing.

Andrew.

She wasn't sure when it had happened or even how it had happened, but her heart ached at the thought of leaving him. She had once considered him a friend. Beth knew that leaving any friend would be difficult. The truth was that Andrew was not simply a friend, and she could deny it no longer. He was much, much more.

By day he haunted her thoughts, and she found herself making excuses to see him. By night he haunted her dreams, causing her to wake filled with longings. She wanted to be with him, day and night, to see his smile, to hear his voice, to feel his touch. She loved him.

She loved him. How had it happened? *Why* had it happened? What on earth was she going to do now? The very idea of love filled Beth with despair. The poets might rhapsodize over love, but Beth knew better. Look what had happened to her mother and Lenore when they had loved.

What kind of fool did that sawbones and his highfalutin lawyer think he was? Peter glowered as he spurred his horse forward. Idiots! They'd offered that piddling amount and 4thought he was dumb enough to take it. Showed what they knew!

Peter dug his spurs in deeper. It was already hotter than Hades, and he reckoned the day was gonna get even hotter. Course if everything went the way he knew it would, he'd soon have enough money to buy himself a dozen icehouses and a purty woman to cool his skin and warm his blood.

Peter looked around. Those were mighty fine houses. It surely wasn't fair that that brat of his was living in one while he was stuck in that tumbledown shack. Not much longer. Lenore's whelp was gonna be his ticket to money—lots of money.

Imagine those fools thinking he would sell her. Admittedly, the brat wasn't worth much now. She might be when she grew up and filled out a bit. Course that would be a few years, and Peter didn't like the thought of having to feed her until she was big enough to sell into service. Lucky for him, it seemed the doc had peculiar tastes and liked the little ones. Peter had no problem with selling the whelp to that fancy sawbones. Let him do whatever he wanted with her; it would serve her right.

Peter tugged on the reins. Might as well get a good look at the houses. He might be living in one next week. Selling Dora wasn't the problem, but it was downright insulting for them to offer such a paltry sum. No, sirree, they weren't going to get Peter Girton's brat for less than any self-respecting slave owner would offer for one of his weakest runaways. No, sirree. Peter was no fool. He knew what things were worth.

Peter whistled as a woman descended the front steps of one of those big houses. She was one good-looking bitch. Peter shook his head. The doc had more money than he knew what to do with. That was plain to see. He wouldn't be living here if he didn't. It was also plain to see that he was dumb. Why else would he be buying a scrawny female like Dora when he could rent one on Canal Street or, if he played his cards right, get one for free? Dumb.

Peter slowed the horse again. According to Wayne, the house was in the next block on that big square. The doc and the lawyer thought they were smart with their fancy education. Peter hadn't missed the way the lawyer hung his diplomas on the wall. Maybe it was supposed to make him feel bad. Well, it didn't. Peter might not have a sheepskin, but he had something worth a whole lot more. He had smarts, and those smarts told him the good doctor had plenty of money in his house, just waiting for Peter to help himself to it.

Yes, sirree. That was why he had set Wayne to watching the doctor's house. Peter was smart. He knew he couldn't risk Beth seein' him, so he gave Wayne a jug of whiskey and told him to report back when the coast was clear. According to Wayne, the doc had taken the bitch and the brat out in the buckboard, and he'd put a basket in the back. That sounded like they were fixing to be gone awhile. Of course, old Wayne—fool that he was—stopped for another drink on the way back, so now Peter would have to hurry. He'd get Wayne for that, but first he had to settle things with the doctor.

It sure was a fancy house. Peter slammed the door behind him, clomped his feet on the shiny floor, and kicked the wall. Damn, it felt good to leave his mark! If he had more time, he'd really give the doctor something to remember him by. But Peter Girton was no fool. The money was what he needed. He could come back later and take the rest.

The money would be in the doc's office, sitting in a big box right on top of the desk where he could count it every day. Peter was sure of that. That's where he would have put it, if he had it. The doc might be dumb, but he wasn't totally stupid. Peter grinned as he kicked the door to the office. Yes, sirree. The desk was right where he'd figured it would be. Now for the money. He looked around. There was no box on the desk. Nothing under the desk. Nothing in that cabinet.

One more cabinet. That must be where it was. Peter flung the door open. There was nothing there but medicine bottles. He reached his arm out, ready to hurl the colored bottles to the floor. And then he heard the voices. Damn it all! They were back! That useless son of a bitch Wayne had drunk away his time. Peter would fix him. And then he'd come back here. Because the money was here. He knew it.

"I'll carry Dora upstairs."

Beth didn't object. The child was sound asleep. It seemed a shame to waken her to mount the stairs, but she seemed to grow heavier each day, and Beth didn't relish the climb. "She was exhausted from all the excitement. I doubt she'll wake even when I undress her."

Beth led the way up the stairs, lighting a lamp to dispel the shadows of early dusk. As Andrew laid Dora on her pallet, he turned to Beth. "If you're not as tired as she is, I thought we might sit outside for a while. There's a nice breeze."

Beth nodded. She would have gone outside—or any-where—with Andrew, regardless of the weather. "I'd like that." Though she had not resolved her dilemma, she had no desire for the day to end, and Andrew, it seemed, shared her reluctance. Only minutes later, she descended the back stairway. As she reached the second-floor landing, Beth inhaled deeply.

"Andrew!" she cried, fear gripping her and twisting her stomach into knots. "He was here." She raced down the remaining flight, filled with an irrational need to be near Andrew.

He had been waiting in the library, but came rushing into the hallway at the sound of her cries. As if sensing how her legs threatened to buckle, Andrew reached out to steady her. "Who?"

The house was silent save for the muffled tick of the mantel clock, the buzz of nocturnal insects, and Beth's harsh breathing. Though Andrew's arm was comforting, Beth's fears would not be denied.

"Peter!" She shuddered and sniffed again, hoping against hope that her nose would deny what she knew. "I'd recognize that smell anywhere."

Andrew inhaled, then shook his head. "I can't smell anything different." But he clearly believed her, for he kept his arm around her waist and asked where the odor seemed strongest. They walked slowly toward the front of the house, pausing as Beth tried to pinpoint the smell.

"Here." She pointed toward the office door. "It's worse here." As they walked into the examining room, Beth shuddered. If evil had an odor, it would be this one.

Andrew settled Beth into one of the chairs, then walked slowly around the room. "You're right, Beth. Someone was here." As a furrow appeared between his eyes, Beth felt fear, colder than any she had ever known, clench her heart. "I'm sure I left this drawer closed," Andrew said, opening one that was slightly ajar. When he looked inside, he frowned. "Someone has moved my instruments."

The fear intensified, and Beth could feel her body begin to shake. "He came for Dora. I knew it!" Somehow he had learned where they lived. Andrew had said that Peter didn't know his name, but even though Buffalo was a city, Andrew was well known. It wouldn't have been too difficult for Peter to learn his identity. After that, finding him would be simple. Beth gripped the chair.

"Try not to worry." Kneeling in front of Beth, Andrew placed his arms around her waist. "She's safe," he said firmly. "I told you I would keep her safe."

Beth wanted to believe Andrew. The alternatives were too awful to contemplate. "But what about next time? What if you're not here?" Beth knew she could not overpower Peter. Silver's bruises were proof of that.

Andrew placed one hand under Beth's chin, tipping it so that she would meet his gaze. "Roberts will move into the house," he said. "You and Dora will never be alone."

It was a solution, but only a partial one. Beth laid her hands on Andrew's shoulders. "What will we do if he brings a judge? He has the right to take Dora."

Beth could see the indecision in Andrew's eyes, and she sensed that he was facing a dilemma as serious as her decision about Mrs. Wilcox's Academy. He was silent for a long moment. Then he said, "I've thought about that, too. This isn't the way I wanted to ask you, but . . ." He leaned back on his heels so that he could watch her face. "Will you marry me?"

Beth's breath came out in a whoosh, and she felt the blood drain from her face as the room began to spin. Marriage! If only Andrew loved her, it would be the answer to so many problems. She would be with the man she loved, and Dora would be safe, for Beth knew that with David's influence and Andrew's position in society, it was likely a judge would allow her to adopt Dora once she was married.

If only Andrew loved her. But he didn't. Beth knew that he cared for Dora and wanted to protect her. Hadn't he told David he would do anything to keep Dora safe? That anything, it appeared, even extended to marrying a woman he didn't love.

For her part, though Beth would do almost anything for Dora, she would not marry a man who did not love her. She could not risk a marriage like her mother's and Lenore's. What would happen when Dora was old enough that she no longer needed Andrew and he started to resent Beth's presence in his life? What if he tired of Dora and treated her the way Peter had?

For a few months, maybe even a few years, it could be wonderful. And then?

"I'm sorry, Andrew. I can't."

# Chapter Twenty

She had refused him. Andrew rocked back on his heels, as if she had dealt him a physical blow. Beth had refused him. He felt the blood drain from his face and pain clench his heart. The bullet wound had hurt less than this. The worst part was, Andrew knew it was his fault. He hadn't meant to surprise her; he had planned to wait another month or so, to be certain she was comfortable with him. But Peter Girton had forced his hand. Damn the man! He had put fear back into Beth's eyes, and that was something Andrew could not forgive.

For it had been fear he'd seen when Beth had refused his proposal. Fear, not surprise. That made no sense. Just as kneeling here like a lovesick boy made no sense.

A sudden doubt assailed Andrew, twisting the cords that encircled his heart. Had Beth somehow guessed the truth behind his lies? Was that the reason she had refused him? He clenched his fists, then released them slowly. He was no longer an eight-year-old, begging for food to save his sister's life. There was no reason to feel the same anguish, the same pain of rejection that he had so many years ago. Andrew rose, then realizing he was towering over Beth, pulled the second chair around so that he faced her. Though the lamp cast a golden glow, her face was unnaturally pale. She was suffering, too.

It was ironic. When he had finally mustered enough courage to do the one thing he had sworn he would never do—

open his heart and his life to another—she had refused him. And in doing that, Beth had opened wounds he thought long healed.

"Why?" he asked when the first spasm of pain had passed and he could once again breathe normally. "I know you want to safeguard Dora." Andrew clenched his fist, then—seeing Beth blanch at the action—forced himself to relax.

"I do," she said. The gleam of tears in her eyes told Andrew that, whatever the reason, the decision was painful for her, too.

"I thought you cared for me . . . at least a little." He couldn't have mistaken her response to his kisses, the warmth in her eyes when she had looked at him. Women could feign many things; Andrew knew that, but he doubted anyone could counterfeit affection like Beth's. Though her feelings might be hidden inside her, he believed them to be as pure as the water from a deep well.

"I do care for you." She spoke so softly that he had to strain to hear her words, and he sensed that the admission was not easily given.

"Then why won't you marry me?" It made no sense. He couldn't have mistaken her feelings. Surely her desire to teach at the school in Rochester wasn't stronger than her love for Dora and her affection for him. She might not love him yet, but Andrew believed the seeds of passion had begun to grow.

Beth leaned back in her chair, giving Andrew the impression that she wanted to put physical distance between them.

"I'm afraid," she said softly, the tremor in her voice telling Andrew she hated to admit it. This was Beth, the woman who valued strength so greatly and who saw fear as a weakness.

"I told you I would keep you and Dora safe from Peter." Didn't she trust him? There was no doubt that Girton was a dangerous bully, but Andrew knew he could protect Beth and Dora.

She shook her head, and a flush stained her face, chasing away that deathly pallor. "I know you'll try your best, Andrew, but it's not only Peter I'm afraid of."

Andrew ran a hand through his hair in pure frustration. What on earth could be the problem? He leaned forward, then when he saw her grip the chair arms, forced himself to relax.

"If not Peter, what are you afraid of?"

She raised those beautiful green eyes to meet his gaze, and the tears that he had seen there threatened to spill onto her cheeks.

"You," she said simply.

She feared him! Andrew shook his head, as if to clear his ears. Surely he had misunderstood. There was no reason on earth why Beth should fear him. He had been careful, so very careful, not to do anything to alarm her.

"I don't understand," he said, trying desperately to hide his bewilderment from her. She was naturally distraught by the fact that Girton had been so close. Perhaps her statements were nothing more than the aftermath of shock. Andrew had seen more than one patient react in a seemingly irrational manner after sustaining a major injury. Though Girton's presence in the house had caused no physical trauma, it would have wrought deep emotional anguish.

There was a long silence during which Beth appeared to be choosing her words carefully. "I can't marry you or anyone," she said in a husky voice. "I've seen what happens to men after they're married."

Andrew forced himself to remain calm. "And what is that?" he asked, keeping his tone neutral. He couldn't, *wouldn't* frighten her by shouting his frustration.

Beth folded her hands together, her fingers pressing so tightly that he could see the skin whiten beneath them. An owl hooted, a carriage rolled by. Outside, it was an ordinary night. It was only here that extraordinary events were occurring.

"Yes, Beth?" Andrew encouraged her to continue. She had no way of knowing that her refusal and now her reluctance to explain were puncturing his heart, leaving a jagged hole and almost unbearable pain.

"Once they're married, men show their true nature," she said at last. Andrew nodded slowly, as if he understood. He

249

did not. Beth was speaking nonsense, but perhaps if she continued, her words would start to make sense.

She was silent for a moment, staring at her hands. Then she raised her eyes and met his gaze. The pain and fear he saw made Andrew flinch. Beth swallowed deeply before she said, "When their wives or children do something they don't like, they get angry. At the slightest provocation—a missing button, stale bread, a dry spell—they become violent." The words poured out of her like a torrent, and the passion with which she spoke told Andrew that her sister's abusive marriage had been only part of Beth's nightmare.

Though he felt a compelling urge to maim whoever had caused Beth such pain, he steeled his face to show no reaction. He must let her finish. If Andrew was right, Beth had just lanced a long-festering wound. She needed to drain all the poison if it was to heal. "Was your parents' marriage like that?" If it was, and if Beth herself had suffered, Andrew could understand her fears.

"Yes." She nodded, her eyes filling with tears.

"And your father vented his anger on your mother?" Though Andrew hated asking the questions, he had to know what had happened. Only then would he be able to help her heal.

"Yes." As tears began to trickle from her eyes, she brushed them away impatiently.

"And he hurt you and Lenore?"

Beth began to sob. "Yes."

With a muffled curse and a wish that her father were still alive so that Andrew could make him pay for his sins, he lifted Beth from the chair. Cradling her in his arms, he strode into the parlor and placed her on the settee. Though he couldn't have explained why, Andrew thought it important to take Beth into another room, one where he could sit next to her.

"I'm not Peter, and I'm not your father," he said firmly when her sobs began to subside. Though Beth was a tall woman, tonight she felt fragile in his arms, as if her pain had weakened her physically as well as emotionally. "I won't hurt you."

The clock chimed the half hour. A single horse rode by. The night was still young; it was only Andrew who felt old. Though his arm around her shoulders kept Beth from moving too far, she leaned back so that she could meet his gaze.

"What if you change?" she asked, and tears began to well again.

"I won't."

"Peter did."

Andrew doubted it. The Peter Girton he had met was a louse, and he doubted he had ever been any different. The evil was too deeply embedded to have been learned; Girton, he was certain, had been born a brute. It was important, Andrew sensed, that Beth recognize that. She would never trust him otherwise.

"Did he change, Beth, or was he just careful to hide his true self from your sister until they were married? I think there must have been hints of his cruelty before that."

Beth lowered her gaze and clasped her hands again. "No," she said. A tear dropped onto her hand. "Maybe. There was the chipmunk."

The note in Beth's voice sent a shiver of dread along Andrew's spine. "What happened to the chipmunk?"

Tears began to stream down Beth's cheeks again. "I found him skinning it. Oh, Andrew, I could see the little creature breathing. I knew it was alive and I tried to stop him, but Peter just laughed. He said I was wrong, that he had found the animal dead. But it wasn't dead. I know it!"

Andrew drew Beth closer and murmured soothing words, though the image made bile rise in his throat. Death was too kind for a monster like Peter Girton.

"Look at me, Beth," he said as her breathing returned to normal. When she faced him, Andrew said, "I am not Peter. I am not your father. I will not hurt you." He spoke slowly, enunciating each word carefully, willing her to believe him. "I took an oath to heal, not hurt people, and I've never broken it." Though there was no telling what he might do the next time he encountered Girton.

Beth nodded slowly. "My mind knows that, but my heart . . ."

His own heart ached at the thought of the pain she had endured, and from the fear, still unquenched, that she would leave him. He had to convince her. "Not all men are like your father and Peter, and not all marriages are like theirs. Didn't you see happy families when you were boarding with students?"

Though she nodded, Andrew could see the skepticism on her face. "There were some," she admitted, "but I thought they were putting on an act while I was there. Peter used to do that when I visited him and Lenore."

No wonder she was so wary of marriage, of any relationship with a man.

"I want to marry you, Beth. I understand you're not ready, but will you stay with me and let me convince you?" Andrew wished he had David's skill at pleading. Surely no case the attorney had tried had been as important as this one. Beth was a jury of one that held his heart, his happiness, and his future in her hands. "Please don't go to Mrs. Wilcox's. Please stay here."

She was silent for a long moment, her eyes searching his face as if it held truths that his words did not. At last, she nodded. "I will."

He had been wonderful, Beth mused as she drank a second cup of coffee. Dora was in the kitchen "helping" Mrs. Kane prepare dinner, giving Beth a few minutes of precious solitude. Though she loved Dora dearly, for the past few weeks she found herself craving time alone to savor her burgeoning love for Andrew and his courtship of her. For it could be called nothing else. His manner was tender, his words romantic, and though he had not once repeated his proposal of marriage, each day he gave her tangible proof of his affection. One day a book she had mentioned wanting to read had appeared next to her dinner plate, its frontispiece inscribed with three lines of poetry that made her heart sing. The next, he'd brought a McGuffey's Reader for Dora. Another day he had made a sweeping bow as he presented her with a tiny bottle of perfume—real French perfume—from Sheppard's. And now this.

Beth sighed. When she had opened her bedroom door this morning, she had found a single white rose lying on top of a cream-colored envelope. The card inside, written in Andrew's careful script, was a formal invitation to join him for a performance of *Twelfth Night* at the Eagle Street Theater.

"I can't," she said when he entered the dining room and poured himself a cup of coffee.

Andrew raised one brow, but waited until he was seated before he spoke. "There's that word again. The one I hate," he said mildly, stirring a teaspoon of sugar into his beverage. "What is it you can't do?"

"Go to the theater with you."

Andrew's blue eyes sparkled with mischief, and she knew this would not be easy. "Why not?" he asked with apparent innocence. "Don't you like Shakespeare?"

"You know I do."

"Perhaps you dislike this particular play."

Beth shook her head. "You know that's not the case." Only the previous week she had told Andrew *Twelfth Night* was one of her favorite comedies.

"Then why can't"—he emphasized the word—"you go to the theater?"

They had had this discussion before, and each time he had dismissed her worries.

"People will talk. They'll say you shouldn't be seen in public with your housekeeper."

"Perhaps." Andrew sipped his coffee. "But no one will deny my right to spend the evening with my fiancée."

"I'm not your fiancée."

Reaching over to lay his hand on top of hers, Andrew said, "In my heart you are."

How could she refuse?

The sun was beginning to set by the time David's carriage arrived. When Andrew had explained that he had invited David and Helen Pratt to accompany them, Beth suspected that he had wanted to ease her entry into society by providing congenial companions and squelching rumors that they were improperly chaperoned. Other rumors, Beth knew, would be more difficult to quash.

"I'm delighted to see you again," Helen said as she arranged her skirts on the seat opposite Beth. Though the carriage was spacious, it had not been built to accommodate two of the fashionably wide skirts on one side. Helen's smile seemed genuine, and there was no hint of condescension in her voice. Tonight she wore a deeply flounced pale blue silk gown trimmed with darker blue ribbons. Beth's own gown was simpler. Though she had acceded to Andrew's request that she not wear mourning and had had a dress made of lavender silk, she had insisted on a simple design that was devoid of trim.

Beth smiled her greeting, not trusting her voice to remain steady. Andrew could scoff at others' opinions, but she worried about how society would receive her and what effect her presence would have on his practice.

David settled next to Helen, leaving Andrew to share a seat with Beth. Surely it was only her imagination that he sat closer than he needed to. If David saw anything amiss, he did not allude to it, saying only, "It's about time Andrew took his rightful place in society." David frowned at his friend. "You were a recluse this summer." For a second Beth wondered what he meant. Then she remembered the weeks Andrew had spent in the attic.

Helen nodded. "You missed so much while you were in New York—parties, the theater, concerts."

"I'm happy to be back." This time there was no doubt about it. Andrew moved so close that Beth could feel the warmth of his arm on hers.

"I can see why." David slanted a grin at Beth, then waggled his eyebrows.

Beth blushed. The night was warm, but that was not what caused her face to flame.

"Now, David, don't tease Beth." Helen swatted his hand with her fan.

He shrugged. "If I don't tease Beth, I'll have to tease you. That could be enjoyable—watching you blush."

Helen's laugh bubbled with mirth. "You can try!"

David's coach was more elegant than Andrew's, with burgundy plush seats and polished wooden doors. Beth settled back and tried to enjoy the brief ride. Though she had walked down Eagle Street and had seen the theater several times, tonight would be her first foray into one of Buffalo's landmarks . . . and into its society.

Andrew helped her descend from the carriage. Though her hand was trembling, she placed it on his arm and kept her head held high. She would not let anyone see the trepidation that filled her heart. As they entered the theater and took their seats, Beth closed her ears to the low murmur that seemed to intensify when the other theatergoers recognized her. She was here at Andrew's request; that was what mattered. Not for the world would she betray the fact that this was the first time she had attended a play, that she found the opulence of her surroundings surprising, and that her heart was beating much faster than normal at the realization that she would spend the next several hours with the man she loved.

Once the curtain rose, the outside world disappeared. It was magic, pure magic, sitting so close to Andrew, smelling his faint citrus scent, hearing his even breathing, sharing the enjoyment of Shakespeare's poetry with him. They laughed together, and when she gasped in delight, he laid his hand on her arm, its warmth at once comforting and, oh, so disturbing.

When the curtain fell for intermission, Andrew and David joined the queue for lemonade, leaving Beth and Helen in their seats.

"Wasn't it wonderful?" Beth asked the petite blonde. The men had taken seats on the ends, leaving Beth and Helen next to each other. Beth wasn't sure if that was customary, but she appreciated not sitting next to David. Though each day made her more comfortable with Andrew, she was still wary of other men.

Helen started to speak, but Beth did not hear her reply, for two women in the row behind her raised their voices.

"I can't imagine what he's thinking of, bringing a woman like that here," the first declared.

"I hear she's a servant," her companion said.

Beth felt her cheeks flush. She had no doubt she was the subject of the women's speculation.

"No one knows where she's from."

"I tell you, Elvira, I heard someone saw her near Canal Street."

"Surely not!"

"She certainly must have hoodwinked the doctor."

"I don't know what I'm going to do with the aphids. They're destroying my roses." As Helen placed a gloved hand on her arm, Beth realized she had been speaking of her garden.

Rising, Beth said, "I think I'd like some fresh air."

Together she and Helen made their way to the theater entrance. The murmurs followed them. Though Beth felt an urge to gather her skirts and run, she did not. Instead, she nodded politely as people let her and Helen pass. And with every step, Beth's eyes scanned the crowd, looking for Andrew. It was silly, of course, to believe that he could protect her. Physical protection was one thing. This was another. If she were to consider marrying Andrew, she would have to face society's scorn. She would have to learn to deal with it. Drawing in a deep breath, Beth smiled at Helen. "Thank you," she said. *For coming with me, for not being ashamed to be seen in my company, for being my friend.* The knowing look in Helen's eyes told her she heard the unspoken words.

They stood near the entrance, not venturing outside, but close enough that a slight breeze reached them. Though they were surrounded by other theatergoers, no one spoke to them. Helen continued to describe her garden, and Beth must have made appropriate replies, for Helen acted as if nothing were amiss. Then her eyes narrowed slightly, as if she were warning Beth of something.

"Good evening, Lucinda." Helen's greeting sounded cordial.

Beth suppressed a shudder. She should have realized that Lucinda Fields would attend the opening night of a play, whether or not she had ever read Shakespeare.

Pointedly ignoring Beth, Lucinda gave Helen a stern look.

"I thought you had more sense than to be seen with a fallen woman."

Helen's expression of puzzlement was so exaggerated that, under other circumstances, Beth would have laughed. "Oh, my dear," Helen said as she looked in all directions. "Has someone taken a tumble?"

Lucinda's lips thinned in obvious disapproval. "You know what I mean, Helen. This creature . . ."

Though Beth longed to flay Lucinda verbally, she remembered a lesson she had learned many years before. "Your gown is quite beautiful, Miss Fields," she said sweetly.

Lucinda glared at her. "I don't recall addressing you."

"That shade of peach is particularly attractive with your dark hair," Beth continued, as if Lucinda had not interrupted.

The dark-haired woman's eyes widened, and she looked down at her gown, as if seeing it for the first time. From the corner of her eyes, Beth could see Helen's faint smile.

"It was so clever of you to order the ruffles made of the silk," Beth said. "Lace or ribbon would have been so conventional. This way, your gown is as unique as you."

Lucinda's lips turned up in a smug smile. "Why, thank you."

"You were wonderful!" Andrew's blue eyes glowed with pride, his approval making Beth's cheeks flush with pleasure. Though he had said nothing at the theater where they could be overheard, now that they were once again home, he had led Beth into the parlor. He poured himself a brandy and handed Beth a glass of sherry.

"You didn't just ignore Lucinda's malice," he continued. "You squelched it."

Beth managed a smile at the memory. "I was so nervous," she told him. "So I pretended that Lucinda was a particularly difficult member of the school committee." She took a sip of the smooth libation.

"If you were nervous, it wasn't obvious. When David and I saw you, you were standing there looking like a queen."

Beth raised her eyes to the portrait over the fireplace. "Or like the Duchess?"

There was a moment of silence as Andrew's gaze turned to the painting of the beautiful yet haughty blonde. Surely it was only Beth's imagination that he seemed ill at ease with her reference to his mother.

"No, Beth," he said at last. "Not like her. Like yourself. Like the woman I want to marry."

That was the problem. Andrew wanted to marry her. It should have been so simple. After all, she wanted to marry him. But Beth could not forget the reception Lucinda and the others had given her.

"Oh, Andrew, you should have heard the women tonight. It wasn't just Lucinda. They all knew I wasn't right for you. I don't come from the same background."

There was another long silence, and this time Beth knew she was not mistaken. Andrew was uncomfortable with the direction their conversation had taken. He reached for her glass and set it on the table next to him. "Would your answer be different if you knew that you came from a better background than I?" Andrew took her hands in his as he waited for her response.

"That's a rhetorical question. I don't see why you're asking it."

He shook his head slowly, his eyes never leaving hers. "It's not rhetorical, Beth. It's the truth. I've been living a lie."

She stared at him, knowing her eyes were clouded with confusion. "I don't understand." Everyone in the city knew of Andrew's impeccable lineage.

He swallowed, his grip tightening as he said, "The woman in the portrait is not my mother."

Beth's gaze returned to the painting. *Not his mother!* The picture of the Duchess was one of the best known in the city.

"Who is she?"

"I have no idea," Andrew said with a shrug. "I bought the painting at a pawnshop in New York and made it part of my life story. The fact is, none of it's true."

Beth sank onto the settee as she tried to understand what he was saying. "Your mother wasn't a duchess who fled Germany with the man she loved to escape a loveless arranged marriage?" That was the story she had heard from Mrs. Kane. Even Silver had recounted the same tale.

Andrew shook his head and took the seat next to her. "Far from it. My parents were poor working people who came to America to give their children a chance for a better life. Unfortunately, it didn't work out the way they had hoped. My father died on the ship, leaving my mother with two children and no way to support them. She tried—oh, yes, she tried—but she died of the grippe soon after we arrived. Mary and I were alone."

Beth's eyes began to fill with tears as she thought of what Andrew had endured. Though he sat next to her, tall and apparently strong, she knew he had not always been that way.

"I did the best I could for Mary." Andrew's eyes darkened, and Beth knew that although he said the words, he didn't believe them. "I worked odd jobs for food, but there was never enough. Then we both got sick, and I couldn't work." Though Andrew's grip was painful, Beth refused to wince. He needed to touch her. She knew that human contact was vital as he told her of losing everyone he had loved. Poor Andrew!

"I tried begging," he said, and the harshness she heard in his voice told Beth how painful the memory still was. She tried not to gasp as she realized she wasn't the only one who bore childhood scars. "No one would give me anything. They all wanted money, and I didn't have any—not one penny. That's why Mary died. I didn't have a penny to buy food for her!"

Beth's heart ached for the young boy who had known such pain. No wonder Andrew had nightmares about his sister. No wonder he considered amassing money so important.

"How old were you?" Beth pulled one hand from his and placed it on his face. Slowly she stroked his cheek, trying to comfort him.

"I was eight; Mary was three."

He had been a child. His sister was Dora's age. For the first time, Beth truly understood why Andrew had resisted her pleas to help Dora. Seeing Dora, knowing she needed medical help, must have raised incredibly painful memories. Beth had believed him heartless when he had refused to help Dora. The truth had been the opposite; Andrew had bled from the anguish of remembering his sister.

"When Mary died," Andrew continued, "I swore that somehow, someday I would have more money than I could ever spend. No one would ever be able to refuse me anything."

Beth felt the tears coursing down her cheeks, and knew that she was crying for both the young boy who had lost so much and the grown man whose loss was still an open sore.

"Don't cry, Beth. I didn't tell you to make you feel sorry for me. I wanted you to see that my life has been a lie." Beth touched his lips, trying to stop the flow of painful memories, but Andrew continued. "You think you're not worthy of me. It's the other way around. My wealthy, aristocratic family—the reason Buffalo society values me—never existed."

Beth shook her head, sensing that, although Andrew might think his wounds had healed, they were still festering. "You're wrong about that. Oh," she admitted, "the story of the Duchess might be important to shallow people like Lucinda Fields, but the others value you for what you've done—your skill as a doctor, who you are as a person."

A glimmer of hope lit his eyes. "What about you, Beth? How do you see me?"

She brushed the tears from her cheeks. "As a man who's kind and good and gentle." Beth smiled, watching his expression change, the spark of hope grow into a fire. She tugged her other hand free. "As the man I love."

She leaned forward, put her arms around him, and pressed her lips to his. Beth had meant the kiss to be one of comfort, to show Andrew how much she cared, but when his mouth met hers, the hunger they shared could be denied no longer. His lips moved beneath hers, tasting, savoring, igniting a flame that would not be doused. He wrapped his arms around her, drawing her so close that Beth wasn't sure whose heart was beating or whose breath warmed her mouth.

"I don't deserve you," Andrew said when they drew apart,

breathless. "But, God help me, I love you." He put his hand under her chin and raised her face so that he could gaze into her eyes. The expression Beth saw in his made her gasp with pleasure and anticipation. "Will you let me show you how beautiful love can be?" he asked.

"Yes!" The fears that had haunted her days and nights melted under the warmth of Andrew's smile. He loved her. He loved her! And what they were about to do was, oh, so very right.

Andrew led her up the stairway and into his room, keeping her hand tightly clasped in his, as if he were unwilling to break the connection between them. They were one, he was telling her, two parts of a whole, and soon those parts would be joined. Though she could see the eagerness on Andrew's face and feel his pulse race beneath her fingers, he moved slowly, almost languorously. He removed his coat and placed it carefully on one of the tall chairs.

"Will you let me undress you?" he asked.

How could she have doubted him? How could she have thought that he had one brutal bone in his body? Andrew was not like the other men she knew, for he would never force her. Even in this simple preparation for love, he gave her a choice.

She nodded.

Andrew stood behind her and pulled one of the pins from her hair. As a long lock tumbled to her neck, he stroked it with his fingertips. "Your hair reminds me of sunset on the lake—so fiery and full of life." He withdrew another pin, and then another. When the final one was gone, he reached for a brush and began to stroke her hair, slowly and deliberately, each movement sending a new shiver of delight through her. And still he did not hurry, though Beth heard his ragged breathing and knew how much the restraint cost him.

When he finished brushing her hair, Andrew began to unbutton her dress, slipping each button from its loop as carefully as if it were made of gold. At last, when the gown slid to the floor, he touched her neck, then her shoulders, his fingers moving slowly, igniting fires in their wake. "Your skin is as white as clouds on an August day," he murmured. But clouds were cold, while her skin felt scorched and her legs threatened to buckle.

As if he recognized her weakness, Andrew motioned Beth to sit on one of the chairs. Kneeling in front of her, he removed her shoes and stockings, each motion as slow, deliberate, and enchanting as the one before. "Have you ever looked at your toes?" he asked in a voice that sent a new tremor of delight along Beth's spine.

She nodded, bemused. Who would have dreamed that a man's touch and such ordinary words could feel so extraordinary? "Of course I have, Andrew. They're just toes."

Andrew shook his head and cupped one foot in his hand. Another shiver swept through her as the warmth of his hand seemed to turn her bones to jelly. "They're not ordinary to me," he said softly. "The nails remind me of tiny seashells. When I look at them, I remember the day we went sailing."

Beth smiled. The man was a magician, his words conjuring happy thoughts, his fingers and lips turning ordinary skin into a fiery surface. For as he revealed each inch of flesh, he stroked it with his fingertips, then pressed soft kisses on it.

Not even in her dreams had she imagined anything so exciting.

When the last garment was removed, Andrew lifted her into his arms and carried her to his bed. "You're more beautiful than anything I ever dreamed," he said as he laid her on the cool linen. For a moment Beth felt bereft now that Andrew was no longer touching her. She reached for a sheet to cover her nakedness, but Andrew shook his head. "Please don't," he said. "I want to look at you."

Though he had moved slowly while he undressed her, his fingers flew as he shed his own clothes. Within seconds, he was lying next to her, his warmth once more heating her blood. His hands cupped her face, turning her so that she could see his expression. And what she saw in Andrew's eyes and in his smile made Beth's heart stop.

"I love you, Beth," he said.

Never again would she doubt that it was true. These were the words she had longed to hear, the ones that would change her life forever. They were wonderful, glorious, and made even sweeter by everything that had preceded them. For Andrew's gentle touches and his passionate kisses told her more clearly than even those priceless words that he loved her.

"Oh, Andrew!"

He grinned, his blue eyes shining with warmth and desire. "I love it when you say that."

Beth reached her hand behind his head and drew his face closer to her. Softly, she pressed a kiss on his lips.

"I love it when you do that," he said.

And then there was no need for words, for his lips clung to hers, drawing the sweetness from hers, giving from his own, while his hands moved slowly, caressing the curves and planes of her body, learning each inch. And every touch, every kiss ignited new sensations. Beth could feel her body change beneath his fingers, warming, softening, opening like the petals of the rose he had given her. And still he continued, stoking the fires of passion, deepening the pleasure. It was sweeter and stronger than anything she had ever known, a sense of intense anticipation, a longing that had no name. *Please, Andrew, please!* She shouted the words in her head as the pleasure became almost unbearable. *Please!*

And then when he joined his body with hers, the pleasure exploded into a kaleidoscope of colors and sensations.

"Oh, Andrew!"

# *Chapter Twenty-one*

"Yes, sweetie, red." Beth smiled as Dora picked up the maple leaf, her face glowing with pleasure as she twirled its stem. Though Beth had always loved autumn and the crisp days that signaled the return to school, never before had the season seemed so glorious. It wasn't simply that the trees seemed to be celebrating, clothing themselves in ever brighter hues, while the sky shone with a blue that rivaled Andrew's eyes in its intensity. That alone would have filled her heart with happiness. But this year, there was more. So much more.

"Ellow!" Dora reached for a fallen elm leaf. They were playing in the backyard. Beth was thankful Andrew's estate was a large one, for Dora was an active child who loved to run. She used to skip ahead fearlessly, then scamper back to Beth on their walks to Canal Street. But those walks had ended abruptly, and now Beth kept Dora confined to the yard.

"Yellow." As Beth enunciated the word, Dora watched her lips.

"Yellow!" she repeated, grinning when Beth nodded.

The progress Dora had made since her surgery had surprised both Beth and Andrew, for it seemed as if Dora were making up for the silent years, learning new words each day and speaking so clearly that a stranger would not have realized she had uttered her first real word only two months previously.

Beth's days were filled with wonder as she watched Dora blossom. And her nights . . . ah, her nights. As she felt the color rush to her cheeks, Beth bent down to pick an acorn from the ground. If Dora saw her flushed face, she would wonder what was wrong. Nothing was wrong. Quite the contrary. Everything was so very, very right.

"Nut." Dora touched the acorn and looked up expectantly. Beth felt her heart swell with pride. Dora was learning so quickly. And it wasn't just Dora who was an eager student. Beth smiled at the thought of everything Andrew had taught her. Who would have dreamt that there were so many ways to find pleasure? Each night, it seemed, he found a new way to delight her. But his attentions were not confined to the nights, for he continued his courtship during the days, surprising her with little gifts, sweet words, and fond looks. Everything he did, everything he said, made Beth feel cherished. And, oh, how wonderful that was.

"Mama." As Dora reached upward, Beth scooped her into her arms.

"Yes, sweetie." She pressed a kiss on the child's head,

then placed her back on the ground. "Let's go inside." Inside, to Andrew. Beth's pulse began to race.

How she loved that man! He made her deliriously happy and caused her heart to sing with joy. That happiness was not one-sided, for Beth knew that, by some miracle, she was giving Andrew some of the deep contentment she experienced in his arms. Somehow her love for him was helping to heal the wounds that his parents' and Mary's deaths had wrought. Though Beth sensed that somewhere in the dark recesses of his fear he still believed that people valued him only because of his fictitious aristocratic lineage, that seemed to concern him less than it had.

The healing was mutual. With each day that passed, Beth loved Andrew more. Now, for the first time in her life, she knew that love was real. It wasn't simply a fantasy storytellers had created. Andrew loved her! He said the words, but—even more importantly—he demonstrated his love in so many ways. Andrew never pressured her. He had not asked her to marry him since that first time, and Beth knew that he was waiting, giving her time to be sure. She was sure. The last of her fears had disappeared, crumbling to dust like the dried leaves beneath her feet. She loved Andrew; she wanted to marry him; and tonight, when they were alone together, she would tell him.

Beth frowned as she and Dora rounded the corner of the house. Dora loved entering through the big front door, and so they had made it a daily ritual, climbing the steps and touching each of the columns as if they were playing tag before they went back inside. Today, though, Beth's pleasure in the simple game evaporated. The pile of pinecones next to the tall spruce had not been there this morning.

With the advent of fall, the Railroad signals had changed. Pinecones replaced the flowers, alerting Andrew to the presence of passengers, telling him he would have to make a delivery tonight. When he returned, he would move the cones to the other side of the spruce, signaling his success.

Though Beth continued to smile as she divested Dora of her cloak, it was a forced smile. While her own fears had diminished, they had been replaced with heart-stopping terror for Andrew. Beth had no doubt that what he was doing was right, but she could not help worrying.

Andrew knew and tried to allay her fears. Since the night he had been wounded, he had changed his route, never taking the same road two consecutive times, and he had sent a message through the mysterious Railroad channels that he could carry no more than two fugitives at any one time. The lesser weight would ensure that his horse could trot if need be to escape a pursuer. But, despite those precautions, Beth's hands grew clammy and her heart pounded each time he took the buggy to the rendezvous site.

Tonight. Tonight when he returned, she would accept his proposal. Somehow she got through supper, pretending that nothing was unusual. Afterward, as she slipped the dress over Dora's head, preparing her for bed, Beth tried to quell her excitement. She wanted Dora to fall asleep quickly, and if the child sensed her anticipation, she would remain awake far too long, demanding yet another story.

It would be so different once Beth and Andrew married. Then she would move to his room, giving Dora one of the empty bedrooms on the second floor. The child was old enough to sleep alone. Though Beth was no stranger to Andrew's bedchamber, she knew that marriage would bring new joys, including the delight of waking in his arms, of making sweet love in the pale light of dawn. Beth's cheeks ached from smiling. Oh, it would be wondrous! Silver was right. The right man made all the difference. Thanks to Andrew, Beth knew that love was a beautiful experience.

"Good night, sweetie." She smoothed the patchwork quilt over Dora's shoulders, then extinguished the candle. Dora would sleep until morning, never knowing that Beth spent most of the night in Andrew's bed.

As she descended the stairs, eager to spend a few minutes with Andrew before he left to make his delivery, Beth's smile was bittersweet. She missed her afternoons with Silver and the children. Andrew was right. She could not risk going to Canal Street until they were certain Dora was safe from Peter, but she still felt the loss of Silver's companionship, and wished she could share the wonder of her love with her friend.

Since the day that they had gone sailing, there had been no sign of Peter. No strangers had entered the house, and if Beth occasionally felt that someone was watching her, she saw no evidence of a spy. Still, she knew better than to think that Peter no longer posed a threat.

"You look more beautiful than usual tonight," Andrew said as she entered his office. His bag lay open on his desk while he rummaged in one of the cabinets. As he did each time that he worked on the Railroad, he was adding extra medicines and bandages to his bag. Just in case. Andrew was still dressed in his black broadcloth suit. He would, Beth knew, change into the threadbare farmer's clothing only minutes before he left. For the moment, he was still Andrew Muller, one of society's most prominent physicians.

Beth smiled, thinking of the other Andrew Muller, the passionate man whose bed she shared. "If you think I'm beautiful," she said softly, "it must be because I'm happy."

Andrew closed his bag and raised one brow. "Dare I hope that I'm part of the reason for that happiness?"

"Yes."

He reached her in three swift strides, his blue eyes sparkling and a sly grin lighting his face as he looked down at her. "Yes, I dare hope, or yes, I'm part of the reason?" he asked with mock severity.

Beth laughed softly. "Both."

Andrew's smile of pure happiness ignited a fire deep inside her. "Oh, my darling," he whispered as he drew her into his arms and lowered his mouth to hers. His lips were soft as a feather, sweet and gentle as they hovered over the edges of hers, teasing her with the lightest of caresses. It was always this way. Andrew's touch inflamed her senses and set her blood to boil. Beth reached for him, drawing him closer, deepening the kiss. "Sweet! So sweet!" Andrew murmured as her lips parted and he tasted the nectar within. Her head began to spin with pleasure.

"Doc! Let me in!" A man's voice and pounding on the door broke the spell.

With a groan of frustration, Andrew released Beth and hurried to the front door. Though they had never before locked the house, after Peter's intrusion Andrew had had bolts installed and had insisted that both doors and all first-floor windows be secured each evening. This was the first night summons he had received since.

"You must come, Doctor." The man's voice was louder now as he entered the house, and Beth recognized it as Lucinda Fields's father's. Her eyes widened in surprise that he had come himself rather than send a servant. Something must be seriously wrong. "My daughter's taken ill," Mr. Fields told Andrew.

"What appears to be wrong with Lucinda?" Andrew asked. They were in the waiting room now, and Beth could hear them coming closer. She hoped Andrew would not bring Mr. Fields into the examining room, for it would be difficult to explain her presence there so late at night.

"Lucinda lost her supper, and she's shaking something fierce." There was no denying the concern her father felt, for his voice shook as much as he said his daughter's body had.

As the clock chimed, Beth frowned. It was time for Andrew to leave.

"Mr. Fields, why don't you sit down while I gather my medicines?" Andrew said in his calmest tones. He closed the door softly behind him, then turned to Beth. "It's probably not serious," he told her, "but I can't take a chance. This once she might be genuinely ill." Andrew opened his bag and took a quick inventory of the contents. "I'll go with her father. Don't be surprised if I'm back in a few minutes."

Beth nodded. Though she was aware of the Fields women's propensity to exaggerate their ailments, she knew Andrew could not ignore their cries for help. And this time, she feared, the illness could be real. Mr. Fields might indulge his daughter, but he didn't seem like a man who would be alarmed by vapors. The fact that he was here seemed to argue for the seriousness of Lucinda's condition.

"What about the delivery?" Beth asked. She handed Andrew an extra bottle of ipecacuanha.

"It can wait until I return. Half an hour won't make any

difference." Andrew had told her that the boats were kept ready for a two-hour period. Timing was critical. Arriving early endangered both the conductors and the fugitives. If too many people gathered at one spot, passersby might notice the unusual activity. Waiting too long meant that the rowers might have gone home, thinking their passengers were not coming.

"But what if Lucinda is truly ill?" Beth couldn't shake the thought that this cry for help was more than a play for Andrew's attention.

Andrew frowned, clearly not liking that possibility. "Then the men will have to wait. They know that if the driver doesn't come, they are to remain hidden until tomorrow."

Beth knew that. She also knew that if she were so close to freedom, even one day would seem like eternity. Look at how long this afternoon and evening had seemed as she'd waited to tell Andrew of her decision. "That's not necessary," she told him. "I can go in your stead."

Andrew closed his bag and walked to Beth's side. Putting his hand on her arm, he said softly, "I don't want you to go, Beth. It's too risky; I'd be worried every minute."

She met his gaze and managed a small smile. "The way I worry about you?" He was silent for a moment, considering the import of her words. At first his eyes were serious; then Beth saw the light of comprehension mix with something else, possibly hope. Could it be that Andrew still did not realize how very much she loved him? When tonight was over, he would never again doubt the depth of her feelings for him.

"Let me go, Andrew." She pled the runaways' case. "I've done it before. I know how to be careful."

Though they could hear Mr. Fields anxiously pacing the outer room, Andrew held Beth close for a long moment. At last he said, his reluctance evident, "You're right. If I'm not back in an hour, go in my place." After giving her a quick kiss, he hurried from the room.

An hour passed, and Andrew did not return. Her heart filled with anticipation and the faint sense of fear that Andrew admitted accompanied him each time he carried slaves on their precarious journey, Beth changed into her somber widow's weeds and drove the carriage to the pickup point.

Two men, one tall, the other short, both so thin that Beth's heart ached for them, climbed into the hidden compartment beneath the floor. Though they were unable to mask their surprise at having a woman driver, they listened carefully when she explained the procedure. "If something should go wrong, I'll slow the horse as much as I can. Get out and run," she told them. Though it was part of the normal set of instructions, Beth hated even voicing the words. She had never thought herself superstitious, but tonight she wanted to think only happy thoughts. Soon these men would be on their way across the river. Soon she would be back with Andrew, telling him of her love. Soon.

They were only a few minutes from their destination when Beth heard the sound of a horse coming from behind her. Her pulse began to race, and she felt her throat constrict with fear. It was nothing to worry about, she told herself. Probably a traveler who had tarried too late at the tavern and now had to hurry to reach home. But Beth clutched the whip handle for reassurance and spoke softly to the men in the back. "Make no sound," she cautioned them, "if I have to stop."

The horse came closer. "Halt! You, there, halt!"

A shiver of pure dread coursed through Beth. She would know that voice anywhere. It was the voice of her nightmares and her deepest fears. By some horrible twist of fate, Peter had found her.

"What have we here? A widow lady?"

Beth said a silent prayer that the combination of her veil and the darkness would keep him from recognizing her. Her prayers were not answered.

As Peter reined his horse next to her, he pointed a pistol at her. "Well, well. If it ain't the little schoolmarm." Shock and surprise drained the blood from Beth's face. If it weren't for his voice, she might not have recognized him. Without his whiskers, Peter looked far different from the man her sister had married. "You ain't gettin' off so easy this time." Peter's chuckle was pure evil, and his scent made Beth want to gag. "Now, stop that buggy."

Beth thought quickly. Somehow, someway she had to elude him. There was no one to help her and the two men whose lives depended on her. Beth knew she had little chance of outrunning Peter. Even to try could be disastrous, for he looked as if he sought an excuse to use the pistol. Though her whip might slow him, angering him would be foolhardy. As he trotted next to her buggy, she could feel waves of fury emanating from him. Beth remembered all too well the danger of provoking an already irate man.

The night was dark and still, and if there were insects or owls about, Beth could not hear them over the pounding of her heart. She was so close to the river. Somehow she had to get the slaves to safety. Beth saw a copse of trees and a thicket a few hundred yards up the road. If she could take the buggy that far, perhaps the men could shelter there. Then she would deal with Peter.

"I said stop!" Peter cocked the pistol.

Beth tugged on the reins, slowing the horse. She would keep moving as long as she could. Each yard they traveled brought the men closer to the thicket. "There's a patient waiting for medicine," she told Peter, trying to buy time. Perhaps if she kept talking, he would not notice that the horse continued to plod. "The man may die if I don't get it to him soon." Her ploy had worked before, but this time Peter was not so credulous.

"What kinda fool do you think I am?" he demanded, coming close enough that his rancid odor assaulted her nostrils. "I don't believe that story about medicine. You cain't tell me it's coincidence that you're on this road the same day some runaway slaves are supposed to be goin' across the river."

Slaves! Beth's heart sank as pieces of a puzzle began to fit together. The picture that emerged was uglier than she had imagined. Peter didn't want her. His objective was something far more valuable.

"Slaves?" she asked, trying to keep her voice from betraying her fear. Now she knew why Peter had taken so many hunting trips. Deer had not been his quarry. "What are you talking about?" The carriage continued its slow but constant forward motion. "I'm delivering medicine."

Peter leaned closer and leered at her. "Then you won't mind lettin' me search the buggy." The way Peter's eyes lingered on her breasts told Beth he wanted to search more than the carriage.

"I certainly would mind," she said in her most official tone. By some miracle, her voice did not waver. "This is private property."

Peter was not impressed. "So are them slaves. Now, give 'em over."

"I've told you that I'm carrying medicine."

"And I told you"—he mocked her words—"that I don't believe you. I may not have gone to that fancy school you did, but I know a lie when I hear it. There are slaves in that buggy, and I'm gonna collect the reward."

Peter's chuckle of delight sent another shiver of horror through Beth. Though his words merely confirmed what she had surmised, the fact that he took such pleasure in destroying others' lives sickened her. "Why, Peter"—she forced a light tone to her voice—"do you mean to tell me you're a slave catcher?" How had Lenore ever married such a monster?

"Sure am." Peter squared his shoulders in a gesture of pride. "I'm a damned good one. Don't need no dogs to catch 'em." The back of the buggy was silent, but Beth knew that the two men hidden in the false floor could hear every one of Peter's vile words. "I caught more than anybody else in this part of the state," he announced.

Though Peter's gloating sickened Beth, the carriage continued to roll forward. Soon they would be close enough that the men could escape. Their safety was all that mattered now.

"If'n I miss one," Peter continued, "I find myself another darkie to take his place."

Beth ignored his words. She wouldn't let her mind register their meaning. "What a fascinating tale, but I must be on my way." Just a few more yards.

"You ain't goin' nowhere, not unless you want a bullet hole in that pretty skin." Peter leaned forward until the pistol was only inches from Beth's breast. "It wouldn't bother me none to kill a lady," he told her, and she didn't doubt the truth of his assertion. "The only thing I hate is killin' a darkie," he continued, "and I only done that once. That fool Rodney figured he could outrun me."

Her horse continued to plod. Peter's kept pace. It was only Beth's heart that stopped. "Rodney?" The blood drained from her face. Though her mind shrieked that there was more than one Rodney in the world, that Peter couldn't possibly be speaking of her neighbor Rodney, her heart knew otherwise.

"Sure enough." The saddle creaked as Peter leaned back, the confident tilt of his shoulders telling Beth how proud he was of his story. "I knew one of the planters would be mighty glad to get a big, strong buck like him. Problem was, old Rodney figured out where we were going and ran away." Peter's hand tightened on the pistol. "I should'a tied his feet as well as his hands. Sure did hate to waste a good darkie, but I couldn't let him get away."

As the darkness started to encroach and her head began to swim, Beth forced herself to take a deep breath. She would not faint, no matter how heinous Peter's crime. There was nothing she could do for Rodney. It was too late for him, but she would do everything in her power to ensure that the two men who had entrusted their lives to her reached Canada.

Tapping her whip handle on the floor in the pre-arranged signal, she said, "You are so clever, Peter." Somehow the words came out as honeyed as she had planned, though her mind still reeled and her stomach churned at the horrors Peter's revelations had conjured. "Lenore used to tell me what a powerful man you were, but she never told me about your cunning." As she had hoped, Peter started to preen at the praise she heaped on him. Thank goodness the man was too stupid to realize she was playing a role. "A man like you ought to be living in a fancy house with servants to wait on him."

"Damn right! Now move over and let me into that carriage."

It was now or never. "Of course." Though the simplest thing would have been to slide over and let Peter climb onto the bench next to her, Beth stood. Apparently gripping the reins for stability, she swayed, as if she had lost her balance and was falling. While Peter tried to catch her, she urged the horse forward. It bolted. She fell back onto the seat. Peter was left behind. "Go right!" Beth whispered to the slaves. Peter would catch the buggy in seconds, but if the slaves could escape and reach the bushes, they had a chance.

As the buggy approached the trees, Beth tugged the reins. "Oh, my," she said to Peter as he pulled up next to her, "I was so frightened. The horse never ran away like that before." She straightened her skirts, hoping that her motions would cover the sound of the men in the back. She could hear their hoarse breathing and the soft thuds as they landed on the ground. Another few seconds. That was all they needed. She slid to the side of the bench, giving Peter the opportunity to climb into the buggy. Then, in an apparently furtive motion, she patted the seat back. As if she had revealed too much, she quickly hid her hand in her skirts.

Peter chuckled in anticipation. "So that's where they are." The carriage swayed as he boarded it. Scarcely giving Beth a glance, he tugged at the seat back. As it started to open and reveal the hiding place, Peter grinned. His grin faded when he saw that the compartment was empty.

"Damnation! There must be another spot." His voice was harsh with fury and frustration. "I know you got darkies in here. Tell me where they are."

Beth kept her eyes fixed on Peter. Not for the world would she look at the bushes and reveal the fugitives' hiding place. "I told you I was carrying medicine." Every second she delayed him improved the slaves' chances.

"You useless bitch," Peter snarled. "I'll take care of you later." He climbed into the back of the buggy and fumbled with the floor. As Beth had known he would, he found the second hidden compartment. It, too, was empty. Peter pounded the floor.

"They were here," he announced, his voice filled with anger and venom. "Look at this." He held up a shred of cloth. "They were here."

"Who?" Beth knew he would not believe her innocence;

all that mattered was buying a little more time for the two men.

"Don't try that act with me, you bitch." Peter gripped Beth's arm and twisted it painfully. "I know them slaves were here. You made me lose them, and you're gonna pay. You and that rich doctor."

He slapped Beth's face. "You're gonna pay, all right."

# Chapter Twenty-two

"Look what I brung, Wayne."

Peter put his hand on the small of her back, propelling her toward the ramshackle cabin. The door opened, the light that spilled out revealing a dark-haired, bearded man whom Beth assumed was Peter's cohort Wayne. Though several yards still separated them, the stench of unwashed flesh and filthy clothing made Beth gag. Peter was loathsome, his accomplice far worse, at least in appearance. Wayne's face was scarred and battered, and when he grinned, Beth saw that several teeth were missing. But physical ugliness was the least of her worries.

"Get movin'."

Beth stumbled as Peter pushed her harder. Though he had untied her ankles so that she could walk from the carriage, he kept her wrists bound, and that threw her off balance.

The ride from the river had taken no more than half an hour; it had only seemed endless. Peter had spent the time boasting of his prowess in capturing slaves, subduing impertinent whores like Silver, and impressing his useless accomplice. Beth had spent the time steeling herself for the ordeal to come. She had no doubt that Peter's idea of payment would be a painful one.

"You brung a redheaded whore!" Wayne crowed, his delight obvious. He reached for Beth.

"Not now, you fool." Peter slapped his arm. "We got important business first."

As they entered the cabin, Peter kicked the door closed behind them. Wayne's eyes widened with recognition. "She ain't just a whore; she's the one that done took your brat."

"Well, what do you know? You ain't as dumb as I thought."

Wayne stretched his hand toward Beth's hair.

"Not now!" Peter snarled.

"Aw, Peter." Wayne's voice rose in a shrill whine. "I just wanted to see if'n it felt like fire. Reckon you owe me that after all the time I done spent watchin' her."

Beth could not suppress a shudder. It hadn't been her imagination. Someone had indeed been watching Andrew's house. To calm her nerves, she looked around her. Though the building appeared to have been used as an icehouse recently, at one time it might have afforded a small family shelter. That time had evidently been decades earlier, for Beth could feel the breeze sifting through cracks in the walls, while stars peeked through sizable holes in the roof. Dust covered the scarred floor, and the scents of mildew and rot competed with the odor of decaying garbage. The room's furnishings were limited to a pile of rags in one corner, a single chair, and a small table that boasted two tin cups and plates next to a large jug that Beth guessed contained whiskey.

"You can touch her later," Peter told Wayne, a smug grin crossing his face. "She's my ticket to riches."

"Riches? How d'you figure that?" Wayne sank into the chair, then rose abruptly when Peter glared at him.

As Peter took the seat he appeared to consider his due, he shoved Beth to the floor. Though her side ached from the impact, she struggled to sit. No matter what the effort cost her, she would not cower before Peter. That was what he wanted. Subservience would only fuel his brutality.

Peter grunted, then laid a hand on Beth's head, apparently taunting Wayne by stroking her hair. Beth ducked her head, moving out of Peter's reach. Though she had resolved she would do nothing to anger him, she would not endure his touch if she could avoid it. *Oh, Lenore,* she thought, *how could you have married him?* Slowly, so he would not notice, Beth slid away from him.

Apparently oblivious to her movement, Peter smirked at Wayne. "If the doc was willing to pay for the brat, think what he'll do for her."

Beth continued sliding backwards until she reached the wall. Resting her spine against it, she considered Peter's words. Though she had known Andrew and David had met with Peter, she hadn't realized that Andrew had offered money for Dora. It seemed wrong, almost like buying a slave, but if the result was that Dora would be free of her father's evil influence, perhaps this was a case where the ends justified the means.

"Good thinkin'." Wayne reached for the jug.

"Not now." Peter leaned back in the chair. "Why don't you go fetch the doctor? Tell him to bring some money with him."

Though he looked longingly at the jug, Wayne moved toward the door. As he passed by her, his hand brushed Beth's hair in a motion that she might have thought accidental if she hadn't seen the satisfied grin that lit his face. It disappeared a second later when he turned back toward Peter. "How much money?"

Peter stroked his chin, apparently pondering the question. "A hundred thousand . . . in gold," he said at last.

Beth gasped. It was a fortune, an absolute fortune. "He won't give you that!"

"Then you better prepare to die," Peter said calmly, if announcing that the stars were shining. "I ain't gonna keep a useless woman around. I already had one of them."

Wayne leaned against the door frame. Though the room was poorly lighted, Beth could not miss the lascivious look in his eyes. It was the same look she had seen on the faces of Silver's customers. "You cain't kill her before we have a little fun with her." Beth watched him lick his lips as if she were a piece of food that he wanted to sample. The thought made bile rise in her throat.

Peter shrugged. "She's a scrawny bitch like her sister. Won't be much fun."

Wayne wasn't convinced, for he said, "We ain't gotta pay for her. That oughta count for somethin'."

"You got a point there." Peter rose and took a step toward Wayne. "If'n the doc don't pay for her, we'll keep her a couple days—use her real good before we kill her. Now," he said, taking another step toward the door, "go get the doctor, and be sure to tie him up good. Hands and feet."

When the door closed behind Wayne, Beth turned to Peter. "Why don't you untie me?" She wasn't sure how she was going to do it, but she had to find a way out of this cabin. She couldn't let Andrew pay the ransom, even if he had that much money. For, no matter what Peter said, she knew he planned to kill her, money or no money. Beth would not let Andrew sacrifice his life's savings on a lost cause. Her only hope was to escape. And since the cabin had no windows and only one door, her options were limited.

"Untie you so you can run away?" Peter sneered. "Naw. I don't think I'll do that. And don't be thinking I'm gonna fall asleep, neither. I ain't that dumb. No, sirree."

His refusal didn't surprise her, and yet there had been a chance. Peter might have done the unexpected and acceded to her plea. Lenore had told Beth that Peter was unpredictable, particularly when he had been drinking. Tonight his foul breath left no doubt that he had been imbibing steadily all evening. As if he could read Beth's thoughts, Peter reached for the jug, then shook his head. "Reckon I can wait until I got somethin' to celebrate." He leaned back in the chair and, propping his feet on the table, stared at Beth.

For a long while the only sounds Beth heard were Peter's loud exhalations and her own heartbeats. She could taste fear and, try though she might, she could not expunge its awful metallic flavor. *Oh, Andrew,* she thought. *I'm going to miss you so much!* And Dora, sweet Dora. How would that wonderful child cope with the loss of yet another mother? The thoughts were too painful to consider, and so Beth relied on the trick she had learned as a child. She removed herself from the filthy cabin and pictured herself sitting in a boat, skimming across the lake while Andrew manned the sail and Dora played contentedly in the bow.

"Where are they?" Peter's words broke the silence and brought Beth back to reality. She wasn't sure how much time had passed. All she knew was that she was stiff from sitting on the floor.

"They're probably not coming," she said. "I told you Andrew wouldn't ransom me."

Peter's boot heels hit the floor. "Andrew, is it?" he demanded. "Sounds mighty personal to me. Like maybe you and the doc knew each other real good, if'n you know what I mean." His leer left no doubt of Peter's meaning. "Tell me, little lady, what services did you give him?"

The instant Andrew's name had escaped her lips, Beth had known it was a mistake. Peter wasn't very bright, but even he wouldn't fail to notice the slip. "I'm the doctor's housekeeper," she said, keeping her voice as neutral as she could.

Peter hooted as he slapped the table. "Funny, ain't it? That's what Lenore called herself. I reckon I know just what kind of housekeeper you were." He managed to make the word sound like an insult. As Peter leaned forward, she caught another blast of his whiskey-laden breath. "Wayne and me's gonna let you keep house here, too."

Beth shuddered, but refused to give Peter the satisfaction of a reply. It was bad enough that he had conjured vile images of his body touching hers, making a travesty of the magical moments she and Andrew had shared. Death, Beth knew, would be a blessed release after those two brutes finished with her.

She settled back against the wall, determined to say nothing more until Wayne returned. At last the sound of a horse's hooves broke the silence. "Reckon that's Wayne." Peter rose to stand in the doorway. "Better hope he's got the doc."

Beth hoped exactly the opposite. Maybe Andrew was still with Lucinda Fields. Maybe he had refused Peter's outrageous demands. Her hopes were dashed when she heard Wayne muttering commands. He wouldn't do that if he were alone. A moment later, Andrew walked into the cabin, his head held high despite the rope that bound his arms behind him. For all the notice he gave Peter or his surroundings, he might have been walking into the Eagle Street Theater.

"I told you to tie his feet," Peter shouted at Wayne as he slammed his fist into his hand in a gesture of pure rage.

"And how was he gonna get outta the wagon?" Wayne asked. "I sure wasn't gonna carry him."

Andrew's gaze met Beth's. Though his expression did not change from the cool hauteur he had adopted, she saw concern, anger, and determination shining in his eyes. Perhaps it was foolish, but Beth couldn't stop hope from bubbling inside her. She and Andrew were together, and maybe, just maybe, they could find a way to escape.

"So, where's the money, Wayne?" Peter grabbed his pistol and started waving it wildly. Beth tried not to cringe, but knowing how volatile Peter could be—and how violent—she could only pray that he would not hurt Andrew.

"Doc says he ain't got it in the house. We gotta wait until the damn bank opens." Wayne sounded as petulant as a child.

"You useless son of a bitch!" Peter's face mottled with anger as he continued to wave his pistol, and Beth wasn't sure whether the rage was directed at Wayne or Andrew.

"Looks like we got ourselves a dee-lay." Peter grinned at Wayne in one of those abrupt mood changes that Lenore had once described. "Reckon we should make our guest here comfortable." He gestured toward Andrew. "Tie him up. And make sure it's tight." While Peter held his pistol on Andrew, Wayne forced him to the ground and secured his legs. "Now, Doc, this little dee-lay is gonna cost you extra. What d'ya think, Wayne? How about a hundred dollars for every hour? Sounds fair, don't it, doc?"

Before Andrew could answer, Beth said, "Don't give it to him. I beg you, Andrew, don't do it. You can't give up everything you've worked for." She wouldn't voice her conviction that the sacrifice would be in vain. "I know how important that money is to you."

"Shut up, bitch. It's important to me, too."

Andrew appeared to ignore Peter. His gaze met Beth's across the room, and for a long moment he said nothing but simply looked at her. "The money is not important." He spoke as calmly as if they were alone in their dining room. "Nothing is important if I lose you."

Beth gasped. How could she have ever doubted Andrew's love? He had shown it in so many ways. Never once had he faltered, not even tonight when faced with Peter's impossible demands. Beth knew what the money meant to Andrew, how he valued it for far more than what it could buy, how it meant security and freedom to him. And he was willing to sacrifice it all for her! Tears welled in her eyes. For the first time in her life she had met a man who gave rather than took. Oh, how generously he gave!

"I'm not worthy of your love," she cried. If it hadn't been for her, Andrew wouldn't be in this predicament. She was the one who had brought danger and the threat of death into his life.

Andrew shook his head slowly, his eyes so filled with love that Beth felt warmed by his gaze. "You're worth everything to me, Beth. Everything." And then he smiled, a bittersweet smile that told her he recognized the precariousness of their situation and that, no matter what happened, he wanted to be with her. Beth's throat was so choked with emotion that she could not speak. Though tears threatened to spill from her eyes, she managed to smile back at Andrew, hoping he would recognize her love for him.

For a second there was no sound. Then Peter slapped his hands together. "Hey, Wayne. You see what I see? Looks to me like the doc fancies the redhead. What d'ya think?"

Wayne guffawed. "I tole you she was a looker."

Peter leaned back in the chair, his gaze moving from Beth to Andrew and back. Then he rose. Grabbing Beth's arms, he pulled her to her feet. Though her legs trembled from fatigue and fear, Beth kept her back straight. There was no telling what was going through Peter's mind. He leered, then drew a long, wicked-looking knife from inside his coat. Beth gasped. He was going to kill her. As if he could read her mind, Peter sneered and brandished the weapon in front of her throat. She stared at him, unwilling to cringe, though her heart was pounding and her hands were moist with fear.

With another evil grin, Peter spun Beth around, slid the

knife between her hands, and slit the rope. She was free!
Beth flexed her shoulders and rubbed her wrists. Peter smiled
at her and Andrew, and for the briefest of instants, she believed the miracle she had prayed for had happened. Peter
was going to release them. Then he spoke.

"The price just went up." He put his arm around Beth,
yanking her close to him and tipping her head. Though Beth
guessed he wanted her to look at him, she focused on the
hole in the roof, the stars, and a sliver of a moon. Outside,
the world was normal. It was only inside this cabin that
everything was so wrong.

Peter chuckled, sending a shiver down Beth's spine.
"We're gonna show the doc what he's missing. Me and
Wayne's gonna have some fun." He ran his hand over her
breasts to make his meaning clear. "The doc is gonna watch.
Then, when we get done, he's gonna give us the money."

Beth flinched as Peter squeezed her breast. Even though
the heavy serge protected her skin, she felt sullied by his
touch. "Now, show us what you learned at Silver's," Peter
continued as his hand moved lower to stroke her waist.
"Show me and Wayne what a good whore you are, and
maybe if you please us real good, we'll let the doc live."

The man was insane! He actually thought she would make
love with him. No, Beth corrected herself. It wouldn't be
making love. That was what she and Andrew did. This would
be nothing more than animal rutting. And he wanted Andrew
to watch. The man was even more depraved than she had
suspected.

Wayne took a step toward Peter and Beth. "Me first," he
offered. When Peter snarled, Wayne moved back.

"Don't do it." The pain in Andrew's voice and the anguish
she saw in his eyes wrenched Beth's heart. He knew how
long she had feared a man's touch, any man's touch. This
was not just any man. This was Peter, the man who had
abused her sister. Andrew knew how Beth loathed and feared
her brother-in-law. What he didn't know was how much she
loved him, Andrew. Beth managed a tiny smile, trying to
reassure Andrew. There was no question what she would do,
for her course was as clear as the night sky above them.

"Shut up!" Peter nodded at Wayne. "Get your shotgun and make sure the doc don't make no noise."

"Don't do it, Beth."

Peter snarled. "Didn't I tell you to shut up? Now, bitch, get those clothes off. I'm in a hurry to see what you're hidin' under there."

Beth reached for the top button.

"Beth!" Andrew's cry was tortured.

Her hands stilled and she looked directly at him, willing him to understand what she was about to do. "Don't you know that there's nothing I wouldn't do for you?" Seducing Peter and playing the whore with Wayne might not save Andrew's life, but if there was the slightest chance that it would, she had to take that chance. She couldn't—wouldn't—let them kill the man she loved. Not if there were even the remotest possibility of saving him.

Tears filled Andrew's eyes. "Don't do it, Beth. I'm not worth the sacrifice."

She returned his own words to him, smiling as she said, "You're worth everything to me, Andrew. Everything." They might not live until the sun rose, and that possibility made it vital that Andrew know how deeply she loved him.

Impatient, Peter slapped her hand. "Get movin', bitch."

"Yeah," Wayne seconded, "hurry."

Beth unfastened the top button with hands that were amazingly steady. Silver would have been proud of her. "You don't have to be a victim," Silver had told her. She was right. What Beth was about to do was not important. She would not allow it to be. She would not let the physical act or the feeling of Peter's hands and body on hers mean anything. All that was important was giving Andrew a chance.

From the corner of her eye she saw that although Wayne kept his gun pointed at Andrew, he was watching her, a dribble of saliva running from the corner of his mouth. Andrew moved his hands slowly, cautiously, and Beth knew he was trying to loosen his bonds. The tiny glimmer of hope that refused to be repressed grew. There might be a chance.

Andrew. It all came back to Andrew. He had taught her that a man and woman can bring each other pleasure, that the simple act of joining their bodies together was anything but simple, for when their hearts and souls joined as well, it brought a joy beyond all others. Andrew had healed her wounds; now she would do what she could to save him, for he was both her love and her life.

Beth released a second button from its loop, then spread her collar, leaving her throat open to Peter's gaze. Moving as slowly as she could, she unfastened a third button, again tugging her bodice open a few more inches. Peter's eyes widened, and she heard Wayne grunt. Beth didn't dare look at Andrew, lest Peter realize that Wayne was no longer guarding him.

Keeping her eyes fixed on Peter and forcing her lips into a smile, she let her hands drop to her sides, and as she did, she felt a tiny object in her skirts. For the first time, Beth's smile was genuine. There might be a way.

"Hurry, bitch!" Peter stretched his hand out to touch her bare throat.

Beth smiled again, hoping that Peter would find it a seductive smile. "I thought you wanted to see what I learned at Silver's," she said in as sultry a voice as she could manage. "You were right, Peter. Silver taught me a lot about men." "She taught me about how to pleasure real men." *And how to protect myself from them,* she added silently.

Peter did not appear impressed. "Get movin'."

On the other side of the room, Wayne shuffled his feet. "What did the old whore say?" Peter glared at him.

Beth gave Wayne a smile, then turned back to Peter. "Silver says real men go slowly. They measure their manhood by how long they can wait." Silver had said nothing of the sort. Though she'd discussed many things with Silver, Beth would never have asked her about such intimate matters. It was Andrew who had taught her about patience and manhood. He always made sure that Beth was ready before he took his own pleasure. She had learned so much from him!

"Is that so?" Though Wayne sounded interested, Beth would not take her gaze from Peter's face. She wanted him to watch her and only her.

"Why, yes," Beth continued, and turned slowly toward the

table. It had been hours since Peter had had a drink. That—
and Peter's undeniable arrogance—might help her plan succeed. "Some of them even enjoy a drink with the ladies."

"I'm mighty thirsty." Wayne's voice sounded closer, and
Beth guessed he was approaching the table. She darted a
quick glance at him. He was no longer guarding Andrew. In
fact, he seemed to have forgotten the other man's existence.

"Wait your turn!" Peter growled at his henchman.

"You could both enjoy a drink while I undress," Beth suggested. Without waiting for Peter's approval, she moved to
the table. Keeping her back to the men, she uncapped the
vial that she had drawn from her skirts and divided its contents between the two tin cups. Then she half filled the cups
with whiskey.

"There you are, gentlemen." She handed each one a cup,
trying not to cringe at the contact with Wayne's sweaty
palms.

Wayne downed his quickly, smacking his lips in apparent
pleasure. A speculative expression crossed Peter's face as he
stared at his cup. Beth's heart plummeted. Had he guessed
that she had given him something other than pure whiskey?
No, he couldn't have seen her. Her skirts were wide enough
that he could not have seen past them.

"Later," Peter said, and plunked the cup on the table next
to Beth. "I wanna taste you." He grabbed the chair and
sprawled on it, stretching his legs in front of him. "Hurry up,
bitch!"

*Hurry, Andrew!* Beth dared not pronounce the words. She
could only hope he heard her silent plea. She moved slowly,
gracefully unfastening the remaining buttons, pausing after
each one to show Peter a bit more flesh. There were no
sounds in the cabin save Wayne's loud breathing and a soft,
almost imperceptible rustling that Beth hoped was Andrew
releasing his bonds. When the final button was undone, she
leaned forward, easing the dress from her shoulders. Peter's
eyes widened, and he began to lick his lips.

"You're gonna taste good," he muttered.

From the corner of her eye, Beth saw a sudden motion.

*Oh, no!* Wayne, who had been leaning against the wall, tumbled forward.

"What the hell!" Peter stared at his accomplice, crumpled on the floor, snoring loudly. Jumping to his feet and kicking the chair aside, Peter shook his fist at Beth. "You bitch! You did it." He grabbed her arm and ripped her chemise from her shoulders. "Hurry, I wanna make a baby tonight!"

"If you do," Andrew said slowly, "it will be the first one."

# Chapter Twenty-three

Beth's heart began to pound with fear as Peter swiveled to glare at Andrew. What was he doing, inflaming Peter? Surely he knew the man was volatile enough without deliberately angering him. The lump that refused to leave Beth's throat grew as a new doubt assailed her. Was Andrew trying to draw Peter's attention away from her so that she could escape? Blood drained from her face at the thought that he would sacrifice himself for her. Didn't he realize that Peter would kill her, too, and that—even if he did not—she did not want to live in a world without Andrew?

"What do you mean?" Peter demanded, his lip curling in a snarl. Though his handsome face was distorted with anger, it was his eyes that frightened Beth, for they were filled with venom. Right now that venom was directed at Andrew.

"I thought my meaning was clear," Andrew said in a voice so haughty that even Peter could not mistake the scorn. "You aren't man enough to sire a child."

If Andrew's intention was to make Peter forget her, he succeeded. Peter took a step toward Andrew, releasing his hold on Beth as he did.

"You lie!" he shouted.

Wayne snored. Andrew raised one eyebrow. Beth moved back a pace, narrowing her eyes. It appeared that Andrew had succeeded in loosening the ties around his wrists and ankles. Though the ropes remained, they no longer restrained him. Why, then, was he still on the floor? As her gaze met Andrew's, she read his warning. *Don't let Peter suspect,* Andrew's eyes urged.

But Peter was too angry to notice loosened ropes. "That little girl you fancy is mine," he declared. "Mine!"

Andrew's eyes moved ever so slightly to the right, and Beth realized that he was looking at Wayne's shotgun. Suddenly, his actions made sense. He was indeed trying to inflame Peter, but for a good reason. For Andrew and Beth to have a chance of living, they needed a weapon. Alone, neither of them could succeed. Together, they just might have a chance. Beth inched toward Wayne. If Andrew kept Peter's attention focused on him, she might be able to reach the gun.

"I don't know *who* Dora's father is," Andrew said calmly. "All I know is that he was a black man."

Beth's step faltered. Could it be true, or was Andrew simply trying to anger Peter? He knew the man was a slave catcher, and it could have been a calculated insult with no basis in reality. Still, Andrew did not sound as if he were bluffing. Could it be true? As she considered the possibility, Beth remembered an afternoon when Lenore and Rodney had emerged from the barn, both of their faces flushed, their clothing in disarray. At the time, she had believed Lenore's story that they had tried to pull a bale of hay from the loft and had lost their balance. Now, Beth was not so certain. The look she remembered seeing on Rodney's face reminded her of Andrew when they lay together in those sweet moments after they had made love.

"Liar!" Peter crossed the cabin in three quick strides and kicked Andrew. "Lenore was a virgin. I know that just like I know the brat is mine." As Beth took another step toward Wayne and his shotgun, Peter's laughter sent a shiver of horror down her spine. "The bitch sure cried like a virgin that first night I had her. Just like you're gonna cry before I get done with you." He kicked Andrew again. "Yes, sirree, you're gonna cry like a baby."

Though tears of anger and sorrow for the pain her sister

had endured stung Beth's eyes, she forced herself to keep moving. She could not help Lenore now, but maybe, just maybe, she could save Andrew.

Beth winced at the sound of Peter's boot connecting with Andrew's ribs. Another step. Andrew gave no sign of the pain he must be feeling. Instead, he raised one eyebrow and asked, "Is that so? If you're her father, why does Dora have curly hair and brown eyes?"

Two feet. That was all that separated her from the shotgun. Beth took another step as Andrew continued his taunting. "You're not man enough to make a baby."

The last step. Beth grabbed the gun.

"You bastard! I'll kill you!" Peter whipped his pistol from its holster and pointed it at Andrew.

There was no time to aim. Beth used the gun as a club, swinging with all her might. She missed. At the last instant, Peter shifted his weight, and the blow landed on his arm rather than his head. The pistol flew from his hand at the same time that Andrew jumped to his feet.

"Run, Beth!" Andrew cried. But she could not, not when it meant leaving Andrew to face the monster alone.

"I'll kill you!" Peter repeated, and lunged at Andrew, knocking him back to the ground. In a movement so swift she barely saw it, Andrew hooked his leg around Peter's. The man fell to the floor like a toppled tree.

Now! Now was her chance to help!

Beth raised the shotgun, training it on Peter's back. Her finger reached for the trigger, then stopped. The two men were wrestling, rolling on the ground, first one on top and then the other. She was too late. Beth dared not shoot now for fear of hitting Andrew. The sounds of thuds and groans filled the small cabin as the two men battered each other, while Beth stood watching helplessly.

"You're gonna die!" Peter grunted and, breaking out of Andrew's grip, reached for his boot. An instant later, Beth saw the glint of metal. A knife! Dear God, she had forgotten he had a knife.

"Andrew!" she cried.

It was all the warning he needed. As Peter raised the blade,

Andrew gripped the other man's wrist, twisting it brutally. But Peter would not drop the knife. "Die!" he screamed. In a desperate attempt to win, Peter jerked free, raising his arm above his head. For the briefest of instants the knife gleamed in the light as it remained suspended over Andrew.

Beth's heart stopped. *Oh, Andrew, I love you!* She dared not say the words aloud lest they break his concentration. Perhaps he heard them, for Andrew grabbed Peter's wrist a second time, forcing it toward the ground, keeping the knife away from him. Suddenly off balance, Peter lurched to the side, and as he did, Andrew took advantage of his momentary weakness to roll on top of him. But Peter continued to roll, dragging Andrew with him.

There were no voices, nothing but the sickening sounds of metal cleaving flesh and blood spurting, followed by a final gasp. Then the cabin held only silence and two blood-spattered bodies.

For a second Beth was speechless, not believing it was over. As realization swept through her, the light began to dim. *No!* She fought against the encroaching darkness. But though her vision cleared, her heart was empty. Once again evil had triumphed. Even in death, Peter had won, for he had taken Andrew with him. Sorrow and the heavy burden of guilt slumped her shoulders. It was because of her that Andrew was gone.

"Oh, Andrew!" Tears filled her eyes and coursed down her cheeks. "How will I live without you?"

"Can you help get this weight off me?"

Beth stood stunned. Her heart faltered, then began to flutter. "Andrew?" She fell to her knees as joy surged through her. Somehow, by some miracle, Andrew was alive! She touched his face with hands that were still wet with her tears. He was alive! "Where are you hurt?" she demanded when they had rolled Peter's body to the side and she had assured herself that Andrew was indeed alive. It was not her imagination. He was dirty and bloody and visibly exhausted, but he was alive. "There's so much blood."

"It's Girton's," Andrew said, running his hands expertly over his ribs. "I have a lot of bruises, but nothing's broken."

"Thank God!" Beth helped him to his feet. For a moment they stood motionless, clinging to each other in a desperate need to prove that they were both alive and safe. Then Andrew looked down at Wayne's inert body and frowned. "Let's tie him up and get out of here. We'll let the authorities deal with him."

A few minutes later, they stood outside the cabin. Beth raised her eyes to the clear sky and inhaled deeply. The same stars that she had seen through the cabin's roof shone brightly, but now they were surrounded only by the purity of the night sky. The ugliness and evil were gone. The nightmare was over. She would fear Peter no longer.

"The air smells so clean." Beth wondered if she would ever forget the sickening odors of blood and death.

Andrew raised his arm to encircle her shoulders. "It's the smell of freedom," he said. "When my passengers would talk about it, I thought it was just their imagination. Now I know better." He drew Beth closer and tipped his head toward the sky. "There's your star," he said, nodding at the North Star. "Your hopes have come true; you and Dora won't have to fear again."

Beth swallowed deeply. "I want to believe that." She had lived with fear for so long that it would take some time before she purged its poison from her heart. "It all happened so fast that I can't believe Peter's gone."

Andrew led her toward the buggy. "I never thought I would kill a man," he said quietly. "When I became a doctor, I took an oath to save lives." The anguish in Andrew's voice was reflected in the pain she saw in his eyes. "Perhaps it's wrong," he continued, "but I'm not sorry that Peter's dead. He deserved to die for what he did to your sister and Dora and all those slaves."

Beth shivered, although whether from the cool night air or reaction to everything that had happened, she could not say. "How did you know that Peter was a slave catcher?" That had come as a shock to her.

"I didn't until tonight. Wayne couldn't help boasting about how good Peter was, and then it all made sense." Andrew tightened his grip on her shoulders, his warmth dispelling the night's chill. "Remember the time David and I met Peter and I told you he seemed familiar to me but I couldn't figure out why? It was the beard that confused me." After lifting Beth into the buggy, Andrew untied the horse and climbed in on the other side. "The first time I saw him, he had whiskers."

Beth slid across the seat and wrapped her hands around Andrew's arm. She had come so close to losing him that just seeing him wasn't enough. She needed the reassurance of his touch. "Where did you see Peter?" It was odd. Her voice sounded normal, as if she and Andrew were having an ordinary conversation, not discussing the evil man who had threatened them both.

"He stopped me on a delivery."

Her calm dissolved, and Beth's hands began to tremble as she remembered the two times Peter had tried to intercept her deliveries.

Andrew laid his hand on hers. When her trembling subsided, he said, "I tricked him the first time. I wasn't so lucky the second." Andrew paused, and she sensed that he was considering his next words carefully. "Beth, I'm sure Peter was the man who shot me."

Not only did it make sense, but it also explained why Peter had been patrolling the same road the night Beth had made her second delivery. She shuddered, thinking of how close Andrew had come to dying at Peter's hand, not once but twice. "He would have killed you. I know it. Peter's the one who killed Rodney."

"Rodney?" Andrew turned the buggy onto the main road.

"My family's free black neighbor." The night was calm, filled with the ordinary sounds of nocturnal animals and the horse's steady clip-clop. It was only Beth's thoughts that roiled. "Rodney was Dora's father."

Andrew tugged the reins, slowing the horse as he turned to face Beth. "Are you sure?" His blue eyes were serious. "I was only guessing when I told Peter that Dora's father was a black man." Andrew stroked Beth's hand slowly. "I know from my research that two parents with blue eyes could not have a brown-eyed child. One of Dora's parents had to have brown eyes. The rest was speculation."

Beth laced her fingers through Andrew's, taking comfort from his touch. "I think Rodney was her father. That would explain why Lenore kept a lock of his hair in her Bible and why she told me that she loved Dora's father." Beth shook her head slowly, remembering the day Lenore had told her that and how incredulous she had been. "I couldn't understand how anyone could love Peter."

"Do you know why she married him?"

"Probably to protect her child. Our father would have killed her if she had had a baby out of wedlock." Beth realized that Lenore had agreed to marry Peter only after Rodney had disappeared. At the time, Beth had wondered about her sister's haste, but Lenore had assured her that she knew exactly what she was doing and that it was the right thing. "Poor Dora," Beth said. "She never knew her father, and she's lost her mother."

Drawing Beth's hand to his lips, Andrew pressed a kiss on her knuckles. "You're Dora's mother now," he said softly. He touched Beth's chin, waiting until she met his gaze before he continued. "And I want to be her father."

"Are you sure?" Though the love Beth saw shining from Andrew's eyes filled her with awe, she needed to ask. "It won't be easy for you if people learn about her mixed blood."

Andrew nodded. "I know that, but I also know the joy Dora will bring us." Though Andrew's eyes sparkled with love, his face was serious. "My darling, don't you know that I want to share everything with you?"

Tears of joy, sorrow and relief welled in Beth's eyes.

"What's wrong?" Andrew asked.

Beth shook her head. "Nothing. Not anymore." She dashed the tears from her cheeks. "I used to ache inside every time that I thought about my sister. It seemed so sad that Lenore had never known the kind of love you and I have shared." Beth brought Andrew's hand to her lips and kissed his knuckles, returning the sweet caress. "Now I know Lenore was happy and loved—even if only for a little while." Beth held Andrew's hand tightly as she said, "I'm glad I have Dora. She's part of my sister and her love."

Andrew looked down at his bloodstained, dirty clothes and frowned. "It never seems to happen the way I plan it, but I can't wait any longer. I need to know. Beth, will you marry me? Will you take me as I am and trust me to keep you and Dora safe and happy?"

There was only one answer possible.

"Oh, yes, my love!"


"It was a beautiful wedding," Beth said as they walked through the front door. Her cheeks ached from smiling, yet she didn't think she would ever stop. Had there ever been such a wonderful day? Had there ever been such a thoughtful husband?

"Thank you, Andrew. I will never forget it."

Andrew's smile matched hers. "I only wish Silver and Tom had agreed to come."

It had surprised Beth that Andrew had been so insistent that her friends receive an invitation, but he had been adamant and had accompanied Beth on one of her visits to Canal Street to add his pleas to hers. Without Silver, he had explained, neither one of them would still be alive, for it was Silver's advice and her drug that had bought Andrew the time to free himself.

"You know they would have been uncomfortable," Beth said, "but it was wonderful, taking them part of the cake."

The house seemed strangely empty. Andrew had given the servants the day off to celebrate, and Silver had insisted that Dora remain with her overnight. "A newly married couple deserves at least one night alone," Silver had declared, giving Tom one of the loving glances that she shared so often with her husband.

Beth smiled again. "I'll never forget how happy Silver and Tom were."

Andrew's grin was mischievous, deepening the cleft in his chin. When Beth reached out to trace it, Andrew forestalled her. "I'm not complaining that you want to remember those things," he said as he swung her into his arms. "That's fine. But, sweetheart, I want you to remember tonight."

Beth laid her head on his chest, listening to the steady

sound of his heartbeat as he carried her up the stairs. Moonlight spilled through the beautiful stained-glass window, coloring the floor. Though the window's hues were brilliant, they could not compare to the scenes that danced in Beth's imagination. Soon! Soon she and Andrew would be together again, sharing the pleasure he had shown her a man and woman could bring each other.

"Close your eyes," Andrew said when they reached the landing. He carried her down the hall, nudged the door to his room open, and set her back on her feet. "You can look now." As her eyes flew open, Beth gasped in delight, for Andrew had filled the corners of the room with bouquets of flowers. Their colors rivaled the stained glass, and their fragrance . . . ah, their fragrance. Beth inhaled deeply. Though the season was late and few flowers were blooming, Andrew must have scoured the city's greenhouses looking for fragrant blooms.

"It's all so beautiful!" She touched the deep green leaves of a heliotrope and breathed in the spicy aroma.

Andrew stood behind her, so close that she could feel his heat and smell his citrus scent. "Nothing is as beautiful as you." He drew her into his arms and lowered his lips to hers, feathering soft kisses on the corners of her mouth, then tracing the outline with his tongue. "Do you know how I've longed to do that?" he asked. "Or this?" He raised his hand and gently stroked her neck. Shivers of delight coursed down Beth's body. Did she know? Oh, yes! She had dreamt of his touch each night, and filled her days with memories of the sweetness of his kiss. Andrew unfastened the top button on her dress.

Beth cupped his face between her hands and smiled. "Do you know how I've longed to have you do exactly that or"— she looked at the bed, its white spread pulled back to reveal the snowy sheet—"how I've longed to wake up next to you in the morning?"

Andrew's eyes were filled with tenderness, love, desire, and a touch of awe. As he smiled back at her, Beth knew that he had seen the same emotions reflected in her gaze. "Your wish will come true," he promised. "We'll waken together tomorrow and every other tomorrow." As he loosened her waist ties, her dress slid to the floor.

Beth reached for Andrew's shirt and started to unfasten it. "I never dreamed I could be this happy."

In the distance a clock chimed and an owl hooted. Andrew touched Beth's cheek, stroking it slowly, almost reverently. "When I was a child, I used to lie awake at night," he said softly. "I'd see stars outside the window and, even though I knew it was foolish, I would wish on one. But the wishes never came true . . . until you."

"Oh, Andrew!"

As their remaining clothes tumbled to the floor, he lifted her into his arms and carried her to the bed.

"I love you, Mrs. Muller," he said, laying her on the smooth sheets. "I will, forever and ever, until the last star has fallen from the sky."

And then his lips claimed hers and their bodies moved in timeless rhythms, tasting, tantalizing, and finally transporting them to a world of their own where the stars of love shone brighter than any in the heavens. Later, much later, in the sweet afterglow of love, Beth smiled.

She touched her husband's lips and murmured the words she knew he loved.

"Oh, Andrew!"

# Lair of the Wolf

## Chapter Ten

### Debra Dier

*Lair of the Wolf* also appears in these *Leisure* books:

COMPULSION by Elaine Fox
includes Chapter One by Constance O'Banyon

CINNAMON AND ROSES by Heidi Betts
includes Chapter Two by Bobbi Smith

SWEET REVENGE by Lynsay Sands
includes Chapter Three by Evelyn Rogers

TELL ME LIES by Claudia Dain
includes Chapter Four by Emily Carmichael

WHITE NIGHTS by Susan Edwards
includes Chapter Five by Martha Hix

IN TROUBLE'S ARMS by Ronda Thompson
includes Chapter Six by Deana James

THE SWORD AND THE FLAME by Patricia Phillips
includes Chapter Seven by Sharon Schulze

MANON by Melanie Jackson
includes Chapter Eight by June Lund Shiplett

THE RANCHER'S DAUGHTERS: FORGETTING
    HERSELF by Yvonne Jocks
includes Chapter Nine by Elizabeth Mayne

On January 1, 1997, *Romance Communications*, the Romance Magazine for the 21st century made its Internet debut. One year later, it was named a Lycos Top 5% site on the Web in terms of both content and graphics!

One of *Romance Communications*' most popular features is The Romantic Relay, an original romance novel divided into twelve monthly installments, with each chapter written by a different author. Our first offering was *Lair of the Wolf*, a tale of medieval Wales, created by, in alphabetical order, celebrated authors Emily Carmichael, Debra Dier, Madeline George, Martha Hix, Deana James, Elizabeth Mayne, Constance O'Banyon, Evelyn Rogers, Sharon Schulze, June Lund Shiplett, and Bobbi Smith.

We put no restrictions on the authors, letting each pick up the tale where the previous author had left off and going forward as she wished. The authors tell us they had a lot of fun, each trying to write her successor into a corner!

Now, preserving the fun and suspense of our month-by-month installments, Leisure Books presents, in print, one chapter a month of *Lair of the Wolf.* In addition to the entire online story, the authors have added some brand-new material to their existing chapters. So if you think you've read *Lair of the Wolf* already, you may find a few surprises. Please enjoy this unique offering, watch for each new monthly installment in the back of your Leisure Books, and make sure you visit our website, where another romantic relay is already in progress.

*Romance Communications*

http://www.romcom.com

Pamela Monck, Editor-in-Chief

Mary D. Pinto, Senior Editor

S. Lee Meyer, Web Mistress

# Chapter Ten

*by Debra Dier*

Meredyth would have retorted to Garon's arrogant quest for her wifely obedience, but she could feel his strength ebb with each succeeding step they took up the stone staircase to their bedchamber. By the time they reached their destination, he was leaning heavily against her. As much as she would deny her traitorous feelings for this man, she couldn't abandon her anxiety for him, it twisted like steel bands around her chest. Many a soldier had died from far less serious wounds than he had suffered this night.

"I swear, Lord Wolf, there are moments when you are the most addle-pated man I have ever met."

Garon laughed, the sound vibrating from deep in his chest. "In that respect, we are well-suited, my lady."

She ignored the barb and slipped her arm around his waist, steadying him as they crossed the bedchamber. Their footsteps stirred the rushes strewn across the floor, releasing the scent of herbs and lavender. Burning logs on the great fireplace cast a reddish-yellow glow into the room, guiding her to the hide chair near the hearth. "I don't understand why you didn't have your men carry you to bed. You'll have that wound bleeding again if you don't take care."

He sank into the chair, his breath escaping on a low sigh. "It would not do to have my people believe their lord is not strong. Not now."

"Pride." She glared down at him. "I shall never understand the foolishness of masculine pride."

He smiled up at her, a wide, boyish grin that tripped her wayward heart.

" 'Tis more than pride, my lady. The people look to their

lord for protection, for guidance, for reassurance that all will be well. We have, at the moment, an uneasy peace within our walls. If our people believed I was near death's door, that peace might be broken."

His casual reference to his own death grated along her spine like sharpened nails. "If you are so concerned about the people of Glendire, you will take care with yourself."

He studied her a moment, a curious expression entering his dark eyes. "You surprise me, my lady."

"In what way?"

"Ordinarily I would think you anxious to have my hide nailed to your wall. Have you at last decided I am not truly your enemy?"

She turned away from him, afraid of what he might see in her eyes. She took a piece of kindling from the box on the hearth and shoved the tip into the fire as she spoke. "Your death would gain me little more than a moment's peace. Longshanks would only send someone else in your stead."

"Aye, he would. But mayhap the new knight would be more to your liking."

She touched the burning tip of the wood to the candles in the branched silver candlestick on the trestle table between his chair and the chair reserved for his lady, still refusing to meet his gaze. She knew he was angling for her true feelings about him. She refused to betray them. "Mayhap he would be a worse tyrant than you. I am accustomed to the Wolf. I have no desire to become acquainted with another of Longshanks' beasts."

"I shall take your words to heart, my lady. And mayhap one day you will learn to accept your husband."

She tossed the kindling onto the fire. " 'Tis difficult to accept a conqueror."

He nodded. "Aye, 'tis difficult. Yet Wales is part of England now, as it has been for nigh on twelve years. If your father and others like him had come to accept their new sovereign, their blood would not have been shed on the battlefield."

"My father and brothers fought for what they believed in. Freedom."

He rubbed his fingers gingerly over the bandage covering the wound in his shoulder. "And when is the fighting to stop? When shall the people stand as one, instead of fighting for a lost cause? When shall the healing begin?"

She curled her hands into fists at her sides, still battling a truth that sank deep into her marrow. " 'Tis not a lost cause. One day Wales shall be free from England's tyranny."

"No, my lady. Wales shall remain always a part of England. You are intelligent enough to know it, even though your heart would cling to a slender band of hope. Edward has the strength and the will to keep Wales in his grasp. And as long as there is rebellion, there shall be bloodshed."

The truth of his words pounded against her heart, demanding acceptance.

She pinned him with what she hoped was one of her chilliest glares. "Give me your dagger."

He lifted one black eyebrow. "You look angry enough to slice my throat from apple to ear."

"Though 'tis a tempting thought, 'tis only the remainder of your tunic I would slice. Else we would jostle your shoulder and cause the bleeding to commence again."

"It takes a certain amount of trust to hand a weapon to an enemy."

"If I had wanted you dead, I would not have shielded you on the stairs."

"Aye. You saved my life." He pulled his dagger from the leather sheath on his hip. Candlelight glittered on the keenly honed blade as he turned it in his hand, offering her the handle. " 'Tis a wondrous beginning."

She gripped the smooth wooden handle and bent to her task. "You should make nothing more of my gesture than my own reluctance to be burdened with another, unknown enemy."

"And should I make nothing of the kiss you gave me?" he asked, his warm breath a soft caress against her cheek.

Her body trembled with awareness of his dangerous masculinity. " 'Tis no secret, Lord Wolf, that you have managed to stir my base-instincts." She eased the blade beneath the shoulder of his tunic. "In this respect I would not attempt to dispute you."

"And you have managed to ignite a fire in my blood, my lady. I find myself thinking of you, day and night."

She clenched her teeth, trying desperately to ignore the warmth his words stirred within her heart. Soft, emerald green wool parted beneath the lethal blade, revealing the smooth skin beneath. "Save your honeyed words. You have no need of them. I shall warm your bed. I have little choice."

"For some time now I've come to think, if given a choice of brides, I would choose no one above you."

Lies from her enemy, she assured herself. He was not to be believed. Yet, a part of her wanted desperately to believe there was a place for her in his heart.

Foolish woman.

Reckless wishes.

The spicy tang of herb soap rose with the heat of his skin, mingling with an intriguing masculine scent that was his alone. The heady blend swirled through her senses, igniting flames low in her belly. She could defeat this desire, she assured herself. Yet the pledge rang hollow inside her.

After removing his wide leather belt, she cleaved the ragged front of the garment and the remaining sleeve. Carefully, she peeled the blood-soaked tunic from his skin. Candlelight poured over the flesh stretched tautly over the broad width of his shoulders. The golden light spilled across the thick planes of his chest, tangling in black masculine curls, illuminating the white linen bandage slicing across them, the blood from his tunic staining his skin, and the white scars carved there as savage reminders of war.

When shall the healing begin?

For a moment tonight, she had thought him dead. In that moment, pain had pierced her so deeply, she had thought she might die. In this moment, as she gazed down at him, it took all her will to keep from making a fool of herself. She wanted to throw her arms around him and confess the terrible secret of her soul. She wanted to cradle him in her arms this night, and all the nights to come. She wanted to give him all the love she had hidden deep inside her. Could it ever be? Would she ever feel free enough to end this war? Did she possess the courage?

She lifted her eyes, meeting his gaze. He was studying her, as though he might dismantle her defenses with that look, peer at all her foolish hopes and dreams. Did he know? Did he realize how close she was to delivering herself utterly into his hands?

"I've brought the warm water and clean cloths you wanted, my lady."

Meredyth started at the intrusion into her thoughts. She glanced at the doorway and found one of the serving maids standing on the threshold, a wooden basin in her hands, white linen cloths draped over her arm. "Place them here, Enid," she said, gesturing toward the table beside Sir Garon's chair.

The young woman crossed the room, her yellow braid swaying, her gaze darting to Garon. She placed the basin and cloths on the table, then stepped back, her head bowed, her gaze fixed on her new lord's half-naked form.

Meredyth handed the bloody tunic to the girl. "Take this."

Enid nodded, her gaze never leaving Garon.

Meredyth prickled at the obvious admiration in the girl's brown eyes.

"That will be all, Enid."

Enid jumped at her sharp tone. "Aye, my lady."

Meredyth followed the girl across the room and bolted the door after her.

When she turned, she found Garon grinning at her. No doubt the Wolf knew exactly how well he could enchant a foolish female.

She marched to the table, grabbed a cloth and the basin, then knelt in front of him. "I should warn you, Lord Wolf," she said, dunking the cloth into the warm water, "I shall not take it docilely should you decide to humiliate me. If I find you rutting with every serving girl in Glendire, I shall do something ugly to you."

"I'm surprised. I had the impression you would prefer I rut with anyone, as long as I stayed away from you."

She twisted the cloth in her hands, sending water splashing into the basin.

"I might not have chosen this marriage, but I expect you to honor your vows."

He slipped his fingers beneath her chin and coaxed her to meet his gaze.

"Why would I want another woman, when I have you in my bed? I may not be a sophisticated man, Merrie, but I do know a jewel when I see one."

She stared up into his beautiful eyes, seeking the lies behind his words but seeing only sincerity. "Are you an honest man, Lord Wolf? Or do you seek only to tame a wild falcon?"

He cupped her cheek in one warm palm, his calluses teasing her skin. "I seek to make a true union with my beautiful, reluctant bride."

She leaned toward him, drawn by the warmth in his eyes. Did he truly care for her?

"I seek to rebuild the glory of Glendire. But I cannot do it alone, Merrie. I want to see the meadows green and rich once more. I want to see the people fat and satisfied from the bounty of our fields. Yet I know little of being a landed lord. I will need your help. Your wisdom. Your advice in many regards."

His words hit her with the impact of a bucket of brine. She pulled away from his touch, counting herself the worst of fools. Gently she rubbed the cloth against his skin, wiping away the stains of his blood.

She had asked for honesty, and she had received it. He wanted her assistance. And he would use his masculine wiles to obtain it. "There is no need for you to pretend any sentiment for me, Lord Wolf. I, too, wish to see the glory of Glendire restored. For the sake of my people, and for the legacy of my father, I shall help you."

He slipped his long fingers around her arms and drew her upward, cradling her between the heat of his thighs. The warmth of his bare chest bathed her face. His spicy scent curled around her. His smile touched her with all the languidness of summer. "Merrie mine, I want more than your sage counsel. I'm a warrior. The delicacies of conversation elude my grasp. I have no experience in shaping the words that would let you know how I feel. But I do know that I want you as my bride, in every way. I will pledge to you my honor and loyalty, if you will give me yours."

Words beat against her throat, seeking release. Yet she could not find the courage to reveal herself so completely to this man. "You ask a great deal of a woman forced into marriage, Lord Wolf."

"No more than I am willing to give." He kissed her brow. "In time, you will see that I am not your enemy."

She withdrew from the compelling heat of his grasp. She lowered her gaze to her task as she cleaned the blood from his skin. Could she trust him? He was, indeed, a warrior. Brutal in battle. Yet there seemed a gentleness in him as well. Was it an illusion? She smoothed her fingertip over a raised white scar that slashed across his ribs. It was but one of many. "You have come close to death many times. Why does a man choose a life of battle and bloodshed?"

"In my case, the choice was the chance to better myself."

"By killing."

"By serving my king."

"A butcher."

"A strong sovereign."

Meredyth dipped the cloth in the basin, and the water turned red with his blood. " 'Tis difficult to accept this man as my sovereign, when I have hated him my entire life. When he has taken from me all that was dear to me."

"There is nothing to be gained in staring into the past, Merrie. What we do now shapes the future we shall live."

She looked up at this man and acknowledged a simple truth: She wanted a future with him. "If you wish for a future, you had better get to bed, Lord Wolf."

"There are things to do this night. Traitors to—"

"Hanes has things well in hand, Garon. You need rest. You can deal with the traitors in the morning. Any reasonable man would see that."

He studied her a moment, and she feared he meant to argue with her.

Instead, he smiled. "I will rest, if you will tell Hanes to

come to me. There are matters I wish him to handle yet this evening."

She smiled, both pleased and amazed that he had deferred to her counsel. "I will fetch him for you, my lord." And she completed her task and left to seek the captain of the guard.

Meredyth found Hanes on the dais in the Great Hall, waiting for Garon. After directing the captain to meet with her husband, she remained in the hall, giving the men privacy. She stood by the great carved chair where her father had once sat, and she observed that three of Garon's men stood guard. Strange, the presence of the English did not stir in her the hatred she had long nurtured. In truth, for the first time in what seemed a lifetime, the burdens of Glendire did not rest so heavily upon her shoulders.

*"What we do now shapes the future we shall live,"* Garon had said.

She ran her hand over the carved oak of the chair. What would her father think of his daughter and the future she would choose? Only a fool allowed guilt to rule her. Her father had not raised her to be a fool. Guilt and devotion to a lost cause led only to destruction. It would take courage to alter her former path in life. Courage and strength to make Glendire whole once more.

Meredyth drew in her breath, silently embracing the challenge before her.

Although her husband was not Welsh, he was a good man. She would stand beside Garon. Together they would restore the glory of Glendire. Her people would thrive. And she would live her life with a man who could make her heart soar. For the first time in a long time, hope blossomed in her heart, crowding out the twisted vines of hatred and bitterness rooted there.

She smiled at Hanes as he approached her upon his return to the hall.

The tall Englishman returned her smile. "My lord would like to see you, my lady."

And she would like very much to see her husband.

With Hanes as escort, Meredyth hurried back to the bedchamber. Hanes left her at the door.

Garon was sitting in the chair as she had left him, smiling at her in that way that sent her heart racing. She answered that smile with a warmth that came from deep within her.

"Are you ready for bed, my Lord Wolf?"

His smile turned devilish. "I will need your help getting out of these clothes."

She rested a hand on his thigh, smiling as the thick muscles flexed beneath her touch. She was beginning to understand the power a woman might hold over a man. If she found the courage to take it. "I think I can manage."

"I think you can manage anything you set your mind to, Merrie mine."

She prayed he was right. She hoped her courage would not fail her or her people.

Garon had never realized that the simple act of holding a woman close to him could be so satisfying. Beneath the soft fur of the pelt covering his bed, Meredyth lay snuggled against his side, her bare breasts smoldering against his skin, one slender arm thrown over his waist in casual possession, her head cradled against his uninjured shoulder. He could sense her softening toward him. He celebrated her courageous act of saving his life. He reveled in the lush heat of desire simmering between them.

He thanked the Almighty for bringing this woman into his life. Silently, he pledged to give to her only the best of him. For this fine, spirited lady deserved nothing less.

He smoothed a hand down her arm, absorbing the luxury of her femininity, of her warmth. The scent of lavender drifted from her hair and skin, spilling through him like a breath of spring. He wasn't certain what he had done to deserve this prize; the single act of taking an arrow for his sovereign did not seem enough. But he did know that he would battle anything and everything to keep her.

Still, a wise warrior knew his enemies well. And something about the events of this night did not settle gently on his mind.

"Merrie," he said softly, "a warrior has always to think clearly. Strategy can mean all the difference in battle. I'm afraid earlier I may have allowed my anger at what happened to you to cloud my thinking, mayhap to blind my judgment."

She shifted beside him, tilting her head to look at him. "What do you mean?"

He drew his fingers through her hair, the short golden strands sliding like silk against his skin. "Did you actually see Sir Olyver strike you?"

She stiffened against him, and light from the hearth illuminated the sudden tensing of her features. "Do you doubt my word of what happened? Do you somehow imagine I arranged for someone to strike me and toss me into the catacombs?"

"No, of course not." He stroked her shoulder. "But how did Sir Olyver learn of the catacombs? Even I didn't know of them until after you told me what had happened."

She frowned. "I don't know. I suppose one of the servants might have told him. Or if he were intent upon committing the evil deed, perhaps he did some exploring and strategizing himself."

" 'Tis not likely." He rubbed her back, drawing serpentine designs against her smooth skin. "Besides, Sir Olyver would gain little by attacking you."

"You doubt he did this? He was with me on the stairs. Who else could have done it?"

Once the red haze of rage had lifted from his mind, the suspicions had begun to enter. "Tell me everything you remember about the attack."

Meredyth pursed her lips. For a moment he thought she would resist. In the end, she released her breath and recounted all she could remember of what had happened on the darkened staircase.

"He warned you to look out, just before you felt a blow to your head?"

"Aye."

A warning from the man who had committed the crime? It seemed unlikely. "And just before you escaped the catacombs, you heard someone coming for you."

"That's right. Sir Olyver."

"Mayhap." Could Olyver have managed to make his way

from the catacombs to the dais before Meredyth entered the hall? As he recalled, the man hadn't so much as a streak of dirt on his person. Nor did he appear out of breath. "Mayhap not."

She sat up in bed, allowing the pelt to tumble to her waist. "Why are you doubting that slimy snake did it? You saw his treachery this evening. You felt the sting of it."

Garon's gaze lowered to her breasts. Firelight flickered against the pale globes that rose and fell with each indignant breath. Heat coiled and tightened in his belly. "He reacted out of fear and anger. I told him I would have him lashed for touching you."

"And now you doubt he did it. The man is jealous of you and all you possess. He would like to see you in your grave."

" 'Tis true, there is no good will between us. In truth, Edward's sending him here as my man was punishing to one so arrogant. Doubtless Sir Olyver Martain would like nothing better than to see me brought to my knees."

"It seems fairly clear, he is guilty."

"He is guilty of something. Yet when I take the sum of what transpired this eve, the pieces do not reconcile." Why would Dame Allison, with all her resentment toward Garon, seek to protect him, her enemy, as she had against Sir Olyver? Did she seek only to help her people avoid possible reprisals? Or was there something more?

"Sir Olyver would gain more by murdering me and placing the blame on one of the Welsh than he would in this attack on you," Garon pointed out.

"That snake was on the stairs with me. If he was not the one directly responsible for the attack, he must have arranged for it to happen."

Garon frowned, shifting the pieces of the puzzle in his mind. " 'Tis true, if someone else had done this, why would they leave him untouched, able to reveal the perpetrator?"

"Precisely." She frowned, digging twin furrows into the smooth skin between her brows. "Still, it was dark, so dark I could not see the stairs beneath my feet. If someone else did this, they might be more concerned with spiriting me away than with dealing with an English knight who mayhap could not see them, either."

"Aye. Still, he lied to me. Olyver said he didn't find you in your chamber." He stroked his fingertips over the back of her hand. "What if the darkness had hidden all from his view? What if all he knew was that you had disappeared when he was responsible for escorting you safely to me? Would he tell the truth if he thought he had allowed you to escape me? Would he have told the truth if he knew you had been attacked, and he had not lifted a hand to defend you? Or would he have lied to save his worthless hide?"

"If not that black-hearted knave, then who is responsible?"

Garon debated the wisdom of revealing what he had learned the day of their wedding. Yet he knew if they were to make a true union of this marriage, it had to be based on honesty. "I received a message from Edward yesterday."

"And it had something in it to make you think that treacherous snake is not responsible for what happened to me?"

"Aye. The message was a warning, my lady. There is a band of outlaws roaming the North of Wales. They took Aberyddlan Castle a little more than a fortnight ago."

She stared at him, her green eyes wide. "They are trying to banish the English."

"These are not men with a noble pursuit. They are seeking riches. They slaughtered men, women, and children at Aberyddlan. Welsh and English. They stripped the castle bare, then left it to rot." He slipped a hand around hers and lifted her fingers to his lips, trying to soften the blow of his words. "Still, could such men convince certain spirited Welsh hearts that they were fighting for the glory of Wales?"

She closed her eyes as though seeking some inner strength. "You think these men might have been behind the attack?"

Garon shuddered inside when he thought of Meredyth in the hands of those murdering butchers. " 'Tis possible."

"They could be in Glendire at this very moment."

He stroked his fingers over the softness of her cheek. "My men are on alert, my lady. Hanes is aware of the danger."

She slowly slid her fingertips through the dark hair shading his forearm, the soft caress shivering across his skin. "I still don't understand. Why attack me and hide me in the cata-combs? Why not simply murder me?"

"You would be a valuable pawn, my lady. Your people would not fight if they thought they might place you in danger. You could also be used to sway me. It would make it easier to take the prize."

She studied him a moment, one delicate eyebrow lifted. "I doubt anyone would believe I could be used to sway your actions, Lord Wolf."

He wished he could ignore the power she wielded over him, but he could not.

He touched her breast, smiling as she sucked in her breath. "What magic have you conjured, my lady?"

"I am not a witch."

"Nay." He slipped his hand around her nape and drew her toward him. "You are a woman, Merrie mine. A woman who has shown this warrior a glimpse of heaven in her arms."

Her lips parted beneath his as he kissed her. The warmth of summer simmered in her kiss, streaming from her into him until heat flowed through his veins, melting all the frozen places in his soul.

He had thought to live his life marching from one bloody battlefield to the next. Never had he imagined he would find softness in his life. Never had he allowed himself to hope for more than an honorable life and death. Yet in a span of days, he had found more than he had ever imagined. She leaned against him, brushing her breasts against his chest. Her soft sigh mingled with his low groan.

"We should not pursue this, Garon," she whispered, pulling away from him. "You will tear open your wound."

He slid his hand along her sleek back. "I need your tender ministering, sweet lady."

She touched the bandage over his shoulder. "You must take care."

He wiggled his eyebrows at her. "There are ways around the difficulty."

She moistened her lips. "Are you certain?"

"More certain than anything in my life." He gripped her hips and drew her between his thighs. A low growl issued from deep in his throat at the brush of her belly against his aroused flesh.

"Garon, I . . ." She hesitated, her gaze darting to the door. "Did you hear that?"

Garon clenched his jaw. "Did you bolt the door?"

"Aye."

Still, the sound of the latch rattling softly was unmistakable. Someone was trying to enter the lord's bedchamber.

*Watch for Chapter Eleven, by Madeline George, of* Lair of the Wolf, *appearing in October 2000 in* Apache Lover *by Holly Harte.*

# MIDNIGHT SUN

## AMANDA HARTE

Amelia Sheldon has traveled from Philadelphia to Gold Landing, Alaska, to practice medicine, not defend herself and her gender to an arrogant man like William Gunning. While her position as doctor's assistant provides her ample opportunity to prove the stubborn mine owner wrong, the sparks between them aren't due to anger. William Gunning knows that women are too weak to stand up to the turmoil of disease. But when he meets the beautiful, willful Amelia Sheldon, she proves anything but weak; in fact, she gives him the tongue lashing of his life. When the barbs escalate to kisses, William knows he has found his true love in the land of the midnight sun.

___4503-6                                    $5.50 US/$6.50 CAN

**Dorchester Publishing Co., Inc.**
**P.O. Box 6640**
**Wayne, PA 19087-8640**

Please add $1.75 for shipping and handling for the first book and $.50 for each book thereafter. NY, NYC, and PA residents, please add appropriate sales tax. No cash, stamps, or C.O.D.s. All orders shipped within 6 weeks via postal service book rate. Canadian orders require $2.00 extra postage and must be paid in U.S. dollars through a U.S. banking facility.

Name_____
Address_____
City_____State_____Zip_____
I have enclosed $_____ in payment for the checked book(s).
Payment <u>must</u> accompany all orders. ❑ Please send a free catalog.
CHECK OUT OUR WEBSITE! www.dorchesterpub.com

They are pirates—lawless, merciless, hungry. Only one way offers hope of escaping death, and worse, at their hands. Their captain must claim her for his own, risk his command, his ship, his very life, to take her. And so she puts her soul into a seduction like no other—a virgin, playing the whore in a desperate bid for survival. As the blazing sun descends into the wide blue sea, she is alone, gazing into the eyes of the man who must lay his heart at her feet. . . .

# Lair of the Wolf

Also includes the fourth installment of *Lair of the Wolf*, a serialized romance set in medieval Wales. Be sure to look for future chapters of this exciting story featured in Leisure books and written by the industry's top authors.

___4692-X                                               $5.50 US/$6.50 CAN

# Lair of the Wolf

Constance O'Banyon, Bobbi Smith, Evelyn Rogers,
Emily Carmichael, Martha Hix, Deana James,
Sharon Schulze, June Lund Shiplett, Elizabeth
Mayne, Debra Dier, and Madeline George

Be sure not to miss a single installment of Leisure Books's star-studded new serialized romance, *Lair of the Wolf*! Preserving the fun and suspense of the month-by-month installments, Leisure presents one chapter a month of the entire on-line story, including some brand new material the authors have added to their existing chapters. Watch for a new installment of *Lair of the Wolf* every month in the back of select Leisure books!

## Previous Chapters of *Lair of the Wolf* can be found in: